DARK AUGUST

DARK
AUGUST

a novel

❧

KATIE TALLO

HARPER

NEW YORK • LONDON • TORONTO • SYDNEY

HARPER

HarperCollins books may be purchased for educational, business, or sales promotional use. For information, please email the Special Markets Department at SPsales@harpercollins.com.

FIRST EDITION

Designed by Jamie Lynn Kerner

Library of Congress Cataloging-in-Publication Data has been applied for.

ISBN 978-0-06-294804-5

20 21 22 23 24   LSC   10 9 8 7 6 5 4 3 2 1

For my sweet ba

DARK AUGUST

AUGUST 2018

HER GAZE SLIPS OUT OF FOCUS, TURNING THE VALLEY OF purple loosestrife into a lavender sea that ebbs and flows in the hot breeze. Smells like cat piss. She continues to push through the scratchy weeds that made their way to North America in the hoof mud of nineteenth-century heifers. Stowaway seeds never meant to cross an ocean.

Big-shouldered settlers took up arms against them. Hacking. Burning them alive. One season to the next. One generation to the next. Fathers and sons. Daughters too. Slashing and burning and cursing the flowery invaders. Held them off for decades until an underground river of toxins turned golden cornfields to black muck and sent a town up in a ball of fire.

With no one left to fight off the loosestrife, it spread. Running rampant across acres of twitch grass and wild rye. Choking every living thing in its path out of existence. Oblivious to the toxic sludge drenching its roots.

Maybe thriving because of it.

Poison doesn't kill everything.

The young woman is overwhelmed standing in their midst.

A speck. A bug. An orphan child. A lone seed.

Twenty years old yet feeling eight.

She shuts her eyes. Grabs hold of that eight-year-old's hand. Holding tight to the past. Holding on for dear life. She picks up her pace. Knees high. Bare legs etched with tiny cuts from the razor-sharp stems. Should have changed into long pants and sneakers instead of jean shorts and flip-flops. But she didn't think.

She just bolted.

Keys. Ball cap. Car. Gone.

Pit stop at the Quickie to fuel up. Then autopilot kicked in. Like it does when she knows thinking is only going to get in the way. Took the 416 out of the city then Highway 5 along the Rideau River. Knows the highway well now. The fork in the road near the rust red barn. The lopsided flea market billboard that marks the halfway point. And the moss-eaten highway that leads straight into a town that once was but is no more.

The town that went up in that fireball. Elgin, Ontario.

A settlement carved from nothing in the 1830s by Mormon missionaries. Made nothing again by greed and spite and toxic wastewater.

The late afternoon sun is baking her brain. She lifts her ball cap, pulls sweaty strands of auburn hair from her neck. Twists and tucks her ponytail under the cap. Her dad's cap. The one from the '87 Masters when a nobody named Larry Mize beat a couple greats of the game. Her dad loved the underdog. Loved the idea that anybody could do something great. Just once. And that would be enough. That would make his life matter forever. At least that's how her mother told it.

He wanted to name you after the home of the green jacket.

The cap is frayed at the bill. Well worn because a twelve-year-old boy never took it off except when his mother insisted at the dinner table. Frayed because that kid wore it right through high school and beyond. It was part of his off-duty guise. Ball cap, T-shirt and jeans, jean jacket, cowboy boots. Same thing worn by every other country boy from small-town Ontario in the early eighties. Now she wears it. It smells like him. At least she imagines it does. Musty. Like grass from the course where he caddied before becoming a cop.

The cicadas buzz incessantly. Her tongue sticks to the roof of her mouth. She could die out here and never be found. Collapse in a heap of dehydrated bones and slowly get sucked underground by the loosestrife. Her body liquefied by the wastewater bubbling below. She could die of a thousand cuts. Die of thirst.

But none of these things is going to happen.

Not today.

Not even the mighty loosestrife can mess with her mission. And even though all roads leading to Elgin are permanently barricaded with concrete blockades bearing warning signs that say ROAD CLOSED. DO NOT ENTER. HAZARDOUS TOXIC WASTE. UNAUTHORIZED ENTRY BANNED. Even though the fields around the town look more like a demilitarized no-go zone than a once-thriving farming community. Nothing is going to stop her.

She drops into the past. Sinking into the cave of her memories. A habit she mastered as a kid in boarding school. It comforts her. And if she tries hard enough, conjures the tiniest scrap of memory—a color, a smell, a sensation on her skin, a word spoken by someone she loved—she can see the past projected onto the walls of her imagination. Once there, she can alter those flickerings to her liking. Reshape the past. Bring people back. Undo the horrible things that happened.

If only for a sweet second.

It's a hard habit to break.

Twenty-five minutes. That's far enough to get her head straight and her feet moving. Twenty-five minutes and a mile back she goes. When she parked in the dirt lane off Highway 15 just east of Upper Rideau Lake. Same shady spot under the weeping willow. Locked the Buick, pocketed the keys, headed out on foot.

Destination: Halladay House.

Two clicks inside the no-go zone, up the rolling hill, over the cedar rail fence. Then along the eastern boundary of the Halladay acreage. Steering clear of the chemical ponds that dot the west side of the property. She knows the lay of the land. Knows the stench of diesel and naphthalene that hangs in the air. Knows the slippery footing along the soggy banks of the creek of wastewater runoff.

Just like the loosestrife, she's a stranger. A trespasser who's made herself at home. She's scaled the barbed-wire fence around the defunct compressor station and yanked ivy from the headstones of graves. She's pried plywood from windows. Walked down the main street, past a grocery store where people once stopped to gossip and buy their milk and eggs. She's even sat on the wooden pews where they prayed every Sunday seeking salvation.

Seems their God wasn't listening.

Now she's back. A can of gasoline in tow. Hiking toward that big old house that sits outside town. A nineteenth-century Gothic farmhouse perched on the brow of a purple knoll. Majestic veranda limping sideways from rot. Moss dripping from its shingles. A widow's walk clings to the rooftop like a spider hovering over its prey.

She has only seen the house once before by moonlight. It's the mansion where Kep Halladay lived. Where he lorded over the county. Stole from the work-worn pockets of his neighbors. Sucked the lifeblood from the very land surrounding his own home. Until he destroyed everything.

She's come to finish what her mother started.

Come to set her eyes upon Halladay House in the light of day, one last time.

Before she burns it to the ground.

TEN WEEKS EARLIER

AUGUSTA LIES AWAKE. IT'S EARLY MORNING. SLEEP ONLY comes in fits and starts these days. Her boyfriend, Lars, is snoring beside her. Her phone vibrates. She grabs it and stares at the name on the screen. Rose Ryan. Her great-grammie Rose. Gus slips out of bed and into the cramped motel bathroom, covering her mouth as she whispers hello.

It's not Rose. It's Miss Santos, Rose's nurse. Calling to tell Gus that she has to come home. The word *home* knocks the wind out of her.

When Augusta was eight, her mother, Detective Shannon Monet, was killed in a car wreck. Gus was left with one relative, Great-Grammie Rose, who was about two hundred years old. Always struck with a migraine or a heavy heart or exhaustion of the bones. Rose lived her feeble elderly years propped in her bed with her Brazilian nurse, Yanna, tending to her every need.

Miss Yanna Santos always reminded Gus of a crow. Thick

coal-black hair dancing on her shoulders like a feather boa. Sour lips sewn shut in a thin cruel line. Basketball tall. But it was her high-pitched voice that was most crowlike. She cawed when she spoke in her sharp Portuguese-tinged English.

Miss Santos was there that night when the female constable brought her to Rose's big house on Island Park Drive. An eight-year-old wearing a pink nightie under a yellow polka-dot raincoat. It was four in the morning. Took three rounds of bell ringing before Miss Santos came to the door wearing a black raincoat she'd thrown over the shoulders of her long nightgown. The wind curled inside the house. The coat billowed like great black wings. Miss Santos stared at the small child on the stoop. Then at the policewoman. Not understanding at first. Then listening, narrowing her eyes, then stepping aside to let them in. She terrified Gus.

From the get-go, Yanna insisted that her new charge call her Miss Santos. And she had other rules. Gus was not to bother her with runny noses or scraped knees or tears or appeals for rides to visit her best friend, Amy. She was to make new friends in her new neighborhood or she was to learn to keep herself company. Augusta was given the periwinkle guest room, all made up with matching bed skirt and wallpaper. But none of her own things. Not her feather pillow, not her doll, Sunny, not her blue toy trunk. Nothing from her old house except a few clothes and her toothbrush. And the puppy her mother had just brought home that summer.

Gus started grade three at a new school and did her best to pretend everything was normal. Like she was happy. For a while, she thought she was. She even made a new friend named Shelly.

But she shouldn't have bothered pretending.

The summer before grade five, voices were raised in Rose's room. Yanna said she wasn't hired to babysit. Threatened to quit. Rose said something about family obligations. Then Yanna said it.

Her or me.

A week later, Rose made her choice. Ten-year-old Gus was told she would be attending boarding school in St. Catharines for a "proper young lady's education." Rose's words. Her feeble attempt to pretend this was for Augusta's own good and not her own. Gus had never heard of St. Catharines. She didn't want to be a proper young lady. She wanted her mother and pizza nights. She wanted to play I Spy in her room with her new best friend, Shelly. She wanted a home that felt like a home.

But no one asked her what she wanted.

Once Augusta left for boarding school, she thought she'd never see or hear from any of them again. Not Shelly. Not Rose. Especially not Miss Santos.

And yet here is that familiar crow voice squawking from her phone.

"Hello? Olá? You on phone? You there?"

Gus can't speak. She manages a croak.

"Shannon, you her dodder, no?"

Gus gently closes the bathroom door. She hasn't heard her mother's name said out loud in over a decade.

"Yes, I'm Shannon's," she whispers. Hoping Lars doesn't hear. He doesn't like it when she's on the phone without his say-so.

"Dis Miss Santos. Yanna Santos. Rose, she gone."

"Gone where?"

"She pass."

"Oh."

Gus stares at the phone. She feels a deep pang of regret that the last tiny thread strung out into the world that connected her to her mother, however frayed, has now been severed.

"How did you get my number?"

"You leave on machine."

Gus vaguely remembers calling Rose a few months back in a red wine funk. She and Lars had been drinking cheap bordeaux in a box. Lars got particularly nasty when he drank wine. But he was also a lightweight so his tirades never lasted long. Usually he ended up puking or passing out. This time he was out cold, and Gus found herself curled in a ball in the corner of the motel room dialing Rose's number. Perhaps hoping her only living relative might ignite in her some courage that would nudge her toward leaving Lars. But no one picked up so she left a rambling message and her phone number. No one called her back. Until now.

"You come home, miss. You come now." And with that Miss Santos hangs up, leaving echoes of the past reverberating in Augusta's ear.

1

THE BALLERINA

GUS REMEMBERS HOW THE LIE CAUGHT IN HER MOTHER'S throat.

Back soon, Sugar Bunch. I promise.

Shannon had those worry lines on her forehead. Gus wanted to smooth away those lines with her eight-year-old hands, but there were too many words in the way. Too many *later*s and *back soon*s and *promise*s. Too many *when you get older*s and *neverminds* for her to get close enough to her mother to rub them away. Gus wasn't strong enough to make things better. Her mother was the strong one. The brave one.

A police officer like her father. A widow. A single mother.

Sometimes Gus spied on Shannon. Listened to her muttering as she scratched notes in her notebook or read newspaper clippings or tapped the keyboard of her laptop. Gus watched her mother's eyes dart up to the photographs and articles pinned on the corkboard above her makeshift desk. Shannon created that desk from her dead husband's tool bench in the garage. It was her sanctuary. Her office. Where she did her secret work. Not for children's eyes. Out of bounds.

But when Shannon was asleep, Augusta would tiptoe into her mother's sanctuary. Gus had one rule. Once she entered that place of secrets, she never stayed longer than it took to count to twenty. She'd stare up at that corkboard and try to see what her mother saw there.

1–2–3

None of it looked like it belonged together. Bits and odd scraps.

4–5–6

A photograph of a boy with his parents.

7–8–9

A page torn from a newspaper.

10–11–12

A Polaroid of a little girl in a tutu and leotard wearing glasses.

13–14–15

A web of red lines drawn across the board from one scrap to another.

16–17–18

A spidery collage that didn't make sense to an eight-year-old.

19–20

One time her mother was working in the garage with the door closed. Gus slowly opened the door and poked her head inside. Her mother was bent over her laptop, bathed in orange light from a lamp clipped to the workbench. Without letting her toes cross the threshold, Gus leaned in to ask her mother a question she'd been pondering for weeks. Using as small a voice as she could muster, Augusta asked who the girl with the glasses was. The ballerina in the photo. She pointed. Shannon slowly looked over at her daughter, eyes sad. Then she rose from her stool, walked toward her, and quietly closed the door. The sharp click of the knob as it settled into place pricked Augusta's eardrums. The orange glow extinguished, she was left on the other side of the door, standing barefoot in a cold blue pool of light from the kitchen stove. A terrible loneliness washed through her chest.

She didn't know who that ballerina was or where she lived or what her name was, but she did know one thing. The girl in the picture was more important to her mother than she was. Gus hated that ballerina and, in that moment, Gus hated her mother even more for shutting that door.

But she's not that little girl anymore.

Augusta pulls her hands away from her face and pushes the past into the farthest recesses of her mind. She's all grown-up and she's sitting on the edge of a bathtub staring at a brown stain ringing the toilet bowl in front of her. She rises and looks at her reflection in the mirror. Her face is partly hidden by her long auburn hair, frizzy from tossing and turning all night. Her freckled cheeks are flushed and hollow. She looks older than her twenty years. Doesn't recognize the weary face looking back at her. But she does glimpse the smallest of flickerings dancing deep in those green eyes and she knows what she must do.

Gus slips out of the bathroom. Pulls on her jeans, T-shirt, jacket, and ball cap. Lars is still snoring. She quietly packs her duffel bag, grabs her purse, and heads for the door. On her way out, she glances at Lars, his mouth hanging slack. She takes four hundred bucks from his wallet and eases out of the door of their motel room.

Hilda, the night clerk, stands in the small portico near the front office. Smoking a menthol.

"Where you off to, middle of the good God night, missy?"

Gus smiles.

"Can't sleep. Thought I'd hit the all-night gym down the road."

She lifts her duffel bag to back up her lie. Before Hilda can blink, Gus turns and strides down the street.

Two blocks over she hops in a cab at the taxi stand.

Twenty minutes later, she's inside the bus terminal buying a ticket to Montreal.

Three hours later, she's on a Greyhound due west.

And two hours after that, she's standing in front of Central Station as the sun rises over downtown Ottawa.

❧

The last time Augusta was headed to her hometown was when she was seventeen. She stood in the school office as papers were signed. Her bags next to her. She'd graduated. Miss Quinte, the assistant to the headmistress, drove her across town and dropped her at the St. Catharines train station. Gus felt like an inmate being released from prison. She'd served her sentence and now she was being shipped back to Ottawa. Back home. To Rose and Miss Santos. Gus was pretty sure the school had neglected to warn either of them of her imminent arrival, so after an hour and thirty-three minutes on the train, Gus stepped onto the busy platform. She was supposed to transfer to an eastbound train to Ottawa. But instead, Gus chucked her ticket in the nearest garbage bin and walked through the station's great hall, out the front doors, and into the glaring glass towers of Toronto. Anywhere seemed better than going backward.

Toronto turned out to be a whole lot bigger than St. Catharines and Ottawa put together. It smelled like seaweed and tar. The sky was packed so tight with high-rises Gus couldn't see the clouds. Intersections were a din of honking horns and crowds hurrying across. It was a river. A rushing river of people bent over their phones floating past toothless hags curled in sleeping bags on the sidewalk.

Gus was young and naïve. She made eye contact with one bearded lady who chased her two city blocks before getting distracted by something in a sewer grate. She bought convenience store sandwiches and placed them in open palms. She tossed coins into cardboard houses and smiled at hobos squatting in doorways. One hobo threw the tuna sandwich back at her and spit in her direction.

She didn't know the rules yet, but she was about to learn them.

2

LARS

⚜

SHE MET LARS IN A LAUNDROMAT OFF DANFORTH. GUS HAD found a job as a dishwasher at Lola Eata, a greasy spoon one block north of the room she rented for $60 a week. Dirt cheap because it was right above a fishmonger. The day she met him, she reeked of french fry grease and cod. The smell clung to her long red hair, her jean jacket, her bedsheets, no matter how much she washed them.

Lars said he liked how she smelled. Told her she was beautiful. Touched her hair. Said it was the color of apricots. He had a flat nose, like it had been broken a few times. Dark blue eyes and a brown mop of hair that he slicked back. Reminded her of James Dean from those old movies she used to watch with her mom.

Lars was the first person to give her the time of day since she stepped onto the platform at Union Station. He offered her a job and she quit the dish pit.

He was in imports and exports. The sales and distribution

end of things, he told her. He seemed worldly, but not worldly like her history teacher at boarding school. Not book worldly. Not nose-in-the-air worldly. Lars was street worldly. He taught Gus which guy in a street-corner huddle was the runner and how to spot a pickpocket about to skin the poke. There was shady stuff going on under the upper crust of life and Lars peeled back the layers and showed her what was underneath.

Gus didn't ask what he was distributing. She caught on pretty quick. Black-market painkillers, tobacco, cell phones, drugs. She told herself she didn't care. Lars taught her how to drive and how to hold a gun. He put his hand on the small of her back like he was showing her off when his buddies were around. He introduced her as his girlfriend and he looked her in the eye when she spoke.

At least he did in the beginning.

Augusta moved into his apartment two weeks after they met. Four days later he got into a fight with the super, busted the guy's nose, and they got evicted. She shoved everything she owned back into her duffel bag, and a long stretch of crashing in motel after motel began. Together, they worked the east to west corridor of the 401 from Cornwall to Brockville to Trenton. Cornwall was close to the border and the bridge to the Mohawk casino. The perfect spot for his drive-through business. Lars moved trunkloads of contraband tobacco and black-market phones in and out of the States by way of the casino.

Easy money. Just how Lars liked it.

He was Gus's first boyfriend. Sometimes he surprised her with chocolate rose bouquets. Other times he slapped her face. He was mean and handsome, sweet and selfish. But mostly Lars was methodical. He obsessed over being organized. He timetabled her days down to the minute. Picked out her clothes and ordered her meals when waitresses asked what she wanted.

Gus never told Lars about her parents or that they were both dead. Said they lived in Vancouver and she hadn't spoken to them in years. It was the one piece of herself she kept all to herself. The rest he could have. Her days. Her hair. Her diet. Her body.

Most mornings before they got out of bed he'd slide on top of her. Same clammy skin, same stale breath, same feeling of homesickness washing over her. Only she had no home to feel sick for, so it felt worse. Like he was opening a wound that nothing could fill. Gus clung to him. He was all she had. He made her feel like she was a part of something. And the adrenaline rush of breaking the law made her feel alive.

This world was the furthest thing from prep school she could imagine and Lars was a sharp edge. The more she leaned on him, the more deeply he cut her. And the pain kept Gus fully on alert. Fully with him. Fully in the present.

Fuck the past.

Gus turned eighteen that first summer with Lars. And as much as she tried to shut out the past, she couldn't help glimpsing the future in the rainy car windshield. A not-so-distant future where she was still running and stealing and dealing at twenty-five. Losing herself in booze and pills at thirty. Jail at forty. Mere inches from sitting in a gutter tossing tuna sandwiches back at do-gooders at fifty.

Shannon would have hated Lars. Been ashamed of her

little girl for jumping into a fucked-up life with a fucked-up guy in the driver's seat. One year spilled into two. And over the course of those two years, Gus grew less careful. Did less shoulder checking and more pedal-to-the-metal risk-taking. Almost daring the cops to come after her. She got stupid and lazy about her freedom and her future. One time she was pulled over for speeding and almost popped the trunk so the cop would find the cases of contraband cigarettes and arrest her. Almost. But she couldn't do it. Not to her parents. Couldn't bring herself to tarnish their good names. Their deep disappointment lurked in her DNA. An ache so profound, she felt it pulsing through her marrow. Always there. Throbbing. Never letting her forget who they were. That they were good. That they were law-abiding. That they were police officers. So she simply smiled and got a slap on the wrist. The highway patrolman liked her red hair.

After two dead-end years, Gus couldn't see her way to an exit. Couldn't bear to think about the future or the past, yet both hovered in her periphery. Never far.

And so it's not at all strange that she finds herself here. June of 2018, sitting in the back of a cab heading down Holland Avenue toward Wellington West.

Heading back.

Augusta asks the cabbie to drop her a few blocks from Rose's house. Needs the walk and her stomach's growling. She grabs a breakfast bagel from the Bagel Shoppe where her mom used to take her Saturday mornings after swimming lessons. Same guy from over a decade ago is still at the cash register. He says he remembers her. Gus can tell he doesn't.

Memories have a way of dancing in your eyes. Like embers in a campfire pit. His eyes don't dance.

Hers do as she walks the familiar streets. Twelve years ago, this was her hood. Her hometown. She used to go to the movies at the Coliseum Theatre on Carling, toboggan at the Arboretum, and swim at Dovercourt Community Centre. She knew these neighborhoods. Hintonburg, Wellington West, and Westboro, one connecting to the next. She knew the bus routes to downtown, the bike paths along the Ottawa River, and the shortcut behind the Beer Store on Scott. And she knows exactly where Rose's house is. That rambling two-story 1920s house, two doors down from the intersection at Richmond on Island Park Drive. A wide avenue where maples border a green space running alongside the road. A prestigious street back in the day. A street lined with embassies and elite private residences.

Gus rounds the corner, barely recognizing the once elegant home. There's a mess of wild crabgrass out front. Craggy overgrown sumacs obscure the bay window. Yellow paint peels off the wood siding. The driveway is a cracked web of moss and dandelions. The garage door hangs from its hinges. The house looks abandoned. Only it's not. A newspaper lies on the stoop and a curtain shifts in the front window.

Someone is watching her.

3

MISS SANTOS

AUGUSTA HEADS UP THE FRONT PATH. UP THE STEPS. SHE IS about to knock when the front door swings open. Miss Santos flies out, stooped to one side, rolling a suitcase behind her. Thick black hair sticks to her forehead. She's wearing what looks to be the same raincoat she wore the night Gus was brought to the house by the female constable.

"You here now. Good. I go."

She bounces her suitcase down the steps. Gus stares.

"Go?"

"I have sister in Kemptville. I go live on her sofa. Like homeless person."

And with that, Miss Santos is soaring down the sidewalk. True to form.

"Miss Santos, wait."

Gus recalls the nurse never having any bedside manner. Before leaving for boarding school, ten-year-old Gus was steered upstairs by Miss Santos. One hand firmly on each of Gus's small shoulders. Without knocking, they entered Rose's bedroom. The old woman's skin was yellow. Goodbyes were brief. Rose blinked through blood-rimmed eyes. Her lips parted to a slight smile. Augusta's two-year-old dog was curled on a turquoise afghan on the bed. Rose's hand reached down to pet his head. He snuggled close to her body. Gus wanted to strangle that stupid mutt. It was so unfair. He got to stay. He was cozy. He was wanted. As she left the bedroom, Gus glanced back at Rose and the dog. Neither looked up as Miss Santos shut the door and took her away.

It was Miss Santos who instructed the headmistress that Gus was to be kept at school for holidays. To stay behind when everyone else went home. When the other girls returned from their Easters and Christmases, they jumped on their beds and laughed about home while she pretended to be asleep, a blanket pulled over her head. None of them cared that Gus had no home and no parents. She felt completely untethered. Set adrift in a sea of dancing, happy girls. Her only relative too fragile and old to toss her a lifeline.

It was there, lying in her bed at school, facing the wall, head covered, that Gus learned to drop into the dark cave of her memories and lower herself deeply and fully into the past. Once there, she'd meander over to one of those Sunday visits at Rose's house with her mother. They'd sit in the garden on yellow plastic chairs and eat cucumber sandwiches with the crusts cut off. They'd sip sweet iced tea and her mother would talk about the unseasonably warm weather. Knowing her daughter was bored, Shannon would tickle her toes with her own under the garden table and make her laugh. Rose, swathed in blankets like a withered baby, would nod and chew as bits of food stuck to the corners of her mouth. In these memories, Miss Santos was somewhere in the background. Off to one side. Sitting near the back door, her bony fingers wrapped around the spine of a book she was reading. Her black hair bobbing in the light breeze.

That same head of hair now dances wildly in front of Gus as Miss Santos veers out into the road, oblivious to oncoming traffic. A car honks and skids to avoid hitting her. Miss Santos doesn't slow down, but Augusta manages to catch up. The nurse's suitcase bumps along behind her as she rants.

"She promise. She wreck her promise. It all in fucking letter. I leave on kitchen table. All your problem now."

They come to a bus stop at the corner of Island Park just as the number seven pulls up. Miss Santos heaves her suitcase up the steps of the bus. At the top, she turns and looks back. Her crow eyes glisten, jaw trembles, lips quiver. Gus knows that look. She's seen it on her own face in the mirror. The stinging expression of someone who's been deeply hurt. As the pain ripples through her facial muscles and racks her bones, Miss Santos tries desperately to hold the hurt inside.

"I put up with bed-wetting, bell ringing in middle of night, this pill, that pill, doctor appointment, cooking meal, picking up dog shit. I say nothing. I do all. For what? For betrayal. Fine. Good. Now I go. Terminei."

And with that Miss Santos disappears into the depths of the bus. The driver shrugs and closes the door. Brakes sigh and the bus pulls away. Sun flares dance across the windows obscuring the view inside. The bus rolls down Richmond, past Hilson, past Kirkwood. Gus watches until it is just a speck of flashing metal in the distance.

That's when she hears the barking.

4

THE PUPPY

S HE WAS EIGHT THE SUMMER SHANNON BROUGHT HIM HOME. After the incident with the photo of the ballerina, Gus decided not to speak to her mother for the rest of summer break. It had been over a week of silent treatment. Shannon baked marzipan bars and played their favorite song by the Four Tops on their portable record player. "I Can't Help Myself." Shannon swayed her hips to the music, but Gus refused to even tap her toes. Nothing but the cold shoulder. Shannon called her "Sugar Bunch" and "Honey Pie" and ordered pizza even though it was Wednesday and not Friday. Finally, when nothing seemed to thaw the deep freeze, Shannon surprised Gus with a new puppy. But it wasn't a real dog. It was a mutt. A mixed breed from the local Humane Society. Part spinone, part golden retriever. Gus refused to play with the shaggy creature. Refused to choose a name for it. She knew the puppy was a bribe. Meant to keep her busy. Out of the way. Gus ignored the scruffy little furball, even when it nudged her arm with its wet nose or licked her ankles with its soft pink tongue. Shannon named the puppy Levi. After Levi Stubbs of the Four Tops.

Most nights that summer ended with Gus storming to her room and slamming her door. Screaming that she hated the stupid dog and she wished her mother was dead.

And just like that, before she could take it back, her mother was dead. Gus had no way of saying she was sorry for not tapping her toes. For not being nice to the puppy. For not being a good girl.

She was eight years old, and she was completely undone.

❦

A sharp, distant bark gets Augusta's feet unstuck. She hikes her purse over her shoulder and quickly heads back toward Rose's house from the bus stop. Her feet thump against the pavement, the present hammering into her bones. She is far from her mother. Far from her childhood. Far from the life she was living just yesterday with Lars.

Far away and right here.

As Gus crosses the street, she spots him. There's no mistaking those floppy ears and raggedy hindquarters. She slows and walks up the path toward the house. He's torn the strap from her duffel bag. Augusta dropped it on the front step when she chased after Miss Santos. The strap has come loose and he's whipping his head side to side, smacking his ears with it.

That's Levi all right. But he's no puppy anymore. A hint of gray sprinkles his brow and he's about forty pounds heavier.

He looks up and spots her. His eyes widen, ears perk, and forehead furrows as recognition jolts some remote nook inside his tiny brain. He drops the drool-soaked strap and bounds over to her. Body wiggling, tail wagging, whimpering like a baby. He leaps at her chest. Claws scratch her collarbone.

"Get off me, dog."

Augusta shoves him off. He's unfazed. He circles excitedly, smells her shoes, then rubs his body against her legs. She feels the familiar pang of guilt. The same guilt she felt as a kid for never letting herself love the dog. But right now, guilt isn't enough to bring her around. She doesn't want him. She doesn't know him. She never did. He was Shannon's, then he was Rose's. He was never hers. She tries to ignore him. Grabs her duffel bag and heads through the open door of Rose's house. Levi races ahead down the wide hallway that stretches from the front foyer to the large kitchen at the back. Gus drops the duffel and follows the clinking of his dog tags. Golden hair flutters off his body.

It all in fucking letter. I leave on kitchen table.

The kitchen smells like brussels sprouts. Augusta crosses to the table. She drops her purse on the floor next to her and plunks down into the chair where she used to sit eating digestive cookies with cheddar cheese while her mother weeded Rose's garden.

Levi flops on the floor like a bag of bones. The excitement has tuckered him out. His droopy neck spreads across the cool pine floors as he lets out a big sigh.

There are two piles of paper on the table. Junk mail and bills. Set apart from these is a plain envelope. Torn open. A letter shoved back inside. It's addressed to Augusta Monet. The handwriting is shaky. Definitely from Rose. In red ink, a *Return to Sender* stamp obscures the address in St. Catharines. Rose thought Augusta was still at boarding school. She'd stopped sending her birthday cards when she was thirteen so it's no wonder she had no idea how old she was. Gus pulls the letter from the envelope. A business card for a Mr. Beath Honey, LLB falls onto the table. She reads the letter.

> *My dearest Augusta,*
>
> *I am sorry I was not a better great-gran to you. I loved your mother very much. She was like a daughter to me. I should have done more for her only child. My deepest regret in my twilight is that I failed you both. I cannot change the past, but I can do something about the future. That is why I have decided to leave you all of my worldly possessions. My house. All of its contents. My money, my car, and my sweet Levi. My lawyer, Mr. Honey, is aware of my wishes and will take care of the arrangements when the time comes. I hope you can forgive my shortcomings.*
>
> > *Yours truly,*
> > *Rose*

The letter is dated just a few weeks earlier. Rose died before it was returned. Miss Santos must have found it while sorting through the mail. And opened it.

She promise. She wreck her promise.

What had Rose promised Miss Santos? Maybe the house.

Gus picks up the lawyer's business card, and with her other hand, she reaches for her purse on the floor. She riffles through it, finds her cell phone, and checks the screen. Ignoring the voice mails and texts from Lars, she dials Mr. Honey's number. He'll take care of things. So says Rose's letter. The lawyer picks up and in a few short minutes it's all arranged.

As she hangs up, a wave of nausea floats up her throat. Augusta looks around for something to eat. She's famished. The kitchen is filthy. Mossy dishes fill the sink. Hairy tumbleweeds inhabit every corner. Tomato sauce stipples the backsplash like blood splatter. Miss Santos might have been capable of administering medication and picking up dog shit, but she was clearly no maid.

Gus gets up. Wobbly legged. She opens the fridge. Big mistake. A head of iceberg lettuce has turned to mush and is oozing a puddle of soupy brown water across one shelf. A moldy jar of applesauce and a supersize bottle of prune juice are stranded in the puddle. Old lady food. Gus covers her mouth to stop herself from puking. Then she spots the bottles of Vanilla Ensure lining the fridge door. She grabs one, breaks the seal, and takes a sip. Tastes like vanilla milkshake. Gus downs two full bottles then collapses back into the chair.

She rests her forehead on her folded arms and drapes herself over the kitchen table. Shuts her eyes as a deep-boned heaviness envelops her, gently holding her down. Levi whines a little as Gus falls asleep, unable to fight gravity or fatigue any longer.

And then just like that, as if no time has passed at all, Gus lifts her head. She gazes out the back door. A purple dusk has descended on the yard. She's napped almost the entire day away. She can't yet lift her leaden arms or fully open her eyelids. She's still drifting somewhere between asleep and awake. Dreams and reality.

Here and there.

Wishing herself gone, Gus carries herself away, to there. To another purple sky.

Beneath its glow, she's eating corn on the cob with her mother on a front porch. She can hear a bicycle clip-clapping as it passes. Playing cards stuck in the spokes. Her mother laughs at the kernels stuck between her teeth. Gus wants to stay in the comfort and warmth of that moment, but it's too painful to linger there long. The evening draft cools her skin and pulls her back to her great-grandmother's kitchen table. She grips the chair beneath her. Trying to stop herself from floating away again. From disappearing completely.

The setting sun suddenly peeks out from below a line of low clouds, streaking the sky with slivers of orange and gold that cascade through the maples at the back of Rose's yard. The rays make their way through the kitchen window and sprinkle the table with dappled light that dances across her fingers. She touches the screen of her phone. It remains black. Battery's dead.

Darkness falls fast. Without turning on any lights, Augusta wanders down to the foyer. Grabs her phone charger from her duffel bag, plugs in her phone, and leaves it on the table in the foyer to charge. Still dead tired, Gus heads into the living room and stretches out on the sofa. She stares at the china cabinet filled with porcelain figurines shaped like horses and hummingbirds. Levi tiptoes into the room and gently hoists himself onto one end of the sofa and nestles in. She tucks her legs away from him into an uncomfortable fetal position. Looks down at him. He's completely at ease lying next to her. Much more than she is with him. Maybe it would be kinder to take him to the pound. Let some really great family with kids adopt him. Kids that would love a dog. The fantasy dissolves into sadness, then quickly shifts to anger. She didn't ask for any of this. Not when she was eight and not now. Tomorrow he's gone. Gus wonders how long the Humane Society will let him live if he doesn't get adopted right away. His problem, not hers.

Augusta closes her eyes and listens to the steady breathing of the old dog. Tries to swallow her guilt. She's got other problems. Another sound radiates from the front foyer.

Buzz buzz buzz.

Her phone quiets. Then the vibrating starts up again.

He's calling again.

Hitting redial over and over.

Lars is pissed.

5

HONEY AND VIRTUE

❦

Augusta is woken from a deep sleep by a knock at the front door.

Lars.

Shit. That was fast. How did he find me?

She slips off the sofa. Heart racing. Eyes darting to Rose's china cabinet. She moves quickly toward it. Grabs a porcelain figurine. The sharpest one she can find. Purple unicorn. Levi lolls on his back. Legs spread-eagle. Great guard dog.

Augusta tiptoes across the foyer and peers through the peephole. The floorboards wince. Not Lars. Some guy in a wrinkled gray suit. Carrying a briefcase. Wiping his sweaty forehead on his sleeve. Bible salesman written all over him. She opens the door. His eyes flit to the unicorn. He clears his throat and smiles.

"You must be Rose's great-granddaughter."

Augusta nods. Definitely a Bible salesman. She places the figurine on the hall tree in the entryway. Hanging from the hooks of the tree are an umbrella and Rose's blue hat with a feather that sweeps across the rim. Old lady hat.

"Rose isn't here."

"Yes, I know. I'm Mr. Honey. Rose's lawyer? Executor of her estate?"

Gus suddenly remembers calling him the day before. He said he'd be in the neighborhood tomorrow and would pop by first thing. And it's now tomorrow.

Levi staggers from the living room, slightly punch-drunk. Stretching his hind legs out behind him, one at a time, like a ballet dancer. He nudges Augusta's calf and yawns.

"My deepest condolences for your loss. There are just a few documents that need signing and then I'll leave you be."

Gus almost laughs when he says this. *Leave you be.* She's all too familiar with being left. But just being and not being told how to be or where to be. That's uncharted waters for Gus. She lets Mr. Honey in through the front foyer of Rose's house, all the while wondering what on earth she'll do when he leaves her be.

SLIPPING INTO A HOT BUBBLE BATH LATER THAT NIGHT, Gus tries hard to let herself be. Too hard. She gives up and simply floats, warm in her watery porcelain vessel. Eyes, ears, and nose just above the surface like the portholes of a sinking ship. Gus lets the day's event replay across her closed eyelids like a bad sitcom, starting with the image of Mr. Honey flaring his nostrils as he enters the kitchen.

The tenacious brussels sprout aroma looms large. She opens the back door to let fresh air in through the screen door behind it. Levi circles. Mr. Honey checks her ID then pulls some documents from his briefcase. Levi whines. Augusta clues in. She reaches for the latch on the screen door, but the dog can't wait. He lunges through the screen, breaking the seal. First patch of brown grass he hits, his hind leg's up and he's peeing.

Gus signs on the Xs of forms while Mr. Honey avoids eye contact. He doesn't want any unseemly tears or embarrassing hand-holding. When they're all done with the paperwork, he hands her a set of keys like she's just won a new car on *The Price Is Right.*

"This one's for the Buick. This one's for the exterior garage door. There's two for the front door, one dead bolt, one main lock. And this one's for the back door."

He assures her that Miss Santos turned over all her keys.

"Don't worry, she won't be causing any more trouble."

He leaves the Proof of Death Certificate on the kitchen table. Says Gus will need it for when she goes to the bank. Says he's taken the liberty of arranging an appointment for her with someone named Trish Virtue at Scotiabank. Rose's bank. For later that day.

He shrinks when Gus asks, "How did Rose die?"

"Your great-grandmother passed peacefully in her sleep with her loving dog by her side."

He sounds like an obituary.

"When?"

"Two weeks ago. It's all on the certificate. She was cremated and interred at Beechwood Cemetery as per her wishes. She had a prepaid plot and headstone. She didn't want a service. And we weren't sure how to contact you. Miss Santos only yesterday managed to find your number so, at the time, it seemed prudent not to wait. No fuss, no muss, you see. And that's that."

"And the trouble with Miss Santos?"

"Oh that. She made some sort of scene at the bank when she tried to access Rose's bank account. She even called my office and was quite rude to my secretary. She was ranting about a promise made to her by Rose. I told her I knew nothing of promises, only last wishes."

Mr. Honey seems proud that he got the better of Miss Santos. Like he beat her at a game of chess. Gus is glad when he packs up to leave.

Floating in the lukewarm bubbles now, Gus can still see the strange little man walking briskly away from Rose's house. The back of his neck glistened with sweat. She thinks about broken promises and the mark they can leave on your heart. She knows the feeling well. Gus imagines the shame Miss Santos must have felt as she scrambled after the broken pieces of that promise made to her by Rose. A promise that wasn't just broken. It was, in fact, a lie.

The images fast-forward and Gus sees herself sitting in the red leather chair across from Miss Virtue in a small, glass-walled office in Scotiabank. After brief *hello*s, *how are you*s, and *so sorry*s, Miss Virtue yo-yos from her office to a printer room down the hall. There and back, there and back, her heels clicking on the polished floors. Her manicured nails tapping on the computer keyboard. A small run visible in her nylons just above the right ankle. A slight twitch at the corner of her mouth as she slowly turns the computer monitor to show Gus the amount left in Rose's estate account after legal fees and bank charges and outstanding debts and property taxes are paid.

That amount now dances across Augusta's eyelids like a flashing neon ticker in Times Square announcing the entirety of her inheritance to the world.

Twenty-two dollars and sixty-eight cents.

Thanks for nothing, Great-Grammie Rose.

Piling on the bad news, Miss Virtue saves the best for last. A few years ago, Rose refinanced the house so she could continue to live in it. Something called a reverse mortgage. Bottom line, the bank wants that loan repaid and Augusta neither qualifies for a new mortgage nor has the money to pay it off. It's due in ninety days or the house belongs to the bank. Miss Virtue hands Augusta the business card of her friend, a real estate agent. The banker knows it before Gus does. The house must be sold.

Augusta sinks underwater. A soft booming throbs at her temples.

Boom. She could go back to Lars.

Boom. She could run away and start a new life in Mexico.

Boom. She could lock the doors and never go outside again.

Gus comes up for air and knows what she has to do.

Tomorrow, she'll call Miss Virtue's real estate agent friend and put the house up for sale.

Levi rests his chin on the edge of the tub. Gus lifts her wet hand and gently rubs the velvety soft tip of one of his ears.

"You love it here too, don't you, dog?"

Gus closes her eyes and tries to be. Just for a moment. She almost does it. Almost believes that her last living relative actually left her a rambling old house that is hers to keep forever. A beautiful home with a pretty picture window and a deep front porch. The kind of house she and her mother used to dream of living in one day. Together.

6

MANSFIELD

⬴

AUGUSTA RACES AHEAD OF SHANNON. TAKING TWO STAIRS at a time. They're good solid family stairs with an oak handrail that doesn't blister her palm. Stairs a kid could run down on Christmas morning to see what presents are under the tree. She makes it to the top and dashes into the first bedroom. It's pink. Pink walls. Pink carpet. White comforter with little pink hearts. Tea set arranged on a tray on top of a pretty white storage trunk. China dolls on a shelf. Teddy bear on the bed. Lace curtains in the window. It's perfect. Shannon is hot on her heels. Augusta spins around and flops back on the bed, then bounces to her feet like a jack-in-the-box.

I call dibs, Mama.

Shannon pretend pouts. Then she folds her arms and scans the room. Her entire face begins to smile starting with the wrinkles fanning out around her eyes and spreading to the creases around her lips.

This room is so perfectly you, Honey Pie. Except for that silly trunk. Your blue treasure chest is much more special than that old thing.

So this room's mine?

Shannon's face gets serious and she rubs her chin as if contemplating the question deeply, then she winks and takes off down the hall. Gus chases her mother with a high-pitched squeal of delight. She races into the next bedroom. Shannon is already calling dibs. Gus stops at the entrance. Mouth open wide. It's an enormous yellow room with a king-size bed at its center. The bed is adorned with a collection of polka-dot and striped pillows. Pretty white sheers frame a set of french doors that stand open to a small balcony overlooking the back garden. Augusta folds her arms and stomps.

No fair.

Shannon smiles. She dances over to her daughter and wraps her arms around Gus. She lifts her up and they spin.

We can share, Sugar Bunch. Trade rooms every other night. Deal?

Augusta tries not to smile as Shannon puts her down. Gus puts her index finger to her chin as if struggling to make a big decision. Then she shakes her head.

No deal. You can have this one, Mama. I want the pink room.

Shannon flops on the bed. The springs groan. Gus flops beside her. They each grab a polka-dot pillow and begin play fighting, messing up the perfectly arranged bedding.

The real estate agent is standing in the doorway. Hands on hips. Brow furrowed. Shannon jumps off the bed, grabs Augusta's hand, and they race past the woman. Shannon tosses her a bone.

I think we'll put in an offer tonight.

They dash upstairs to the third-floor loft. The agent follows them like a mall security guard. She stays mute. Pretty sure they're messing with her but not willing to blow a potential sale. Shannon rambles on.

Open concept, hardwood floors. Perfect for my office. Love it. Kitchen needs some work but who needs to cook when there's takeout pizza.

Shannon's beyond excited. Gus loves it when she gets like this. It's been the best day ever. They've found their dream house this time.

We'll speak to our financial adviser and get back to you.

Shannon takes the agent's card. Gus loves that her mother says *we*.

The big three-story brick house on Mansfield Drive is amazing. They skip the rest of their Sunday open house excursion and head straight to the nearest Mac's Milk to buy a scratch-and-win lottery ticket. All their dreams will come true on Mansfield. Augusta will have a pretty pink bedroom. They'll put their wet boots side by side on their new welcome mat in the front foyer and they'll paint the kitchen walls robin's-egg blue. They'll order pizza every night and they'll be happier than they've ever been in their whole lives.

They scratch and don't win the jackpot. Not even a free ticket. Shannon's eyes get glassy as she stares at the worthless ticket. She flips it once, her face flushing as if genuinely surprised. Caught off guard that they aren't lucky enough to have the lottery gods shine down upon them.

Shannon rips up the ticket. Says it was stupid to think they belonged in a house like that. They have everything they need. Perfectly good house even if the roof leaks a little and there's hardly any backyard. They'd be lost in that big house just the two of them. Shannon says they aren't going to waste any more Sundays on open houses.

Then she goes into her office and stays there.

Gus spends the rest of Sunday riding her banana seat bike around the neighborhood. At night, she plays in her room inside the small tent in the corner where she keeps her stuffed animal collection. She sits in a circle with her bear Claudius, her frog Louis, her lion Praline, and her purple giraffe Girly. She reads aloud to them. Quietly. Holding a flashlight so she can see the words. *The Paper Bag Princess* is their favorite. When she can't keep her eyes open any longer, she kisses the tops of their heads, then curls up and sleeps.

In the morning, Augusta makes herself banana pancakes for breakfast. She packs four syrup-soaked pancakes in a plastic container for her lunch, then goes off to school.

When Gus comes home the kitchen is clean. The front curtains are open. Shannon's making cookies. Whistling to herself.

How was school today, Sugar Bunch?

This is their normal. It's the way things are. Shannon is like every other mom. They all forget to tuck in their kids once in a while. It's part of being a grown-up. Even when her best friend, Amy, tells her that her mom never forgets to pack her lunch, Augusta knows she's lying.

It's normal to eat chocolate chip cookies for dinner once in a while. It's normal to feel horribly alone when the house is so quiet except for the rain pattering on the roof. It's normal to have to check that all the doors are locked before putting yourself to bed.

Amy says no. Says it's not normal.

Gus doesn't believe her. She can't be the only one who's

ever crept into her mother's bedroom only to be told to get back to bed in a voice so sharp it stings her eyes and makes her heart ache. Amy's heart must ache sometimes. Amy says it doesn't.

Gus thinks she's a heartless liar.

She envies her.

It would be easier to have no heart.

7

HALEY-ANNE

Ɒ

G US WAKES FROM A STICKY SLEEP TO A BRIGHT AND SUNNY Saturday morning. She's anything but sunny. In fact, a blue melancholy seems to have crept into her bed overnight. She rises and stumbles downstairs to escape it. And before her morning coffee can make its way into her bloodstream, the real estate agent pops by for a *look-see*. Haley-Anne crunches her nose at the smells radiating from the musty armpits of Rose's house. High heels clicking across the hardwood like two tiny hammers tapping away at the soft tissue of Augusta's fragile dream-soaked brain.

"The place definitely needs some serious spit and polish, top to bottom, inside and out. And then it'll be all about the staging for MBV."

Haley-Anne blinks. Gus stares at her like she's speaking Swahili.

"Maximum buyer visualization? MBV. I came up with that. A potential buyer needs to be able to see themselves cooking dinner for the fam, planting petunias in the garden, entertaining the in-laws, even if her mother-in-law is a judgmental old B. It's the life that we're selling, not the house."

Gus gets that.

"That crack in the ceiling." Eye roll.

"That yellow toilet." Nostril flare.

"That torn screen." Big sigh.

"And that hideous brown lawn." Shoulder slump.

"Weed that garden, roll out some fresh sod, put a couple of potted mums on the porch, et voilà! Curb appeal!"

Haley-Anne hands her an inventory of to-dos as she leaves. Gus promises she'll get right on it. The bank has given her three months, so the sooner they list the house, the better. Gus posts the to-dos on the fridge under a puppy magnet. She stares at it.

How hard can it be to create curb appeal and clean up a little?

Harder than she thinks.

Gus spends the weekend moving from room to room like a balloon bouncing off the furniture. The melancholy follows her as she hovers in doorways. Gets sucked down halls. And occasionally clings to a wall while Lars sends her text after text.

> Babes, where you at?
> What the fuck, Augs?
> Please come back.
> You're dead to me.
> I love you, Auggie.

She runs her fingers along dusty windowsills where paint peels away in lovely cracked patterns that remind her of the backs of Rose's wrinkled hands. She stares through cobwebs crisscrossing the front window as the world outside moves past, a carousel of mothers and strollers, dog walkers, a postman shouldering a heavy bag, a garbage truck wincing as it stops and starts. All moving past Rose's house. Unaware that Gus is watching from behind the cobwebs.

Miss Santos probably looked out this same window as life passed her by. Waiting for an old woman to take her last breath so she could collect on a promise.

Gus has been at Rose's house since Thursday evening. It takes her until Monday to move herself into the room where Miss Santos used to sleep. The smallest, starkest bedroom in the house. The one with the single bed in the corner and the TV sitting across from it, knowing its blue flickering will keep her company at night. She closes the door to the periwinkle guest room that used to be hers and leaves it closed.

Levi has been sleeping on Rose's bed. Every evening after supper, Gus hears his nails *tick-tick-tick* up the wooden stairs and down the hall. Then the soft squeak of the box spring as he hoists his old bones up onto the bed.

Tuesday, Gus stumbles into the kitchen wearing one of Rose's long flannel nightgowns. She found a stack of them neatly washed and folded on top of a hamper. Made of soft cotton that reminds her of the nighties she used to wear as a kid. Gus sits at the kitchen table with her coffee, just like she has the previous four mornings. The to-do list waiting on the fridge. Levi at her feet.

Wednesday, she pokes around upstairs. Opening the drawer in the small teak table next to Rose's bed. Three linen dollies, a melted candle, matches, a Bible, and a small handgun along with a box of bullets tucked underneath a half-dozen *Reader's Digest*s.

In the closet, Gus finds a collection of hatboxes, a different colored hat inside each. Pink, plum, daisy yellow, and pistachio. Sunday hats. Each a delicate pastel bouquet resting inside a satin coffin. Some gilded with pearls. Others decorated with feathers or tiny silk roses. She opens the daisy yellow box and tries on the hat. Sitting in front of Rose's vanity, she pulls a strand of gray hair from the rim. It's caught in a pearl.

A remnant of Rose.

On the vanity sits a hand-carved jewelry box. Its velvet-lined pockets are brimming with bangles and shiny rings and rhinestone necklaces coiled like sleeping snakes. Costume jewelry. Cubic zirconia and simulated diamonds. Lars used to deal in junk jewelry. She knows it well. Gus clips on a pair of dangly earrings and looks in the mirror.

A child playing dress-up stares out at her.

She dips back in time.

8

ROSE

෧෧

GUS IS FIVE WHEN SHE'S CAUGHT SNOOPING IN ROSE'S jewelry box. She's never seen Rose that angry before. Rose was always so kind. She gave her powdered green mints from a candy dish with a glass lid. She let Gus play on the living room carpet with her Russian nesting dolls. But in that moment, she's a different person. Her pastel lips pull back to reveal yellow teeth like fangs.

How dare you touch my things.

She snaps the jewelry box shut. Grazes the back of Augusta's hand with her fingernail, leaving a scratch that almost bleeds. Gus is so ashamed of what she's done that on the way home in the car, when she finds a ring on her baby finger that she forgot to take off, she howls and throws it out the window. She falls into a fit of hysterics. Her mother has to pull the car over. Shannon doesn't know what's happening and Gus can't find the words to explain how Rose turned on her so unexpectedly. Shannon rubs her back and tells her she's overtired. Probably ate too many of Rose's mints.

But Gus isn't tired and she didn't eat too many mints. She's horribly sad. She's discovered that there are lines only grown-ups can see. Lines children are not supposed to cross. But these lines are invisible. And these lines are everywhere. From that day forward, Gus watches for them. Her nerves fray from looking so hard. From trying to spot them.

She crosses another when she's eight.

When she asks her mother about the photo of the ballerina.

Gus stares in the mirror. She's twenty now. All grown-up. No one can *how dare* her anymore. She can drink coffee from Rose's crystal, eat mac and cheese on the fine china, and wipe down the wet dog with the good towels if she so chooses.

This is her house. For ninety days at least. So there.

Gus tosses Rose's yellow Sunday hat on the carpet and storms down to the kitchen. She looks around. Then she pulls the table closer to the back door so the morning sun will cascade across it when she's having her coffee. She duct-tapes the broken screen back in place and tosses the crusty dishes into the trash bin under the sink. Then she spends the rest of the afternoon stretched out on her belly on the living room carpet playing with Rose's collection of Russian nesting dolls. She opens each maiden until she finds the smallest one hiding inside. The small ones have nothing inside them. They're solid. Not hollow like the others. These are her favorites. Gus opens all ten nesting dolls, then lines up the ten smallest in a row on the front windowsill so they can watch the carousel pass by.

Thursday, Gus browses through Rose's LP collection that

sits in a wire rack next to a turntable inside a wood cabinet. *Lawrence Welk and His Champagne Music. Patsy Cline's Greatest Hits. Pat Boone, Frank Sinatra, Johnny Cash.* Old lady music. Gus plays Sinatra's "My Way" cranked up loud. She spins around the living room letting her grannie nightie float like wings around her.

Friday morning, eight days since arriving at Rose's house, Gus is pouring her second cup of coffee when Haley-Anne phones to see how the to-do list is coming along.

"Oh, it's going great," Gus lies. Not wanting Haley-Anne to come over and burst her cocoon. If mail didn't tumble through the slot every afternoon, it would seem impenetrable. Gus could stay inside Rose's house forever. Ensure is amazingly filling.

"Give me a week and I'll give you curb appeal."

Levi walks into the kitchen as Gus hangs up. He's got one of her sneakers in his mouth. She darts at him, tries to grab the runner, nearly passes out from hunger.

Might be time to get some real food. She ventures out. Heads to the Metro grocery store around the corner. Fills a plastic basket with bananas, bread, a bag of mini Mars bars, a box of Honeycomb cereal, a six-pack of pink cream soda, and a chew toy for Levi. At the checkout counter, the guy stares at his register, then at her.

"That'll be twenty-four fifty-one. Cash, credit, or debit."

She can't believe she forgot her purse. Crap. She flushes red. He raises his eyebrows. She checks the back pocket of her jeans. Hits pay dirt. Change from the twenty she used to buy the bagel sandwich. Since she was a kid she's been shoving odds and ends in her back pocket like a squirrel and now one of these little acorns has come in handy. She tells the checkout guy to take off the cream soda. He does.

"That'll be sixteen sixty-one. Cash, I'm guessing?"

Back home, Levi ignores the chew toy. Instead, he sits in the front foyer staring up at her sneakers on the top shelf of the hall tree. After an hour of trying to will them to fall off, he lumbers to the kitchen and eases his arthritic hindquarters slowly to the floor. He stretches out on his belly and begins to gnaw the wooden leg of the kitchen table. Gus checks her phone. Twenty-two new texts from Lars.

> Auggie, baby girl. It's Lars.
> You can't just fucking ghost me.
> Honey, I miss you, Miss me?
> Answer me, bitch.

She doesn't bother reading the rest. Deletes them. Gus has bigger problems. Cash flow. The money she stole from Lars won't last. She could sell some of Rose's collectibles, but where? She's clueless. She's been living under a rock her whole life. Been taken care of by someone else. She doesn't know how to pay bills or clean a house or even boil an egg. All she knows how to do is microwave a frozen dinner, shoot a gun, and hot-wire a car. She needs a paycheck. A job. A real job.

Levi has one. Chewing. Gus watches as the dog chews the leg of the table. It's what Levi does best. Every stick of furniture, every baseboard, the lower rungs of the banister. All of it is scored with teeth marks. Dog's spent a decade chewing his way through this house. She watches his white whiskers quiver as he gently grinds his teeth. He's getting old. Doesn't eat that much. Hardly ever barks. Doesn't seem to care if she walks him or not. Mostly sleeps all day. No trouble at all when she really thinks about it.

Humane Society can wait. Gus gently slides his muzzle away from the chair leg.

"No, Levi."

He rolls casually onto his side, stretching his neck toward the leg, and goes back to gently gnawing on it. She lets him.

For the next week, they settle into a daily routine. They meet at the top of the stairs and head down to the kitchen together. Gus makes coffee and mashed bananas on toast sprinkled with Honeycomb. Levi eats his kibble then pushes past the duct tape and out through the broken screen, disappearing into the thick honeysuckles at the back of the yard. Some secret spot where he does his business.

Their routine includes a morning excursion to the dog run at Hampton Park. Levi likes to romp with a Great Dane named Eugene whose owner hasn't bothered to share his own name. He's a lanky man with a pointed nose and a pinched mouth. Resembles Eugene. The dogs smell each other then deke and dodge like they're playing tag. They're both slow. Levi's slowed by age and Eugene by his size. He's all legs. Eugene's owner talks nonstop. Gus doesn't mind. Sometimes he's the only person she talks to all day. And she might be the only person he talks to. They have nothing in common except their dogs. He tells her how Eugene's been off his food lately. How his poop hasn't been solid for days. How the vet charges an arm and a leg for Eugene's low-fat GI food. Sometimes he catches her off guard. Like when he said he wasn't sure he could go on without Eugene. She doesn't tell him that most days she feels like a small wooden doll living deep inside layers of bigger wooden dolls. How she's been nesting for days. How she's hiding but she's not sure from what or who.

Back from their morning walk, Levi stares at Augusta until she gets him a cookie from a jar in the kitchen. She asks him to sit. He looks at her. Tongue out, eyes wide. She asks him again. He scratches one ear with his hind leg. She gives up and tosses him the treat. He tries to snap it out of the air but misses and has to scramble after it. She pours another coffee and sits at the table. Levi settles at her feet and chews contentedly.

Gus loves the view out the open back door. The warm breeze of the fan. The cool floors on her bare feet. There's only one thing wrong with her kitchen world. That door next to the pantry. The basement door. As a child, she hated looking down those stairs when it stood open. Deep into the basement with its dark corners and hairy walls.

Gus decided a few days back to pretend that there was no basement in Rose's house. That a simple hook-and-eye latch was sufficient to keep any basement monsters down below where they belonged.

Not all doors are meant to be opened.

THAT NIGHT, A RAGING THUNDERSTORM ROLLS THROUGH THE neighborhood. Levi scurries into her bedroom. Panting. Body trembling. She pats the bed and he jumps up and snuggles close, burying his nose in her armpit. She strokes his ears. He puffs short, shallow breaths. He's terrified. She lies back, watching the fierce wind paint tree shadows on the walls. Lightning flashes. It's breathtaking. She always loved thunderstorms. Loved jumping in her mother's bed. Pretending she was scared so she could sleep next to her.

Sometime in the middle of the night, Gus wakes from a restless sleep to a strange sound. Levi isn't beside her anymore. A sharp squeak like someone's moving furniture comes from down the hall. She slips silently out of bed. Inches into the hall. The noise is coming from Rose's room. Her mind dances to the gun in Rose's bedside table. Levi hasn't barked once. She grabs a plunger from the bathroom. Envisions the dog, lying dead on the carpet. Lars waiting in the dark to murder her before taking his own life. Gus tiptoes toward the half-open door. Plunger out in front of her, mind reeling, she slowly peers inside Rose's bedroom. It's dark. There's a commotion. She can hear Levi snarling. He's alive. She feels along the wall for the light switch. Flips on the light.

There's no one in Rose's room but the dog. The crazy dog. He's perched on the edge of the bed, leaning over, bum in the air, furiously tearing chunks from Rose's mattress. He's managed to rip holes down the length of the mattress all the way to the corner. Ignoring Gus, he jumps off the bed and starts pulling great swaths of cotton stuffing out of the mattress. With each yank, the entire bed shifts and squeaks against the floorboards as he disembowels the mattress.

"Levi. No! Bad dog."

Momentarily, he lifts his head and looks over at her with big dumb eyes, clumps of stuffing hanging from his drooling lips. He hacks violently as the stuffing catches in his throat, then he returns to eviscerating the mattress. Gus drops the plunger and grabs Levi by his neck fur. She pulls him away from the bed. He vomits a soggy wad of fluff.

"Jesus, dog. Really?"

She shoves him, and he slides across the floorboards. Then he slinks to the corner. Tail between his legs.

Gus stares at the mess. The mattress is toast. She picks up the wad that Levi hacked up. She gags. Searches for a garbage can. There's one next to the bedside table. She's about to toss it in when she spots a face in the wad. The Queen's face. She gently pulls the soggy wad apart. Inside is a chewed-up twenty-dollar bill.

She looks at Levi who's standing in the corner. He wags his tail.

She looks at the mattress.

Gus kneels down and reaches her hand into one of the holes. Feels around. Nothing but stuffing. She digs deeper. Up to her elbow. Then she touches something plastic. She yanks, but it's stuck. She gets both hands inside the hole and is able to grip the plastic. Uses her feet against the bed for leverage. Then, like a baby being born, it slides out of the open wound in the mattress. A large plastic garment bag. The edge is torn where Levi got his teeth into it, the rest vacuum-sealed flat and zippered tight. Gus lays the bag on the floor. Straddles it. Grabs hold of the zipper and opens the bag. She stares at the contents, then looks over at Levi.

"You waited two and a half weeks to show me this, dog?"

By the time she's finished counting the bundles of twenties and hundreds at the kitchen table, the sky has turned a milky blue as night gives way to a cloudy morning. Gus has no doubt that Levi saw Rose sock away that money in her mattress. Sensed they were down to their last bag of kibble and decided to share what he knew. Or maybe everything just looks like a chew toy to the dog. Either way, he's earned himself a full pardon. And that ten grand stuffed in Rose's bed means Augusta can postpone her job hunt for now.

Gus leans back and sips her coffee, pondering what other riches might be secreted away in Rose's house.

She looks over at the door to the basement.

Another kind of hunt comes to mind.

A treasure hunt.

9

BLUE

❦

GUS IS EXCITED FOR THE FIRST TIME SINCE ARRIVING AT Rose's house. Stored away in that basement might be a few precious items from her life with her mother. Unlatching the basement door, Gus stands on the top step. She can do this. She's twenty. She peers into the pitch-black void. Damp air fills her nostrils. She feels for the string at the top of the stairs. Pulls it. A dim bulb illuminates steep wooden steps leading to a concrete floor. She grabs hold of the dusty handrail and descends. The stairs groan.

A spongy white fluff pushes through the cracks in the cement floor. A couple of broken kitchen chairs and a dozen stackable bins are piled next to the firewood along a far wall. A water heater, a fuse box, and an old furnace occupy a corner. A freezer hums off to one side next to a shelf of rusty paint cans and a red tin toolbox.

Gus crosses to the freezer. Lifts the lid. No dead bodies. Just a lifetime supply of Weight Watchers frozen microwave dinners. Shrimp Marinara. Cranberry Turkey Medallions. Salisbury Steak. Ready-made meals encased in frost. Right up her alley.

One by one, Gus opens the stackable bins. Each time, she holds her breath. First, there's the sewing bin. A collection of fabric samples, jars of buttons, felt squares stuck with rows of sewing needles, and an array of spools of thread. Next, there's the one with the Christmas decorations. Bulbs missing their hooks, tinsel, tangled strings of multicolored lights, and a plastic star with three broken points. Then a bin full of cards. Birthday, sympathy, thank-you, anniversary. Bin after bin. Full of the stuff of Rose's life. Her hobbies, holidays, memories. But nothing of theirs. Nothing of hers and Shannon's. No cards, no photo albums, no treasures from their life together. As if that life never existed.

Gus sits back on her heels after closing the last of the bins. She bites her lip. This is the real reason why she hadn't come down here yet. She was hoping. And hope is stupid and childish and fucked up. Augusta rises and violently kicks the nearest bin as hard as she can.

"I hate this house!"

She limps to the stairs and grabs the rail. It snaps off in her hand. Stupid old-lady house. She whips the rotten rail to the floor. It clangs off the edge of a box tucked under the stairs and skids across the floor. Gus leans sideways to get a better look. It's not a box.

It's a trunk. A blue trunk.

She knows it. She drags it out from under the stairs. Pins and needles prick her neck.

It's *her* trunk.

The one she named Blue.

The one her mother called her treasure chest. A place to keep her most precious things. It used to sit at the foot of her bed in their house in Hintonburg. She can't believe it. She touches it gently with one hand, rubbing dust from its lid.

How did it end up in Rose's basement?

Levi has come to the top of the stairs to see what all the commotion is. She looks up as he lowers his chin.

"Guess what I found, dog?"

With all her might, Gus drags the trunk upstairs. Levi scoots under the table as she pulls it into the kitchen. Gus sinks to her knees. Grabs the lock. She knows the combo by heart. Her birthday. 5–2–9–8. She rotates the numbers until they line up and it clicks open. She lifts the lid, holds her breath, and looks inside.

It feels like mere seconds since she last peered inside her trunk. But here are all her things. Right in front of her. Proof that time can stand still. Her Hilroy notebooks filled with doodles. Her plastic art kit, pastels, crayons, and colored pencils worn to the nib. Sunny, her yellow-haired doll with the ceramic feet, wearing the same pink pinafore with the lacy pockets. A collection of clip-on earrings in the emerald silk bag. Her Barbies. Her beanbag frog, Louis. Class photos from Junior K through grade three. Swimming medals. Olympic coins. Her sticker collection. And rolled up right where she left it. Her pink pashmina scarf. The one her mother gave her their last Christmas together.

Levi ambles over and sticks his head inside the trunk. He gently takes Louis in his mouth and walks away. She barely notices. She softly closes the lid. Tears in her eyes.

It's not until much later that day, well after dark, fortified with sweet sherry from Rose's dining room hutch and dressed in her grannie nightie, that Gus drags Blue down the hall and into the living room. She swigs sherry straight from the bottle as she opens the trunk. And sitting on the carpet, she slowly pulls out each item and arranges them in front of her. Lovingly touching her plastic earrings. Lining up her Barbies side by side. Sipping sherry. Wallowing in these treasures from her past. In her childhood. Touching the worn ends of the pink and green and orange pastels in her art kit. Placing her stickers in neat little piles, next to a row of Olympic coins and her swimming medals.

Levi peers in the living room, thinks better of it, and heads up to bed.

Gus picks up the stack of class photos from the bottom of the trunk. Each is framed in a cardboard sleeve. She sits cross-legged with them in her lap and prepares herself for a sherry-soaked trip down memory lane. One more swig and she starts. Junior Kindergarten. Opens the sleeve. A column of names is written carefully in pencil on one side, opposite the class photo. Three rows of four-year-olds pose next to their teacher, Miss Temple. Miss Temple's smile is distorted because the photo is bulging where her face is. Gus tries to smooth it, but there's something behind the photo. She lifts the edge and peers underneath. There's a piece of paper tucked in behind it. Despite her sherry fog, Augusta can clearly make out two words.

Missing persons.

Gus leans closer. The other folders tumble from her lap. Grade two flips open. She lifts the corner of that class photo. A newspaper clipping is tucked behind it. She checks the others. Behind Senior Kindergarten is a legal document. Behind grade three is a collection of photographs. Behind grade one, a photocopied image. She slips each item out from behind the class photos, then gathers them into a pile. Two newspaper clippings, a photocopy of what looks like a security camera image, a handwritten document, a missing persons report, and three photographs.

She knows these things.

She's seen them before.

Above the workbench her father built in Kingston. The one Shannon insisted the movers bring to their new house in Ottawa. The bench where her mother set up her makeshift office and where she spent most of her evenings poring over documents and photos.

These documents. These photos.

Gus closes her eyes and curls her feet up inside her nightie. She topples to one side in a fetal position. Her head spins.

Sleep tugs her eyelids closed. She can hear a noise. It's in her bedroom. She forces her eyes to open. It's her mother. Gus wants to call out, but her mouth won't open. She's too sleepy. Shannon's face pops up from behind the open lid of the trunk at the end of her bed.

Mama.

She smiles. Wipes her tired eyes.

Go to sleep.

Gus closes her eyes like a good girl.

Back soon, Sugar Bunch. I promise.

Augusta drifts off to sleep.

Then and now.

Not sure which is which but sinking deeply into both.

10

HENRY

CRUSTY-MOUTHED, GUS ROLLS ONTO HER BACK. NIGHTIE twisting around her legs. Pain stabbing her temples. Sherry pain. She peels a photo off her cheek.

Levi is sprawled across the foyer. He lifts his head as she stirs. He's been waiting. Daylight slices through the curtains. Daggers in her eyeballs. Augusta sits. Nausea swims up her throat. She squints at the photo, a snapshot of a young man flanked by two adults. They're all smiles. He looks about seventeen. High school graduation. Gown. Cap in hand. Dark hair and dimples. Handsome.

Augusta drops the photo and crawls to the sofa. Pulls herself to her feet. The room sways. She vows never to drink sherry again. Levi heads for the kitchen and Gus stumbles after him.

Put kibble in dog bowl.

Set coffee to brew.

Down jug of water.

Open back door to let dog out.

Coffee. Black.

Gag.

Dry toast with mashed bananas.

Gag.

Three Advil.

Nibble Honeycomb.

More coffee.

Rest forehead on kitchen table awhile.

Breathe.

Watch dog slip back inside through broken screen.

Glance at Haley-Anne's to-do list.

Shake pins and needles out of legs.

Throw up in garbage can.

Stumble back to living room.

Stare at mess on carpet.

Spot photograph.

The Polaroid.

The one she's never forgotten. Gus knows every detail of that picture of the ballerina. The awkward little body in the sagging white leotard circled by a pink tutu. The bony shoulders strapped with butterfly wings. The Coke-bottle glasses and that jet-black hair tied in a messy bun with a pink bow. The girl is about seven. Her small hands are clasped above her head, arms forming a halo. She's posing on the edge of the veranda of a big house.

Gus picks up the Polaroid. Holds it close. The girl's eyes are far away and her smile is only half there. Gus flips the photo over. On the back, there's writing in red marker. It's upside-down. She turns it so she can read what her mother wrote.

Gracie Halladay, April 2002.

All these years, Gus never knew the girl's name. It was on the back this whole time. She'd never dared touch the photo to flip it over. But the name was there. Shannon was hiding it. She was protective of this girl. This photo. Of all her things. Everything in her workspace in that garage. It was off-limits. Gus was to stay out. She even had to keep her bike in the front hall. Shannon didn't share her work with anyone. Colleagues. Fellow cops. Friends. Not even Uncle Rory who stopped by every Christmas. He was a policeman too, but that didn't matter to Shannon. Her work was for her eyes only.

And now, the very photo that made Shannon shut the door on her daughter's face is the same photo Shannon put in Augusta's trunk. Along with her most private papers and documents. Things that preoccupied her days and nights. Things she held close. She took them off her corkboard and she hid them. She was afraid someone might see them. She was protecting the little ballerina. Just like she'd always done.

Fuck Gracie Halladay.

Augusta rips the Polaroid in half and tosses it into the black hearth of the fireplace. Her fingers are suddenly icy cold. She shivers, trying to shake off the chill.

Levi barks and scratches at the hall tree in the foyer where his leash hangs. Gus turns to snap at him, but the look on his face is priceless. Tongue hanging out, mouth wide. He looks like he's smiling ear to ear.

"You're right. Let's get the fuck out of here, dog."

After throwing on a T-shirt, jeans, her sneakers, and a ball cap, Gus heads outside with Levi. An orange sun warms her face as they walk. The chill inside her begins to thaw a little with each step. Levi is bouncier than usual. They make their way down the tree-lined drive, winding uphill toward Byron. They veer off the main road and take the walking path that skirts alongside the Tramway Park where empty swings rock in the light breeze.

Gus empties her brain of Gracie and Shannon and focuses on the soft patter of the dog's paws and his light sweet breaths. He sniffs garbage cans and the occasional passing dog's bum. He pees every couple of blocks. Saving it up for this curb or that hydrant. Marking his territory. Claiming it as if he's the last dog who'll ever mark that patch of grass. She sinks into the simplicity of Levi's world.

Augusta and Levi loop back to Wellington Street where she stops to grab a coffee at the local Bridgehead. She wraps his leash around a metal bike rack, then goes inside to order. When she comes out, a slim woman in neon-pink jogging pants is petting his head. The woman places her *Ottawa Citizen* newspaper on a nearby table and stoops to one knee so she can ruffle Levi's ears. He's eating it up. Augusta tells her his name as the woman presses her face to Levi's snout and talks baby talk.

"Who's a beautiful boy? You are. You're a beautiful boy. Yes, you are."

Gus places her coffee on the table so she can untie Levi. The picture on the front of the newspaper catches her eye. It's of a young man. She picks it up.

COLD CASE MYSTERY SOLVED: BODY FOUND FIFTEEN YEARS AFTER BOY'S DISAPPEARANCE.

She knows that face. It's the boy from the photo. The one she peeled off her cheek this morning. She scans the article for a name. Henry Neil. She glimpses random phrases.

No foul play suspected.

It was just an accident.

She tears the front page off the newspaper and, before the woman can object, Gus frees Levi and hurries down the street. The woman hollers something about Gus owing her money for the paper, but Augusta can't hear her. She's tuned in to the fierce and steady drumbeat of her heart. To the two words that *thump thump thump* across her brain.

Cold case.

❧

Shannon and Augusta are sitting on the front porch eating spicy Thai noodles out of greasy cardboard cartons.

What's a cold case, Mama?

Gus heard the word on a rerun of *Murder, She Wrote*. She'd heard her mother say it too. Shannon chews her noodles.

It's a case nobody's solved yet.

Why cold? Does it need warming up?

Shannon smiles.

It does. If it's not kept warm, people might forget about it. Then no one'll ever know the truth.

They twirl their noodles around chopsticks.

Is that what you do in the garage? Keep cold cases warm?

Shannon stops twirling and goes quiet, chewing slowly. Gus holds her breath. Has she crossed one of those invisible lines? She wishes she could swallow her words. But then Shannon softens.

I try, Honey Pie.

❧

Levi naps on the kitchen floor. The walk tuckered him out. But Gus is wired. She has the torn front page of the newspaper in her hand. She feels an overwhelming sense of déjà vu. As if she's seen something so familiar, something she knows so intimately, only she shouldn't know it at all. This feeling carries her down the hall and into the living room.

Gus drags the standing lamp that sits in the corner over to the main wall. Pulls off the lampshade and floods the room with light. She steadies herself. Then she goes to work.

She hauls the furniture away from the wall. Then begins to clear it off. The Canadiana wildlife paintings of the bald eagle and the wolf pack. The mounted wooden box that holds Rose's teaspoon collection bearing the crests of each province and territory. It all comes down.

Now she needs supplies. She hunts the house for Scotch tape. Finds it in a kitchen drawer. She rummages through the red toolbox in the basement. Finds a hammer. Back in the living room, she removes the leftover nails with the hook of the hammer.

Sitting on the sofa, staring at the blank wall, she lets her gaze slip out of focus. Then she takes hold of her eight-year-old hand and goes back with her.

∾

Shannon is asleep. Augusta sneaks downstairs. Goes into the garage. Into her mother's office. She blinks, sleepy-eyed, at the corkboard above the bench. There are faces and sentences and numbers. There are lines drawn in red marker between the pictures and words. Augusta's eyes follow these red lines, leading from one photo to the next, one piece of paper to the next. Numbers are written on top of these lines.

❧

The world around Augusta rolls back into focus. Those same faces and sentences float in front of her on Rose's living room wall. Before they can disappear, Gus gathers the items scattered on the carpet. One by one. The pieces her mother left in her trunk. She attaches tape to the top edge of each newspaper article, photo, and document. Then sticks them helter-skelter to the wall. She steps back.

It's all wrong.

She looks at the front page of the newspaper that she took from Neon-Pink.

COLD CASE MYSTERY SOLVED.

Compares the picture with the grad photo of the boy and his parents. Yep. Same guy. Henry Neil. Was this the cold case Shannon was keeping warm? Just an accident. It makes no sense. Feels too easy. Too simple for her mother not to have figured out. Shannon didn't obsess over an accident. Didn't shut out her own daughter because of some missing teenager.

Gus stares at the misshapen collage on the wall. At the pieces that look like they have nothing to do with Henry Neil or each other. She closes her eyes. Searches for a strand. A stray memory she can tug on. Unravel. She lets her breath guide her deeper. Then she finds one.

Gus opens her eyes and grabs Henry's grad photo off the wall, then retapes it dead center where it belongs.

Yes, says a voice in her head. *That's more like it.*

But it's not her own voice. It's Shannon's. Maybe her mother wasn't hiding these things in her trunk so much as leaving them for her as a gift. Gus reaches toward the wall but doesn't touch it. She senses her mother's presence close by. Her scent. Her cells. Her DNA is deposited on these documents and photographs like a fine dust. The fragments begin to re-assemble in Augusta's mind's eye. And as they do, she moves each piece into its proper place.

Good girl.

The missing persons report for Henry Neil goes below the grad photo. Below that goes the photocopy of the grainy security image. In it a young man is walking onto a porch toward the front door of a house. His face is turned away from the camera. A hand can be seen holding the door open. The date stamp says July 14, 2003. Written across the top of the photocopy, in her mother's red marker, is a simple question.

Henry?

To the left of the wall space dedicated to Henry, Gus tapes the newspaper clipping from a publication called *Lakes and Islands*. The headline reads, "Local Woman Killed in Freak Accident." Gracie's Polaroid belongs directly above this article. Gus reaches into the fireplace and picks up the two pieces of the ripped Polaroid. She carefully tapes the picture back together and sticks it in place.

Everything comes into focus.

The handwritten document called a deed of trust and a business article from the *Globe and Mail* go to the right of Henry's zone. And last is the photo taken from inside a car looking out toward an intersection. A man is crossing in front of the car. Gus tapes this photo underneath the business article.

She stands back. She's done it.

Each item is arranged exactly as it was on her mother's wall in the garage. But there's something missing. She sinks down into the sofa. An oddly contented feeling envelops her entire body. The sofa feels warm and solid beneath her sitting bones.

This is a beginning. Even if incomplete and uncertain. Everything feels right and real to her in this moment.

And yet Gus has no idea what she's looking at. If Shannon were sitting next to her, she'd put her arm around Augusta.

Do you see it, Gus?

Augusta closes her eyes.

Not yet, Mama.

11

SENATOR HALLADAY

LATER THAT NIGHT, A CRANBERRY TURKEY MEDALLION dinner in her belly, Gus reads the full article about Henry Neil that she stole from Neon-Pink.

He went missing in July of 2003 and his remains were discovered this week by a group of spelunkers exploring an abandoned mine near Newboro, Ontario. Fifteen years ago, Henry had been studying earth sciences and geophysics at Western University in London, Ontario.

A promising young man with a bright future ahead of him is how one of his former professors describes him.

His parents reported him missing when they didn't hear from him for a week. At the time, he'd been away on a summer internship conducting mineral surveys in the Township of Rideau Lakes. He was billeting in Elgin, Ontario, with a local senator who was overseeing the mineral study. A man named Kep Halladay. No foul play was suspected, and a body was never found. The case went cold. Until now. The article says police have closed the case. He fell. It was just an accident.

Gus grabs the Scotch tape and sticks the newspaper clipping on the wall near the other items about Henry. She traces her finger across Henry's story. From his body being found this week, to a possible sighting on a porch in 2003, to his missing person's report that same year, to his graduation a few years earlier. It's a timeline. She gets a sudden flash of Shannon absently twirling a red marker between her thumb and index finger.

That's when it hits her. She knows what's missing.

Gus riffles through Rose's antique roller-top desk in the dining room. Inside she finds stacks of old receipts, a stapler, envelopes, a box of paper clips, and a drawer full of pencils, pens, and markers. Bingo! A red marker.

As if her hand has a mind of its own, Augusta picks up the red marker, moves to the far left of the wall, places the tip under the Polaroid of Gracie Halladay and slowly draws a thick red line down the plaster wall, through the *Lakes and Islands* article, across and through the missing persons report, the deed, all the way to the photo of the man crossing the intersection. Her line connects with red lines already marked across some of the documents by her mother. Remembering the numbers, Gus sidesteps back to the ballerina and scans for dates in the bylines of articles, next to signature lines of documents, and on the backs of photos. She writes these dates in red marker at various points along the red line.

September 2002. Freak accident.

July 2003. Disappearance.

August 2003. Signing of the deed.

January 2004. Land deal.

Gus takes a step back. Stands at the far side of the room to survey her work. Twirls the red marker between her thumb and index finger and smiles.

Now that's her mother's wall.

A timeline of events that took place over the span of less than two years, connected by evidence. She can't believe it took her this long to remember the red timeline, considering remnants of Shannon's marker still streak and circle parts of each piece of evidence.

This is what preoccupied her mother. A cold case that's about more than just one person. A case she seemed compelled to keep warm.

Gus admires the beautiful transformation of her great-grandmother's living room wall into Shannon's wall. No longer a place for miniature teaspoon collections and kitschy art. It is now hers and her mother's. A work of art they created together.

Augusta's phone vibrates. Haley-Anne. She looks up at the wall and cringes a little. Oops. What would the real estate agent think if she saw the state of the living room? Not likely the staging she had in mind. Gus ignores the call. She's not ready to sell just yet. A sense of purpose begins to slowly seep into her bones.

Gus takes a close-up photo with her phone of each item on the wall so she can carry them with her for quick reference. Then she grabs a pen and a small spiral notebook from a collection she found in Rose's desk. Opens the notebook to a blank page and begins examining each piece of evidence more closely, jotting notes as she goes. Shannon was always taking notes. It feels right to do the same. Even though Gus isn't exactly sure what she's looking for or why she's even doing any of this, she feels her mother's guiding hand with every stroke of her pen.

Levi is long gone to bed. It's after midnight. Gus is wide awake.

She starts with the Polaroid of Gracie Halladay. Writes Gracie's name and the date written on the back of the photo. April 2002. She skims the *Lakes and Islands* article dated September 3, 2002. The headline reads, "Local Woman Killed in Freak Accident." It's a brief notice more than a full-blown article.

> June Halladay, 23, was tragically killed in a freak accident early Monday when she was struck by her own car in front of her childhood home in Elgin, Ontario. The young heiress suffered severe head injuries and later died in hospital. Her seven-year-old daughter, a minor who cannot be named, was in the car at the time of the accident. No charges have been laid. The victim's father, prominent local businessman and political figure Senator Kep Halladay, was home at the time of the accident. June Halladay's daughter, now sole heir to the Halladay fortune, remains in the care of her grandfather.

In red marker, Shannon had circled Kep Halladay's name. Gus checks her notes. She does the math. The Polaroid was taken a few months before the accident. Gracie looks about seven. June's twenty-three. If Gracie is her daughter, then June would have been fifteen or sixteen when she got pregnant. Gus writes June Halladay in her notebook. Then

Kep Halladay. Adds the date of the accident next to June's name.

Gus skims the missing persons report. July 16, 2003. Not much to it. The report was initiated by Ida and Ron Neil and filed at the Kingston RCMP detachment by Sergeant Marty Stanton. Henry was nineteen when he was reported missing. It names Senator Halladay among those interviewed, as well as his eight-year-old granddaughter, Gracie Halladay.

So Gracie was the minor who could not be named. Daughter of June.

Gus smiles. She's enjoying connecting the dots. According to the statements given by those interviewed, Henry was last seen two weeks earlier collecting mineral samples seven miles from the town of Elgin. Again, Shannon has circled Kep Halladay's name. Gus jots Henry's name, age, and the date he went missing in her notebook.

She compares the two photos of Henry. One with his parents. A beaming young high school grad. The other on a porch. The image is grainy. Taken at night. Almost looks like a robber caught by a security camera. Tough to tell if it's Henry. By the question mark after his name written across the top of the photocopied image, Gus sees that Shannon wasn't sure either. And someone else is there. A hand is opening the door. There's a large brass knocker on the front of the door shaped like a lion's head.

Gus moves on to the deed of trust. It's full of legal mumbo jumbo and lists a bunch of names and places. The town of Elgin is mentioned along with some longitudes and latitudes. There are thirty-three signatures at the bottom of the deed. And below those names is another signature. A thirty-fourth.

Set apart from the others. Kep Halladay's. The deed appears to be some sort of land deal relating to mineral rights. The rights are being signed over to Halladay by all the others. Halladay's name has been circled in red marker. The deed was signed, notarized, sealed, and dated August 26, 2003, by the county records office of Leeds Grenville. The records office address is neatly typed across the bottom of the document.

Next is an article from the *Globe and Mail* dated January 22, 2004. Some five months after the deed was signed. The headline reads, "Prominent Tycoon Inks Landmark Mineral Rights Deal." Senator Halladay is named as the tycoon. It details how Halladay just announced that he has negotiated a mineral rights deal with a Toronto land brokerage firm representing an American oil and gas company. His name is circled again. Another of her mother's red bull's-eyes squarely aimed at Senator Kep Halladay.

The final piece of evidence on the far right of Shannon's wall is a photograph. Gus remembers it. Remembers never letting her young eyes linger on it too long because she didn't like it. To an eight-year-old, the man in the photo looked like a ghost.

She leans in close now. Curious and unafraid. The photo was shot through the front windshield of a car from the driver's seat. Looking closely, she can make out the edge of the tan dashboard and the blue hood. Her mother's Corolla was blue with a tan interior. The figure is crossing the intersection in front of the car. Must have been taken when the car was stopped at a red light. He's moving fast so his lower body is a blur. He's broad shouldered. His arms swing. He's wearing a white hoodie. His upper body and head are in focus.

His face is in profile, partially hidden behind the hoodie, but his left ear pokes out. It's deformed. A mass of wrinkled scar tissue that's almost as white as his hoodie. Augusta flips the photo over. Shannon's red marker has scrawled two words on the back.

Grease Monkey.

Gus flips the photo back over. In the background of the image, behind the man, is a storefront. Slightly out of focus, but the sign is readable. *Elgin Apothecary and Gift Shop.*

Gus reviews her notes and underlines key names and dates.

Gracie Halladay (7), photo dated April 2002.

June Halladay (23), died September 2, 2002.

Henry Neil (19), reported missing July 16, 2003.

Deed of trust, signed August 26, 2003.

Land deal, announced January 22, 2004.

She adds the words *Grease Monkey* to the list.

Gus picks up her red marker and circles Senator Halladay's name in the article about Henry from today's newspaper. Just like her mother would have done.

That's when she spots it.

A tiny smudge of red ink at the bottom of the police report. Only this is more than just a remnant of a line or circle made by Shannon years ago. This smudge is a fingerprint. Only part of a fingerprint. Made accidentally. But it was made by her mother. Gus shivers. She presses her index finger against Shannon's print. Feels herself being led. But where? And toward what? Augusta's eyes search the evidence and a place jumps out. A town. Then it clicks. That's where Shannon used to go and Gus is certain she must go there too.

She remembers her mother telling the babysitter, Annalee,

that's where she was going. More than once. She can almost hear them now.

She's finished her French dictée homework. She's settling in next to Annalee to watch a movie. The fifteen-year-old loves dance movies. Has DVDs of all the latest releases. *Shall We Dance, Dirty Dancing: Havana Nights.* The pair barely look up as Shannon stands at the door giving last-minute instructions before she rushes off.

Okay, I've set the alarm on my watch for 10 P.M. like usual. I'll head back then. Call 911 if the house catches fire or if anyone accidentally gets stabbed.

Annalee laughs and waves.

Don't worry, Mrs. Monet. We're good.

I'm serious. Call 911 if anything happens. You might not be able to reach me. Cell service drops out in that part of the county, especially around Elgin.

Another time, Augusta is waiting in the parking lot of the Independent Grocer while Shannon's inside. Gus has her feet on the dash and is doing a tap dance on the glove compartment when it pops open. A crumpled map tumbles out. Augusta opens it. Eastern Ontario. She finds Ottawa on the map. Then she notices a circle drawn around a town not far away.

Elgin.

12

JAMES

◈

AUGUSTA WAKES TO LEVI LICKING HER FACE. SHE'S LYING ON the sofa in the living room. The sun's up. She must have fallen asleep sometime after two in the morning. Her eyes adjust to the light flooding in the front window. She looks up at Shannon's wall. Levi follows her gaze. His eyes scan the red markings crisscrossing the collage of photos and papers. He looks at her. She shrugs. Dog doesn't get it. Neither does she really, but she's happy with what she's done. Her mother now inhabits Rose's house along with her and Levi. She ruffles the top of the dog's scruffy head.

"Road trip?"

A half hour later, Augusta and Levi are standing in front of the rickety garage door. She opens it. A dust cloud billows from inside. Levi wags his tail. Next to a few rusty garden tools and cracked planters sits Rose's beige Buick Skylark sedan. Levi barks. He knows the car. She puts the dog in the back, gets in, holds her breath, and turns the key in the ignition.

The old Buick whirs then sputters and stalls. She floors the gas pedal like Lars taught her. Flushing the air out of the gas line. Tries again. The Buick chugs then turns over. She exhales and backs out of the garage. Levi settles down across the back seat.

Gus has her new satchel on the seat next to her. It was the first thing she bought with Rose's mattress stash. Found it in a little luggage store a few blocks from Rose's. To replace the purse Lars picked out for her. That one's in the dumpster behind the Metro. This one's less faux designer. More functional. Large enough to carry her phone, notebook, pen, red marker, two water bottles, and a couple of egg salad sandwiches wrapped in tinfoil for lunch.

One for her, one for Levi.

The Buick is a beast but Gus is comfortable driving it. The weight of it feels solid underneath her. No weird pings or moans are coming from its belly so hopefully it's road-ready. Gus pulls into a gas station to fill up. She gets the attendant to check under the hood while she goes inside to buy a map of Eastern Ontario.

Gus likes maps. Likes the feel of the paper. The folds and the grids. The feeling that all the world can be seen from overhead in a glimpse. That everything has a place and connects to everything else. An illusion she finds comforting. Lars used to laugh when she'd suggest they buy a map instead of using his GPS. But to Gus, it's much weirder to have a disembodied digital voice telling you where to turn and when. What if it steers you wrong? Paper feels more reliable. Besides, she's pretty sure the phone Lars gave her isn't that smart.

Opening the map, Gus finds the town. It looks to be about

eighty miles from Ottawa, in the middle of a system of lakes and rivers. Looks remote. Not close to any major highways. A few small towns dot the county twelve miles away on either side, but Elgin seems to sit apart. Closest city is Kingston, which is about a forty-minute drive southwest. She circles Elgin with her red marker. Just like Shannon did. Gus leaves the map open on the seat next to her as she drives out of town due south. They're in farm country inside twenty minutes. Rows of green corn stand at attention along the roadside under a baby blue cloudless sky. It's a full hour before Augusta sees the first sign.

Elgin 50 km.

She rolls down the windows. The breeze turns her red hair into a cat-o'-nine-tails. Levi sticks his head out the window. Tongue flapping. Cheeks billowing. Eyes shut. Blissful. They pass acres of summer-soaked alfalfa fields. Cross a long bridge over a wide brown river dotted with cottages. A ghost tree sits solitary on a grassy hill at the far side of the bridge. All its leaves and bark are stripped away by wind, sun, and age. Nothing left but naked white bones reaching for the sky.

Elgin 35 km.

Augusta turns on the radio. It's tuned to public broadcast. CBC. A noon call-in show. Some heated debate over whether or not elementary-school children should get two nutrition breaks versus one lunch break. Angry parents call in to give their two cents. A child psychologist offers her expert opinion. Gus can't imagine getting so worked up about two twenties versus a forty. It's the same thing. Kids eat either way.

Shannon usually forgot to pack Augusta's lunch. If she remembered, it was some prepackaged salami-and-cheese combo in a plastic tray with a mini Kit Kat and a tutti-frutti juice box that turned Augusta's lips blue.

Gus punches buttons on the radio until she hears the sweet rippling voice of a woman singing a bluesy folk song. Or is it two women singing together? In harmony. Lars never wanted to listen to anything but hard rock or heavy metal. She didn't mind because the deafening noise drowned out her thoughts. This song does the opposite. It brings them achingly into the foreground.

> *Take me oh take me back,*
> *Take me oh take me back,*
> *To where I was when our world blew apart,*
> *To how it felt when you wrecked my heart.*
> *I want to live in the space between our kisses,*
> *I want to wander through all our near misses.*
> *Take me oh take me back, to that place we once called*
>   *home,*
> *Take me oh take me back, to that feeling of being so*
>   *all alone.*

She turns off the radio midsong. Instead, she tunes in to the dog snoring in the back seat. The hum of the Buick's engine. The hiss of tires across hot asphalt.

Elgin 10 km.

The road slowly changes the closer she gets. The pavement becomes more and more riddled with cracks. Crumbling at the edges. After a few miles, the landscape changes too. Lush farmland gives way to dusty barren fields or great swaths of purple flowering weeds that cover huge tracts of land. Rock formations weave across the fields, jutting from hillsides and edging the cracked highway.

As she continues, Gus sees something blocking the road up ahead. She slows, then stops. A cement barricade runs across the two-lane highway. Blocking the road to Elgin. Dead end. She must have missed the warning signs.

Augusta leaves the car running and gets out to stretch her legs. Levi jumps out. Bolts off the hot pavement and pees on the purple loosestrife in the dry ditch. Augusta walks to the barricade and reads the sign bolted across it.

ROAD CLOSED. DO NOT ENTER. HAZARDOUS TOXIC WASTE. UNAUTHORIZED ENTRY BANNED.

At the bottom of the sign, there's some smaller writing.

BY ORDER OF THE COUNTY OF LEEDS GRENVILLE PUBLIC WORKS AND RECORDS OFFICE AND THE CHIEF MEDICAL OFFICER OF THE ONTARIO MINISTRY OF HEALTH.

After taking a photo of the sign, Augusta jumps back into the Buick. Levi follows. She checks the map then pulls a U-turn, heading north on Highway 15.

There are other roads into Elgin.

She takes a right on 42, following the detour sign she missed before. All the side roads off the 42 that lead toward Elgin are closed from Lockwood Lane to Hartsgravel Road. She drives through the town of Delta and finds another detour sign rerouting her back to the 15 via Lyndhurst Road. This detour takes her through the village of Lyndhurst, past three more barricades at Old Briar Hill, Sweet Corners, and Back Street, which lands her right back on the 15, well south of Elgin. Reaching a T-junction at the 15, she checks the map again. She's done a 180 around Elgin, never getting closer than three miles to the town. No back lanes. No cut-throughs. All blocked. And if the map's right, there's no access on the far side, either. Just a maze of rivers that connects Sand Lake, Murphy's Bay, and Opinicon Lake.

She can't drive in. Now she's even more curious about this town her mother used to visit. She'll have to park somewhere and walk in.

Gus turns right, passes a graveyard surrounded by a low fence bearing a sign that says DESIGNATED CEMETERY. Farther up, she passes a deserted gas station. Weeds spiral around the abandoned pumps. Past the station is another barricade. She pulls off the highway onto a dirt lane sheltered by a large willow. Parks in the shade and decides to eat before beginning the three-mile hike into town. She grabs an egg sandwich and tosses Levi half. He chokes it down whole, then nudges her shoulder for more. Gus ignores him, closes her eyes, and listens to the willow branches swishing lightly in the breeze. Levi delicately pulls the half-eaten sandwich from her hand. She doesn't care. She leans her head back as the branches stroke the hood of the Buick. The song from the radio wafts back.

> *Take me oh take me back, to that place we once called home,*
> *Take me oh take me back, to that feeling of being so all alone.*

Levi barks. His sharp angry-dog bark. Augusta's eyes snap open. She's disoriented. The sun slants low across the field of purple loosestrife. It's late afternoon. She's slept the day away. Again. Something she seems to have mastered since arriving at Rose's. Gus rubs her eyes and shakes off the nap. Levi barks again.

"I'm up. I'm up."

Then she hears it. A soft rhythmic drumming in the distance. Gus looks through the back window of the car. A man bobs on the horizon, then he rises up over it, perched on the saddle of a large white horse. The horse comes into view as the pair trots toward her. Clouds of purple seeds waft up in the horse's wake.

Gus gets out of the car. Levi follows, cowering behind her legs. The rider slows the horse as they approach.

"Howdy."

Sounds like a farmer. Looks like one too. Jeans, plaid shirt, tan suede vest, and a cowboy hat that shades his leathery, stubbled jawline. Looks about sixty, though his eyes, spidered by wrinkles and sunken by heavy lids, seem much older. He chews on a thick blade of grass.

"Howdy," Gus says, even though she's never used that word in her life.

"Car break down?"

He brings the horse into the shade of the willow. Its muscles shine with sweat.

"Just passing through. Pulled off the road to eat lunch. Fell asleep."

She feels the need to explain herself to this stranger. Might be his land.

"This your farm?"

"Was once. This field and up beyond that hill too."

He twists in his saddle and stares across the field.

"Just a few hundred acres of dust and weeds now. At one time, barley and corn grew better than them wildflowers. Not no more."

He laughs, but his face doesn't. He pats the side of his horse's neck.

"Me and Jocko, we ride out here time to time. Just to look around. We live about ten clicks that way so it's a nice ride when the winds aren't coming from the east."

Gus decides to pick his brain since he knows the lay of the land.

"Is there any way to drive into Elgin?"

Levi inches slowly toward the horse. The large animal chews at the willow fronds, keeping one eye on the dog. Levi circles. Staying well back. He slowly lowers to his belly and sniffs the horse's sweaty aroma from a safe distance. The farmer looks at Gus, then points behind her, across the road.

"You see that gap over there?"

He points to a massive rocky ridge in the far field. A deep gully runs down the middle of the ridge, scarring the landscape. This great gash seems to stretch for miles in either direction. She nods.

"That's a five-hundred-million-year-old crack in the earth."

"Oh yeah?"

Gus leans back on her car and waits. Sensing a history lesson coming. She does her best to look interested.

"A geological anomaly. That's what that is. See, there used to be mountains around here back in the days of T. rex. When the mountains eroded, they left great big cracks and those cracks filled up with minerals. Limestone. Dolomite. Fast-forward five hundred million years and some dipshit discovers a vein of shale running the length of the Frontenac Axis. Gas companies love them some shale. They start pushing toxic wash deep underground to get the gas outta those minerals. Fracking, they call it. Only what they don't know is that big vein of shale sits right next to a monster artery. A T. rex–size crack in the earth. That crack."

He points to the canyonlike gully across the road.

Gus sits up. Listens, fascinated now.

"Runs straight through the county. Straight through the town of Elgin. First it breached underground, but they didn't stop fracking. Toxic wash got into the groundwater. Killed the crops first. Then the livestock. For miles. Finally, they did a little digging and figured it out. Only it was too late."

"And the town? Why the barricades?"

The horse stomps. Jocko's getting restless. Levi cowers behind Gus again. The farmer isn't bothered by the horse's skittish dance. He goes on.

"People started getting sores and bloody noses and bad coughs. You could smell gas coming outta the sewers. Ticking time bomb. Then it blew. Whole town went up. Gas company paid off the surviving townsfolk. They boarded up the town. The county put up them signs. And the gas company said sayonara. Overnight, practically. The place became a ghost town."

"When was this?"

"It's just over five years now. Town burned for weeks."

"No one came back?"

"It was too dangerous. Three-headed babies dangerous."

"Wow."

"That's my roundabout way of saying no. There ain't no way to drive into Elgin. No call to neither. Like I said. It's a ghost town. You don't wanna go anywhere near that godforsaken place."

He pulls on the reins of his horse and circles once.

"Name's James Pratt."

He tips his cowboy hat.

"I'm Augusta and this is Levi."

"Best you two head back the way you came. There ain't nothing left to see in these parts save the stink of chemical waste and greed."

"But how is it that you can still live out here?"

"We got lucky, me and the missus. Our farmhouse is ten clicks over yonder. It's just the town itself that's still stewing with toxins and 'bout a five-click radius all the way 'round her. Pretty much right up to them barricades. The county comes 'round to test the water and soil every year. Some folks say it'll take generations to come back. But nature usually finds a way."

"So why ride out here if there's nothing to see?"

"Guess part of me's still hoping for signs of life."

He looks toward his forsaken fields. Up the hill into the setting sun.

"Hope springs eternal, Miss Augusta."

And with another tip of his hat, James Pratt rocks forward in his saddle. Jocko instantly takes off in a gallop. Before long they are across the field and up on the ridge. Augusta waves but he doesn't look back. Then he's gone and she realizes she forgot to ask him if Senator Halladay is still around.

It's late in the day so Gus takes the farmer's advice. Gets in her car. Dog in the back. Pulls onto the deserted highway and drives away from the barricade, past the gas station, past the cemetery. Time to go home. Regroup. Come back another day when she has more daylight ahead of her. Sounds like the town of Elgin isn't going anywhere. She glances at the cemetery in her rearview mirror.

Something about the sad little plot of headstones makes her turn back. Maybe it's the saggy wooden fence surrounding it or the crooked headstones sitting alone in the middle of a dead field. Or maybe it's because she can picture her mother walking up the grassy slope toward the cemetery.

Even before Augusta hikes herself over the wooden fence, her eyes are drawn to the large plot at the center of the graveyard. A family plot that dominates the cemetery. Towering over the others. Surrounded by an ornate iron fence with an archway. She moves closer. The name carved in the archway comes into view. Halladay. The plot is overrun with wild bracken and ivy. Unkempt. Neglected.

Levi is busy burrowing his nose through the long dry grass that weaves between the graves. Augusta steps inside the Halladay enclosure and pulls ivy from the largest of the headstones. A carved granite spire topped by two bronze winged angels.

KEP JACOB HALLADAY

MAY 30, 1935

AUGUST 4, 2006

And just like that, she's found him. There are no words of sorrow or love or mentions of resting in peace written on the headstone. Nothing. She takes a photo.

Right next to this massive winged monument is a smaller headstone with only one angel on its top. This one looks older than the other one.

AMELIA GRACE HILLCOTT-HALLADAY
BELOVED WIFE OF KEP JACOB HALLADAY
BORN APRIL 22, 1955
DIED JUNE 17, 1979
AGE 24

Husband and wife. Next to these two but set back a few feet from the others is a small plain headstone. It's crumbling. Cheap. Engraved on it is a name. *June Halladay.* The one who died in the car accident. Nothing else. No dates. Not even a mention of June's daughter, Gracie, who was left behind. There's a mean-spirited energy inside these iron fences. Gus scribbles the dates and a few notes in her notebook and snaps shots of the Halladay gravestones.

As she steps out of the family plot, she sees a small grave. Close, but not inside with the others. It's modest but sweet. Carved with a simple daisy chain design that circles writing at the center. Gus stares at it in disbelief.

IN MEMORY OF OUR DEAREST GRACIE ANNE HALLADAY
ONLY DAUGHTER OF JUNE
MARCH 31, 1995–APRIL 1, 2013

DIED TRAGICALLY AT THE TENDER AGE OF 18.
SHE WILL REMAIN FOREVER ALIVE IN OUR HEARTS.

Gus sinks to her knees. She's found the ballerina. The girl on Shannon's wall. Not knowing it until this very moment, she was so hoping to find Gracie alive. To talk to her. To see if she knew why her mother kept her picture and obsessed over her.

But Gracie died five years ago. She's a ghost.

Gus is sad for her. She lost her entire family. And yet, she was set apart from the others in death. Outside their inner circle. Gus wonders who chose the headstone, if they were all gone, and why they chose to place her outside the family plot. She ponders the tender words.

She will remain forever alive in our hearts.

Whose hearts?

Gus takes a photo of Gracie's gravestone.

Levi's found a stick and is twisting his head back and forth, bending low then jumping and turning. He wants to play. The sun has set. Only a hint of lilac on the horizon suggests that it was ever there. Standing amid the dead, Gus shivers.

Levi drops the stick and barks. He's looking behind her. Lip curled. Augusta turns. A distant figure stands on the horizon about two hundred yards away. A man in a red lumberjacket over a gray hoodie. Tall rubber boots. She can't see his face, but he's looking in her direction. It's not James, the farmer. Smaller build. Different clothes. She calls out to the stranger and waves. But he simply turns and walks away, limping slightly like he's got a stone in his boot. Levi growls. The man disappears over the hill and out of sight. Augusta suddenly feels incredibly vulnerable. In the middle of nowhere. By the side of a deserted dead-end road. No one for miles.

Gus and Levi make their way quickly across the ditch and jump into the Buick. Soon they're heading down the 15 toward Ottawa. Augusta can't shake the feeling she's missed something, like a lone spider crawling up the back of her neck. Something she saw. Not the man on the hill. Something else. Then it comes to her. It was right in front of her eyes.

She slams on the brakes, pulls onto the gravel shoulder. Grabs her phone and flips through the photos she took at the cemetery. Now it feels like a million tiny spiders are crisscrossing her entire body. A car whips past, rocking the Buick. She finds the photo. Tingling head to toe. There. The one she took of Kep Halladay's headstone. She pinches the image to enlarge it. To confirm her hunch. She reframes it so she can read the dates on the headstone. Specifically, the date of his death.

August 4, 2006.

It's right there. Carved in stone.

How could she have missed it?

August 4, 2006.

A day she thought she'd never forget.

The exact same day that her mother died.

13

CHARLIE

❧

BEFORE HEADING BACK TO ROSE'S, AUGUSTA ROLLS THROUGH the neighborhood where she once lived with her mother. Edge of Hintonburg. West of downtown where small two-story houses stand inches apart on narrow one-way streets. Shannon bought into the neighborhood when it was considered sketchy. A Hells Angels hangout. A halfway house on every block. Prostitutes perched at corners after sundown.

Up-and-coming, the real estate agent called it. He was right. Twelve years later, it's hip. The "in" place to live according to *Ottawa At Home Magazine*. Two yoga studios, three coffee shops, a juice bar, a vegan bakery, and an organic market. Yuppyville central. From Rosemount to Bayswater, hints of the rough edges still linger, but most of the old rooming houses have been converted into high-end condos and the riffraff's been moved out. Gus pulls up to the address on Hilda Street where they used to live.

Darkness has fallen. Streetlights have flickered to life. And in that lonely muddy light between dusk and nightfall, Gus wants nothing more than to go inside their old house and curl up in her old bed.

But it's gone. Replaced by a modern town house all glass and chrome and sharp edges. She can see her reflection in the floor-to-ceiling windows. Distorted. Unrecognizable. Just like the old neighborhood. Levi is curled up asleep on the front seat, tail swept across his face. Dog's at home anywhere.

Gus remembers what that felt like.

❧

Her mother buys it sight unseen. She reads Gus the description. *Cozy two-story cottage with covered front porch. Needs some work. Priced to sell. Up-and-coming area.* They're leaving Kingston and moving to Ottawa. Gus has just turned five.

A roof over our heads, a cozy bed, and a front porch. What more could two gals moving to the big city ask for?

Shannon is right. They move and they're happy. Summer nights when the upstairs gets too hot, they camp out on the front porch. Side by side on the wooden swing, wrapped in a cool bedsheet, rocking to stir up a breeze. Gus loves those nights. Just the two of them. Rebels. Sleeping wherever they want. Breaking the rules. Sometimes, when they're sitting there quietly, she asks her mother how she met her father. Shannon laughs.

Sugar Bunch, I've told you a million times.

Augusta snuggles closer and asks for a million and one.

It was the first week of basic training at Depot Division in Regina. Day one of Police Defensive Tactics. Shannon took an instant dislike to the tall, brash redhead. He was all talk.

Too sure of himself. Cocky. His name was Charlie Monet. She preferred the quiet guy. Rory Rump. He was safe. No trouble. Easy to be friends with. But nothing more.

Rory's one of the good guys. Did the best he could.

Shannon described him like she was making excuses for him. But Rory was no Charlie. Rory stood at the back and had a nervous stutter. Charlie sat up front and showboated when he knew the answer, and even when he didn't. Rory held the door for her. Charlie didn't think he had to. Rory abided by the rules. Charlie liked to bend them. They couldn't have been more different. Charlie had a big mouth and a big heart. His energy was infectious. He took Rory under his wing. Everyone loved Charlie. Shannon tried not to. But once Charlie decided he wanted her, she was done. His green eyes seemed to read her mind. She hated that. And loved it too.

By week four, the three musketeers were inseparable. Out every weekend, running track together, practicing ground fighting, studying together. They were best friends. Having the time of their lives. Shannon was one of the guys. Just how she liked it.

She graduated top of the class. Charlie a close second. Rory passed with a little help from his friends. Thirty-one cadets graduated following twenty-six weeks at Depot. After the swearing in, the parade, the drill, and the badge ceremony, the graduating troop gathered for a formal banquet and right after dessert, in front of everyone, Charlie dropped to one knee, looking devastatingly handsome in his red serge, and proposed to Shannon. She said yes.

They were married that summer at the Sandbanks Winery in Prince Edward County. Small ceremony. A few friends from Depot. Some from high school. Mostly Charlie's. Both Shannon and Charlie had lost their parents young and neither had siblings so there was no family. Shannon's only living relative was her grandmother Rose and she was too frail to travel. Rose sent her love in the form of cash. Rory was not only Charlie's best man, but he also did double duty and gave away the bride.

Four weeks after graduation, they got their rookie postings to O Division in Kingston. The three friends were posted together. They moved into the same apartment complex. Rory into a bachelor. Shannon and Charlie into a one-bedroom. They shared Sunday dinners and talked about the future over spaghetti and beer.

That's where Shannon's story usually trails off.

Sometimes she gets all the way to the part where she got pregnant a month after they got married. Was pulled off patrol training. How Rory and Charlie got fast-tracked to assignments in the Border Response Unit. How she got slow-tracked to a desk job.

The end of the story, Gus only hears once. It comes out of nowhere when Gus is seven. They're making tuna casserole in the kitchen one day after school. Shannon tosses some cheddar cheese in a pot of hot milk on the stove. She stirs while Gus opens the can of tuna and pours the contents into the bowl of cooked macaroni. Shannon doesn't look up from stirring the cheese. She just begins.

I was making tuna casserole for dinner that night.

What night, Mama?

You should know what happened. So you're not wondering your whole life.

Then she tells Gus how her father died.

It was 1998. Late April. Shannon was due in two weeks. Less than a year into Rory and Charlie's stint with the Border Response Unit. They were partnered this one night because both their training officers were out sick with a bug that was going through O Division. Charlie and Rory were following up on a tip about a possible parole violation at a residence on Howe Island. Should have been a routine call.

But it wasn't.

They drove straight into a pile of shit. Shannon's words. The residence was deep in the woods at the end of a laneway. Their cruiser rolled down the laneway. Came to a clearing by a large cabin where three males and a female were smack in the middle of loading eighty bricks of cocaine into a Ford cargo van with no license plates. Chaos erupted, shots were fired, and the foursome jumped in the van. They floored it, slamming into the RCMP cruiser and bouncing it out of the way. A high-speed chase ensued across the island, onto the mainland, and down the 401. Charlie and Rory called for backup as they gave chase toward Kingston at upwards of a hundred and ten miles per hour.

Charlie was on the radio giving updates as to their location. Rory was driving. The van took an exit at the edge of Kingston. Charlie called it in. But instead of Battersea Road, he said Montreal Street, which is what Battersea turns into once you're on the south side of the highway. Charlie got it wrong. Same road, different name on the north side.

Deadly mistake.

Backup got turned around. The van made a hard left into a salvage lot. Too hard. It crashed into a fiberglass sign at the edge of the property. One guy took off on foot. The van spun its wheels, dislodged, then raced off, bumping down the dirt road between the rows of derelict vehicles. Charlie jumped out and went after the runner. Rory gunned it in the cruiser after the van.

A nasty flu bug, the wrong street name, late backup, and a lone runner all converged to bring Charlie racing full speed around the hood of a rusty '78 Chevy Malibu and straight into the raised muzzle of an AK-47. Rory doubled back when he heard the shot. Found Charlie on his back in the mud, a hole blown through his chest. Eyes wide.

Officer down. Officer down.

Shannon heard the call come in over the police radio that she kept on the windowsill. She stopped stirring her cheese sauce and listened. Waiting to hear Charlie's voice. A name. Anything but the voice she kept hearing over and over. The tearful broken voice of Rory.

Officer down. 10–64 ambulance required. Oh God. Oh God.

Backup arrived within minutes and managed to corner the shooter. He didn't put up a fight. And later, when ballistics and fingerprints matched, they had the guy dead to rights, but none of that mattered. Charlie was gone.

The sauce burned black as she sat at the kitchen table until they came.

Rory tried his best to help with the arrangements. To field phone calls. To be a shoulder for her to lean on. But he was no Charlie. He drove her to the hospital when the baby came ten days later. Brought them home. Got her groceries and diapers. But it was pointless. She didn't want his help. Shannon wanted her husband back. She wanted him to be there to kiss their new auburn-haired baby girl. She didn't want to go it alone. This wasn't what they'd promised each other. Wasn't even close.

Your daddy could take up all the space in a room and yet he always made everyone around him feel important and safe and loved.

Shannon distanced herself from Rory even though he lived down the hall. His voice reminded her too much of Charlie's last moments. She stopped asking him over for Sunday dinners. He got pulled off patrol a few weeks after Charlie's death. Lost his nerve. Ended up in a basement job. Archives and records, then the property office.

Shannon did the opposite. She threw herself into work. She cut short her maternity leave, got full-time daycare, and got reassigned from desk jockey to patrol. She needed to be out on the streets doing what she was trained to do. It made her feel closer to Charlie. Shannon and Rory said *hey* when they passed each other in the hall at the apartment building or at work. Sometimes he babysat when she couldn't find a sitter. But mostly they were like strangers.

He was Uncle Rory to Augusta.

Even after they moved to Ottawa, Rory still tried. The week before Christmas, he'd drive the two hours from Kingston to bring a Beanie Baby or a new Barbie for Augusta. He always brought a box of Black Magic chocolates and a small bouquet of white roses for Shannon. She'd apologize and tell him they were just on their way out the door, then she'd watch him drive off from behind the front curtain. Augusta would ask where they were going.

Nowhere.

The last part of Shannon and Charlie's story is not Shannon's to tell. It's Augusta's. She knows it by heart. She was eight. Awakened by a policewoman who turned on the ceiling light in her bedroom. Blinding her. She could hear Annalee crying. The woman told her that her mother had been in a car accident. It was a muggy summer night.

The kind of night when it was best to sleep out on the front porch.

The kind of night it is tonight, twelve years later, as Gus sits in the Buick and looks into the windows of a stranger's house that now sits where their front porch used to. Gus knows the story of her parents, but she wonders about Rory. What became of him. Where his story took him. If he found love. If he ever got over Shannon and Charlie and the good old days.

Uncle Rory was at the funeral. His forehead sweaty. His face puffy and pasty white. He hugged Gus too tight. His hands were shaking. She felt sorry for him, but she wasn't sure why. Maybe it was because he looked a hundred years old even though he was only in his late twenties. Gus remembers thinking it would probably be the last time she'd ever see him.

And it would be.

Until today.

14

RORY

⁓

Augusta watches Rory from across the parking lot of the high school. School must be letting out for the summer soon. It's almost July. Levi rests his chin on the back of her seat. He huffs. Bored. She tosses him a cookie and he settles down, grinding his teeth into the hard biscuit.

Rory is skirting the brick wall. He approaches a group of young boys. About fifteen years old. One boy is taking a drag from a joint. The kid drops it when he sees Rory. Digs it under his heel. Rory folds his arms. The kid picks up the butt and tosses it in a coffee can by a back door. Rory nods then turns and walks away. Behind his back, the kid flips him the bird. The other kids laugh. One imitates Rory, walking with his belly pushed out, legs bowed, arms wide like he's six hundred pounds.

Rory has put on a few pounds since she last saw him. His neck balloons over his collar. He's wearing short sleeves and short pants like he's going cycling. His police revolver sits in a pocket on his belt. Shiny badge on his chest. Hat tipped slightly off to one side. He looks like a kid playing dress-up. Goofy as ever. Just as she remembers him.

Must be about forty. Graying sideburns. Chewing gum. She realizes he's about the age her father would be if he'd lived.

Augusta gets out and stands next to the Buick. He glances in her direction. Nods then turns and heads toward the front doors of the school. Doesn't recognize her. Then something registers under that tilted hat. He glances back. One eyebrow raises. He squints as recognition floods his puffy face. He moves closer, head tilting one way then the other.

"It can't be!"

He's shouting across the parking lot. The boys are staring. He's so embarrassing. Gus wants to hide.

"Is that my Little Monet? All grown up?"

She wishes the boys would go back into the school. Rory strides over and before she can stop him, he bear-hugs her, lifting her off her feet. She can't help herself. She giggles. Feeling like a five-year-old. Rory could always make her laugh. He drops her gently then steps back. Chewing his wad of gum.

"And those freckles. Still got those freckles and your pop's red hair."

He tells the school office he's going on break and ten minutes later they're sitting across from each other in a booth at Timmies. She's explaining how she tracked him down. How she called the Kingston detachment. How the desk sergeant on duty told her Rory was a school liaison officer in Kemptville. At North Grenville District High School. A forty-five-minute drive from Ottawa. So she drove out to see him.

"Quite the detective."

"I told the desk sergeant who my parents were and he opened right up."

"That'd do it. They're legends down Kingston way. Everybody knows them." He grimaces. "I mean, knew them. Sorry, kiddo."

"It's okay, Rory."

He slurps coffee spillage from the plastic lip of his triple triple. Augusta inches the conversation forward, not wanting to coldclock him until she's warmed him up. She casually asks him what, exactly, his job entails. Big mistake.

Rory launches into a half-hour description of life as a school liaison officer. The day-to-day school patrol, the drug counseling, the special event chaperoning. His favorite duty by far is organizing the Cycle Safe rides each spring for their sister elementary school. Teaching first-time riders the rules of the road. He sets up an obstacle course with little stop signs and yield signs dotted across the parking lot. Some of the kids are still on training wheels. He calls it a *hoot*. Gus smiles and eats another Timbit.

When he finally takes a sip of his coffee, Augusta cuts in. It's now or never.

"Um, Rory? I came to see you for a reason. See, my great-grandma Rose died."

"Oh gosh, I'm sorry to hear that."

"I inherited her house, sort of, and I found some of my mother's things in the basement and I was looking through them. I thought you might be able to help me figure out what they are. Fill in the blanks since you knew her back then."

"Blanks?"

"Like, for example, what Kep Halladay's got to do with my mum's death?"

Rory snorts coffee out his nose. "What the? Who?"

He dabs his chin with a paper napkin. She pushes on.

"I was out there. Near Elgin. Saw his grave. He died the same night she did? August fourth, 2006. It can't be a coincidence."

"What the heck have you been up to, Little Monet?"

"I think Shannon was investigating something that had to do with Halladay. A land deal or something. I don't know. But this boy went missing and now his body's been found, and Gracie is dead, and it's all connected, Rory."

He holds up his hands in a stick-up position. "Whoa, slow down, girl. You're six horses ahead of me and I haven't even broke outta the barn yet. You're talking about Senator Halladay from Elgin. That Halladay?"

"Yes. They died the exact same night. Isn't that weird?"

"I'm sure other people died that same night. Doesn't mean their passings are related."

He's not getting it. Gus bites her lip to keep from snapping at him. Takes a deep breath and tries a different tack.

"Tell me about the night she died."

"Don't you remember?"

"Bits and pieces, but mostly nothing."

"You blocked it out. That happens."

"All I have is what she left me. But it's just more bits and pieces."

"I don't follow. What'd she leave you?"

"Come. I'll show you."

She gets up and grabs her satchel, then waves for him

to follow. He grabs his coffee and jacket and an hour later, Augusta and Rory are standing in Rose's living room. He's staring at the wall. The one she's written all over with red marker and plastered with newspaper clippings, documents, and photographs. Gus grabs her red marker and continues the red line past the evidence. Above the line she adds the date *August 4, 2006*. She caps the marker then steps back beside Rory.

"It's a timeline. See?"

Rory slowly nods. He opens a pack of Nicorette gum and pops a couple in his cheek, his eyes never leaving the wall. He hasn't spoken since entering the room. Gus pretends to look at the wall, but she's watching him out of the corner of her eye. He steps forward to take a closer look at each item. He touches the documents, runs his finger along the red line, taps each photo, one after the other.

All the while, Levi is sniffing Rory's lower thighs just below his short pants. Now he's licking the top of one of Rory's police-issue oxfords. Rory chews his gum slowly. After what seems like an eternity, Rory folds his arms across his belly and takes a deep breath.

"Impressive."

"This is exactly how she had these. In the garage. In her office. Above her desk. At our old house."

"So you do remember?"

"I remember this."

"But not what happened that night?"

"Some stuff I see just like a photo projected onto my brain. It's like I'm standing in that garage, looking up and seeing it. Clear as day. And then some memories are all muddy like they're under water or something. I can't make them out but I know they're there."

"Where'd you say you found all this?"

"She hid them in my room. In a toy chest at the foot of my bed. I found the chest in Rose's basement. Somehow it ended up here."

Rory looks like he's having trouble connecting the dots. Not digging deep enough. She tries to prompt him.

"See how Senator Halladay's name is circled everywhere. I didn't do that. Shannon did that. Well, I did that one."

Gus points to the recent article about Henry. The Halladay she circled.

"But she did the rest. See?"

Rory doesn't see. Gus wants to grab him by the shoulders and shake him hard until he does. But she holds herself steady, speaks clearly and slowly, as if to a small child.

"I always thought it was a dream. Her coming into my room that night. But it wasn't. This is why she was there. She was hiding evidence in my trunk. For me to find. All this has something to do with a cold case she was working. I'm sure of it, but I don't know what any of it means. What does it mean, Rory?"

Augusta suddenly bursts into tears. She has no idea why, but it feels so good to cry. Rory looks scared. He pats her shoulder. She hugs him and cries into his shirt. It's good to share her wall with someone other than the dog.

"Now there, there, Little Monet. Come on. Buck up."

He pats her head lightly. She dabs her eyes with her fingertips and looks up at him. His eyes glisten too. He swallows hard.

"Sorry I've made you sad, Rory."

"No, no. It's just that you remind me of your mother. How she was before."

She smiles. "Before?"

"Before your dad passed."

"Not after?"

His eyes wander across Shannon's wall. "She wasn't herself after that. Then that whole business with June Halladay happened. Shan got caught up in it. Got too close. Not saying Shan wasn't a good cop. She was. The best. Just lost her way."

"Do you mean this business?"

Gus points to the newspaper clipping about June's accident, trying to get him to open up. He does know something. But just as quickly, he shuts down. Slaps his hands together. Tucks his belt under his belly and turns to Augusta. His tone official like he's delivering a press conference.

"I'm sorry. Your mother meant a lot to me. I don't want to speak ill of the dead. Especially her."

And with that, Rory checks his watch, picks up his hat and keys, and heads for the door. Levi bounces after him hoping for a walk.

"The ladies in admin will think I've fallen off a cliff."

Gus can't believe he's leaving. They were just getting started.

"We'll talk more soon, Little Monet."

He waves awkwardly as he opens the front door.

"Did I say something wrong, Rory?"

She follows him outside. So does Levi. Rory stumbles across the lawn toward his cruiser. Dark clouds roll across the sky. Gus stares at him. He sighs. Can't look her in the eye.

"Tell me the truth, Rory."

He fumbles with his keys.

"Truth is, Little Monet, that I don't know what happened that night. I know she didn't see eye to eye with Senator Halladay. I know that. But Shannon wasn't talking to me. Hadn't spoken in months. Wasn't talking to anyone on the force since her suspension."

"She wasn't suspended."

"You were a kid. She didn't tell you. But you asked for it and there it is."

He opens the cruiser door and gets in. Gus holds on to Levi's collar so he doesn't jump in with Rory.

"You got that same look in your eyes that she had."

He starts the engine, shuts the door, then rolls down his window.

"That wall in there? Might look like something you remember from when you were a kid, but it's nothing but thunder and lightning. Leave it be, Little Monet. Leave it be so you don't end up like her."

Augusta watches in stunned silence as Rory's cruiser backs out of the driveway and heads down Island Park. The afternoon sky darkens and thunder rumbles in the distance. Levi turns tail and scoots back inside the house.

A syrupy yellow aura descends on the neighborhood, making it feel more dreamlike than real. Clouds gather and a flash of lightning streaks the sky. Augusta can smell the rain coming. Can feel the electricity in the air. The solstice has just passed and the hot, muggy, midsummer months are heavy on the horizon.

A storm is approaching.

She takes a deep breath and braces herself.

15

LUCKY

꩜

WITH JULY'S RELENTLESS NIGHTTIME HEAT WAVES COME vivid dreams. When Augusta wakes, she often feels like she's left a part of herself behind in the dream. Sometimes she's brought someone from the dream back with her into the waking world. Usually, it's her eight-year-old self.

Maybe it's the thick humidity or the electric summer storms. Pressure systems building and shifting energy both inside and out. Or maybe this always happens, early July, as the anniversary of her mother's death looms.

Augusta sits up in bed. Her phone is lit up on the side table. She picks it up. Three texts from Lars.

> Okay I've given you your space. Time to come back, babe.
> Auggie, I've been patient but I'm gonna lose my shit if you don't text me back.
> The fuck.

As Gus reads, she becomes aware of breathing under the bed and for a split second her heart stops. That anxious eight-year-old still inside her head. She slowly dips her head and looks under the bed. It's Levi, hiding from the thunderstorm that tore through last night. He's fast asleep. Her shoulders relax. She lies back and looks out the half-open blinds. The sky over Rose's backyard is a deep cobalt blue.

Gus lifts the window. Below in the yard, she can make out the crab apples strewn about the lawn like beads let loose from a broken necklace. The crows gossip across the high maples.

An hour later, Augusta is sitting on the back stoop, a mug of fresh coffee warming her palms. Levi is happily digging at the base of the crab apple tree. The rising sun slowly transforms the dawn. Illuminating the yellow-green ferns lining the back fence. She tries not to let Rory's words nudge at her.

Leave it be so you don't end up like her.

Something splashes into her mug. A clump of dirt floats on her coffee. Gus looks over at Levi. He's feverishly digging with his front legs. Sending chunks of dirt in the air behind him. Belly blackened. Head deep. He's excavated a large hole at the base of the crab apple tree. Gus dumps her coffee, runs over, and hauls him out of the hole by the collar.

"Seriously, dog? Chill out."

He squirms free and dives back into the hole. She pulls him back out. This time he's got something in his mouth. A craggy root. Gus yanks it from his teeth. It's no root. It's a skeleton. A cat skeleton. The four legs dangle from the small hollow rib cage. Yuck. She flings it away. Rose's cat, Lucky.

Levi scrambles after it, grabs it up in his mouth, and races into the house.

"No! Levi, stop."

Gus runs after him. Follows a trail of muddy paw prints through the kitchen, down the hall, and into the living room. Finds him on the sofa. Sitting pretty. Like he's done nothing. Just chilling out. Happily licking dirt from his paws. Lucky's bones lie abandoned on the carpet.

Augusta heaves Levi off the sofa. He picks up the skeleton and slinks under the dining room table, hiding behind the lace tablecloth that's draped over it.

As she scrubs the sofa cushions with a wet dish towel, the rising sun reflects off the windows of the houses across the street and bursts through the bracken obscuring Rose's front window. It dapples Shannon's wall with orbs of golden light.

The wall comes to life.

Gus stops scrubbing and approaches the wall. She runs her fingers across each photograph, each article. Along the red lines. Searching for patterns. Feeling for clues. Like her mother did. Rory was right about one thing. She *is* like her mother and the way forward is here. Surrounded by her mother's work. Somewhere on this wall. She just needs to find one detail. One clue. One step. Somewhere to start.

Gus looks over at Levi. She can see him, through the lace tablecloth, gently licking Lucky's skeleton. She doesn't remember when Rose's cat died. Gus was very young at the time. The cat was ancient. It scratched her once when she tried to play with it. Hissed at her. She never liked it. And now her dog is gently chewing on that grouchy old cat's tiny spine. And enjoying every minute of it. His eyes are closed. His mouth quivers. Drool drips from his tongue.

Augusta looks back at the wall and her eyes come to rest

on the newspaper article about June Halladay's car accident. She thinks back to what Rory called it.

That whole business with June Halladay.

Gus reads the byline on the header of the article.

Written by Renata Corrigan.

There's a detail. She finds her notebook and writes down the name. Beside it she writes *journalist* and *June Halladay article.*

Gus flips through the pages of her notebook. Comparing her notes to the photos on her phone. Looking for more details. She finds another. It's in the photo she took of the barricade outside Elgin. The sign on the barricade says it was erected by order of the County of Leeds Grenville Public Works and Records Office and the Chief Medical Officer of the Ontario Ministry of Health. She hears the farmer's words.

Whole town went up. Gas company paid off the surviving towns-folk. They boarded up the town. The county put up them signs.

She examines the deed of trust hanging on the wall. Yes. His name is among those who signed away their mineral rights. James Pratt. The farmer. And an Alison Pratt is named too. Gus notices something else. The deed is stamped with a Leeds Grenville County Public Works and Records Office crest. Their address is at the bottom. It's in Brockville, Ontario. Same office that put up the sign on the barricade. She writes the address in her notebook.

"That's a step, right, dog?"

Levi ignores her. He's busy chewing on old bones.

16

BEBE

⟨꩜⟩

Gus spreads her map on the kitchen table. Brock-ville looks to be a little over sixty miles away, a straight shot south of Ottawa, on the St. Lawrence River. Forty-five minutes east of Elgin. The Records Office is on Central Avenue. Pen, notebook, map.

Who needs a GPS?

Gus puts on her dad's ball cap. Grabs a box of raspberry Pop-Tarts for the road. In the foyer, she laces up her sneakers. Levi peeks from under the lace tablecloth. Head framed like he's wearing a wedding veil. Gus rolls her eyes.

"Up for another road trip, dog?"

Levi springs from under the table. Tail wagging.

An hour later, Augusta is standing in front of Bebe Foot-hold, the official gatekeeper of Leeds Grenville County's records. Bebe sits at a desk behind a large window. Her name-plate is propped on the counter in front of her. She has long dark braids, golden skin, piercing brown eyes. Massive biceps and freakishly broad shoulders. Bodybuilder for sure. Or she-goddess. Early forties. Tight white blouse. Sleeves rolled up like she means business. Bebe isn't to be messed with.

A steaming bowl of noodles sits in front of Bebe, next to a tall glass of white pus that looks like raw egg whites. Gus tries not to gag. Bebe looks up but doesn't speak. Instead, she slowly puts down her plastic chopsticks, making it very clear that her lunch is being disturbed. Gus keeps things short and sweet. She tries playing the age card.

"Sorry to interrupt your lunch, ma'am, but I'm doing some research for this, like, school project about the fire in Elgin, Ontario. Think it was in 2013 maybe."

Bebe rolls her eyes. "That's a new one."

Without looking where she's reaching, Bebe grabs a pink form from a slot in her metal desktop organizer.

"Fill this out so we can get this party started, hon."

Bebe shoves the form and a pen across the counter toward Gus. *Hon?* Maybe Bebe's not as stone-cold as she looks. Bebe picks up her chopsticks and starts twisting her noodles. Augusta takes the form.

"You lift weights?"

Bebe looks up and stares. Gus gulps, then smiles and nods toward the woman's biceps.

"Impressive is all."

Bebe stares. Brownnosing is not working. Gus shrinks away and takes a seat on the wooden bench across the lobby. The building is old. Government issue. Circa 1950s. Shiny institutional floors that smell like lemon polish. Reminds her of Ridley College in St. Catharines.

"Two-ten."

Gus looks up. Bebe's no longer staring at her. She's lean-ing over the counter, stirring her egg pus. Her shoulders are relaxed. Jaw unclenched. She liked the compliment after all. Seems Bebe's a woman of few words but *two-ten* is definitely the icebreaker Gus needs to keep things moving.

"Two-ten?"

"Two hundred ten pounds. That's what I can bench-press."

"Wow."

Bebe's eyes smile, even though her mouth remains perma-nently locked in a straight line. Gus has no clue if two hundred and ten pounds is good or not, but it's clear Bebe thinks it is.

"World record tops three hundred."

"No way."

"Way."

Bebe downs the egg whites in a single gulp as if to prove her point. Augusta's eyes widen in awe. Bebe's mouth wavers and the edge of a smile emerges like a crack in a huge iceberg. She waves her over. Gus approaches the counter.

"You're one of them, aren't you, hon?" Bebe says, her tone warming.

"Who?"

"Gas company paper pushers."

"I'm a student."

"I get it. Procedure. Forget the form. I know what you're looking for. You people should just call ahead."

Bebe disappears through a swinging door behind her that leads to a back room. Gus glimpses rows of filing cabinets and shelves stacked high with boxes. She waits at the counter. Bebe takes her time. Gus wanders over to the front door and checks on Levi. He's sitting up in the car. He barks when he spots her. She ducks back toward the counter. Out of his eyeline.

Bebe hip-checks the swinging door and comes out. Arms holding a large file box marked *Office of the Ontario Fire Marshal, April 1, 2013, Elgin Fire.*

The date rings a bell.

Bebe shoves the box across the counter.

"I'll need a picture ID."

Gus opens her wallet and hands over her Ontario driver's license. Bebe examines it briefly then places the ID below the counter.

"You can use the table down the hall. You'll get your ID back when you're done."

Gus hoists the heavy box into her arms with some effort.

"Like I told the others. There's been no new filings this past six months. No amendments or addendums or motions or appeals. Nothing. No new lawsuits relating to the original fire marshal's report. Nothing new of any kind."

"Really, I'm not . . ."

Bebe holds up her hand. "I know, I know. Due diligence and such. Have at it, hon."

Gus doesn't bother arguing. And besides, she's about to drop the box. She makes it to the table and plants it with a thud.

"You can make copies there." Bebe points to a photocopier at the end of the hall.

"Can I take photos with my phone?"

"Suit yourself."

That's why the date rings a bell. Gus has seen it before. In one of the photos on her phone. She scans through them and finds it. Gracie Halladay's gravestone.

March 31, 1995–April 1, 2013:

She died the day of the Elgin fire. She was just eighteen.

Gus opens the file box lid.

An hour later, she's done. Done skimming and photographing documents and taking notes. She can hear Levi barking. Time to go. Gus heaves the box onto the counter. Bebe swivels in her chair and picks up Augusta's ID. She looks at it one more time.

"Augusta. You know there was a Saint Augusta. Of Treviso. Fifth century. Her own father pulled out all her teeth then decapitated her for converting to Christianity."

"Wow. My dad just liked golf, so he named me after Augusta, Georgia."

"Can't pick your parents."

They both smile.

Levi barks.

Bebe hands Gus her ID.

"Find what you were looking for?"

"Not sure yet."

Levi howls like a wolf.

"You're not with the gas company, are you, Miss Augusta of Georgia?"

Bebe leans on the counter and winks. Despite her muscle-bound exterior, she's really a big softie inside. Gus smiles.

"Thanks for all your help."

Gus heads for the door.

"You want to know all about that town, Miss Monet?"

Augusta turns back.

"Talk to Renata. She sat on the Heritage Society board for years. Wrote for the daily paper for most of this century. Renata was in here all the time doing research. Knows Elgin like a mama knows her child."

Gus flushes. Feels like Bebe has read her mind.

"Renata?"

"Renata Corrigan."

Gus remembers writing that same name in her notebook that very morning. Bebe scribbles something on a Post-it note. Holds it out for Gus.

"You'll find her here. Retirement home in Smiths Falls."

Gus walks back to Bebe, takes the note, glances at it, then slips it in her back pocket. Levi howls again.

"Thank you, Ms. Foothold."

"My pleasure, Miss Augusta. You talk to Renata."

Outside the Records Office, Gus lets the dog out of the car. He's got amazing willpower. Has a super-long pee against the curb. Then they head back toward Ottawa. About twelve miles down Highway 15, she passes the sign to Smiths Falls. She decides against popping by to see Renata Corrigan. She'll make an appointment tomorrow.

Gus has someone else she wants to meet first.

The sole survivor of the fire in Elgin.

As she drives back toward the city, her mind flits across the contents in the fire marshal's box. Photographs of the charred aftermath of the fire. Statements from the mayor, the fire chief, local residents, police officers, and the ambulance attendants first on the scene. All cataloged. The photos and accounts describe the terrible devastation. Scorched storefronts. Heat-warped roads and telephone poles. A toxic black plume that turned day to night and wafted across the US border all the way to Chippewa Bay. From the photographed evidence, it's impossible to imagine anyone surviving such an inferno. But one man did. His name dances across the windshield of Rose's Buick.

Desmond Oaks.

The fire marshal's report said he sustained devastating injuries. Medical forms list his current address as an apartment in Vanier in the east end of Ottawa.

She's hoping he still lives there.

The fire officials were detailed in their final report. Listing each resident by name, age, and occupation. The entire population of Elgin was accounted for. All three hundred forty-two. All except five. On that particular day in April, the town had been shut down. Most of its residents were at the annual spring agricultural fair in Merrickville. *A stroke of luck*, the town's mayor declared in his statement. He offered his *thoughts and prayers* to the families, coworkers, and friends of the five souls who perished. Bodies were never recovered. But everyone knew who they were just the same. They were the five who went missing that day. Never seen again.

Lois Greenaway, 63, Dance Academy Proprietor, Mortuary Cosmetologist.

Edgar Greenaway, 23, Unemployed.

Margo Dargavel, 83, Pensioner.

Rhonda Dargavel, 83, Pensioner.

And *Gracie Halladay, 18, Assistant Mortuary Beautician.*

Gus already knew Gracie was dead. That much was obvious from her gravestone. But until now, she had no idea how Gracie died. Now she had the written evidence. She was one of the victims of the Elgin fire. The others, Lois and Edgar, were mother and son. The Dargavel sisters were identical twins. Hadn't stepped foot outside their childhood home in sixty-eight years according to the town librarian who brought them books every Friday. *Agoraphobic bibliophiles*, she called them in her statement to a fire marshal official.

It's these statements made by the decent folks of Elgin that stick with Augusta most. Claims of close personal relationships. High school chums. Valued customers. Good friends. Longtime neighbors. Seems everyone had a claim on one of the dead.

All except Gracie Halladay. Most maintained they knew nothing about her. Some described her as different. Odd. One even called her the town freak. Another divulged that Gracie had a thing for roadkill. None expressed sorrow at her passing. Most focused on what they had lost instead. Their homes. Their livelihoods. Their cherished possessions.

Ironically, the sole survivor didn't even live in Elgin. Desmond Oaks. He said he was passing through that day. Stopped for gas. Wrong place, wrong time. The Red Cross Emergency Response Team and the Prescott paramedics who coordinated his airlift to the Ottawa General were credited with saving his life. Paperwork documented the personal injury claim filed by Reed, Howe, Lowell, and Associates on behalf of Desmond Oaks against the gas company, insurance companies, the province, the county, and the town. Astonishingly, documentation from the fire marshal's office indicates that officials deemed the incident a natural disaster. Caused by an earthquake. They cited a fracture in an active fault line, which led to a catastrophic explosion at the town's epicenter. Concluding there was no definitive link between the fiery explosion and the fracking activities in the region. One insurance form called it an *act of God*. In the end, the gas company paid out less than two hundred grand in cash settlements just to make any future lawsuits go away. The money was divided between Mr. Oaks and a half-dozen relatives of those who died in the fire.

Gus drives on. Back to Ottawa. She glances at the map next to her where she's circled the town of Elgin in red. A town her mother circled on another map years ago. Seems they're both captivated by this place marked by tragedy. By accidents, disappearances, deaths, a terrible fire that took lives and, ultimately, destroyed the town. And then there's the stranger. Maimed for life just because he stopped for gas in that same town. Looks like no one but God has been held to account for what happened in Elgin.

Gus wonders how Desmond Oaks feels about that.

And what else he might have seen that day.

She aims to find out.

17

DEZ

❧

GUS PULLS INTO THE PARKING LOT BEHIND THE LOW-RENT apartment complex off Montreal Road. A late day tangerine sky hovers over the outdoor pool. She leaves the dog asleep in the Buick and approaches the metal gate surrounding the two-story stucco building. There's an intercom panel attached to the gate. Nameplates sit next to each button. She scans the list. Finds it. Oaks. Unit 202. She buzzes. Waits. Nothing. She leans over the gate to see if anyone's in the courtyard. It swings open. So much for security.

Augusta follows a cement path leading to a rusty staircase at one end of the complex. Two flights up, a long balcony stretches the length of the building. The air stinks of curry and mildew. Paint chips are piled like flakes of coconut along the sills of each apartment window. Most have their curtains drawn. Cracks in several windows are bonded with duct tape.

Gus knows what it's like to live in a place like this. The dreary sad-sack atmosphere of a seedy motel. Familiar from her days with Lars. Seems like years ago, but it's only been three weeks since she lived in a place just like this. The lackluster decor. Each unit indistinguishable from the next. Stained carpets. Fake-wood laminate furniture. Musty beds. Every motel was the same. The predictability became strangely comforting. Until it wasn't. Until there was nowhere for her imagination to wander. No way to fix what was broken or paint what needed painting because none of it belonged to her. They were just passing through. Everything was temporary so what was the point of fixing or painting or imagining? They were just good places to hide out. Even better places to put in the rearview. No heartache. No fond memories.

The sad thing about Desmond Oaks's apartment complex is that it isn't a motel. People live here. Permanently. Gus shudders. How do they stop from throwing themselves off the balcony knowing this is their home?

Augusta knocks on the door of apartment 202. Silence. She knocks harder. Leans her ear close to the door, careful not to touch it. She cups her hands to the front window. Blinds are drawn.

"Lookin' for someone, Miss Nosy Parker?"

The voice echoes from the courtyard below. She jumps. Turns. Crosses to the balcony rail and looks down at the pool. At first she doesn't see anyone. Then she spots him. He's sitting on the far side of the pool under a cockeyed umbrella. The pool has been emptied for some reason, despite the sweltering heat. There's a shallow black puddle in the deep end where a few pop cans have drowned. The man's lying on a plastic chaise lounge. It's difficult to make out his face because he's hidden in the shade of the tipped umbrella.

"I'm looking for a Mr. Oaks."

"That guy's a right fucking a–hole, you ask me."

He crushes a can in his fist and chucks it into the pool with the others. He grabs another from a cooler beside him and sticks a straw in it. Gus scans the courtyard. The place is deserted.

"Are you the super?"

He doesn't answer.

Gus heads down the two flights and works her way along the pool fence to a gate. She enters the enclosure just as the lampposts crisscrossing the apartment complex sizzle to life. They cast a cool blue light across the pool deck. The man sips from his straw. She skirts the pool and approaches him.

"Do you know where I can find Mr. Oaks?"

He tips the umbrella to reveal his face.

She freezes. Unable to speak or look away.

The man has no face.

She wants to run. Scream. But doesn't.

Gus holds her gaze steady. Searching for eyes.

"You're lookin' at him. In the flesh."

Where the man's face should be is a bulge of twisted raw scar tissue. His ears, his eyebrows, his lips are gone. His nose has been burned off, leaving two nostrils that flare like pitted black olives. She finds his eyes deep inside two small desiccated holes. A pair of tiny white pupils streaked with blood. A single tuft of black hair juts from his skull. Swollen scars circle his head like a Medusa tattoo. He wears white gloves. His long fingernails have poked holes through the tips of each finger. They look like claws. He's wearing a white Adidas tracksuit zippered high up the neck. Plastic straws stick out of a chest pocket in the track-suit. A ripple of withered flesh bubbles over his collar.

Gus coughs to snap herself out of the coma that has her entranced.

"Um, Mr. Oaks, I'm Augusta Monet."

She holds out her hand. He raises a gloved hand toward hers. Gus leans closer and shakes his gently. It's ice-cold. He smells like the Neosporin cream her mother used to put on her scraped knees.

"Nobody calls me Mr. Oaks 'cept my drug dealer and my priest."

The flesh around his mouth hole stretches into a macabre smile, exposing yellow teeth and purple gums.

"Monet. How come I know that name?"

She shrugs.

"Any relation to Picasso or Pollock?"

She smiles. "I was hoping to ask you a few questions."

"You the fresh meat?"

"Sorry?"

"Not as sorry as you're gonna be."

He takes a sip of his cream soda to wet his whistle.

"Last goody-two-shoes social worker they sent me couldn't take a joke."

"I'm not a social worker. I'm nobody."

His beady eyes glisten deep in their sockets. "You like cream soda, Miss Nobody?"

"Have my whole life."

"Amen to that. Sit."

He reaches into his cooler and hands her a can.

"Mr. Oaks, I was hoping to ask you about the fire in Elgin."

She pulls a plastic chaise closer. It squeaks as it drags. He flinches. She's not sure if it's because of the mention of Elgin or the squeaking.

"Call me Dez now that we're cream soda buddies."

He holds out his can and they toast. Then he drops his cream soda with a splash. She bends to pick it up, but he waves her off. She leaves it. The soda foams across the patio stones and trickles into the pool. He grabs a fresh one.

"Why does a young girl like you want to know about some fire in some nothing town?"

"My mom was a police officer. She used to go there."

"Don't recall a lady cop at the fire."

"She wasn't involved in the fire investigation. It's complicated."

"The past is complicated."

"Can you tell me anything you might remember?"

"Remember my face melting off," he croaks.

Gus tries not to look away.

"How'd you find me?"

"Leeds Grenville County Records Office. Fire marshal's report."

"You're a regular Sherlock you are."

"My mother was the detective. I'm just following some of her leads."

"Leads?"

"Just some old photos and papers she left me. Probably lead nowhere."

"Well, I do recall the tank full of ice they put me in. Wanted me to stay under only I kept floating to the top. Scum always rises to the top, isn't that what they say?"

"I think it's cream."

He shifts in his chair. Wincing as he repositions his body. His breaths are raspy. She waits for him to recover.

"Truth is, I don't recall fuck all. I got no clue how I ended up in that fuckin' town or what happened after I got there."

He pops the lid of his new soda with one thumb, dips his chin, and purses his mouth hole around one of the straws tucked in the pocket of his tracksuit. He lifts the straw out and places it into the can with surprising mastery.

"Do you remember seeing a young woman that day? Dark hair?"

He sips as if he hasn't heard her. She keeps trying to jog his memory.

"She would have been about eighteen. She died in the fire."

"Psychogenic amnesia. Doctors say parts of my brain got lightly baked."

"I was hoping you might know something about her last moments. Maybe you saw her?"

"Why do you give a shit about some dead girl?"

Gus considers reviving her school project routine, but she's pretty sure lies won't cut it with this guy. He's been lied to a million times by lawyers and insurance adjusters, by county bureaucrats and company representatives. She knows this from the fire marshal's records. She cuts to the chase.

"I think my mom was investigating something that had to do with Gracie Halladay . . . the dead girl."

Oaks makes a slight gurgling noise in the back of his throat.

"Your mom?"

"The detective. Shannon Monet."

"Thought you said her name was Gracie."

"My mother was Shannon."

"And she died in the fire?"

"No, but she is dead."

"Did she like cream soda?"

Gus is getting nowhere. He's drooling soda foam.

"She did."

Gus realizes it was a mistake coming here. Even if the un-cooked part of this guy's brain could remember the fire, he was a stranger passing through town. He's a bum lead. He didn't know Gracie. He was just an unlucky passerby.

"Thank you for your time, Mr. Oaks."

Gus downs the dregs of her cream soda. He doesn't seem to be listening anymore. She shoves the empty can in her satchel. Slaps her knees. Time to leave. Desmond Oaks is blowing into his straw. The bubbling soda overflows and drips across his white gloves and into his lap. He looks up.

"Dez. Call me Dez."

"It was nice meeting you, Dez."

"You too, Gracie. Sorry about your mom."

Augusta feels nauseated from the sugary pop and from staring at this pathetic bag of charred bones. Is he messing with her? Trying to confuse her? Does he know something? She tries to meet his gaze but can't find it. Tries to see the man he might have been. A big man. Broad shouldered, thick arms, barrel chest. Strong once. Now withered and broken by trauma and pain. Although not entirely feeble. He can crush a can in one hand and do straw tricks with his nonexistent mouth. But when she does catch a glimpse inside the hollows of his eyes, they look dead. Vacant. She can't tell how old he is. Could be thirty or seventy. The only thing she is growing more certain of as she looks at Desmond Oaks is that he can't help her. He's a lost cause. Literally burned out. Gus wants to leave, but he's not done with her yet.

"Wait. Have another soda."

He wants company.

"You miss your mom?"

His words are a gut punch.

"I do."

She swallows hard.

"I don't want to take up any more of your time."

"A face I don't have. Time I got plenty of."

She steps toward him and gently shakes his hand.

"I really have to go. My dog's waiting in the car."

His grip tightens. He's definitely stronger than he looks. He tries to hold on. Too long. Gus manages to gently free her hand. She gives him a little wave and heads for the gate.

"Places to be, people to meet, I get it," he calls out after her. She feels horrible.

"See you around, Dez."

"Not if I see you first, Augusta Monet."

She's surprised he remembers her name.

Gus heads out the gate. Around the side of the building. Picks up her pace to a jog. Eager to put space between her and that creature by the empty pool. Something about him scares her. And it's more than just how he looks. It's his whole vibe. There's a creepiness about him. She shudders at the thought of what he's been through. No wonder he's weird.

Who wouldn't be? She turns to look back. To make sure he's not coming after her. Knowing she's being silly. He probably can't walk, much less run.

She turns back and that's when she does a face-plant, literally, straight into the chest of a man coming around the back of the building. He's solid and the jolt stuns her for a second. She lets out a tiny involuntary scream. Embarrassed, she keeps her head down and dodges past him. Sending a breathy "sorry" over her shoulder. That's all he gets.

Levi barks as Gus jumps in the car. Glances back toward the apartment building before peeling out of the parking lot.

Dusk descends from blue to black as Augusta drives down the Queensway, heading toward the Island Park exit. Back to Rose's house. She turns on the headlights. Rattled by her visit with Desmond Oaks.

Driving calms her. Always has. Even when she was a kid, Gus loved the feeling of being carried safely along while her mother's sure hands rested on the steering wheel, fingers tapping lightly to a song on the radio. Maybe it's the light rocking of the old Buick or maybe it's being completely alone with her thoughts as neighborhoods zoom past. But these days, driving is where she feels most content. Sees most clearly. Where she regroups and finds her bearings.

She knows she's been circling the truth. Not talking to the right people. Rory. Dez. Wrong people. Wrong questions. She's been going about this backward. The fire is the end of Gracie's story. The end of Elgin. She needs to go back to the beginning. Back to when the town was still there and Gracie was still alive. Gus reaches into her back pocket and pulls out the Post-it that

Bebe gave her. A phone number and address for the Chartwell
Willowdale Retirement Home in Smiths Falls.

You want to know all about that town, Miss Monet?

Talk to Renata.

Gus takes the exit and heads home. Despite the dark, she
can see the road ahead.

18

RENATA

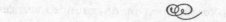

AFTER A NIGHT SPENT IN A BOTTOMLESS SLEEP, GUS PROPS herself in her usual spot at the kitchen table sipping her morning coffee. She calls Chartwell Willowdale Retirement Home. Tells the receptionist she's a student writing a thesis on the history of Eastern Ontario. She'd like to interview Renata Corrigan. Today if possible.

Elevator music kicks in. She's been put on hold.

Ten minutes later, the receptionist is back. Renata will meet her after lunch. At 2 P.M. Before Gus can confirm, the woman hangs up. Friendly place.

Gus arrives at the appointed time. Approaches the young receptionist at the front desk and asks for Renata. The girl is texting. She looks up and points to an elderly woman across the room. Just as Gus starts to head over, the girl shoots her a word of advice.

"She's pretty with it today, but don't be surprised if she sails off to la-la land."

Gus nods and the girl goes back to her phone.

Renata is waiting in the far corner of the main lounge in one of two pink floral wingback chairs. Gus knows it's her. She's the one waving her tiny webbed hand. The Weather Network plays on a TV in the corner, but no one is watching. Gus approaches Renata. Walks past a lady having an animated conversation with the cushion next to her. Several other residents are nestled in armchairs scattered about the room. Blue-haired. Most in housecoats and slippers. The odd billowy knit sweater. Each a shrunken or plumped-up or crumpled version of her younger self. Each looking like she's off somewhere else or fast asleep.

Except Renata.

She's sitting up straight. Waiting. Eyes bright. Each delicate elbow resting lightly on the arms of the wingback chair. Augusta smiles, reaching out her hand as she takes a seat in the companion chair next to Renata.

"Renata Corrigan? I'm Augusta Monet."

"Oh my goodness, what absolutely lovely hair you have. Bet your mother was a ginger too."

"My father actually."

"Ruadh gu brath!"

Gus stares, not understanding.

"It's Gaelic. Redheads forever."

Then Gus understands. She sees it in the freckles that dot the bridge of Renata's nose and trail across her cheeks forming an intricate map around her smile lines. Renata was a redhead too. Now, just a hint of pale copper gilds the tips of her silver wisps.

"So tell me, what's your thesis statement, dear?"

Renata's handshake is feeble, but her voice is strong. She's small. Has an open, curious face. Reminds Gus of a child about to get a cookie.

Augusta likes her instantly.

Renata's olive eyes glisten from beneath fleshy wrinkled eyelids. Her ruby lipstick smudges the front of her white dentures. A pearl necklace loops across her gooseflesh neck and accents her yellow blouse. She wears a pair of shiny black penny loafers and tan nylons. Renata has dressed up for the occasion. She'd look good in one of Rose's Sunday hats.

"My thesis? Well, it's about Elgin. The town. Um. Really, it's about a family from that town. The Halladays? It's about them, I guess."

"Well, is it or isn't it?"

Renata is no-nonsense.

A heavyset man wearing kitchen whites sets a small tray on the table between them. Gus is off the hook for the moment.

"Ah, tea has arrived. Thank you, Vern. That'll be all for now."

She shoos him away with a flick of her hand as if he's a servant and she's the Queen of England. Vern stares at her, opens his mouth to speak, then changes his mind and leaves. Renata winks at Gus and calls out to Vern.

"I'll ring for you when we're done."

He slows momentarily, then keeps walking.

Renata looks at Gus with a girlish grin.

"Can't take the heat, get out of the kitchen."

On the tray sit a steaming teapot, two turquoise china cups with matching saucers, a milk and sugar set, and two silver teaspoons. Renata lifts the lid of the teapot, nods her approval, then carefully grasps the handle. She pours the tea with a few shakes and spills. Gus doesn't reach out to help. She knows both young and old are often made to feel inept. Renata wants to play host. Gus lets her.

"This was my grandmother's tea service. Nothing like a little piece of the past to remind one of what really matters."

Renata nods for Gus to help herself to the sugar and milk. Gus adds several spoonfuls of sugar to her tea. Renata stirs milk into hers. They both settle between the wings of their chairs and sip their warm tea.

"Okay, dolly, let's start over. There is no thesis. So what gives?"

Augusta and Renata smile at each other. Renata feels like a kindred spirit. Perhaps there's an old woman inside Gus who sees the young woman inside Renata and vice versa. Perhaps their kindredness has them meeting somewhere in between.

"I heard you were the one to talk to if you want to know about the history of Elgin."

Renata leans toward Gus.

"Hah, flattery will get you everywhere. But really. One ginger to another, you didn't come to sip tea and chew on the early days of some one-horse town. You're on a mission. I know that look. Wore it myself for years. You're investigating a story."

Gus looks into Renata's eyes and is suddenly filled with regret at trying to manipulate her. This woman is smart and deserves her best.

"I didn't mean to lie or insult you. It's just that I'm after the truth."

"Oh, precious, I'm not insulted, I'm intrigued. You remind me of me in my glory days. And Lord knows I need reminding."

She cackles. Gus smiles and dives in.

"I think you can help me. I want to know why my mother died on the very same day Kep Halladay died. I want to know what happened to June Halladay and her daughter, Gracie, and why Henry Neil disappeared and why a whole town got wiped off the face of the earth just like that. I want to know the truth."

Renata sets down her tea.

"That's more like it."

Renata reaches down beside her and retrieves a large blue scrapbook resting against the leg of her chair. Augusta hadn't noticed it before. Renata lifts the book and places it on her lap. She puts both hands on top of it and stares at the book lovingly. After a few seconds, she looks up at Augusta and reaches out to lightly touch her wrist.

"First, I'm sorry about your mother, young miss."

This is the second time Gus has heard this sentiment in the last twenty-four hours. Dez said almost the same thing. Only coming from Renata, there's a sweet sting to the words that catches Gus off guard. She pushes against the agonizing pain that racks her chest whenever someone manages to stir that pot so tenderly.

Renata leans back. Opens the book to the first page. Scans the newspaper clipping glued there then slowly flips pages. There are clippings glued to each page. Oversize articles are folded like origami to fit inside the book. Renata is very still for a moment. She appears to glaze over ever so slightly as her fingers play over the folds of newsprint. Gus can tell the older woman is trying to remember why she's looking at the book. Then a cog clicks into place and she speaks.

"My life's work was the story of that town."

Augusta stays quiet. She can see the past lapping at Renata's eyes, however gingerly. She lets her find her way.

"I loved Elgin. Her narrow streets lined with shady oak and willow and sumac that turned bright red in fall. I grew up there. Riding my bicycle up and down her sidewalks. Running through the fields at the edge of town. Picking black-eyed Susans for my mother's supper table. By the time I was your age, I was working at the local library on Main. Dreaming of the big wide world that existed in all those books. Of one day getting out of the stacks and becoming an investigative journalist just like Nellie Bly. Traveling the world. Exposing injustices. Such courageous writing."

Renata's hand rests on her heart like she's pledging allegiance to the dreams of the young woman she once was.

Gus reaches into her satchel. She pulls out her notebook and pen. Without taking her eyes off Renata. Doesn't want to break her flow. Gus makes a note to look up the name Nellie Bly while Renata continues talking.

"Lord knows I was tenacious. I pitched my ideas. I wrote mock-ups of articles, week in, week out. I handed them in to the local newspaper, trying to get my foot in the door, but I got rejection after rejection. It didn't matter what I wrote or how well I wrote it. It was just too big a stretch for the gentlemen running the paper. They couldn't wrap their pea-brains around the notion of a woman doing a job that had always been a man's. It took seventeen years for those old boys to acquiesce to letting a woman join their ranks. 1979. The year Margaret Thatcher was prime minister of the United Kingdom and Renata Corrigan finally became the first female reporter of Elgin, Ontario. The county of Leeds Grenville had entered the twentieth century."

Renata flips to the first page of her scrapbook.

"It was called the *Lakes and Islands Times* back then. Community news and the like. Chicken dinner stories, they called them. But to the locals they were the stuff of life and death. Weather forecasts mattered to farmers. Who got appointed chair of the local wheat board mattered. Day-to-day life and death mattered. People mattered. That's what history's all about, little miss. People and what happens to them when lightning strikes or droughts come or prime ministers appoint senators or county fairs happen to fall on the same day that a fire burns down an entire town."

Renata's eyes drift to a faraway memory. As if it's painful even thinking about the fire. She clears her throat and picks up her teacup. Then she takes hold of the teaspoon and adds sugar to her tea. She looks in the cup. Then she adds more sugar, stirs, then places the teaspoon in between the seat cushions of the chair she's sitting in as if to hide it there.

Gus glances over at the receptionist who happens to be staring at them. The girl shrugs as if to say, *Told you so.* Maybe this is what she meant by la-la land.

Renata notices the scrapbook in her lap, as if seeing it for the first time. She touches it, her bony fingers searching for meaning in its pages. She finds it.

"Everything I ever wrote for that publication is in this scrapbook. *Lakes and Islands Times.* Heritage Society newsletters. All of it. History. That's what I was writing. A record of the facts as I saw them. Or at least as they were presented to me. Did the best I could with my God-given talents."

Renata's face glows a little as she remembers. She looks like a woman who lived her life with purpose. Then she turns the book toward Gus so she can see what's glued on that first page.

"This is where it all started for me. I had just turned forty-seven. Left the library and got my first job in journalism after years of banging hard on that door. The editor wanted to ease me in slow so he put me on birth and death notices. The Irish comics, they called them."

Gus doesn't get the joke, but she smiles and pretends she does.

"But, as fate would have it, I didn't get some old geezer dying in his sleep or a set of triplets born to a dairy farmer. Not Renata Corrigan. I hit the mother lode. A double whammy."

She pokes her bony finger at the article.

"I got the baby girl who was born with a death rattle in her little hand."

Gus leans over. Glued side by side are two short articles. A birth announcement and a death notice. Written on the same day. The former announces the coming into the world of June Halladay and the latter marks the departing of Amelia, her mother who died during childbirth.

In her mind's eye, Gus can see the dark branches of a tragic family tree. The Halladay women are hanging from this tree. Amelia; her daughter, June; and then June's daughter, Gracie. Mother, daughter, granddaughter. All dying so young. She remembers Amelia's gravestone in the Halladay family plot. Dead at age twenty-four, it read. June was dead at twenty-three. Gracie, still younger, at eighteen. Gus feels the sway of these branches against her skin as goose bumps form on her arms. Augusta knows she was meant to come to see Renata the moment she wrote her name in her notebook.

Renata glances at the tea set on the table beside her. Her brow furrows as if she's forgotten what she was going to say. Her shoulders sag. Augusta lightly touches Renata's hand and the woman starts, gets her bearings by referencing the page in front of her.

"June 17, 1979. A dark day for the town of Elgin. Especially for one of its founding families. The Halladays."

Renata falters again. She looks at Gus. Her eyes dim. As if somewhere deep inside the old woman's brain, a light flickers precariously.

Renata defaults to her manners.

"I'm sorry. I'm boring you, Miss Halladay."

"Not at all. It's Monet."

"That's right. Doing some detective work. I remember you. Was it Kep you asked about?"

Her eyes come alive. Before Gus can answer, Renata is off again. Rolling down memory lane, the wind at her back, Kep in her crosshairs.

"I went to Elgin Grammar School with Kep Halladay. I was three years ahead of him, but I knew who he was. We all knew the Halladays. They lived on Main Street in the prettiest house you ever saw. Until his parents were killed when he was ten. It was grade five as I recall. Terrible bit of business. They'd just purchased that fancy new Chrysler. It was the talk of the town. They went for a Sunday drive. There was a head-on collision with a combine. A local farmer named Jenkins. He said he pulled out onto the highway and they came out of nowhere. They were going so fast he couldn't get out of the way. They drove right into the metal teeth of his thresher. Killed them both, instantly."

Gus shudders at the thought of how terrible that moment must have been. How horrific the aftermath. A pang of sadness throbs in her chest for the boy who was orphaned so young. She knows the pain of such great and sudden loss. The open wound it leaves that never quite heals.

"The house in town was sold and young Kep was sent to live with his grandfather just outside town in the mansion on the hill. Jacob Halladay was his name. He made his fortune in the twenties as a bootlegger during Prohibition. He ran a network that stretched clear across the county and down into the States. Elgin was perfectly situated for his business to thrive. Far enough out so as not to attract attention, but close enough to the border to launch boats from Gananoque and island hop to Grindstone, stateside. Jacob amassed a fortune rum-running. He bought out the owner of the local feed company with his profits and expanded that legitimate business clear across the province. He built that mansion with his riches. It was his very own castle on the hill. He wanted to show everyone in town how well he was doing. How prosperous he'd become. He named it Halladay House. It was a huge property. Underground he dug a network of tunnels leading from the house to the barn where he operated his distillery. Spidering under his property and beyond. He had an army of men moving crates of moonshine through those tunnels. Paranoid and greedy, old Jacob was. When the law tried to crack down on his operation, he used loopholes in the Dunkin Act to get himself out of hot water. He claimed he was exporting alcohol for medicinal purposes and the local judge always threw out the warrants. Jacob Halladay even paid the county doctor to write prescriptions for medical tonics and elixirs. He had the scrips tied to the bottles. The law backed off and business boomed. That is, until Prohibition was repealed in Ontario in 1927. That's when Jacob closed up those tunnels and turned his attention to his more legitimate ventures."

Augusta is on the edge of her seat, enraptured by Renata's storytelling, taking notes. Renata likes that. She turns a page in her scrapbook and unfolds another newspaper clipping. She runs her finger across the typeface. Eyes closed as if touching braille. As if the memories live inside the layers of ink and the folds of newsprint. Carefully preserved and glued into place. Yet elusive and fragile.

"By the late 1980s, I was the resident history expert at the paper. I got my own column. Took almost a decade, mind you. They called it Stepping Back in Time. I wrote about note-worthy moments in the history of the county. People loved it. They used to stop me on the street to ask when the next Stepping Back was coming out."

Renata stops once in a while. Sips cold tea to wet her dry lips, but mostly she keeps talking. Going through the chapters of Elgin's history with each flip of the page. The scrapbook jogging her memories when she falters. She recounts how the town of Elgin flourished after Prohibition and became one of the most prominent communities in South Crosby Township. That's what it was called back then.

"A thriving center for farmers, merchants, mining com-panies, not to mention tourism what with all the surround-ing lakes and cottages. Elgin was prospering and for a time it seemed there was enough good fortune to go around. Enough for everyone. Save for one man."

Renata's face darkens. Augusta holds very still. Feeling the tiny hairs on the back of her neck rise as if someone has just sent a breath across her nape.

Renata slowly flips to an article she wrote in August 2006 about Kep Halladay, the week after he went missing at the age of seventy-one from Halladay House. Missing? Gus wonders what happened to him. How he died. Renata turns the scrapbook so that Gus can take a better look at the full color photograph of the man.

"This was the official portrait taken of Kep Halladay when he became a senator in 1985. He bought that seat with the fortune he inherited when his grandfather died a few years earlier at the ripe old age of ninety-nine. Jacob's money might have been enough if Kep's lovely Amelia had lived. But that wasn't to be."

Gus gets her first look at Kep Halladay. His name has been swirling through her life for days. On Shannon's wall circled in red. On gravestones and police reports and deeds. But this is the first time she's seen his face. Gus kicks herself. She could have easily found his picture with a simple computer search at a library. She's no detective. No investigator like Renata.

"His daughter, June, had those same steely blue eyes."

Gus thought there'd be a family resemblance to Gracie. But the thin frame and dark hair of the ballerina in the Polaroid are nowhere to be seen. In fact, he's quite the opposite. He wears a suit, perfectly tailored to fit his bullish chest and trim waistline. Full head of slicked-back blond hair. Square jaw and deep-set eyes. His expression is unwavering as he stares into the photographer's lens, a mix of disdain and pride subtly etched across his brow.

Renata turns the book back to face herself. Stares at Kep before taking a deep breath. Gus sees the old woman is tiring, but she doesn't stop her. Lets her dip deeply into the past. Into Kep Halladay's story.

Augusta senses that it's now or never.

19

KEP

☙

KEP WAS THE ONLY SON OF THEODORE AND DOROTHY HAL-laday. His father, Theo, was born with a silver spoon firmly clamped in his mouth. Likable fellow, but a flake. Theo dabbled in farming equipment, then in local mining, then in some spring water scheme that went belly-up. Each venture was bankrolled by his father, Jacob Halladay. Old man Jacob hoped his only son would eventually make something of himself. But Theo didn't have a head for business. He preferred living on a monthly allowance from his father.

"And Theo and Dottie wanted what they wanted. The latest-model car, weekends in New York, garden parties for their visiting American friends. Theo had little interest in making something of himself. Jacob gave up on the boy. He saw his son as his greatest failing and turned his attention to shaping the character of his young grandson, Kep. When Theo and Dottie were killed on that fateful Sunday drive, Jacob vowed never to indulge Kep as he had his only son.

"A hard road lay ahead for the young master.

"At thirteen Kep was shipped off to military school in Connecticut. He'd always been a soft sort of bully in grammar school. Pushing and shoving and shouting. But Kep's reputation hit new lows at military school. Perhaps it was losing both parents so suddenly. Perhaps it was his grandfather's iron hand. More likely Kep was just born rotten and boarding school transformed him from bully to sadist in short order. His grandfather had to intervene his sophomore year when a freshman came forward with sexual abuse allegations. Jacob opened his wallet. Kep got a slap on the wrist and the freshman got expelled. The incident was wiped from the school's records. Until years later when a certain feisty female reporter came along and sweet-talked the retired headmaster into revealing the truth. Off the record. Shame is a terrible gatekeeper."

Renata pauses, looks up, and smiles at Gus.

"You?" Gus asks.

Renata winks.

"By his senior year, rumors of Kep's cruel streak had darkened the back hallways and lower stairwells of the school and instilled terror among the freshman ranks, so much so that an unwritten code was put into place.

"Stay out of Kep's way and never get caught alone with him.

"Kep's valedictorian speech to his graduating class was likely one of the defining moments of his life. I interviewed a former schoolmate of Kep's for the article I wrote after he disappeared. He told me all about Kep's legacy at the school. He remembered Kep standing at the podium, like a god looking down upon his devotees, boys he'd molested, boys he'd ruined, boys who hated him. A look of pure joy on his face."

Renata shifts in her armchair. Augusta's hands are clammy as she listens to Renata. She knows in her gut that Kep Halladay is at the center of everything. The dark center. A nurse comes by to check on the older woman, but Renata shoos her away. She's deep into her story. Doesn't want to be interrupted or thrown off track. Gus can see that stories are what make Renata's heart soar.

Renata flips back to the first page. The side-by-side birth and death announcements. Gus leans in to look closer. There's a picture of Amelia on the death announcement. A pretty young woman with chestnut hair and big brown eyes. She's wearing a wedding dress. Odd considering it's a death announcement.

"After attending Harvard Business School, Kep came home and Jacob put him to work in the feed business. His grandfather decided good old-fashioned hard work was what Kep needed to scuff up his polished Ivy League manners.

"Kep started at the bottom. Sweeping the factory floor. The old man had no problem boxing Kep's ears in front of the other workers if he slacked off. He even threatened to leave all his inheritance to charity if Kep didn't live his life as Jacob saw fit.

"For two decades, Kep was at his grandfather's beck and call. He rose up the ranks of the feed business, sat on the Grain Board, bartered with local farmers, was introduced to his grandfather's government connections in Ottawa, and finally became Jacob's right-hand man. He was good at it. A smooth talker. A quick study, but he hated the feed business.

"It was the late seventies. Jacob was well into his nineties and still a formidable businessman. He was always looking for ways to expand, to cement his reputation and to make more money. As if wealth could ward off death. Jacob wanted to take over his biggest competitor. A successful businessman from Perth. The man wouldn't sell. Then Jacob stumbled upon a way to remove the thorn from his grandson's shady reputation and from their family's good name. Kep would marry the only daughter of his rival in Perth. Her name was Amelia Grace Hillcott. Conveniently, the union would also solidify the Halladay legacy by linking his family to the Perth Hillcott dynasty.

"Jacob arranged for his grandson to meet the girl. Kep was forty-two. Amelia was just twenty-two."

Gus flashes, momentarily, to the cemetery. She sees the gravestone.

AMELIA GRACE HILLCOTT-HALLADAY
BELOVED WIFE OF KEP JACOB HALLADAY
BORN APRIL 22, 1955
DIED JUNE 17, 1979
AGE 24

Gus shivers, knowing the story isn't going to end well for Amelia. Glances at the obituary. Renata continues.

"For a man whose heart seemed hardened from years of living as his grandfather's goat, Amelia was Kep's salve. Sweet, kind, shy, and utterly lovely. He was smitten from the moment he saw her. No woman had so much as turned his head in his forty-two years until Amelia. A brown-haired beauty with pale skin and big green eyes, she took his breath away. He proposed on their second date. They married and a year later, Kep's grandfather died of walking pneumonia after refusing to stop working and rest. He died on the factory floor giving orders. Just collapsed in a heap.

"In that moment, Kep's world seemed to right itself.

"First Amelia and now freedom. He sold the feed business. They traveled to Europe and when they returned home, Kep seemed a changed man. Lighter. More like his parents. He even smiled at people when he passed them in town. Amelia wanted to live in Halladay House so they made it their own. Gussied it up with velvet curtains and imported antiques from Italy. She built a large rose garden with a greenhouse out back, white picket fences, a trellis, and hedgerows. Summer evenings they were often seen strolling hand in hand down the sidewalks of Elgin after getting ice cream cones at the dairy bar."

Gus is smiling despite herself. Carried away to a summer evening long ago. Transported by the pictures Renata paints with her words. But those pictures quickly shrivel and darken.

"Then news came that she was with child. Kep was forty-four. He handed out cigars at the barbershop and he bought fresh cut roses every day for his wife at the general store. He stopped people on the street to talk about the weather. Townsfolk warmed to the man for the first time in decades. Everything seemed to have worked out for one of their founding sons.

"Then one unusually crisp June morning, Amelia died giving birth to a healthy baby girl."

Augusta feels that breath on her neck again. Her mother's breath. She trembles involuntarily. Renata doesn't notice. She's staring at the pages in her lap.

"When Kep heard, he refused to believe it. He nearly killed the doctor who told him the news. Once he saw her for himself, he blamed the doctors, the nurses, the priest, the whole town. But in the end, he could only find one person to truly blame. The baby. Kep wouldn't touch her or name her.

The nurses chose a name for the birth certificate. June for the month she was born. Little June Halladay was alone the moment she entered the world."

Gus bites her lip. Wondering why life can be such a warm refuge for some, but for others, it's nothing more than a cold, bottomless pit. Gus has been down there. She feels herself slowly digging her way out, the more she searches and finds pieces of the truth. Moves toward the light. The warm surface. But baby June never felt her mother's warm breath on her neck. Likely never found her way out. At least, it's doubtful she did. Augusta knows how June's story ends.

Renata continues.

"Folks used to say Kep's marriage only masked who he really was. Like a Band-Aid over a festering wound. With his beloved ripped away from him, the real Kep seeped out. He buried his wife, squared his shoulders, and began rebuilding his grandfather's empire. Bought back the feed business. Bullied local merchants into cutting their prices. Intimidated competitors. The local farmers despised him. He held them hostage. Raising prices, monopolizing the market, cutting off their supply routes. By the early eighties, Kep Halladay owned a piece of every business in Elgin, from the local paper to the motor inn. He had politicians in his back pocket. Transport officials and law enforcement on his payroll. It was rumored he even had a police officer or two on the inside doing his bidding. Then he bought himself a political seat.

"At the age of fifty, Kep Halladay was appointed to the Senate by Prime Minister Brian Mulroney. Halladay House was revived and a new heyday began. An endless stream of bigwigs from Chicago and Washington, Ottawa and Toronto came to Halladay House. Local teenagers were hired to work the parties, serving drinks and food. Boys mostly. The gossip bubbled around town that some of the boys were earning extra money for favors. Party favors, they called them. These rumors were fueled by a bruise seen on a boy's neck or a heated argument overheard between a father and son in the drugstore. The high school crowd that used to gather on summer evenings outside the bowling alley, laughing and jostling, now huddled together and whispered in hushed tones. Most weekends, Kep's parties went well into the night and the town braced for the worst and hoped for the best come Sunday morning. No one dared shut them down or stand up to Kep Halladay.

"And no one gave much thought to June Halladay."

20

JUNE

❧

RENATA FLIPS ANOTHER PAGE IN HER SCRAPBOOK. GUS NO-tices the old woman's eyes twinkle as if, in the turning of the page, time is flickering before her like an old movie. Unraveling itself. Not only illuminating what happened back then, but also showing her who she once was. A young female reporter assigned to write a story that is now a newspaper clipping glued forever in place. A copy of that same article is taped to Shannon's wall. Gus recognizes it. The one about June Halladay's accident.

Gus feels compelled to inch closer to Renata and her scrapbook. She leans in, barely breathing. Drawn toward the faded ink and yellowing newsprint just as Renata is. Gus can almost smell the wood pulp. Renata's mouth quivers. Gus waits. Ears perked. Knowing Renata is about to reveal so much more about the girl who was June Halladay.

"She lived up in Halladay House. Alone with her father. The housekeeper said she made the child supper and a school lunch before leaving each day. The groundskeeper who mowed the front lawns said June played out back in the derelict greenhouse. He was told not to clean out the greenhouse or weed the rose garden or trim the hedges or tend to the mess of tangled shrubs behind the house. It was all left to rot.

"People worried that little June was neglected too.

"She walked herself to school from the age of five. Her teachers said she was a good artist. She drew pictures of a mother and child. A blue ocean and a field of daisies. Her teachers marveled at her bright spirit, her artistic talent, and her sweet bearing. Attributing it to her mother's genes. Kep never attended school art shows or plays or end-of-year parties. Not one parent-teacher interview. Not one graduation. Not primary school. Not middle school. Not high school. June raised herself.

"She grew leggy and pretty with long yellow hair and deep blue eyes. She joined the cheerleading squad and had lots of friends. At fifteen she started seeing a local boy. Todd Hammond. He was sixteen and worked part-time as a stock boy at the grocery store. People saw them walking together down by the creek or along some lane next to a cornfield. Never holding hands for fear of it getting back to her father. They were just talking and walking.

"This went on all summer. Everyone knew except Kep. No one said a word to him. Then one evening, he was driving through town and saw them sharing a milkshake outside the drugstore. Todd ran off when Kep pulled up to the curb. The whole town heard June screaming as Kep dragged her by the hair into the car. A week later, Todd and his family packed up all their belongings, stuck a For Sale sign on their front lawn, and drove off in a U-Haul. Everyone knew they'd been run out of town by Kep's men. A couple of tough guys he had on his payroll. They did his dirty work. Townsfolk said nothing. They were afraid. They knew he could turn on any one of them in the blink of an eye.

"Then June started to show. She was pregnant. That was it. Any friends she had turned their backs on her. The whole town did for fear of showing her a kindness and having the wrath of Kep come down on them and their kin.

"Little Gracie was born the spring of '95. The town was shocked that Kep let her keep the baby. Some say he didn't have a choice. June wouldn't have it any other way. June loved that baby. She had no idea how to be a mother. And no one in town was brave enough to give her work or even help her take care of the baby, so she was stuck living with her father in Halladay House. Those girls she used to be friends with would cross to the other side of the street when she came along pushing her pram. Cowards, the whole bunch. No wonder she dipped into the sherry once in a while.

"June didn't care about any of them. She had raised herself and she would raise her baby. Her little Gracie. A quirky, pale-skinned, dark-haired babe who looked nothing like her pretty mother. Or young Todd for that matter. Gracie was an odd duck from day one. She went from skinny toddler to gawky preschooler. June enrolled her in dance lessons, took her swimming at Little Lake, and ordered dresses for her from the Eaton's catalog. Did her best, despite her drinking. Did her very best to ease her little daughter into a world Gracie seemed misshapen for.

"Every Sunday evening they walked through town. Once

Gracie was old enough, she rode a pink bike alongside her mother. They would pass by the house where Todd once lived. It unnerved the folks who lived there. They'd heard the stories. Didn't want the attention. Gracie was seven years old the last time those folks saw the pair of them pass by.

"That was the year June died. 2002."

Renata brushes a tear from her cheek. Augusta is taken aback that the retired journalist is so choked up by her own story. But then Gus realizes she too has a lump in her throat. The old woman's words are more than just stories. They are homages to real lives lived and lost. At least the words about Amelia and June and Gracie seem to be. They are about mothers and daughters. They are about a family of cursed women. Gus can't help but think of her own mother. Of Rose too. Another family of women, not so much cursed, as splintered. Not a family at all anymore. Gus clears her throat, trying to swallow the lump away.

One of Renata's crooked bony fingers rests lightly on the article she wrote about June's accident.

"I didn't write what I wanted to write. What I knew I should write. I wrote around the truth. I skirted it like a croc in a pond. I was a coward too. Just like the rest of them."

Renata wipes her cheek with the small paper napkin from under her teacup.

"The truth will come back to bite you if you're not careful."

An exceptionally tall nurse stands at the far side of the lounge. She catches Augusta's eye and taps her thin wrist. Time to wrap it up. The nurse folds her gangly arms. She reminds Gus of an ostrich. Long-necked and awkward. Her mouth forms a thin stern line under her nose. Her bug eyes are unwavering. She looks like a tough cookie despite the pastel floral uniform. Gus gives her a nod, pretending she's on board.

"Renata. What didn't you write?"

Renata stares at her. Blank. She looks at the napkin, turning it in her hands as if she's never seen one before. Gus knew the roll Renata had been on was too good to last. She tries to help her remember. She points to the clipping about June's accident that sits in Renata's lap.

"You said you wrote around the truth. What truth, Renata?"

Renata shakes her head and furrows her brow. Frustration closing in.

"I don't know anyone named Renata."

The nurse is on the move. Shit.

"Everything okay here, Mrs. Corrigan?" the nurse says in a loud patronizing voice as if Renata is stone deaf.

"Stop bothering me, June." The old woman snaps at the nurse and tries to shoo her away. The nurse is having none of it. She stands her ground and whispers to Augusta as if they're coconspirators.

"Like the wind. She just drifts off and there's no telling when she'll come back."

Gus sits forward in her chair. Not ready to give up.

"But she was fine a minute ago. More than fine. I'm sure we're good."

The nurse smirks at the naïve young woman.

"And I'm sure you've had a lovely time chatting about your little school project, but Renata needs to rest now. She rarely gets visitors just popping by."

The nurse grabs the scrapbook, tucks it under her arm,

then takes hold of Renata's elbow, and makes her stand. Gus resents the implication and the way she's manhandling poor Renata.

"But I didn't just pop by."

"Time to go to your room for a little nap, alrighty, Mrs. Corrigan?"

The nurse tries to maneuver Renata away, but the old woman pulls from her grasp and grabs hold of Augusta's wrist. She leans over and whispers to her.

"Please don't go."

The nurse peels Renata's hand from Augusta's wrist.

"That's quite enough, Mrs. Corrigan. You see, miss, you've upset her."

Gus is livid at this ostrich of a woman. "You're the one who's upsetting her by grabbing her arm."

Renata leans closer to Gus. "Don't go back there."

The nurse glares at Augusta. "Do I need to call security?"

Gus is really beginning to hate Nurse Ostrich.

"Don't go, Shannon."

Augusta flinches. An orderly comes to help the nurse and all Gus can do is watch them lead Renata away. She rises and calls out before Renata disappears, "I'll come back tomorrow."

The nurse shoots her a look that says, *Not bloody likely.* Gus makes her way to the front door, glancing down the hall. She sees the nurse leading Renata slowly into her room.

Outside the retirement home, Gus inhales, welcoming the fresh air into her lungs. The smell of urine and old skin lingers on her clothes. An elderly resident sits hunched in a wheelchair. Strands of wispy white hair float about her face. She gives Augusta a scrawny-fingered salute. Then she mutters through smacking gums, "If you've seen my Bucky, you tell him I've made roast beef and Yorkshire pudding with brown gravy. Just like he likes it. You tell him."

Augusta gives the woman a thumbs-up. She heads across the parking lot toward Rose's Buick, going over her encounter with Renata. How sharp and fluid the woman's mind could be one moment, then suddenly and without warning betray her the next.

She recalls what Renata said to her midway through their meeting.

Doing some detective work. I remember you. Was it Kep you asked about?

At the time, Gus had brushed off Renata's use of the word *detective.* Thinking it was just a figure of speech because they'd been talking about her investigating the story of Elgin. Of the Halladays. Of Kep. But when Renata called her Shannon, Gus knew it wasn't a figure of speech at all. It was a tiny sliver of a memory slipping through a crack in an old woman's fragile mind. Poking out for Gus to see. Her mother had also sought out Renata. When she too would have been looking into the town of Elgin and into Kep Halladay's past.

Shannon was there with them today.

Renata knew it.

Augusta knows it too. Knows it deep in her bones.

She felt it in the lump in her throat and in the goose bumps on her arms.

Gus is following in her mother's footsteps.

21

ALICE

AUGUSTA BARELY SLEEPS THAT NIGHT. RENATA'S STORIES spin round and round her brain. Stories of the Halladays. Of Elgin. The woman's a living encyclopedia of the town. It makes sense that Shannon sought her out. The whole history of that town and one of its founding families is laid out in that scrapbook, but Gus believes much of that history isn't written in ink. It's etched on the dim walls of Renata's delicate brain. Gus wants to shine a light in those dark places. Wants to hear it all. Every detail. She has to go back to see Renata. Fuck it if the Ostrich doesn't like it.

At the break of day, Levi in the back seat, Augusta heads back to Smiths Falls. She doesn't call ahead this time. Better to ask forgiveness in person than get shut down on the phone. Surely they won't deny Renata a little visit after a full night's rest.

Gus strides confidently into the lobby and approaches the front desk. Same receptionist from the day before. The girl is busy swiping the screen of her phone with one finger. Gus clears her throat.

"I'm here to see Renata Corrigan."

The girl doesn't look up.

"Not here."

"Oh. Where is she?"

The girl tears her eyes from her screen and looks up.

"You related?"

Recognition dawns. They both know she isn't. Nurse Ostrich steps out of the office behind the receptionist and gives Augusta the stink eye. Hands on her pointy hips, neck craned, she ignores Gus and instead talks to the receptionist like Gus can't hear them.

"This is the one I was telling you about."

The girl doesn't give a shit. Fakes interest.

"She's the reason poor Mrs. Corrigan is in the hospital."

The girl glances at her phone, then gives Gus a look that says, *Why am I part of this conversation?*

"It's not looking good. No thanks to her."

Nurse Ostrich could use some anger management training.

"What do you mean? She was fine yesterday."

"I think you should go."

The nurse snorts at Gus as her mind whirls in confusion. Did her visit upset Renata that much? Did Ostrich do something to Renata after she left?

"What hospital?"

The receptionist gives Gus a *what the fuck* look. The Ostrich has had enough.

"Please leave before you give another one of our residents a stroke."

Augusta is taken aback. A stroke? Renata's mind wandered but she wasn't sick. Gus gets a woozy feeling in the pit of her stomach. Maybe she pushed her too hard. Could digging into old memories actually be harmful to a fragile mind like Renata's? Gus reels. It's all her fault. She covers her mouth as Renata's words come to her.

The truth will come back to bite you if you're not careful.

Nurse Ostrich gestures toward the door.

But Gus can't bring herself to leave. Something has her frozen in her tracks.

Fear.

But not fear of what she might have done to Renata. And not fear of the purple-faced nurse glaring at her. It's fear of letting her mother down. Shannon wouldn't give up now. She'd push. Hard. Gus can hear her saying what she always said.

If you want something, little girl, you have to go after it with everything you've got. Life's too short for eggshell walking and pussyfooting.

Gus steps forward, with her mother by her side. She shakes off the guilt over Renata and takes one last kick at the Ostrich. More than ever, Gus needs to get at the truth. And if Renata can't help her find it, maybe that scrapbook of hers will point Gus in the right direction.

She smiles innocently.

"Do you think I could borrow her scrapbook? For my school project?"

Nurse Ostrich smiles.

"Why, of course. How about some of her jewelry too? Maybe a nice watch. How 'bout her TV? You go on and help yourself to whatever you want."

Gus turns beet red. So much for not pussyfooting. The

receptionist snickers as she texts. Likely sharing this fiasco with one of her many friends. Feeling small and stupid, Augusta awkwardly turns to leave. At the door, she slams her hand across the wheelchair access button. The doors magically part. Too slowly. She shoves them open and takes off across the parking lot as humiliation turns to anger.

Screw Ostrich-face.

Gus wants that scrapbook.

She has to have it.

Gus drives two blocks over and parks on a side street. Levi's fast asleep as usual. She cracks the window, shoves her keys and phone in her back pocket, then strolls back toward the retirement home. When she reaches the edge of the property, she ducks low behind the front hedge. She crawls across the lawn from shrub to shrub until she's pressed against the side of the building. She skirts the corner and finds a kitchen door propped open at the back. She walks in.

Act like you belong and no one will suspect a thing.

Gus strolls alongside the steel countertop, nodding to a prep cook who barely looks up from his onion chopping. She runs her finger across the counter and examines it for germs, pretending to be a health inspector. She makes it across the kitchen and peeks out the swinging doors into an empty dining room. She can see the lounge and the reception desk beyond. No Ostrich sightings. The receptionist has her head bent over her phone. Gus makes her move. Pushes through the doors, crosses the dining room, and heads down the hallway where she saw Renata being led to her room the day before. She moves fast, but not too fast. Renata's room looked to

be about halfway down on the left. She checks the nameplates.
She passes an open door. The nameplate says Alice Myers. Inside sits the wispy-haired biddy who spoke to her outside. Alice sits reading in a large yellow armchair, next to her electric
wheelchair. Gus tries to slip past, but Alice is already peering
over her spectacles.

"You can call me Alice, but don't call me late for tea."

Alice giggles.

Afraid to linger in the hall, Augusta steps into Alice's room.

"I'm just on my way to Renata's room. You have a good day."

"She's not in her room."

"Oh yes, I know that."

"They don't tell us diddly-squat, but I think she's gone up
there."

Alice points upward. And since there's no second floor,
Gus figures she means heaven.

"No, she's just in the hospital. I'm her niece. Come to get
a few things for her."

"Probably the beans that caused it."

"Beans?"

"My late husband, Bucky, once had to go to emergency,
but it was just gas."

"That's good."

"Did you see Bucky on your way in?"

"I didn't."

"Renata doesn't have a niece."

Gus smiles. She's underestimated Alice.

"Renata plays her radio loud sometimes. Walls are paper
thin. Her room is right next door to mine."

Gus nods. She checks if the coast is clear. It's not. A male nurse is heading toward her pushing a cart of pill bottles. She closes the door. Alice smiles.

"He asked about you. Told her to spill the beans."

"Who?"

Alice pulls herself to the edge of her chair and whispers loudly.

"The man. The one that came to see Renata in her room last night. Cardboard walls you see. I could hear him asking her what she talked about with the girl. I knew you had to be the girl. Only visitor she's had in forever."

"What did he look like?"

There's a knock on the door. Gus presses herself behind it as it opens.

"Mrs. Myers? Time for your meds."

"Let's get it over with then."

The nurse guides the cart into the narrow room. Hands her a small container and a glass of water.

"Here you go, Alice."

Alice quickly swallows three large white pills with a gulp and sticks out her tongue. The nurse backs the cart out of the room and shuts the door.

"Alice, did you see the man?"

"No, I can't see through cardboard."

"I really should go."

"Me too. Got a date with a chopper pilot from Trenton. Don't tell Bucky."

Alice winks. Augusta winks back, then peers into the hall. Coast is clear. She slips out just as the Ostrich rounds a corner. The nurse is looking down at her clipboard giving Gus the milli-

second she needs to scurry into Renata's room. Augusta locks
the door. Takes a deep breath. The room smells like Listerine
and lavender. It reminds her of Rose's bedroom.

She gets down to business. Lifting pillows, checking the
bookshelves, the closet, opening drawers, stooping to look
under the bed. She can't find the scrapbook anywhere. Maybe
the mystery man took it. Or maybe Alice just heard the radio.
She lifts the corner of a blanket lying across the arm of a pais-
ley easy chair by the window.

There it is. Tucked down the side of the chair under the
blanket. She picks up the scrapbook and holds it close.

Just then someone tries the door.

Almost at precisely the same moment, her back pocket
pings loudly. She frantically grabs for the phone and turns off
the volume. The screen lights up with another text from Lars.

> You think I don't know where you are? Think again. I'm
> coming for you, Auggie.

Keys jingle. Shit. Augusta pockets her phone and scans the
room. She yanks the window open with one hand, shoves the
screen off its frame, tosses the scrapbook outside, then pulls
the window shut.

The Ostrich enters.

Augusta is sitting in the easy chair with her head in her
hands, pretending to cry.

"Jesus Christ! How in God's name did you get in here?"

The Ostrich stomps one of her orthotic shoes into the beige
carpet. Augusta looks up at the nurse, trying to muster tears.

"Poor Renata."

"Right, that's it. I'm calling the police if you don't get out this instant."

Nurse O holds the door open and sweeps her hand in the direction of the front lobby. Gus obeys. The girl at the front desk perks up when she sees Gus being ushered out. More drama to text about. Before Gus can escape, the Ostrich grabs hold of her satchel. Rummages through it and finds nothing. She lets go. Augusta gives her a *you should be ashamed of yourself* glare and walks out the front doors. Again. The Ostrich watches her until she's off the property.

Back at the Buick, Levi's up and barking. She lets him out to pee, then holds out a cookie for him. He snaps it from her fingers, his teeth grazing the tips. She drives farther into the neighborhood. Down a crescent where the houses back onto the grounds of the retirement home. She parks. Checks her phone. Fuck Lars and his ridiculous stalker-texting. He could have given her away before she even got into Renata's room. Gus makes a mental note to figure out how to block his number. But right now she's got a mission to complete.

She spots a house with no cars in the driveway. Doesn't look like anyone's home. Gus tells Levi to chill. He's busy chewing. She locks the car, walks up the driveway, and enters the backyard. She crosses the yard, then pushes through the hedge and scrambles across the grounds of the retirement home. She makes it to the side of the building, feeling like a ninja inching her back along the wall. She finds Renata's window and voilà! The scrapbook is right there in the grass where she tossed it. She grabs it and dashes back the way she came. As she reaches the hedge, she glances back at the retirement home. That's when she spots Alice waving frantically from one of the big glass windows in the lounge. A huge smile on her face. Gus waves back just as the Ostrich appears at Alice's shoulder and looks out to see who she's waving to. Gus ducks into the hedges and disappears.

Back on the highway toward Ottawa, her heart is still racing. Racing because something doesn't feel right. It's the man Alice heard talking to Renata the night she had a stroke. Maybe Alice conjured him up, just like she does her dead husband, Bucky. Or maybe the man is real. And he's asking about Gus. Following her. And maybe it was *him*, and not her, who pushed Renata over the edge. Augusta's head tells her she's being paranoid, but her heart won't stop racing.

Racing because with every step she feels pulled by her mother's wake.

She likes the feeling.

22

STANTON

AFTER A NIGHT SPENT PORING OVER THE SCRAPBOOK AND phoning three hospitals, Gus found her. Called her room and a nurse answered.

Can I speak to Renata, please?

I'm afraid that's not possible.

Please, I just want to know she's okay.

And you are?

Her niece.

Then you're aware that she's lost the ability to speak. Permanently.

Poor sweet Renata.

Augusta wakes the next morning to the low hum of her phone vibrating. The sound drags her from the fog of a deep sleep. As she opens her eyes, she knows she was having one of her vivid dreams. And this one will be hard to shake off.

In the dream, she was visiting Renata in a derelict hospital. They were the only two in the entire building. The halls were empty as if abandoned. Renata lay in a rusty metal bed under a thin sheet. Gus sat on a chair across the room. A red leather chair like the one in Miss Virtue's office at the Scotiabank. Gus was sitting so far away from Renata that she had to shout to talk to her. When she rose to move closer, Renata's mouth began to disappear, and her eyes became terror-stricken. Then, slowly her horrified mouthless face morphed into the deformed hunk of flesh that is Desmond Oaks.

Then Gus woke, leaving Renata all alone.

Augusta's phone vibrates again. She grabs it off the side table next to her bed and expects to see another text tirade from Lars. It's not him.

It's Rory calling. She picks up. He needs her to come to RCMP headquarters. Gives her the address on Leikin. His boss, Sergeant Stanton, wants a word. Rory says he'll meet her at the main gate in an hour. Sounds like she has no choice. She doesn't ask what it's about. She's pretty sure it has something to do with Nurse Ostrich and trespassing. Being summoned to RCMP headquarters seems a tad extreme for a petty crime.

Augusta gets up, brushes her teeth, doesn't bother showering, feeds Levi, then lets him out back to pee while she sips her coffee. She stuffs a Pop-Tart in her mouth and heads for the front door. She glances at herself in the mirror of the hall tree. Glimpses her mother's angular cheekbones. Runs her fingers through her long red hair. Dark circles rim her green eyes. Her pale skin, dotted with freckles, looks almost translucent. She needs to eat better.

As Gus opens the door, she looks back at the dog. Levi pouts, chin on paws. He doesn't like being left behind.

"Back soon, promise."

The headquarters are on the edge of the Barrhaven suburbs situated in an open field. The large parking lot is surrounded by wrought-iron fencing that wraps around the entire complex of unremarkable gray brick buildings. There's a small security outbuilding at the edge of the parking lot where visitors check in. Gus registers her ID with a constable at the desk, gets a plastic clip-on visitor's pass, then waits on a hard plastic chair in the glass lobby.

Eventually, Rory rushes in, huffing and puffing.

"Sorry I'm late. How've you been, Little Monet?"

"Keeping busy."

"So it seems."

He leads the way. Avoiding eye contact. Either he's sorry for the way he acted last time they saw each other or he's nervous about what's about to go down.

Rory guides her through a turnstile, scanning the pass that hangs around his neck so each of them can move through the electronic arms. They cross a courtyard to the main building, go through a large foyer, up an elevator, down a long hall. Finally, they arrive at a closed office door bearing a sign.

SERGEANT MARTY STANTON, HEAD OF YOUTH SERVICES

Gus cringes. She might only be twenty, but this is ridiculous. Rory smiles awkwardly at Gus as he knocks lightly.

"Enter."

Stanton is a brick of a woman. About sixty. Gus was expecting a man with the name Marty. Stanton's ample chest pulls open the buttons of her blue shirt. Her white bra peeks out. Her neck puffs over her collar like pizza crust. Gus shakes her spongy hand and sits across from her. The jacket of her uniform hangs on a metal coat-tree in the corner. Her office is small. Stanton sits back in her chair and jostles the coat-tree. Gus can tell from her tense jaw that this happens every time she sits down and it's slowly driving her crazy. A large computer crowds one-half of her desk. A stack of file folders, about to tip over, crowds the other. Yellow sticky notes decorate the edges of her computer monitor. A window looks out to a brick wall. Her office is a prison cell.

"I knew your parents well."

Stanton shuffles paperwork. Doesn't look Gus in the eye or introduce herself. She doesn't want to be dealing with this. Rory stands behind Gus.

"Fine people. Good police officers."

"The best," Rory pipes in.

Stanton shoots him a look before continuing.

"I was in charge of rookie training in Kingston when they joined the detachment back in '97."

"Your mom worked for Sergeant Stanton when she was in the family way. With you that is."

Rory can't keep his mouth shut. Stanton raises an eyebrow. Rory gets the message, excuses himself, closing the door behind him.

"Have I done something wrong?"

Gus feels like a kid in the principal's office. Stanton adjusts her tight belt then clasps her hands. Time to get down to business.

"I understand you have RCMP evidence in your possession."

Augusta wasn't expecting that.

"You mean a few old newspaper clippings?"

"And a little collection of photographs and a police report, among other things. Copies or not, they are police evidence."

She can't believe Rory told Stanton everything.

"They're my mother's."

"They belong to the RCMP."

"She was trying to solve a cold case."

Stanton rubs her chin.

"Can I call you Augusta?"

"Sure. What can I call you?"

Dipshit comes to mind but Gus doesn't say it.

"Augusta, Constable Rump tells me you've been engaging in a little amateur detective work. You've been poking around a restricted area out in the county south of Ottawa."

Damn Rory. Thanks a lot.

"Your parents were outstanding police officers. But you, young lady, are not a police officer. I want you to stop pretending you are. Am I clear?"

She rises. She's done, and Gus is dismissed. Gus hates her condescending tone. Calling her mother's wall a "little collection." As if it were an assortment of teaspoons like the ones that used to hang on Rose's living room wall. Stanton might be done with her, but she's not done with Stanton.

"Were you the one who suspended her?"

Stanton sits back in her chair. It whines under the strain.

"Actually, no. I was the one who got her off the desk and back out on patrol. Then June Halladay's accident landed on her shift. The case got to her. June's girl being so young, losing her mother. From then on, she had it out for the senator. Head office transferred her out of there. To Ottawa. But she never let it go. She still poked around. Looking into the Halladays.

Then the Neil kid went missing and she was like a dog with a bone. Somebody in the senator's office got involved and that was that. Ultimately, your mother got herself suspended."

Gus is trying to take it all in. Connect the dots.

"Henry Neil? They just found his body. He was living at Kep Halladay's when he went missing."

"Doesn't mean the man killed him."

Stanton looks like she wants to eat her words.

"Is that what my mother thought happened to him? To Henry?"

"No. Yes, but it was a wild theory based on nothing."

"So it wasn't an accident. I knew it."

"I think you misunderstood what . . ."

Gus cuts her off. "Did you know my mother died the same day Kep Halladay disappeared?"

Stanton looks at her, steadies herself.

"Two unrelated incidents, I assure you, young lady."

Gus doesn't buy it, but she lets it go for now. Stanton's a gold mine.

"What happened to Gracie Halladay once her grandfather was gone?"

Stanton wipes sweat from her brow. She's trying not to lose her cool.

"As far as I remember, the house got boarded up. Some woman in town took her in. Lois somebody. I recall, she was a dance instructor in Elgin."

Lois. The name's come up before, but Gus can't think where. Stanton continues.

"A few months after Kep Halladay's murder I was transferred to Youth Services here at headquarters so that's all I know about that."

Stanton is trying to wrap things up. But Gus is startled by this revelation.

"Murder?"

"That's right. His body was never recovered, but at the time, forensics found physical evidence that pointed to it being a homicide. The case went cold. It remains unsolved to this day."

Gus opens her mouth to speak, but Stanton gives her a look that shuts it.

"We're done, Miss Monet. I called this meeting out of respect for your parents, but the interrogation is over."

She rises and so does Gus. They shake hands.

"So we're clear?"

Gus nods. Rory is waiting outside like an eager puppy. In the elevator, he looks down at his hands.

"Stanton might be a bit of a bull in a china shop, but she's just looking out for you. Me too."

"Is that why you told on me, Constable Rump?"

He turns and takes her gently by the shoulders. She stiffens at his touch. Not quite ready to forgive him.

"You're young. You should be going out on dates and shopping at the mall and looking to the future instead of digging up the dusty old past."

Then she realizes forgiveness is exactly what it's going to take. Taking a deep breath, Augusta forces herself to relax, then wraps her arms around Rory and squeezes him tight enough to make the lie that's coming feel true.

"You're right. I guess I just wanted to be close to her. Got caught up in it. I know there's really nothing there in all that evidence. I'll leave it alone. I promise."

"That a girl."

Gus can't help but smile. She loves her uncle Rory. Her mother did too in her own way. A pity-filled love, but a love nonetheless. Shannon understood something else about Rory that Gus is just now realizing.

The less Rory is involved the better.

THE REST OF THE DAY IS STINKING HOT. GUS TAKES LEVI FOR A cool evening walk. As the rosy sky turns a lovely marine blue, Gus mulls over what Stanton told her about Henry. About Kep's murder. About Shannon being like a dog with a bone. About her wild theories. Gus desperately wants to sit next to Shannon in her office in the garage, look up at that corkboard of evidence, and talk to her about what she knows for sure and what she only suspects. She wants to hear all of Shannon's wild theories and so much more.

Gus realizes there is one other person, besides her, who saw her mother during those last days and nights of her life. Augusta's babysitter, Annalee. Maybe she remembers something. Has some fragment of information that the police don't know or won't share.

Gus does the math in her head. Annalee was fifteen when she babysat for Shannon. She lived on the same street two blocks down. Number 256. That was twelve years ago. She'd be in her late twenties. Probably moved out by now.

But maybe her parents stayed put.

Back at Rose's, Gus makes a quick call to 411 and gets the

phone number. The Franklins still live at 256 Hilda. Ken and Beckie. She calls.

Beckie answers. She remembers Gus and her mother, Shannon. Says she could never forget either of them. Says it like their story is one she's shared often. Beckie tells her that Annalee now works as a hairdresser at Supercuts in Kanata. Lives with her boyfriend out there. They don't see her much anymore. Her voice cracks a little. She tries to keep Gus on the phone, asking her questions about her own life. Gus lies about having a job and about going to university, then she asks for Annalee's cell number. Says she wants to touch base. Grab lunch. Beckie says her daughter will be so happy to hear from her, but at the moment she's backpacking across Europe. France, she thinks. Maybe Spain. She's not sure when she'll be back, but if Gus does eventually speak to Annalee, Beckie tells her to be sure to say hello from her. Like she can't call her own daughter. Something is broken between them. The wavering in Beckie's voice tells Gus this fracture causes her a lot of pain. Gus is happy to hang up. Mother pain is the worst.

She dials Annalee's number. Voice mail. She leaves a message, asking her to call when she gets back from her trip. As Gus hangs up, she suddenly feels unreasonably desperate to speak to Annalee. As if in doing so, her babysitter will be able to shed some incredibly bright light on her mother's movements the night she died. On her motivations. On her innermost thoughts. Gus knows she's being completely irrational, but it feels good to pretend that a young woman in Spain or France is carrying around some fragment of the truth about her mother in her backpack.

It's just past nine when Gus retreats to her bedroom. Her

oasis. Turns off the lights and turns on the TV. Settles next to a tray of her favorite snacks. Peanut butter on Ritz crackers, a mini Mars bar, dry Honeycomb cereal, and cream soda. The blue flickering of the TV dances across her comforter as she watches an old movie with Cary Grant. It's about a reporter getting a scoop on an escaped convict. Gus is not really following the plot. Her mind dips in and out of another story that hangs suspended above the bed. The one Renata shared about Kep Halladay's life. The article about his life mentioned that he'd not been seen since August 4, 2006. That's it. No blood. No suspicions or theories. Almost dismissive of foul play. As if he decided to retire to Mexico and live out his days drinking margaritas.

Maybe Renata wrote around the truth more than once.

First about June's accident. Then about her father's disappearance. Or maybe the police hid the facts from the press.

Levi's gone to bed in Rose's room.

The old movie pulsates. Light banter hums from the screen. Screwball antics. Swelling music. Reminds Gus of lazy Sunday afternoons when she'd lay spooned against her mother on the sofa, watching black-and-white movies. Warm. Safe. Monday hovering closer with each passing hour. Back to school. A distant, bitter pill stuck to her tongue.

What was her mother thinking as she lay with one arm across her daughter? Monday looming for her too. Where did she go when she pretended to go to work? Out looking for Henry? Out poking around Kep Halladay's hometown?

Questions bubble over into full-on pins and needles in her legs and arms. Gus gets out of bed. Too restless to just lie there. She heads downstairs to her mother's wall for answers. She doesn't have to turn on the light in the living room. The blue moon lights up the wall. Gus blurs her eyes. Looks closely at the shapes of the collage in front of her. A pattern slowly reveals itself in the shadowy light. She can see three distinct blocks of evidence on the wall. Three bones that her mother couldn't let go.

The first is all about Gracie. The little girl who captured her mother's heart.

June's girl being so young, losing her mother.

Henry is in the second. He captured her attention. He was the reason she was drawn back to investigating Halladay. Stanton said it.

Then the Neil kid went missing and she was like a dog with a bone.

The third block is what kept her mother digging. It's all business. Kep Halladay's. Each block is connected. Each leading her mother to the next. Each holding her tight.

Gus scans this third block. The one with the newspaper clipping from early 2004. The article about Senator Halladay's landmark business deal with a gas company. It details how a previously undiscovered vein of shale was unearthed, stretching clear across the county. The business tycoon didn't own the land, but he owned the mineral rights. The deed, signed just a few months earlier, details his purchase of those rights from thirty-three local farmers.

Gus ponders his timing. Extremely fortuitous. Like he had a crystal ball and knew those rights were about to come in handy. Make him a fortune. And Henry was conducting mineral surveys for the senator. Maybe he was the crystal ball.

Augusta steps closer to the missing persons report filed by Henry's parents. In his statement, Kep Halladay confirms the boy hasn't been seen by anyone at Halladay House in over two weeks. He says this on July 16, 2003. Gus examines the date on the surveillance photograph where her mother wrote Henry's name beside a question mark. It's date-stamped July 14, 2003. There's a door knocker in the photo. A lion's head. She's seen it somewhere else. She scans the other photos on the wall and finds it. Behind Gracie, the ballerina, posing on the veranda in the Polaroid. It's the same porch. The lion's head door knocker is in both images. Henry was at Halladay House. That has to be where the girl is standing.

Augusta's brain is woozy with truths and lies and questions. She stares at her mother's wall. One minute it feels like the stars are about to align and then nothing. She's left with a vast universe of random ideas colliding then drifting away.

She lets the nothingness prevail for now and ambles back to bed. Pulls the comforter to her chin and settles deep into the pillows and drifts off.

Suddenly everything falls away. Ice-cold water hits Augusta's eight-year-old face. She's stricken with a terrible sickening jolt in her belly. It's so dark. Glass shatters and pricks her skin like a million bee stings. Water rushes over her small arms, up her neck and over her head.

She can't breathe.

Augusta tries to suck in air.

Opens her eyes.

Gasps.

Begins to breathe again.

She sits up in bed. Soaked with sweat. Trembling as a terrible knowing creeps across her wet, tingling skin, chilling her to her core.

These vivid midsummer dreams are more than just dreams.

They are memories.

23

ELGIN

ِِِِ

AT SUNRISE, GUS AND LEVI HAVE ALREADY LOOPED DOWN the ramp on the Queensway that splits south toward the 416. Windows rolled down. Summer heat rippling across the pavement despite the early hour.

Eighty miles later, they're parked under the willow where they ran into James Pratt and Jocko and have begun to walk. Past the blockade. Straight down the cracked highway toward Elgin. Gus has her satchel looped over one shoulder. The usual supplies. With one add-on. Rose's gun. Last time she was out this way, there was someone watching her in the cemetery. Might still be around. Better safe than sorry.

They crest a rise in the road. There it is. They can see the edge of town.

An abandoned water tower stands just outside Elgin like a rusty sentinel watching over the town's ghosts.

It's midmorning as they enter the town, passing a sign that says WELCOME TO ELGIN, POPULATION 342. Someone has spray-painted an X across the *342* and added a zero next to it. The sign is mounted in a cobwebbed wrought-iron frame. The lower part of the sign is a tourist map. Its bright colors are muted by a thin layer of grime. Gus wipes a palm across the map so she can get a better look at the town. The map lays out the dozen or so streets that make up the two-by-three-mile hamlet. A numbered legend runs alongside the map pinpointing the town's key features. The two churches, the general store, the funeral home, the town barber, and the central square at the crossroads of Main and Halladay. The square looks to be a couple of miles away in the heart of the town.

Gus and Levi head straight down Main Street. Side by side.

It's like walking into Armageddon. Gus feels like they are the last beings on the planet. The streets are deserted. Silent. Except for the rustling of a hawk picking at bugs in the eaves of a boarded-up house. Gus and Levi walk on either side of the broken yellow line in the middle of the road toward the heart of Elgin. Glancing into the smashed-out windows of a hardware store. The goods on its shelves coated with soot. There's a diner where a few dirty dishes litter the tables. A funeral home that leans awkwardly to one side. A grocery store, many of the shelves bare, as if someone scavenged all the packaged and canned goods. The meat and produce were left to decompose into piles of ash and bone or to be eaten by rodents and raccoons. The sewer catch basins are rimmed with yellow grease that runs down the trough next to the curbs. An oily river.

"Stay close, dog."

Most striking of all is the stench. Like a barbecue over a neighbor's fence, only the steak's rotten and burned to a crisp. Gus wonders how safe it is for them to be breathing in the pungent air. Levi finds a broken spatula. Picks it up and begins dancing like a puppy with a stick, trying to make her play keep-away.

"Drop that."

He ignores her and dances closer to the oil slick at the side of the road.

"Levi, no. Heel."

She lunges for the spatula, but he dekes. Then she remembers the dog cookie in her satchel. She finds it and holds it out. He drops the spatula and bounces over. Bites the air. She pulls it away.

"Gentle."

She rolls her eyes. He stares. She gives up. Hands him the cookie and he snaps at it, nipping her fingers.

"Ouch. That's not gentle."

She grabs his collar and hooks on his leash.

They continue down Main. Just past a crossroads, Augusta stops. Something isn't right up ahead. The road looks warped in the distance. As they continue walking, everything becomes hideously black. Rooftops of buildings are bubbled. Hardening into tumorous aberrations. Hydro poles are twisted where they stand. Power lines litter the street like streamers left over from a parade. Shards of burnt wood and bricks and glass confetti the pavement. Only this was no parade. Something far more sinister blew through town, turning everything in its wake black as night.

The yellow line at her feet is gone. A layer of soot coats the road, the sidewalks, shops, signposts, newspaper boxes, abandoned cars, a fire hydrant, and a bicycle tipped to one side in a metal stand. All are smeared with black death.

Still some distance from the center of town, they begin to see it. A massive blackened crater the length of a football field. The epicenter of the explosion. Nothing at the heart of town escaped the scorching heat. Not a tree. Not a bench. It's all gone. There is no town square. The small hamlet that Renata spoke of so lovingly has no heart. It was forever changed that day.

Gus inches her way toward the edge of the crater. Levi barks and pulls in the opposite direction just as the earth beneath her feet shifts and falls away. She scurries back to solid ground. He sensed it before she even noticed.

She looks down. Just a few feet in front of her, the ground is moving. It's barely perceptible. As her eyes track toward the center of the crater, the earth is turning faster. Looks gooey. Like quicksand. At its core the molten liquid swirls clockwise and disappears into a bubbling hole.

The crater is alive. Breathing and sputtering.

Augusta looks for a way around. She moves to her left. Big mistake. The hard earth crumbles, giving way to a muddy pool underneath. Her shoes disappear into a murky soup. Levi scrambles away. She drops his leash, but he doesn't run off. He barks and lunges for her. Augusta falls backward toward him, landing on the edge of the crumbling earth. He takes hold of her jean jacket in his teeth as she crab-walks backward and drags her heels out of the mud with Levi's help.

Back on solid ground, she wraps her arms around her dog. Holds him tight. When she lets go, he shakes off the dirt but stays close.

They both look around. Taking in what's left of downtown Elgin. The catastrophic explosion obliterated the main intersection and caused a fire to rage through town, rendering most of it a wasteland of broken trees and burned-out vehicles. A war zone. She can see why no one bothered coming back. No one could live here.

As terrible and strange as this place looks, somehow Gus gets it. This wasteland. Where the everyday stuff of life has been ripped away in a split second. She knows how that feels. To be worried about homework one minute and wondering what to wear to your mother's funeral the next. Everything normal ripped away like a Band-Aid torn off an open wound. There's something strangely comforting about this blackened town. Strangely familiar. Gus rubs her dirtied hands on the backside of her jeans. Reaches into her satchel for her phone. Takes photos of the barren streets surrounding the warped crater. A hawk loops overhead. Levi barks.

"He's not circling for us, Levi."

The dog barks again. She looks at him. He's not looking at the hawk. He's staring across the crater. She follows his gaze. A lone figure stands in the middle of the road on the far side. A heat mirage obscuring their warbly face. Levi growls. Gus lifts her phone to take a photo, but the figure disappears behind a building. Gone before she can snap it. She's reminded of the man on the hill near the cemetery and wonders if it's the same person. A caretaker? Security guard? Former resident who never left? Maybe a squatter or a hiker just passing through?

She decides to find out.

Gus picks up Levi's leash. They head down a side street, giving themselves a wide berth around the crater. She's hoping there's a way to circle the town's epicenter. The farther away from ground zero they get, the more Mother Nature has managed to poke her head up from the devastation. Moss creeps along cracks in the sidewalks. Dandelions crowd around fire hydrants. Ivy winds up posts on front porches. Crabgrass steals across potholes and into basement windows.

A few blocks from the crater, Gus lets Levi off the leash again. She takes pictures of derelict houses, shops, a swing set in a small park, an abandoned school bus, a street sign, and a bus shelter. Levi eats the heads off dandelions but stays close. The pair comes to a dead end where a small white brick building sits. It's covered in a mess of pink wisterias. An unexpected burst of color amid the decay. She takes a picture. The flowers remind her of the purple loosestrife covering the fields outside town. Thriving where little else does. A plastic sign hangs from the building.

LOIS GREENAWAY'S DANCE ACADEMY

Bells ring in Augusta's brain. Stanton mentioned the name Lois. A dance instructor. The one who took Gracie in when her grandfather disappeared. Has to be the same woman. Lois Greenaway. Gus knows the name from somewhere else too. She digs through her satchel and finds her notebook. Flips through the pages. Lois Greenaway and Edgar Greenaway. Two of the victims of the fire.

Under great clumps of wisteria and encased in Plexiglas, a bulletin board hangs on the side of the dance academy. Augusta pulls back the flowery vines from the Plexiglas. Tacked to the board are a collection of photographs and a dance class schedule from 2013. The year of the fire.

One photo features a group of dancers wearing identical red sequin leotards with large white maple leaves attached to their shoulders like wings. Fifth-place medals are strung around their necks on ribbons. They're all smiles. Red lips. Teeth showing. Eyes painted like showgirls. Can't be more than seven years old. One tiny dancer in the back row has half her face hidden behind the wing of another, but Augusta recognizes her right away.

"Look, Levi, it's Gracie."

She takes a photo. Turns and realizes Levi's not beside her. Then she hears him barking in the distance. She can't spot him.

She jogs away from the dead end to a cross street. Sees him just as his bum squeezes under a fence. She runs over. A sign lies on its side against the fence. JUNKYARD BLUES AUTO SALVAGE. She's never been a fan of salvage yards since hearing the story of how her dad met his end. Wonders if it's an omen. She hesitates, then just as she's about to launch herself up and over the fence, Levi reappears, squeezing back under. A stick of black licorice hangs from the corner of his mouth. He chokes it down in one bite.

"Where did you get that?"

Gus stands on tiptoes and peeks through the fence. A rusty car blocks her view. She grips the top and hoists herself up to get a better view. Just as her head pops up, a large knife hurtles through the air and sticks into the fence inches from her face. She lets go of her grip, pitches backward, and falls on her back. Without thinking, Gus riffles through her satchel for Rose's gun. She finds it and fires a shot in the air. Levi nearly jumps out of his skin. He lands legs spread, still as a statue. The shot crackles across the abandoned town.

"Time to go."

Gus grabs Levi's leash and starts running. They hit the main drag full stride. Neither looks back until they're well past the water tower outside town. Only then does Gus dare to glance over her shoulder to make sure no one's following them. Hopefully the shot scared them. Gun at her side, she slows to a light jog but keeps moving toward the Buick. Both of them are panting.

That knife came way too close for comfort.

Then Gus stops in her tracks.

Up ahead, in the direction of her car, a man is running full speed toward them. She doesn't know what to do so she drops to one knee, aims the gun, and fires at him. He dives for the dirt and covers his head.

"Are you nuts? Hold your fire."

Lying flat on his belly, he riffles in his back pocket, pulls out what looks like a wallet. He holds his arms high like he's flying, flips open the wallet so it's facing her.

"Drop your weapon. RCMP."

Gus flushes, realizing he's holding up his police badge. She rises, but keeps the gun leveled at the stranger. Levi starts galloping toward him.

"No, Levi, stop."

It's too late. Levi's closing in fast. The guy takes cover, arms over his head. Levi pounces and starts licking the man's ears. The man starts laughing, then he rolls over and ruffles Levi's neck. She lowers the gun to her side.

"If you're a cop, where's your uniform?"

The man sits up and wipes off the front of his T-shirt and jeans. Gus keeps her distance. Levi rubs up against the man, then gallops back over to Gus.

"I'm undercover. I mean, damn it, I'm trying to look in-conspicuous."

"Not doing a very good job."

"Yeah, I see that now. It's my first week on the job. On surveillance, I mean."

He stands up. Hands raised slightly like he's showing his cards.

"You're tailing me?"

"No. Sort of."

Déjà vu washes over her. Like she's seen him somewhere before. Then it dawns on her. Even before she was called to Stanton's office, the RCMP have been following her. They know everything she's been up to. This is all Rory's fault. It's not on this guy. He's just some dumb rookie assigned to babysit her. She feels like a fool.

"Name's Lashey. Constable Stu Lashey."

He holds up his badge for her to see. Levi leaps for it when he spots the quick flash of metal and leather, thinking it's a chew toy and the nice policeman wants to play.

"Levi. Heel."

The cop stifles a laugh. Pulls the badge away from the dog's open mouth, pockets it. Then he leans over and pets the top of Levi's furry head.

"Spinone?"

"Mutt."

"Hey there, Levi."

"Sorry I shot at you."

He stops petting Levi and gives Gus his full attention.

"Augusta Monet, right?"

She nods. Of course he knows her name. He continues.

"Listen, I shouldn't have come at you like that. It's just that I heard the gunshot and figured, better to blow my cover than have something awful happen to the person I'm supposed to be watching."

Great. He does think he's babysitting.

"I can take care of myself."

She puts the gun back in her satchel even though she'd rather not. Someone still threw a knife at her head and who knows where that someone is right now. Gus glances over her shoulder toward town.

"Are you sure you're okay, miss?"

When she turns back to face him, he's smiling. Little dimples pinch the sides of his mouth. His whole Boy Scout vibe is bordering on nerdy, but somehow she's finding it hard to resist. She tries not to smile back. He's so clean-cut and fit and blond and blue-eyed. A touch of acne at his temples. Probably still lives at home and gets his mom to iron his shirts.

Levi circles his legs and licks his shoes. Gus moves closer to try to get Levi to behave. A scent wafts from the young constable. A clean smell like sandalwood soap and oranges. Yep. Mom definitely does his laundry. She tries to grab Levi by the collar.

"Sorry about him. He has a thing for footwear."

"He's just friendly. Aren't you, boy?"

As the constable roughhouses with Levi, Gus forgets where she is for a moment. Time slips away and suddenly she's standing in front of her father. A young rookie. New to the job. About her age when he went out on that last shift. She almost reaches out to touch the young man in front of her but stops herself. Knowing Charlie's not there.

"Miss Monet. Hello?"

Gus shakes off her father's ghost.

"Sorry. What?"

The young constable is staring at her.

"I asked what you two were doing out here. It's pretty dangerous in these parts. And off-limits. You know that, right?"

"We got turned around on our walk, that's all."

"And I'm sure you have a permit to carry that gun."

He nods toward her satchel.

"It's at home."

Lashey nods. She can tell he doesn't believe her, but he drops it. Seems at a loss for words so he gently brushes dog hair off his jeans. In the awkward silence that falls between them, she realizes that he's just as out of his element as she is. Both of them rookies.

"Thanks. For, you know, doing your job, I guess."

He looks up, having gathered a ball of stray Levi hair in one hand. He holds up the ball between his finger and thumb, like it's evidence of a crime.

"You know I'd be well within my rights to take you two in."

She tries not to smile. Points to Levi.

"He's the menace to society, not me."

"He got a record?"

"Wouldn't you know? You're the one following us."

"Following? More like protecting and serving, ma'am."

He salutes.

"Levi can protect me just fine. Thanks."

Constable Lashey gives her a nod. Reaches down to give Levi one more pet on the head, then turns and walks away.

"I'll be seeing you, Red."

He continues walking down the road that leads back to her car. Must have parked near the barricade. Near the willow where she parked.

Gus feels like an idiot, but she has no choice. She follows him. She keeps about forty paces back. Levi ambles ahead and keeps pace beside Lashey. The dog looks back to make sure she's coming. Augusta watches the pair walking side by side along the moss-ridden highway. On either side of them, swaths of purple loosestrife sway and ripple across the deep ditches.

The rancid scent of Elgin is a few miles behind them now. Gus can breathe deeply again. The pissy weeds smell sweet by comparison. Lashey never looks back. Keeps walking until he reaches his car. A dark gray Pontiac Grand Am. It's sitting across the road from the willow where she parked the Buick. He gets in and waits. He's making sure she leaves the area. Levi paws at the passenger door of his car. Beet red, Gus has to walk over and drag the dog to her car.

Driving back to the city, Augusta periodically checks her rearview mirror. Constable Lashey's Grand Am follows at a distance. The setting sun bounces off his windshield so she can't make out his face. He tails her most of the way back on Highway 15. Then when she takes the split onto Fisher, he continues on, leaving her alone. For now.

Augusta pulls into Rose's garage. She opens the door leading into the kitchen. Levi follows. Sluggish from the day's excitement. His old bones are tired. She fills his water dish and tops up his food bowl with kibble. He drinks all the water and eats a few morsels of kibble before disappearing upstairs. She hears the creaking of Rose's bed as he jumps up and settles. Gus sets her satchel on the kitchen table and stands still. Quietly listening.

Something is off.

She inhales and that's when she smells it. Aftershave. Old Spice.

Augusta pulls Rose's gun from her satchel and checks the back door. Locked. She moves slowly down the hall and checks the front door. Bolted. She looks upstairs. Levi would have barked if someone was up there. She steps to the entryway of the living room. Spots the dirt first. Near the front window. Then she turns. Surveys the room and can't believe her eyes. She lowers the gun, drops it on the table in the front foyer, and stares.

Her mother's wall. It's gone. All of it. Vanished. Other than a few bits of Scotch tape and a stray corner torn from one of the documents.

A melancholy washes over Augusta as she runs her palms over the barren wall. Across the space that her mother had come to inhabit in Rose's house. Shannon's wall has been violated. Torn away. Her heart aches. But just as quickly it hardens.

She knows who's done this.

JUST BEFORE DAYBREAK THE NEXT DAY, AUGUSTA DRESSES AND heads downstairs. Levi eats, then goes out to pee, then races back inside. He can sense something's up. A road trip maybe. He chases his tail excitedly while she digs into her satchel. Finds the address scribbled on the back of the card he gave her. Gus heads out to the car, Levi by her side.

Rory's house is at the far end of Kemptville, about a forty-five-minute drive from Ottawa. A small bungalow set back in the woods, off a rural road. The property borders a maple-lined creek. A long narrow lawn, in desperate need of a good mowing, winds alongside the gravel driveway leading to the house. It's quiet, isolated. A modest cottage with white siding and blue shutters. There's a tin awning over a small porch. A couple of lawn chairs sit next to a barbecue. Rory's red Honda is parked beside the house. No signs of life.

Gus opens the unlocked side door and slips into the kitchen. Levi stays close to her, sniffing the stale kitchen air, then flopping near her feet. Gus takes a seat at the table and waits. Levi begins grinding his teeth into the wooden leg of the chair. Before long she hears the floorboards groan and a door whine. Feet patter across the hardwood. Then silence. Then the sound of pee flowing into a toilet. Soon, the feet patter toward her and a long fart echoes down the hall. Rory steps into his kitchen and nearly jumps out of his boxers when he sees her and Levi.

"Jesus H Christ, girl! I coulda shot you."

"With this?"

She motions toward the police revolver and holster sitting next to her hand on the table.

"What in the heck are you doing in my kitchen at this hour?"

His left eye twitches badly. Terrible actor.

"You broke into my house yesterday. Thought I'd return the favor."

"I never."

"I know it was you."

His puffy face begins a slow descent toward crumbling.

"You destroyed her wall."

"I'm sorry."

"What did you do with all of it? The evidence? My mother's things?"

"Gone. I tossed them in a dumpster. I'm so sorry. It's for your own good."

Gus glares at him. Levi gnaws contentedly, ignoring the two of them.

Rory bites his lower lip.

"I swear I did it for you, Little Monet. And for her. For Shan."

"She left them for me. You had no right."

"She wasn't thinking straight. She wouldn't have wanted you knowing any of it. She wouldn't have wanted you digging into the past."

His eyes well up. He's hijacking the situation with his blubbering. She spins the bowl of fruit on the table between her palms, trying to keep her cool.

"Tell me the truth, Rory."

"The truth's a shit pile."

She really wants him to stop feeling sorry for himself.

"You're a shit pile."

Augusta tosses an apple at his head. It bounces off his forehead and he looks like he's going down. He grabs the counter and steadies himself. Levi scrambles after the apple. Realizing it's not a ball, he leaves it where it lies and ambles off into the den.

"I didn't help Shan twelve years ago. But I'll be damned if I don't help her kid now."

He turns his back to Augusta and wipes his forehead with a dirty dishrag. He takes a deep breath and stares into the sink. Then he tells her about her mother.

24

DETECTIVE MONET

⁓

I̶T WAS 2002. WE WERE BOTH WORKING AT O DIVISION IN Kingston. With your dad gone four years, Shan had been back on patrol for a while. Theft and property infractions unit. Rural district that included Elgin. Cow patrol. That's what we called it. I was filling in on dispatch that day. It was a Monday. Early September as I recall. I heard the call come in. There was trouble out at the Halladay place. Your mother was the first one on the scene. She radios in. June Halladay's dead."

Gus can see her mother. Squad car. Uniform. Badge. She can hear Shannon's smooth, confident voice coming across the radio. Strong. Unwavering. Knows her job. Gus feels a burst of pride. Her mother was a police officer. A good one. Whatever Rory is about to tell her, Gus knows in her heart, this is the truth. She was good.

"We were short of men, so Stanton, squad commander at the time, sends a couple of us desk jockeys over to help process the scene. When I get there, Kep Halladay's right in Shan's face. He doesn't want any fuss. He wants the body taken directly to the funeral home. She's telling him there's procedures to follow. The body can't be moved till the coroner comes and forensics has looked over the scene and checked the vehicle. I know the guy. Halladay isn't used to being told what's what. He's out of his mind. He takes her badge number. Makes some calls. Then just like that a hearse comes by and takes the body away before the scene's even processed. Shan loses her cucumbers. She tries to question June's daughter, who was just a wee thing. Only seven years old. And injured. Kep won't allow it. Kid's taken away in an ambulance. Stanton's furious with the way it all goes down. She says as much, but it's clear the sarge has her hands tied by someone higher up the food chain. She tells Shan to write up her report and move on.

"That day forward, your mom has Kep Halladay in her sights. She refuses to believe June's death was an accident. She says she knows something bad's going on up at that house. She says she's gonna prove it one day. She keeps digging and pushing. Stanton tells her Halladay's got friends in high places. She's gotta watch herself. I even tried talking some sense into her. I told her she was messing with fire."

Gus listens. Says nothing. Her heart beats faster with every sentence he utters. Knowing his words explain so much about her mother, and yet not wanting to believe a single one of them.

"Sure enough she gets burned. It was her own doing. About a year later, Shan's still digging into Halladay's business. Then she takes the girl. Gracie Halladay. She picks her up when she's walking home from school and takes off with her. Later Shan tells Stanton she was just taking her for ice cream on account of it being the anniversary of her mom's death and all. Halladay hollers kidnapping. Stanton saves your mom's butt. Stops her from going to jail by getting her a transfer to Ottawa. Shan ends up pushing papers at headquarters. That was the fall of 2003. Shan was only twenty-six. You were just a little tyke. Five at most so you probably don't remember the move to the city or any of this."

He's wrong. Gus does remember the move. Remembers sitting in the back seat of her mother's car, wedged between suitcases stacked so high on either side she couldn't see out. Remembers eating Chinese takeout from the carton for their first dinner in their new home. Remembers using a big cardboard moving box as their dining table. Remembers lying on the floor in a sleeping bag that first night. Her mother crying in the kitchen as she quietly unpacked cutlery and dishes.

"I barely saw her after that. I tried. The few times I did, she wasn't the old Shan. A couple of years later, she made detective and got assigned to the Canadian Police Centre's Joint Task Force for Missing and Exploited Children. Working at the national coordination center. It could have been a new start. But then sometime '05, maybe '06, she came across the Henry Neil file and saw Kep Halladay's name all over it, and she was at it again. Digging for dirt on Kep Halladay. He caught wind and she got suspended.

"The night your mother died, I don't know if she went out to Halladay's place. I don't know what went on or what she did. All I know is he disappeared and was likely murdered that night. Maybe she was still trying to save that girl. I can't say for certain. But cops protect their own."

Augusta's mind can't process what he's telling her.

Disappeared. Murdered. Protect their own.

Her brain feels as if it might splinter into a thousand pieces. Rory sheepishly turns around to look at Gus. Her tangled and tormented expression makes him bow his head in regret. Shoulders slumped.

"I know it's hard to hear, Little Monet. But Charlie's passing and then June Halladay, then that Henry kid going missing, it all drove her into the deep end. She never came up for air. It cost her everything. Her life. If she'd just let it go, things woulda turned out different. That's why I tore down that wall of evidence you created. I got rid of it so you don't end up going down that same road as her. So you don't find a truth at the end of that road that makes you think less of your mom. I would hate that."

Augusta is infuriated that Rory thinks she needs protecting from her own mother. Who does he think he is? Making decisions for her. Acting the hero. Beating around the bush to spare her some terrible truth, instead of just coming out and saying it. Before she can find the words to express her rage, he hits her with another round.

"Maybe she was nowhere near Halladay's that night. Her car accident was quite a ways from Elgin. But those fresh tire tracks on the edge of the Halladay property matched her vehicle. Like I said, we protect our own. I can't say the old man didn't deserve what he got."

Augusta strains against the pressure building behind her eyeballs and ripping at her gut as the truth burrows into the pit of her stomach, then slowly rises up her throat.

"Cuppa coffee, Little Monet?"

She can't speak. A scream might burst out if she tries.

Gus rises, her chair tumbling backward. Levi comes into

the kitchen as she grabs her satchel. Sleepy-eyed, Rory reaches a hand out, but she pushes past him and heads out the screen door, leaving it wide open. He calls out as Levi races past him and out the door after her.

"She was not in her right mind, you know. Never got the help she needed."

Gus crosses the porch praying that he'll stop talking.

"If you want to hear everything, you have to hear this. She had thoughts."

Gus spins around. Rory stands on the other side of the screen, his face distorted through the mesh.

"She sometimes said she didn't care if she lived or died. She wanted to care. Care for you."

Augusta trips over Levi and nearly falls off the edge of the porch. She turns away from Rory. Stumbles down the stairs. He has to be lying.

Gus staggers toward the Buick. She doesn't want him to utter another word. She can hear the squeak of the planks as he crosses the porch. She searches her pockets for her keys, then tries her satchel. Damn it. She left them on the table. She looks over and Rory's got the keys in his hand.

"I was trying to spare you this pain, Little Monet. That's why I didn't tell you before."

Gus walks over and reaches out for her keys. Feeling like she's being held hostage. Feeling out of control of her own destiny. Feeling alone. He doesn't hand her the keys. Instead he meets her gaze and holds it. Then he delivers the final blow.

"The call came over the radio. Someone saw a vehicle go in the lake by Bruce Pit. I got there before paramedics or the police so it was me who pulled her out. But I was too late. She was gone. There were no skid marks. She never hit the brakes. Shan drove straight into that lake like she meant to. Like she couldn't live with what she'd done."

Augusta's heart sinks. Rory looks like he wants to eat his words. He tosses her the keys and Augusta lurches for the car. Opens the door. Levi jumps in and so does she. Gus turns over the engine and guns it down the driveway. The Buick kicks up a cloud of gravel as she peels out onto the main road, nearly sideswiping a car coming the opposite direction.

A long horn blast sends her speeding away.

Gripping the steering wheel tight so she doesn't hurtle into oblivion.

25

GOOD DOG

⟨∾⟩

Back home, Gus parks in the garage. She sits in the car, in the darkness, very still until Levi whines. Gus slowly gets out, her mind blank. She enters the kitchen. Drops her satchel on the table. Levi follows but stops in the doorway.

"What? Hungry?"

As she's pouring kibble into his bowl, she notices the back door. It's wide open. Her heart skips a beat. Her mind skitters back in time. Did she forget to close it this morning after Levi went outside for his pee? Yes. She was so focused on Rory, she just took off. She relaxes. Regretting the entire expedition out to Kemptville.

Gus fills Levi's bowl and then stands aside and waits. He doesn't move.

"Okay. Eat."

The dog has never refused a meal in his life. He's not himself. Maybe his belly's off because of the early morning car ride. Hers sure is. Augusta stands by the open back door and breathes in the fresh air. She can't even stomach the thought of coffee. Needs to dull her senses, not wake them up. Gus leaves the back door open for the dog and wanders into the dining room. She checks Rose's liquor cabinet. She finds a tall bottle of something called limoncello. She grabs it. Through the clear bottle, she can see a thick yellow liqueur. She takes a swig. Tastes like lemon meringue pie. Yum. She goes into the living room and plunks down on the sofa. Levi slinks into the room. Head low, tail tucked, as if he's done something bad.

"What'd ya do, dog? I'm not in the mood."

Then Levi lifts one ear and looks over his shoulder toward the stairs.

Midgulp, she hears it too.

A floorboard creaks above them.

Gus feels all the blood in her body rush directly to her brain, leaving her heart to fend for itself, beating so fast it's pushing against her ribs.

Someone's in the house.

And she's pretty sure she knows who that someone is. She'd forgotten all about the text that nearly gave her away at the retirement home. The one from Lars.

You think I don't know where you are? Think again. I'm coming for you, Auggie.

She shudders. He wasn't joking. He's come for her.

Augusta rises and carefully tiptoes into the dining room and through to the kitchen. She reaches into her satchel for Rose's gun. It's not there. Then she remembers. She left it on the table in the front foyer the day before. Gus peeks down the long hallway toward the table. The gun's not there. Another creak. She can't think. Run or hide? He's likely got the gun, so running is out. She can't risk Levi getting shot in the cross fire.

Gus scans the kitchen and grabs the first thing she can find that looks like a weapon. A cast-iron frying pan hanging next to the stove. She slips into the pantry. Levi follows. She gently closes the door. They wait. A low growl rumbles in Levi's throat. Augusta taps his nose. He stops growling. She pets his head.

Light footfalls pad down the stairs above the pantry. He's coming. She grips the frying pan tighter. Then the front door slams. She presses her ear to the pantry door but has a hard time hearing anything except the blood surging through her eardrums like ocean waves.

Augusta counts to fifty before easing the door open. She crosses the kitchen and inches down the hallway, holding the pan over one shoulder like a baseball bat. Levi cowers in the pantry, lowering himself to the floor slowly. He's not budging. She moves down the hall, glancing up the stairs through the banister. Gus approaches the front door. Leans toward the peephole. Nothing but a Camaro parked across the street. But no Lars. Damn. Her knees weaken at the sight of Lars's car. She was so wrapped up in what Rory had told her about Shannon that she hadn't even noticed it was parked across the street when she had gotten home. Her grip on the frying pan falters as her palms grow sweaty. Levi growls from the far end of the hall. She turns, knowing they should have stayed hidden.

Lars is standing in the entryway to the living room.

"Not too shabby."

His voice sends a chill down her spine. He looks around the house like he's a prospective buyer appraising the property.

The little scar on his upper lip, the one he got in a knife fight at a strip club in Toronto, quivers ever so slightly.

Gus tries to stop the frying pan from vibrating, grasping it tighter with both hands. He taps his leg with something. Rose's gun. Lars smiles, but not a smile that says, *Hey baby I'm so glad I found you*, but more like, *Hey baby you're fuckin' dead*.

"No kiss goodbye?"

"My great-grandma died."

"Fingers broken? Couldn't shoot me a text?"

"I meant to. I've been taking care of things."

"I don't care that you stole money outta my wallet like I was some mark."

"I needed to get home."

"Home?"

He laughs and twirls the gun on one finger. Augusta can feel his temper bubbling to a boil. She slowly lowers the frying pan, hoping to defuse his anger. She jumps when he speaks.

"See, what I do care about is what you been up to since you left."

"I told you. My great-grandmother . . ."

He cuts her off by raising the gun. Steps toward her. Levi growls.

"Don't fuck with me, Auggie. That phone I gave you? I installed this little app on it that lets me know exactly where you are at all times. I did it 'cause I wanted you to be safe. But now I see you've been busy, as you say, taking care of things. All over the county in fact. Up and down the 15. Over in Brockville. Funny how that's right along our old 401 route. Co-in-kee-dink? I don't fucking think so. You've been setting up your own thing? Who you been working with? That fucker Ozzy down in Prescott?"

In spite of her fear, Gus rolls her eyes. Can't believe he thinks she's been masterminding some criminal takeover. She almost bursts into hysterical laughter. Why did she waste so much of her life on this moron?

"Jesus, Lars. Don't be an idiot."

Poor choice of words. His chin quivers. Even though she's expecting it, he lunges suddenly. She flings the frying pan at him. It misses, crashing to the floor with a brassy clatter. He grabs for her arm and she manages to twist free and spin past him. Tries to scramble up the stairs, but he's on her fast. Grabs a handful of her red hair. Hauls her neck backward and pulls her onto her back down the stairs. She twists and claws for the banister before landing with a thump at the bottom. Straddling her chest and arms, Lars raises a fist, greasy strands of hair dangling at his cheeks. She closes her eyes.

Instead of a punch to the face, she feels a light dusting of fur on her cheek and opens her eyes to see Levi body-slam Lars. Levi rolls into the living room. Lars topples sideways into the hall mirror. It shatters, showering him with glass. He drops the gun. Levi scrambles to his feet, eyes wild. Gus feels a surge of mama pride well up inside her as Levi goes for his leg. Clamps his jaw around Lars's kneecap and shakes like he did her duffel bag strap. Only this time there's blood and high-pitched screaming.

Lars tries to break free by punching Levi on top of the head. Gus sees red. The dog yelps and lets go, but stands his ground. Teeth barred, frothy blood dripping from his curled gums. Augusta grabs the gun and races to Levi's side as Lars yanks a shard of mirror out of the back of his hand and pulls himself to his feet.

Despite her racing heart, Augusta steadies her breath as she points the gun at Lars, one hand reaching down to touch Levi's head to make sure he's not injured. He licks her hand. The fear fizzles out of her bones. Her shoulders release. Jaw loosens. She empties. Clears space. Allows herself to see him through Shannon's eyes.

"I'm done with your shit, Lars. Done with you. I'm living here now. And if you want to know the truth, my parents don't live in Vancouver. They're dead. I've been looking into how my mother died. That's what I've been busy taking care of. So I'm only gonna say this once. I'm not coming back to you. Ever."

"I thought you said your great-grandmother died."

"Get the fuck out."

Blood soaking through his jeans and dripping from his fingertips, Lars tries to stare her down. But she holds his gaze. She wants him to see what's in her eyes. It's not something he's seen there before. An unwavering loveless stare that bores straight into his soul. Usually she looks away or softens. But not this time. Not now. Something's changed. There's a confidence lurking deep inside those black pupils of hers. She means what she says.

Lars fakes like he's coming at her, then pulls up. She doesn't flinch. He mutters under his breath, flips his greasy hair, and smooths it into place.

"Fuckin' mutt should be put down."

Then he slowly turns to leave, moving as casually as his injured knee will allow. He swaggers down the steps, leaving the door wide open. Halfway down the front path, Lars turns to look at her. His voice cracks a little as he attempts to sound tough.

"You're nothing without me and you know it. You'll see."

Augusta kicks the door shut, latches the dead bolt, then leans her back against the door. Relief washing over her, she stays very still until her heart steadies and her breathing returns to normal. She listens as his Camaro pulls away from the curb. Lars honks twice like he's going out for groceries. She sinks to the floor, realizing she's completely drained.

Levi ambles over to her. He stares at her with wide adoring eyes. His expression says it all. He will, unquestioningly and without hesitation, do anything for her. She is overwhelmed by the pure love she feels for this creature as she gently pets the top of his furry head and pulls him close. He is hers. And she is his. He licks her cheek.

"Good dog."

Then she remembers Rose's money. Augusta runs upstairs to Rose's room and races to the closet. She flips through Rose's sweaters and dresses until she finds the plastic garment bag at the back of the closet. She checks inside. The money's all there. Lars didn't find it. She decides she needs a better hiding place for all this money. She finds one in the trunk of Rose's Buick. She stuffs the garment bag inside the Buick's spare tire, then pulls the tight vinyl cover over it before laying it back in the wheel well under the carpet. Perfect.

Fifteen minutes later, she gets a text message from Lars.

It's a photo of his penis.

And that does it. After making sure Levi eats something and double-checking all the locks in the house, Augusta heads to the mall with a wad of Rose's cash in her back pocket. She walks west. Down Richmond Road to Carlingwood Mall. At the Telus store, she buys herself a new phone and asks the sales guy if he can put all the photos from her old phone onto her new one. He says it's no problem.

The sales guy is in his early twenties. Wears a starched, green polo shirt bearing a Telus logo, but somehow he manages to look cool despite the corporate uniform. Might be the small nose ring or the way his hair is slicked over his head revealing a closely shaved underside. He talks superfast and asks a million questions and has a million special deals. No. She won't be keeping her old phone number. No. She doesn't want a data plan. She's used to not having one. Lars only gave her a phone so he could always reach her. And track her movements apparently. She opts for what she's always had. A text and talk plan only. Mr. Cool tells her that she has to have data if she wants to use the phone's GPS or apps like Snapchat or WhatsApp or Tinder or post her pics on Instagram. Gus tells him she doesn't want to do any of those things. No apps. And she doesn't need GPS. She has a map. He smiles.

"Off the grid. I like it."

Gus doesn't know what he means. He tells her his grandfather is off the grid. Helpful. She's like an old man. The rep says she can always come back and add a data plan if she changes her mind. She nods, knowing she won't.

"For now, you can text, call, and take photos. But you can't share them. Cool?"

Gus feels anything but cool. She's not like people her own age and being around a contemporary who is übercool just makes her feel all the more irrelevant and out of touch and odd. She wishes he'd just wrap it up. Instead he's checking out her ball cap.

"Retro."

Once she's paid, she can't get out of the mall fast enough and hopes never to step foot in there again. Too many kids her age wearing clothes she doesn't wear and using words she's never uttered in her life. Like Snapchat and Tinder. She feels like she's back in high school when everyone thought she was weird for not being on Facebook.

Gus had always gravitated toward a sort of no-man's-land back then. Far from the popular circles. Well outside the in-crowd. Hoping no one would notice her clothes or her freckles or the color of her hair. She had this one homework buddy named Nigel who lived on the outside too, but mostly Gus kept to herself. The last thing fifteen-year-old Gus wanted to do was create a profile where she was supposed to share her past, her photos, her every fleeting thought and passing interest with all her friends. She didn't have friends, and a running tally announcing that fact to the world would have been mortifying. Being invisible, even weird, felt safer.

Back home at Rose's now feels safer too. Later that afternoon, after smashing her old phone with the cast-iron frying pan, Augusta plops down on the sofa across from Shannon's empty wall. She texts her real estate agent, Haley-Anne, her new number. Time to list this old house. Now that Shannon's wall is gone, there's nothing holding her here except a looming mortgage debt. She also texts the new number to Annalee. Still no response to the message she left her two days ago.

Levi pokes his head into the living room, then looks up at his leash hanging from the hall tree. She ignores him. Her bones are heavy, her head aches from where Lars yanked her hair. It seems like days since Rory's bombshell about her mother, but it was just this morning. It's been a long day. Levi's walk can wait. She tips to one side and hits her head on the bottle of limoncello that she left on the sofa earlier. She sits back up and takes a long swig.

Levi hangs his head and eyeballs her sideways then slinks upstairs. She can hear the clicking of his nails down the hall, then the wincing of Rose's bedsprings as he settles on the blanket. She can picture him curling himself in a tight ball, tail tucked over his nose and mouth for comfort. Augusta draws her knees to her chest, wishing her life was as simple as Levi's. She takes another big gulp of Rose's limoncello and listens to the whisperings coming from the wall. The soft sound of a woman's voice singing along to the Four Tops and getting the words wrong.

Honey pie sugar bunch.

A woman's laughter echoes down the empty hall, resounds through the kitchen, and rattles the windows of the old house. The day fades away as Gus empties the bottle and the shadows on the wall in front of her disappear as the room and her mind both dim.

Mercifully, Gus passes out.

26

CONSTABLE LASHEY

A SHARP KNOCK DISRUPTS HER LEMONY COMA. GUS OPENS her eyes. Finds herself on the floor, curled against the wall. No idea how long she's been there. The house is dark. She rolls onto her side then sits up. Tries to stand. One of her legs is asleep.

Knock knock.

It's the front door. Levi pads down the stairs to see who it is. Gus pounds her fist into her hamstring to wake it up, wipes drool from the side of her mouth, and staggers to the front door. The hallway slopes to one side. Either there's been an earthquake or she's stone-cold drunk. She peers through the peephole. It's the baby cop. She opens the door. The sky is deep blue. Evening. Levi pushes past her and jumps up at Constable Lashey's chest. Then he spots a squirrel and takes off across the front lawn. Gus calls after him.

"What the fuck, dog?"

She perfumes Lashey with lemon fumes. He motions to the dog.

"Sorry about that."

He's taller than she remembers. His tight T-shirt stretches across his biceps. Kind of built for a nerd. She brushes a tangled clump of hair from her sweaty cheek.

"Constable Lashey, I presume? Reporting for duty?"

She salutes, bonking herself in the forehead. He tries to cover up a laugh by running his fingers through his wavy blond hair and turning away.

"You want me to go after your dog?"

"Leave him. Mangy mutt's probably gone and left me like everyone else."

"I came to say I was sorry. About yesterday."

"I shot at you. Why are you apologizing to me?"

"For surprising you like I did."

"Nothing surprises me. I am unsurprisable."

"You okay?"

She snorts. He continues.

"So I just wanted to say that if you see me around, it's nothing personal. It's the job."

"Wouldn't you be doing your job if I didn't see you?"

"I suppose."

Gus leans on the door and almost falls over. He grabs her arm to steady her. She pulls away.

"Did you know my mother drove into a lake? Did you know that?"

"I didn't know that, I'm sorry."

"Why do you keep saying you're sorry, Constable Dumdum?"

Levi runs up behind Lashey with a tiger lily dangling

from his mouth. He races back inside the house. Lashey looks at his watch. Gus folds her arms in triumph.

"Told you he'd come back."

"I should probably go and let you sleep it off."

"Great talk."

He's about to leave, then reconsiders.

"Listen, Miss Monet, if you ever need an ear to bend, I'm here."

He writes his number on a slip of paper, holds it out to her, and smiles.

"I've got big ears. So feel free to call me."

Gus takes the paper and shoves it in her back pocket.

"You have got seriously big ears. And pecs."

She leans toward him and presses her hands against his chest.

Gus stumbles off the threshold and pitches forward. He tries to block her fall and the collision sends them both tumbling onto the front walkway. He's on his feet in seconds, leaning over her and cradling her head.

"Don't move. You might have broken something."

He feels the back of her neck for injuries.

"Does it hurt anywhere?"

She tries to sit up too fast and they bash foreheads. He shakes it off and sits back on his heels.

"Let's get you to your feet."

He helps her up. She teeters against him, one hand on his chest, the other grabbing hold of his bicep and squeezing like she's testing the ripeness of a peach.

"Hello, Mr. Bicep. Work out much?"

He gently guides her hands off his body and leads her back up the steps. Once she's firmly planted inside, he lets go.

"See you later, Red."

"And you can tell your bossy-boss Stanton that she can call off the dogs. I mean she can call you off. Call off the baby cop. 'Cause I'm done with all this bullshit. Over and out."

She closes the front door and sinks to the floor.

Standing isn't working anymore.

She slumps sideways and closes her eyes.

27

TODD

LEVI IS LICKING HER NOSE. AUGUSTA PUSHES THE DOG'S FACE away from hers and gazes down the long hallway that leads toward the kitchen. The dog circles then stretches out in the entryway to the living room on the cool hardwood floor. He stares at her. Her view of rock bottom is made more poignant by the sound of Rose's clock. Each tick accentuating her old lady existence. Each tock echoing into the emptiness of the big old house. A boozy sadness washes over her. A tidal wave thick with futility. With wasted days spent driving the countryside in a rusty Buick with a geriatric dog as her sole companion.

Gus eases herself up off the floor and crawls to the kitchen. Head throbbing as the blood begins to flow to her extremities. Three cups of coffee and a bowl of dry Honeycomb later, the fog slowly lifts.

Faint recollections flit across her lemon brain.

Lashey. He came to the house.

Oh shit. Did she kiss him? She couldn't have.

Nah. Touched him inappropriately?

Maybe she dreamed it. Yeah, just a dream.

Augusta cups her forehead in her hands and takes a deep breath.

She drags herself upstairs. Takes off her clothes, leaving them in a pile on the bathroom floor, and stands under a cool shower. Letting the past wash into her pores.

❧

Shannon is standing her ground. The line at the cash is ten deep. She won't budge. To make matters worse, it's the express cash. Everyone wants to get out of there fast. Impatience pushes them forward. They check watches and sigh loudly. It's so embarrassing. Gus is red-faced. She buries herself in a *People* magazine from the rack. Maybe they won't think she's with the obnoxious woman arguing with the cashier. Gus moves closer to the man next to her. Trying to insert herself into his life and out of her own. Trying to escape the drama that is Shannon.

Right here in black and white. It says I get twenty-five bonus air miles if I spend over thirty bucks.

Shannon holds up the coupon for everyone to see. The cashier is stone-faced. Red splotches on her neck, the only sign she's rattled. Her voice is dronelike.

And like I said, ma'am, that total is before taxes and your before-tax total is $29.59, not thirty dollars.

Gus cringes. Shannon hates being called ma'am.

I'm done here. Get me the store manager.

The man behind them grabs his Wonder Bread and 2 percent milk off the conveyor belt and huffs over to another checkout, muttering to the rest of the line, *Crazy person on the loose.*

Shannon glares at the man. *I heard that.*

The cashier presses a button on the intercom phone and her voice blasts across the store's PA system. *Manager to cash one. Manager to the express cash.*

Then the cashier slides Shannon's groceries to the end of the counter and asks her to stand off to one side so she can help the other customers waiting in line. She says it like she's a brain surgeon and Shannon is preventing her from performing lifesaving surgery.

Shannon and Gus wait. The other customers move through the checkout line, each being extra polite to the cashier to prove themselves superior to Shannon. Each ignoring the pair as they wait. Each leaving the store and setting off into the world. Free. Gus wants to wait outside, but she doesn't. She doesn't move or speak. After about ten minutes, the assistant manager, who looks about seventeen, arrives. He overrides the system using his passcode so that Shannon can have her twenty-five bonus points. The cashier hands her a plastic bag and turns to serve someone else. Shannon can pack them herself.

On the way home, one of the bags splits open and a carton of eggs falls out. Raw yolk splatters the sidewalk. Shannon bursts into tears.

Gus is scared. Her mother never cries. At least not in the middle of the street. Gus tries to gather up the broken eggshells.

Don't cry, Mummy. You won. You got the air mile points.

Shannon stares at the shells in Augusta's gooey hands.

Everything's broken.

She's not sure if her mom's talking about the eggs or something else.

They walk home in silence.

❧

Augusta remembers how the leaves on the maples were turning gold and red and orange all around them. How she used some of them to wipe the egg from her palms. How she put one particularly bright red heart-shaped leaf in her back pocket.

She can see that lovely red leaf even now as she walks through the maples of Beechwood Cemetery. She'd hung it in her bedroom window on a small piece of string. Long gone now. These trees, lining the rows of headstones, are tinged orange and brown and red. But not autumn-tinged like the ones in her memory. These trees are thirsty. It's been a dry summer.

Gus weaves her way through the cemetery toward the headstone. She knows where it is even though she's only been here twice. She hates cemeteries. The first time was a few years before her mother's funeral when Shannon had Charlie's ashes interred in a plot she bought for the two of them. Tall white granite double headstone. Soft curving rose garland design. Engraved on the front.

CHARLIE RAYMOND MONET

MARCH 15, 1977–APRIL 23, 1998

BELOVED HUSBAND AND FATHER

The second time Gus was here was when her mother joined her father. Her name engraved beside Charlie's.

Shannon Marie Monet
October 16, 1977–August 4, 2006
Beloved wife. Mother of Augusta Maggie Monet.

A bouquet of tiny white roses withers in a glass vase propped at the base of the headstone. Augusta kneels, sitting back on her heels. She touches the flowers. They disintegrate.

She closes her eyes. She can hear the soft rustling of a chipmunk or a bird scuttling across a stone path. The light breeze in the trees above. A distant woodpecker tapping the trunk of a tree. A small plane whirring overhead.

Everything but what she wants to hear.

Her mother's voice.

Then a man clears his throat behind her. Letting her know he's there. Gus twitches, but doesn't turn to see who it is. She knows. Slowly, she stands. Keeping her back to Rory. He puts a hand lightly on her shoulder. She recoils.

"Sorry I was so blunt yesterday."

Augusta turns to look at him. He's holding a fresh bouquet of white roses. He leans down and carefully replaces the old with the new. She softens.

"You loved them, didn't you?"

He flushes.

"You don't have to watch over me. I'm all grown-up."

"I know."

"I don't need the RCMP following me around."

"I wasn't following you. I come here all the time. Cross my heart."

"I'm talking about the rookie Stanton has tailing me."

Rory has perfected his poker face, but she's not buying it.

"Tell Stanton I'm done playing detective. You were right about my mom. She wasn't always in her right mind. I'm glad you took down her wall. I'm glad it's gone. It was just pieces of paper anyway. Meaningless. I'm done with her just like she was done with me."

Before he can respond, Gus makes a beeline across the cemetery. She's sick of Rory and Stanton and Lashey. Sick of being checked up on. Like she's a child. Coming to her house whenever they like. How dare they? She's committed no crime. *Youth Services, my ass.* Stalkers, the lot of them. Hopefully Rory believes her and gets word to Stanton.

In the words of her immortal mother, *Fuck them all.*

Back home, her hangover fading, Gus sits at the kitchen table. She chews on a Salisbury Steak frozen dinner while leafing through Renata's scrapbook. If Rory bought her act, Stanton will move Lashey on to something more important. Like rescuing a cat from a tree. Gus doesn't care as long as they stay out of her way.

Why? Because Gus is not moving on. She has the photos of her mother's wall on her phone. All her notes and Renata's articles. She doesn't believe for one second that her mother is a murderer. Why Rory believes that is a question for another day. Right now, Gus needs fresh leads that can help prove her mother's innocence, if only to herself.

Gus leafs through the articles one by one, scanning for details she might have overlooked. She verifies dates, cross-referencing them with photos, and adds new notes next to some of the names in her notebook.

Henry Neil. Seen by someone at Halladay House two days before he was reported missing. On the report, Kep claimed no one had seen him for two weeks.

Kep Halladay. Presumed murdered. Body never found.

Lois Greenaway. Took in Gracie after Kep's death.

And Gracie. She stares at the torn image of the ballerina on her phone.

They are more alike than she first thought. Augusta can empathize with the girl in the Polaroid. Wonders what other traumas she endured besides her mother's death. No mother. No father. An orphan like Augusta. Then she remembers. Gracie isn't an orphan. She did have a father. Renata said he was run out of town. She checks her notes for the name of June's boyfriend.

Todd Hammond.

Augusta leaves the dog behind, much to his dismay, and drives over to the library on Rosemount. Snags a computer in one of the carrels and does a name search. There are twenty-five Todd Hammonds listed on Facebook. One lives in Ontario. Amazingly, he lives in Ottawa and he's clearly not figured out how to use his privacy settings. Not that Gus has any clue how to do it herself, but she's not on Facebook. All his personal information is there for the taking. Status: married. Age: thirty-nine. About the right age. Two kids. Works at Home Hardware on Bank Street. Likes MMA fighting and bird watching. Hometown: Elgin, Ontario. Jackpot.

Before leaving the library, Gus does one more quick search on the computer. Renata spoke of her days as a young woman dreaming of becoming an investigative journalist like Nellie Bly. Gus had written the name in her notebook. She looks her up. Turns out, Nellie was an American pioneer in the field of investigative journalism. Bored with writing about fashion and gardening for the women's pages, at twenty-one she went undercover in an insane asylum to expose the deplorable conditions. Her writing was a sensation and she became famous for her gritty exposés. Gus remembers how Renata described her.

Traveling the world. Exposing injustices. Such courageous writing.

Gus likes the sound of her. Spurred on by the spirit of Nellie, Gus summons her own youthful grittiness and heads off to find Todd Hammond. Renata would approve.

GUS DRIVES THROUGH CHINATOWN VIA SOMERSET AND HITS Bank Street. She parks at a meter then walks down Bank until she's across the street from the Home Hardware. She buys a sausage on a bun from a street cart vendor and settles on the bench in a bus shelter. Her sleuthing has given her an appetite. Time for a little stakeout. She chomps on the sausage, contemplating what to say to Todd, if he's even working today. She stops chewing, realizing she should have called ahead to make sure he is. Okay, so she's no Nellie Bly but she's working on it. She tosses her mustard-covered napkin in a trash bin and crosses the street. A bell on the door jingles as she enters the hardware store.

Wandering the paint aisle, Augusta spots Todd across the store. Looks just like he does in all his Facebook photo albums. Incredible how much of themselves people willingly share with total strangers. It baffles her. He's helping a customer find the right toilet plunger. Prematurely graying. Kind blue eyes. Chubby. Disarming. The customer moves on and she approaches him.

"Todd?"

"That's what they tell me."

He taps his name tag and smiles.

"What can I do you for?"

"My name's Augusta Monet. I want to ask you about June Halladay."

His salesman smile stays plastered on his face, but spasms at the edges like he's being gently electrocuted. She's definitely found the right Todd.

"Junie?"

"My mother was the police officer at the scene of her accident."

He flinches. "Accident. Yeah, right."

He says it like he doesn't believe it. Emboldened, Gus keeps going.

"Some people think my mother killed Kep Halladay."

"Jesus Murphy."

He knocks over a container of broom poles. They clatter to the floor. A stock boy darts over to help corral the brooms. Todd shoos him away. He's flustered. Todd rights the brooms, straightens his starched shirt, and nods toward the front door.

Outside, Augusta follows Todd around the corner of the building. She leans against the brick wall while he lights a cigarette. He offers her one. She shakes her head. They stand side by side below a sales banner that says Clean Sweep Broom Sale.

"I hope he was killed. The SOB would've deserved it."

"Sure doesn't sound like a good guy."

"You think your mum did it?"

"She was investigating Halladay. But she was a cop. Justice in her mind would have been seeing him locked up, not dead."

"She go to prison for it?"

"No. She died. Same night as Kep disappeared."

"Whoa. That's terrible. I'm so sorry. What did you wanna ask me about Junie?"

"I was curious why you didn't go back once Kep was out of the picture?"

"No reason to. Junie was long gone and I'm not one for visiting graveyards."

"But what about your daughter?"

He takes a long drag from his cigarette, then drops it and stamps it under his heel. Todd's eyes continue to look down as he talks.

"My mum was born and raised in Elgin. It broke her heart the day she had to leave the house she grew up in. And for what? Junie and me. Kids being kids. Junie was the first girl I ever kissed for Christ's sake. And for that, the almighty Kep Halladay made it so me and my folks couldn't live in our own house anymore. Our home."

He's shaking with anger. Gus waits for him to continue. But instead, he begins to move away toward the front entrance of the store. He tilts his head in the direction of the entrance.

"Listen, I should really get back."

Gus knows she's losing him. Knows there's more to Todd's story.

"I get it. Sometimes it's easier to make a clean break with the past. You didn't want to be a father. You were young."

He flinches. Stops walking but doesn't look at her.

"The baby wasn't mine. Junie and I never."

"You're not Gracie's father?"

Painful memories dance behind his eyes. Gus decides to keep poking at those memories, ever so gently.

"I'm sorry. So June was with someone else then? Another boy?"

Todd looks over his shoulder to make sure no one has come around the corner. He doesn't want to talk. He's holding back. Staring at his hands, he mumbles something inaudible.

"What was that?"

Todd clears his throat and begins to speak in a whisper. As if a secret whispered isn't really being revealed. Gus moves closer to hear.

"Junie was raped. She was fifteen. I was the only one she ever told, and I've never told another soul until now."

Gus immediately regrets poking at his wounds. She touches his shoulder and pats it lightly.

"It's okay, Todd."

"I said it was mine 'cause she begged me to."

"You must have loved her a lot."

He nods. Choking back tears.

"My family was better off away from that town. Away from Kep Halladay. We would've lost everything in that fire anyway if we'd stayed. But a part of me always regretted not going back for Junie. Not getting her away from him. When I heard what ended up happening to her a few years later, I knew it was no accident. The only justice for Junie was that old man disappearing into thin air and leaving his fortune to June's little girl. What goes around comes around."

Gus tries to take it all in.

"Do you know who Gracie's father was?"

"Junie said they were teenagers. A couple of players from the annual high school rugby tournament that was in town. The tournament was sponsored by her father. Two boys took advantage of her. They were not much older than her. The smaller one held her while the bigger lad raped her. She never heard names. She said when it was happening, all she could do was stare at the green-and-gold crest on the front of his shirt."

Todd's eyes glisten as tears stream down his pockmarked cheeks. Gus sees the young, pimple-faced boy Todd once was. The helplessness he felt then and feels to this day. She's sorry she stirred it all up.

Augusta wants to tell him to forgive himself. That it wasn't his fault. That he was just a kid. But she knows words won't matter. They never do. Once regret seeps into your bones, it lives in your marrow until the day you die.

28

MANNY

A UGUSTA CAN HEAR THE WIND WHIPPING VIOLENTLY AT the trees outside her bedroom window. Red veins dance across her eyelids like lightning. She tries to open them, but sleep drags her deeper. She can feel someone lying next to her. Breathing on her arm. Hot breath. She's scared. Can't move. Trapped by lifeless limbs that seem paralyzed. Clawing from the deep, Augusta wills herself to consciousness. Her eyes pop open. She sits bolt upright and leaps out of bed.

"Who's there?"

Her eyes adjust. It's Levi.

He wakes up with a great sigh. Stretches his back legs and exposes his belly for a rub. He must have left Rose's bed in the middle of the night to join her. Seems to be his habit when the winds begin to whip branches against the old siding of Rose's house. Gus calms her racing heart, sits on the edge of the bed, and rubs his belly.

Only justice for Junie was that old man disappearing into thin air and leaving his fortune to June's little girl.

Todd's words come to her as she throws one of Rose's knit sweaters over her nightie and heads downstairs. Gus wonders what happened to Kep's fortune when Gracie died.

While the coffee's brewing, she leafs through Renata's scrapbook and finds the article she's looking for. One of the last articles Renata wrote before she retired. Gus hadn't read it closely before because it didn't seem relevant. Just a short notice really. About the bank closing in Elgin. A CIBC branch. The article is dated August 1, 2011. Two years before the fire. The town was already dying. The bank manager at the time was Manfred Clocktower. He's quoted. Calling it a sad day for Elgin. Says the bank had no choice. With businesses closing and people moving on, they had to relocate. He says he's being transferred and he'll be happy to continue to serve the good people of Elgin at the new branch in Perth, just twenty-five miles away. Renata's article goes on to list other businesses that have closed in the past year. The bowling alley. The local pub. Her article ends with an announcement that the newspaper itself will be publishing their final issue at week's end.

Gus sips her coffee.

If anyone knows about the Halladay fortune, it's the bank manager. And Augusta's lucky streak continues. Manfred Clocktower is easy to find on the library's computer. He's everywhere. Has his own website, blog, Facebook page, and Twitter account. He's all over social media but doesn't have many followers. His bio says he retired from banking in 2014 after sixteen years. He now goes by the name *Manny the Happy Medium*. His life journey, as he calls it, has taken him on a new and exhilarating path. He has become an online practitioner of the mystical arts. His spiritual retreat is located just outside Perth, Ontario, in the small hamlet of Glen Tay. Augusta uses Manny's online reservation tool to book a spiritual reading for later that morning.

His schedule is wide open.

LEVI COMES ALONG FOR THE RIDE. HE LIKES ROAD TRIPS. AND he's good company. The dog sticks his head out the window for the first few miles, then curls up on the back seat and snores the rest of the way. Gus is beginning to love that sound.

Manny's spiritual retreat turns out to be a dilapidated mobile home in a place called Sunset Veranda Trailer Park. Gus pulls into the narrow stone lane next to his unit. The lane is bordered with plastic pink flamingos. Manny is standing on a small vinyl porch that clings to the side of his trailer. He's smoking what looks like a joint. Above his head, a hand-painted sign hangs from a rod.

MANNY THE HAPPY MEDIUM
YOUR BRIDGE TO THE SPIRIT WORLD

Manny snuffs the rolled cigarette into a small metal container in his palm and snaps it shut with his thumb. He's quite a sight. His fingers are adorned with silver rings that snake down to his knuckles. He's very short. Almost as tall as he is wide. He's got man boobs that bounce as he descends the narrow steps to greet her. His purple sweat suit and lime-green flip-flops make him look more like a cartoon character than a spiritual bridge. Manny's not the most attractive man. And the lip liner, chin stubble, and fake eyelashes don't help. But his big smile and gushing enthusiasm instantly put her at ease. His total lack of shame and his head-to-toe weirdness are actually quite endearing. Reminds Gus of a gaudy showgirl.

They shake hands, but instead of letting go, Manny holds hers tight. Augusta gets a warm feeling from him. She figures there's no point in lying. She confesses immediately that she's not come for a reading. She's come to talk about Elgin. He smiles, nods, and says he knows. The slight lift of one eyebrow tells her that he had no clue.

He sets them up in a couple of faded lawn chairs on the porch, offers her a diet cola, and they settle in. Gus explains that she's investigating some cases in Elgin. She drops Renata's name. He brightens at the mention.

Manny goes on about his job at the bank. About the town before it fell apart. Nothing she doesn't already know, but it's a good warm-up to the main event. Asking about Halladay's money. Gus feigns interest and slowly she eases the conversation toward the Halladays. Asks if he had any dealings with Kep.

Manny pauses. His boobs heave as if the memory of the man exhausts him.

Augusta waits. Manny closes his eyes. She's pretty sure he's pretending to conjure up the past. And he does. She opens her notebook.

"The man was a skinflint through and through, Kep Halladay was. A cheapskate. And paranoid. Woof! He always insisted on doing his banking behind closed doors in my office. Too good to mix with the rabble waiting for a teller. He didn't want anyone looking over his shoulder. Knowing how much he had. He'd take me to task over a two-dollar service charge even though the man was worth millions. He wouldn't deal with cash directly, though. Everything was bank drafts and checks and transfers. He actually hated touching the stuff. He said it was covered with the filth from grubby-handed farmers. Bit of a germaphobe. I think he thought himself something of a Howard Hughes type. Kep met the man once at a CNE air show in Toronto. From then on he carried hand sanitizer in a little spray bottle. Squirted the armrests of the chairs in my office, doorknobs, pens if he had to touch one. The man wouldn't even shake my hand."

Manny opens his eyes. Looks down at his fleshy palms. Gus can see that these encounters with Kep Halladay actually hurt his feelings more than they annoyed him.

"But what I remember most about Halladay was the aroma. Antiseptic. The second I'd see his Cadillac pull into the handicap spot, I'd practically smell it. I couldn't shake it for the rest of the day once he'd left. Slightly minty, but not in a good way."

Gus wants him to focus on something other than Kep's personal hygiene.

"Did you know his granddaughter, Gracie?"

He seems startled by Augusta's presence and quickly looks down at his rings, twirling one between his fingers. His glassy eyes flit up to look at her. He's definitely stoned.

"How old are you? Seventeen? No, eighteen?"

"Twenty."

He quickly looks down again.

"Must be the fiery hair that gives you that youthful glow."

Gus begins to wonder if this is why people open up to her so easily. Renata, James Pratt, Todd, even Bebe, the records office lady. They see a young girl in her and let their guard down.

But Manny seems to be stalling. He's not opening up. Gus can tell it's not because he doesn't want to. There's a sadness in his eyes. He knows things and he's either ashamed or disturbed by those things. Gus isn't sure how to get him to talk. She just wants him to know it's safe to do so. She tries honesty.

"Sometimes I feel so young. Like a child. Like I'm stuck there and I might always be stuck there."

He looks up at her. "The past can be sticky like that."

He takes a deep breath, as if collecting himself.

"But I can see you're no child."

Gus and Manny look at each other, and both of them smile. He doesn't look away, but absentmindedly fiddles with his silver rings as he tells her what he knows.

"Kep brought the little girl in just once. Gracie. She was about nine or ten. Slip of a thing. She was wearing her Sunday best. His lawyer was with them. He'd drawn up papers making her the beneficiary of his fortune. It was all to be directed to a living trust. All those royalties he was getting from the local farmers' mineral rights were to be transferred to that account as they came in. Everything was in her name, to be held in trust until she turned eighteen. It was all legal."

Shame catches in his throat. Gus makes a note about the trust.

"Funny word for it. Trust. It was a charade. That trust was completely revocable. I knew what was going on. He knew it. His lawyer definitely knew it. And they both knew I knew it. The girl was never going to inherit a penny. The trust was a tax scheme. The assets could be transferred back to Kep and the whole thing dissolved whenever it suited him. It was simply a way to make Kep Halladay richer as the mineral royalties flowed in practically tax free. Meantime, across the bank floor at the teller's wicket, local farmers were getting by on Kep's fumes. Arrogant bastard never even tipped his hat to a single one of them for all they'd given him."

Gus looks up from her notetaking. Manny looks stricken, like Kep is standing right in front of him. Like he's back in his office at the bank in Elgin.

"You ever smell evil?"

"I don't know. Maybe."

She thinks back to the stench rising from that black crater in the middle of Elgin. That came close.

"Well, it smells like mint. Like it's masking something horrifying."

Then Manny shakes off the past and it seems to literally lift from his shoulders. He shrugs, smiles, and sits back in his lawn chair with a sigh. Augusta gets Manny. Gets how he slips in and out of time and place. She does it too. He smiles at her.

"What is it you really want to know from an old banker?"

"I want to know what happened to the Halladay fortune."

"The girl cashed out."

"Gracie Halladay? What do you mean?"

"Well, the day she turned eighteen. She inherited it all. And withdrew the lot."

Gus flips back through her notebook. "March thirty-first. 2013."

He nods. "You've done your research."

She scans her notes. "This was the day before she died in the fire. April first, 2013."

He nods again. Then he leans closer. "I shouldn't be telling you any of this, Miss Monet."

"I think all this has something to do with my mother's death. But I don't know what or why. Manny, it's important."

He leans back. Stares at her. She holds his gaze. He blinks. Then tells her about Gracie.

"The girl was only eleven when Kep left her that fortune, but she couldn't touch a penny of it. So for seven years, she lived like a pauper while the royalties kept flowing into the trust. The bank closed, moved to Perth, and the trust moved along with us. Then in 2013, a month before her eighteenth birthday, she showed up. She wanted to get things in order. The balance was over two hundred and sixty million at that point. I verified signature cards and set her up with a savings account so that the day the trust matured, the balance would be transferred over to her account. Then she came in a week before her birthday and said she'd changed her mind. Said she wanted to pay off any taxes owed and cash out. She arranged for a bunch of certified bank drafts. She wanted nothing left in that savings account that I'd set up for her just a few weeks before. I got everything ready. Then the day came, and Gracie Halladay walked out of the Perth branch of the Canadian Imperial Bank of Commerce with one hundred seventy million dollars' worth of bank drafts in her purse. Made out to cash. No names. No expiry date."

Gus makes a note of the amount. Trying to picture what size mattress you'd need to fit that much cash inside. Manny continues.

"I strongly advised her against it. I told her it was highly irregular, not to mention flat-out dangerous to be walking around with that much money in drafts. Anyone could cash them. She wouldn't listen. She didn't want a record anywhere of who the money was going to. She wanted it the way she wanted it. Odd young woman."

Gus flinches ever so slightly at his descriptor: "odd young woman." Gracie's behavior sounds specific and defiant, but odd? Funny how people can toss out judgments about someone when they don't understand them. Gus feels like she's beginning to figure out who Gracie is. Damaged. Different. But that only looks odd to those walking around whole and ordinary. Manny breaks her train of thought.

"Then the poor thing died the next day. So to answer your question as to what happened to the Halladay fortune? At the time, I imagined it burned up in the fire along with the girl. But I had no clue. And that's exactly what I told her father when he showed up the next morning asking about the money."

Gus nearly falls out of her chair. He knows he's just dropped a bombshell from the stunned look on her face. Momentarily, she forgets how to breathe. She can't speak. He pauses to let her catch her breath, and for dramatic effect. Then he forges ahead with gusto, like he's revealing the sleight of hand behind a magic trick.

"Remember I told you I opened her a savings account? Well, it was a joint account. With her father. The pair of them came in together. She insisted on it being a joint account. Bank card. PIN. The whole bit. She was going to give him full access to the entire fortune."

"Her father. You mean Todd? He was posing as her father?"

Augusta's head is spinning as she tries to match up Manny's words to the image of a teary-eyed Todd standing outside the Home Hardware. She can't. It couldn't have been Todd. Unless

Todd lied, and Gracie knew who he was, *and* she wanted him to have her money. Gus is beyond baffled. Manny helps her out.

"Gracie vouched for the guy so what could I say? At first, I figured she wanted to share the wealth with kin, but when she came back into the bank a few weeks later, without dear old Dad, I got the feeling she'd had a change of heart. So, like I said, he shows up that fateful morning. A few hours before the fire in Elgin. The guy went white as a ghost when he found out the money was all gone. Then he laughed. Said I was messing with him because it was April Fools' Day. He thought it was a joke. I told him I most certainly was not joking since that would be highly inappropriate given my position at the bank. Then he blew a gasket. He started ranting about how the bank doors opened not ten minutes before and there was no way the money could be gone because today was his daughter's eighteenth birthday and her trust didn't come due till today. It was not lost on me that this rogue's plan all along had been to come grab the cash as soon as it was transferred into that joint account. Otherwise, why come in without her?

"That's when I told him that Gracie Halladay's eighteenth birthday was in fact yesterday. Not today. He got this blank look on his face. Then his body shuddered like a realization had just sunk deep into his bones. I could tell he knew he'd been made the fool. He called me a liar. I told him I was surprised he didn't know the date of his own daughter's birth. That was when he tried to clock me, and security tossed him to the curb."

Manny looks proud of how he handled the situation. He folds his arms across his man boobs. Gus can't wrap her head around any of it, and yet Manny's acting like he's just wrapped up his story with a nice tidy bow. Meanwhile, Augusta's mind is racing ahead, searching for what comes next. There has to be more.

"So Kep's entire fortune burned in the fire."

"Didn't say that. Said at the time I imagined it did. But over the next few months, those bank drafts started getting cashed. None in our branch, but mostly branches scattered across the province."

"Gracie's father?"

"Hard to say. Maybe he somehow got his hands on them. Stormed out of the bank like he was on a mission. But I doubt it. She had me put each one of those bank drafts in a separate envelope instead of all in one. Seems they weren't destined for one place or one person. Maybe she mailed them before she died."

Gus tries to get inside Gracie's head, but she can't see her way past the fact that Gracie called someone her father. That she pulled some sort of scam or trick on him. And if her father wasn't Todd, if this person she brought into the bank was her real father, then was he the man who raped June?

"Do you remember her father's name?"

"Desmond Oaks."

Manny says it so matter-of-factly that it skips in one of Augusta's ears and out the other before flitting back inside her skull then burrowing like a knife into the back of her brain. As if paralyzed, Gus loses all the feeling in her arms and legs. She drops her diet cola. It pools around the legs of her lawn chair. She stares down into the black foaming puddle forming at her feet, can see her face distorted in the murky slick.

Gus manages to croak out his name.

"Dez."

That charred shell of a man sipping cream soda by the pool? That Dez? Maybe that means he wasn't some random stranger passing through town like the fire marshal's report said. Her mind reels with a million questions.

"What did he look like?"

"Jet-black hair. Big man. Stocky. High cheekbones. He was sporting a cauliflower ear. The left one, I think. Or was it the right one?"

Manny tips his head as if he's trying to picture which one of Desmond's ears he's looking at. Gus shakes the shock from her limbs, opens and shuts her eyes, trying to refocus.

"Cauliflower ear?"

"You know, sort of chewed up. It's what happens to a rugby player's ear when it's been ripped to shreds one too many times."

Gus pulls her phone from her satchel and scrolls through her photos until she finds the image from Shannon's wall. She holds it up.

"Like this?"

Manny looks at the picture of the man crossing the street in Elgin. The picture taken from inside Shannon's car through the front windshield.

"Yup, that's a cauliflower ear. Same build. That could be him. I would have to see his face to be sure, though."

Gus is having a hard time picturing Dez as anyone other than that frail and deformed cripple by the pool. Definitely not a rugby player or a rapist or a grease monkey, whatever that is. For the moment, it's just a term Shannon wrote on the back of a blurry photo. And yet Dez has suddenly become all these things and more.

Manny leans forward in his lawn chair.

"You've met him."

Augusta nods.

He takes her hand and closes his eyes. Gus winces. She doesn't want him reading her mind. Seeing her pain. She pulls her hand away. She gets up to leave. Her lawn chair topples.

"Sorry. I should really get going."

"She's proud of you, Augusta Monet."

Gus cringes away from him and makes her way down the steps. Why do people keep saying things about her mother like they knew her? Manny pulls himself up from his chair, with some difficulty.

"It's okay."

Gus hates pity. She flips out.

"Is she really proud of me, Manny? Did she tell you that? Then ask her why she left me all alone. Why she made such a mess of things. Why she left me to clean it all up. I didn't ask for this. She did this."

Gus realizes she's shouting at a sweet man she's just met. She's woken the dog. Levi's barking from the car. Manny looks startled and quite hurt by the unexpected outburst. She feels terrible.

"I'm sorry. I'm not myself. Please forgive me."

"No, I'm sorry. I'm a complete fraud. I looked your name up online. Found your mother's obituary. Made it all up. Just felt like telling you that. I've been wanting someone to tell me that for years and thought you might like hearing it."

He looks like he might cry. Gus climbs back up the steps toward him and takes his hand in hers. Just like he did when she arrived. She holds it.

"It's okay. You've been really helpful, actually. You're a good medium. And I'm sure your mother's proud of you too, Manny."

He smiles and lowers his glistening eyes. She tries to pay him for his time, but he refuses to take her money. She gets in her car and Manny guides her vehicle as she backs out of the narrow lane. As she pulls slowly past him, he stops her. She rolls down the window.

"She didn't leave you. She's right next to you."

Augusta knows Manny is full of shit, but his words are just what she needs to hear. Driving out of Glen Tay, she tries to focus only on the long road ahead. On her sweaty hands on the steering wheel. The hum of the pavement under the Buick's bald tires. Levi's hot breath on her neck.

But as much as she tries to leave him back there with Manny, Dez has come along for the ride home. Gus definitely talked to him about Gracie. Asked him about her and he didn't let on that he was her father or that he went to the bank with her weeks before the fire. Desmond Oaks was after her money. And if Manny's story is true, it seems Gracie might have known it and got the better of him.

A couple of miles past the town of North Gower, Augusta merges right into the slow lane as a black car approaches fast in the left. She's coming up to the overpass, aiming to cross the highway then merge onto the 416 north to Ottawa. Levi rests his head on the seat just beside her shoulder. He pants lightly in her ear.

The black Impala gets closer. Its windows are tinted so she can't make out the driver. She watches as it approaches. It's about to pass on her left, when Augusta hears a pop like a firecracker. She's not sure if a rock hit her car. The Impala noses next to the Buick, then swerves and slams into her bumper. She fishtails across the overpass and thumps against the guard-rail. Levi tumbles behind the seat. Gus grips the steering wheel tight. Her wheels catch the edge of the pavement, the car lists and careens into the deep median, bumping across the rough grass then abruptly jerking to a stop. Gus lurches forward, her chest slamming against the steering wheel, her head bouncing off the windshield before the seat belt whiplashes her backward. No airbag.

The Impala slows and U-turns, kicking up gravel from the shoulder and taking off in a cloud of debris. She watches as it gets smaller and smaller in her rearview mirror. She catches an A and a V on the license plate. Nothing more.

It's hard to breathe. She turns to check on Levi. Spots a hole in her back windshield. A bullet hole. Levi scrambles up from the floor and jumps back onto the seat. He sniffs the passenger headrest, tail wagging. There's another hole in the headrest, likely where the bullet ended up. Her neck begins to ache. Her breathing is shallow.

"You okay, dog?"

Levi rests his chin on the back of the seat and pants. She dials 911, then lifts her hand to gently touch her dog's nose. It's warm.

29

GREASE MONKEY

෨

S HE'S IN SHOCK."

"Get her some water."

Gus is slowly helped from the car. Levi stays close. She's not sure how long she's been sitting there. She remembers going off the road, but why it happened is a blur. A blanket is draped across her shoulders and someone hugs her. She pushes away. Then she realizes it's Rory and stops pushing. Collapses against him. Lets him hold her weight.

"You're okay, Little Monet. Thank Christ, you're okay."

She doesn't want to go to the hospital. Seems like overkill to her. The paramedic isn't convinced. He says if she refuses to come with him in the ambulance, she needs to stay with someone who can watch her. She shouldn't sleep right away. She likely has a concussion. Rory says he'll watch her. His place is close by. As luck would have it, the accident happened on the highway near Kemptville. A few miles from his place. He tells her she can stay at his little house on Harris Road as long as she needs to.

It's the hospital or Rory's house, so she agrees to go with him even though she just wants to go home. Rory takes charge. He arranges for her car to be towed to his house. He thanks the paramedics and gently puts her and Levi in his police cruiser. Gus rests her head against the window and lets him take control.

The house backs onto Kemptville Creek. Levi discovers his love of dog-paddling and mud-rolling that first day at Rory's. His house is far enough off the road that Gus doesn't have to worry about the dog wandering the property off leash. For two days she binge-watches old movies from Rory's VHS collection on the ancient VCR that sits atop the PVR that he has no idea how to operate. Just like Rose's house, Rory's world is stuck in another time.

Gus gives him her new cell phone number so that he can check in on her when he's out at work or running errands. When Rory comes home after work, they watch one of his favorites. *The Godfather*, *Serpico*, or *Chinatown*. Gus stares at the screen without really watching, Levi curled at her feet. His wet fur stinks of creek water. Rory brews her chamomile tea and brings it to her in a yellow happy face mug.

"Here you go, Little Monet. This'll warm your belly."

Rory tries to tidy up the place. Neatly stacking his *Sports Illustrated* magazines. Dusting off the TV with his sleeve. Or brushing crumbs under the sofa or toward Levi. He even bakes chocolate chip cookies from premade dough.

Their third night staying at Rory's, Gus sits in her usual spot in his den. She drifts in and out of tonight's movie. Some guy has Jack Nicholson up against a wall with a knife shoved inside his nostril. Then the man slices Jack's nose open.

"That's my favorite part," Rory says, ducking his head into

the room from the kitchen. He's got oven mitts on his hands, but no cookies. He smiles an evil smile at Gus. She rolls her eyes.

"You know you can stay as long as you want. You hear?"

"You don't have to keep telling me that, Rory."

She can smell the cookies.

"You think I'd kick you and Mister Levi out? Not a chance. Not me. Nope."

Now Rory's acting weird. Talking too much.

"Did you burn the cookies?"

"Heck no. They're cooling."

He coughs.

"You seem nervous."

"Who me?"

He flings his arms about in protest and one of the oven mitts goes flying.

"What is it?"

He looks down. She knows he's done something she won't like.

"What?"

"Stanton's coming by. She needs to talk to you."

Gus pouts and folds her arms.

"I really don't get her. What's so fascinating about me? She's an RCMP sergeant in charge of Youth Services. Has she got nothing better to do? I'm not some troubled youth that needs a good talking-to, am I?"

"Look, I've known her a good long while. Since I joined up. She got sidestepped early on in her career. Passed over. One too many herniated discs and messy divorces, and I think she's just bored pushing pencils. Humor her. She's not all bad."

Rory pulls off the other oven mitt and folds his arms while

he waits for the cookies to cool in the kitchen. Gus mutes the movie and props herself up.

"Why did you join up, Rory?"

"The force?"

He flushes a little like he's surprised she's interested. Rory can be sweet. In this moment, she feels like she's seeing the real him. The young cop. The friend to her parents. The quiet one. The good guy.

"Well, here's the thing of it, Little Monet. I grew up in a rough part of Toronto. Jane and Finch. A housing experiment gone wrong. Gangs. Drugs. I got into sports at school. That's how I stayed out of trouble. I also got lucky. I had both parents at the dinner table. A warm bed. At least compared to some of my friends. One kid I knew, his mom was a drug addict. She started dealing and doing worse. All to support her habit. His house was full of good-for-nothings. He snuck in my window and slept at my place most nights. He kept his nose clean awhile, then he went off the rails. He got into dealing. Then there were a couple of arrests. Juvie. Unlucky. That was him.

"So there you have it. Two kids from the same neighborhood. Life gave him lemons and me lemonade. I guess I joined so I could help kids like him stay outta trouble. Does that make any sense at all?"

Augusta nods and smiles.

Rory walks to a bookcase propped against the far wall. Yearbooks, a couple of dusty trophies, and a collection of paperbacks clutter the shelves. Mostly western novels. She can make out a few names across the worn spines. Zane Grey. Louis L'Amour. A photo sits on the top shelf. He picks it up and hands it to her. It's a picture of three young boys.

"That you?"

She points to the kid on the right. Unmistakably Rory.

"That's me. And that's my buddy. The one I was talking about. And his kid brother. They had different dads, I think. It seems a lifetime's gone by since this was taken."

Gus examines the small black-and-white picture. Rory looks about the same age as the bigger kid. Both about eleven or twelve years old. The little one in the middle. He looks three at most. They're perched on overturned milk crates in an alley next to a brick wall. They're making peace signs and smiling at the camera. Messy hair. Dirty faces. Bruised knees. Boys being boys.

"What happened to them?"

"Oh. Lost touch a long time ago."

There's a rap on the screen door off the kitchen. Rory jumps to attention. Augusta hears the hinges whine as Stanton lets herself in.

"Anyone home?"

Rory heads to the kitchen to greet Stanton. Levi drags himself off the sofa to investigate. Augusta hears mumbling but can't make out what's being said. She clicks off the TV. Pulls the blanket around her. Tries to shake off her sulky eight-year-old self, but she won't budge. She hangs on to the edge of the blanket.

Sitting across from Stanton in Rory's den, Gus waits for the sergeant to explain her visit. Levi is stretched out on the floor sniffing Stanton's shoe. Too tired to bother begging for belly rubs from the company.

"Looks like someone ran you off the road."

Coming out of the kitchen with a steaming mug for Stanton, Rory gasps. He places the mug on the coffee table, wanders back toward the kitchen, but doesn't leave. Instead, he leans on the doorjamb. Stanton continues.

"Any idea who might want to cause you some harm?"

Augusta's mind dances immediately to Lars, then just as quickly dismisses him. The penis pic was definitely his last hurrah.

She shakes her head. Stanton persists.

"No jilted boyfriend?"

"Nope."

No point in siccing the cops on Lars and making that loser feel important.

"You been anywhere unusual recently?"

Stanton's playing with her. She knows damn well Gus has been out to Elgin.

"Nope."

Gus looks away.

Stanton glances around Rory's cramped den as she sips her coffee. Sweat dimples her forehead. She's having a hot flash.

"Well, if you think of anything."

She leaves it at that. Puts down the mug and backs up her chair to rise.

"Oh, I almost forgot. Your friend had an accident."

Stanton catches her off guard. Just like she meant to. Gus stares at her.

"What friend?"

Stanton nods for Rory to give them some privacy. Rory skulks into the kitchen.

"The Happy Medium."

Stanton had been holding on to this nugget since she arrived.

"He was taking a walk. Seems he got hit by a vehicle,

dragged, and then left for dead in a ditch. A passerby found him and got him to Emerg in Perth just in time. Hit and run."

"Holy shit. Manny? Is he okay?"

"Looks like he'll make it, but someone did quite a number on him."

Gus can't speak. She flashes to the figure across the crater in Elgin. And the one on the hill beyond the cemetery. Then she sees her movements of the past few days and a jumble of thoughts flood her brain at once. Images of a stranger visiting Renata, a black Impala trying to run her off the road, shooting at her. And now Manny. Poor Manny. Dragged by a car. She can almost see his purple sweat suit tattered and covered in blood.

She shivers. Someone doesn't like who she's been talking to. What she's been looking into or what footsteps she's been following. Gus wishes Stanton would leave so she could think this all through, but her head is throbbing from the effort.

And Stanton's not done yet.

"I understand you had just come from Mr. Clocktower's residence when your car went off the road."

"How do you know that?"

She wants Stanton to admit Lashey is still following her.

"Manny's got a nosy neighbor who likes to photograph license plates. And we checked his appointment schedule on his computer. You were in it."

Gus knows she's caught.

"Mr. Clocktower worked in Elgin once upon a time. Seems you've been digging into what I told you to leave alone. Neighbor said there was yelling."

"What? I didn't hurt him. Manny was fine when I left."

"And that bullet hole in the back windshield of your car?"

Stanton nods toward the driveway where Rory had her Buick towed.

"Guess you don't know how that got there, either."

Augusta shrugs.

Stanton looks pleased with herself. With how she's played her cards. With how she's made the young woman in front of her feel inferior and young and stupid. Gus can't stand her.

"Your mum and I had our differences, but she was a good cop, until she wasn't."

Gus opens her mouth to speak, but Stanton cuts in.

"Shannon bent the rules till they broke."

Gus looks away. Stanton's voice softens.

"I get it. You're looking for answers about your mum. But there are some things you don't know."

"Oh, I know. Rory told me everything. All about the night Kep Halladay went missing. The tire tracks from her car found out at his house. About how she drove her car into the water and how he pulled her out. I know the whole story."

Stanton's eyebrows rise.

"Someone's painted himself a hero."

"You're not a very nice woman, are you?"

"No, probably not."

"Well, I'm not a kid."

"Clearly."

Stanton leans back.

"I don't need babysitting."

She looks blank. Gus is done talking to this old windbag.

"I'd like to rest now."

"Take care of that head."

Stanton rises. Just as she enters the kitchen, Gus calls out, "And you can stop having me followed."

The sergeant mumbles something over her shoulder but Gus can't make it out. The woman heads into the kitchen. Gus can hear Rory's and Stanton's voices in hushed tones. Then the back screen whines and shuts. Rory comes back into the den and stares at Augusta.

"Bullet hole? What in the heck is going on?"

"Can we just go get a pile of junk food, watch old movies, and forget everything for tonight, Rory?"

He zips his mouth with two fingers indicating that he's done with questions.

Ten minutes later, they're at the local B & H Grocer. Augusta fills her cart with sugary childhood memories. Caramel corn, cream soda, and mini powdered donuts. Rory chitchats with the deli clerk while the man slices cold cuts.

Augusta wanders the store. That's when she sees Miss Santos, Rose's old nurse, in the dairy aisle inspecting each egg inside an open carton. Miss Santos glances up and spots her. Gus looks away then feels badly so she glances back and gives Miss Santos a quick nod before turning her back on her. She heads over to Rory, taps his shoulder, and tells him she'll meet him at the front cash.

On the way back to Rory's, they stop for chocolate sundaes at the local Dairy Barn. Sit at a picnic table near the take-out window. They don't talk. Just enjoy the summer evening and their ice cream. Levi licks the sticky ground at their feet. That night, they rewatch *Chinatown* and both Gus and Levi eat too much caramel corn. The dog vomits on the carpet. Gus goes to bed feeling sick.

Sometime in the middle of the night, Augusta wakes with a start. She's been dreaming about Lars. About the first time she saw his facade crumble. She was waiting in the car in the casino parking lot. Late at night. Lars was standing in the headlights, talking big in front of the Akwesasne Mohawk district chief and his men. Thought he could put the screws to the chief and get stingy with the casino parking lot percentages. The guy let him yak, then one of his men slapped Lars right across the face. Not a punch. A slap. Like he was a girl. Caught Lars by surprise. Shamed him. Lars didn't say another word. Came back to the car. Yelled at Gus for looking at him. Called the guy who slapped him a fucking grease monkey.

Sunday morning, her head still misty, Gus asks Rory to drop her at the public library while he goes to church. He thinks church would do her good, but she says she'd rather browse through the books. He doesn't push. Once there, she uses one of the computers to look up the words *grease monkey*.

Grease monkey.

A mechanic.

Maybe.

Someone who is greasy and unwashed.

Doubtful.

A hand job with lube.

Jesus no.

Someone who gets things done. A hit man or hatchet man.

Yep.

Gus checks her phone and flips to the photo from her mother's wall. The one Gus showed Manny. The one that might or might not be Desmond Oaks. The one with the weird ear. The one her mother wrote "Grease Monkey" on the back of. Her mother suspected it was a guy who gets things done. A hit man or hatchet man. Or maybe she knew that's what he was.

While she's waiting for Rory on the sidewalk in front of the library, a gray Grand Am pulls up to the curb in front of her. The window rolls down. She can't help but laugh when she sees who's behind the wheel.

"You're so bad at this."

Constable Lashey shrugs sheepishly.

"I wasn't following you. Scout's honor."

He places two fingers on his chest. She smiles, shaking her head.

"I swear, Red. My sister lives in Merrickville. It's just up the highway. I was there for brunch."

"What's your sister's name?"

"Phyllis."

"Kids?"

"Two."

"Their names?"

"Kyle and Rachelle."

He's not missing a beat. Seems more relaxed and sure of himself. She likes this side of him. She giggles. Gus never giggles and quickly stops herself. He leans out the window.

"Where's the pooch?"

"Still checking up on me?"

He raises both hands in surrender.

"Not me. Off duty."

Rory pulls up across the road. She waves at Rory and heads across the street.

"See you around, Rookie."

Lashey smiles and hollers back, "I swear, if I was following you, you'd never know it."

She tries not to blush as he drives away. Gus jumps in Rory's car.

"Don't ask."

Rory stays quiet. She can tell he knows exactly who Lashey is.

THAT NIGHT, STRETCHED OUT ON THE SOFA UNDER A BLANKET that smells like Rory's aftershave, Augusta drifts in and out of sleep. Half dreaming until her bruised brain drags her under, fully and deeply.

Jack Nicholson is in the driver's seat of her Buick. He smells like Old Spice and he's driving way too fast. He's got a bandage across his nose. She can see it through the rearview mirror. She's sitting in the back seat. It's dark outside. Beams of light skim across her face, one after the other as the car hurtles into the darkness. She's tired so she slips down to the floor behind the seat and curls in a ball under a blanket. When she peeks out, all the lights are gone. Jack is gone. Out the windows is black nothingness.

She hears a strange gurgling noise. It's her mother. She's choking.

Then the deafening sound of metal crunching and glass breaking pierces her eardrums.

Augusta awakens with her mother's name on her tongue and the residue of the dream swirling around Rory's den. It felt so real. She can't shake the vision of herself behind the back seat. Something about it felt so familiar.

Suddenly, Gus sits up. She remembers. A chill washes over her. It wasn't the Buick. It was her mother's car. She was there. Eight years old. In the back seat under a blanket. Hiding so her mother wouldn't find her and take her back home. Curled up in a ball as Shannon drove the car straight into the lake.

The water was so cold.

30

ANNALEE

❧

THE NEXT MORNING, AUGUSTA AND LEVI ARE SITTING IN Rory's kitchen when he comes in wearing his uniform. Tucking his wrinkled shirt into his pants. She's sipping coffee. He gives Levi a neck rub. She wants to slap him for not telling her the truth, but she doesn't. She decides to give him a chance.

"What were you doing out there?"

"Well, if you must know, I was brushing my teeth, among other things."

"Out near Bruce Pit, the night Shannon drove into the lake."

His face falls.

"Oh, out there. As I remember it, looking into a guy on probation with a court-ordered curfew. Routine bed check. Nothing special."

"I think about that night sometimes. Remember things."

"Yeah, me too."

She sips her coffee. He's not going to fess up. He looks at her. Worried.

"You gonna be okay if I go to work? I could call in sick?"

"I'll be fine, Rory."

Gus knows she was in the car with her mother that night. Rory knows it too. But he won't tell her unless she hits him over the head with it. Then he'll blubber and beg forgiveness for simply trying to protect her. She doesn't want any more blubbering. She wants answers.

And she's about to get some. But not from Rory.

Rory pours coffee into a thermos, wraps a muffin in a paper napkin, and heads off to work.

"You need anything, holler. I'll come by at lunch to check in."

"Am I on probation too?"

She smiles.

He nods awkwardly and heads out the door.

About two minutes later, just as Gus is letting Levi outside, her phone dings. A text. She hesitates before looking at the screen. Hoping Lars hasn't found a way to reach her on her new cell. Hoping Rory hasn't sent her another silly emoji.

But it's not Lars. And it's not Rory. It's Annalee Franklin, her old babysitter. Finally.

It's short and sweet.

> Hey Gus. It's Annalee! I got your messages. Sorry for being MIA.

A chill runs down her spine. Annalee was likely the last person to see Shannon before the car accident. Her timing couldn't be more perfect. She might be able to shine some light on the dark patches in Augusta's memories.

> Hi Annalee. How was Europe?

Gus doesn't care, but figures she better ease toward the nitty-gritty.

> Awesome. The Dutch are crazy!
> LOL

Gus cringes at having typed these three ridiculous letters.

> What's up with you, kiddo? How old RU?
> Twenty
> 4COL

Gus has no idea what that means so she cuts to the chase.

> Do you think we could meet? I want to ask you about my mother.
> Shannon? What about her?
> Do you remember the night of her car accident?
> Yeah.

Gus can tell, even over text, that Annalee's tone has changed.

> Can we chat in person, Annalee?
> I'm super busy what with work and just getting back.

Annalee is blowing her off.

> Quick coffee?

Long pause.

> Sorry, Gus, I gotta run. I'm at work. Let's touch base next week. Bye.

Gus stares at her phone. Waiting for Annalee to change her mind, but she doesn't.

BY LATE MORNING, GUS IS PACKING. SHE HAS TO SEE ANNALEE face-to-face today. Gus convinces herself it's the right move, even though an uneasy rumbling churns in the pit of her stomach. She alleviates the belly tremors by reassuring herself that she'll be extra careful. Make sure she's not followed. Doesn't want anyone else getting hurt. But she can't stop now. Just like Shannon, she's a dog with a bone.

Gus crams her clothes into her duffel bag, eager to get out of Rory's place. He ratted her out to Stanton, he broke into her house, he destroyed Shannon's wall. He treats her like she's still eight years old. She was foolish to stay with him. To trust him. He doles out the truth when it suits him and then acts like it's for her own good.

It's time for her and Levi to take care of themselves.

She breaks the news to Rory when he comes home for lunch. He begs her to stay, but she stands her ground. Says her head's feeling much better. Says she's imposed for too long already. Says she needs to get back to Rose's.

Levi sticks his head out the back window as they drive away. The dog's going to miss that muddy creek. Rory stands on his back porch. Hands shoved in his front pockets, head bowed, like he's the last kid picked for the team.

Gus pulls onto the highway. They head back toward the city. She's not sure if the car behind her is a tail, but just in case, she veers away from the turnpike into Ottawa at the last second and swerves onto the underpass going in the oppo- site direction, cutting off a Ford pickup in the process. The driver lays on the horn as they head west toward the suburb of Kanata. Back at Rory's she called four different Supercuts in Kanata before finally finding the one where Annalee works.

"Yes, Annalee's in today but she's all booked up."

Gus hangs up. She doesn't need an appointment. She'd rather make a surprise visit. Annalee can't blow her off if she's right in front of her.

Gus finds a spot in the mall parking lot, cracks the window for Levi, tosses him a treat, and walks across the concourse to the Supercuts. Annalee spots her through the window. Her former babysitter is now a bleached blond with purple streaks. Her glittering eye shadow sparkles as she glances at Gus then quickly looks away. Clearly not pleased to see her.

Annalee continues styling her female customer's long bru- nette hair, running her brush through it and curling the ends as she blows it dry. Her back to the front door.

Gus enters. Another hairdresser acknowledges her with a quick nod.

"We're all full up today, miss, but gimme a sec and I'll put you in the book for tomorrow."

Gus ignores the woman and makes a beeline for Annalee. With a salon full of clients and coworkers eyeballing them, Annalee pretends she was expecting Gus.

"I thought that was you, Augusta. Same baby face from when you were a kid."

Annalee gives her an air kiss on both cheeks, then continues to dry the brunette's hair. Gus has to shout over the drone of the blow-dryer.

"I'm sorry to just pop by but I really wanted to finish our talk."

"Like I said. I'm at work. So . . ."

Annalee points to the head she's blow-drying.

"I just want to know how she seemed that night."

"Who?"

"My mom. Shannon."

"Oh."

"Was she herself?"

Gus is irritated with having to shout their entire conversation to a room full of perked ears.

"Um. She was pretty amped up, I guess. She was never like that. Your mom was the queen of cool."

"Like what?"

"Like she tracked mud into the house and didn't even notice. Didn't care. I asked her if she was okay and she said she needed me to stay longer. She said she had to go back out. So she did and, well, you know."

Annalee looks around the salon, not wanting to say the words. Gus shouts.

"She didn't say anything or do anything weird?"

Annalee pulls the brunette's hair by accident. The woman glares at her and pushes her hands away. Annalee turns off the blow-dryer and begins perfuming the long mane with a cloud of hair spray while shielding the woman's eyes with one hand. In a more hushed tone, Annalee answers Gus.

"Not that I can remember. It was a long time ago and I try

not to think about it. I know you miss her but really, do you think it's a good idea to go over what happened that night?"

"Yes. It was my mother who died. And if she killed herself I want to know."

Gus realizes she's still using her blow-dryer voice and the entire salon is dead silent. Watching the pair through the wall of mirrors. Augusta's cheeks burn hot and her neck turns blotchy red. Gus feels like she might pass out.

Annalee goes white with worry. Stops spritzing the brunette and takes Augusta's arm. She pulls her across the salon, down a back hallway, and into a staff kitchenette. Annalee turns to face her. She takes Gus by the shoulders.

"Oh my gosh, Augusta. Your mom wasn't suicidal. Not by a long shot."

"But she drove into a lake."

Annalee bites her lip. And just like that, there's the sweet teenager Gus once knew. The one who loved dance movies and caramel corn.

"I've been a total bitch, haven't I? It's just that I haven't talked about that night, ever, and I thought I'd never have to. I always felt so guilty about it."

"Guilty?"

"After your mum went back out, my boyfriend, Chet, you remember Chet, well, he came over and we smoked some weed and had some of your mom's wine and after he left I passed out and the next thing I knew the police were at your door and your mom was dead and I'm so sorry, I was a terrible babysitter and I'm an even worse person."

Tears drip from Annalee's glittery eyes. Gus hugs Annalee tight. Annalee lets out a deep breath. One that she's been holding since the beginning of her confession. Gus releases her and looks her in the eyes.

"You didn't do anything wrong."

"But what if she tried to call me?"

"Do you think she did?"

"No. But what if she had?"

Annalee's wet eyelashes bat up and down as she tries to stop crying. Gus picks up a small paper napkin from a stack on the counter and holds it out to Annalee. The hairdresser takes it and dabs her eyes. Gus reaches out and gently touches Annalee's shoulder. She looks at her until Annalee finally makes eye contact.

"Annalee, I don't care about what didn't happen. I just want to know everything that did."

Annalee sits down at the small plastic table in the middle of the kitchenette and motions for Gus to join her. Gus sits. Annalee fiddles with a tiny salt shaker, examining it, as if she can see the past in its tiny crystals.

"I know people say they do but I remember it like it was yesterday. After your mom got home she went into the garage. She came back out with some papers and her camera. The one she bought the week before. Remember she was showing us how it could shoot in the dark? Infrared or something. She videotaped you eating your supper with all the lights out and you didn't want to be filmed so she filmed the puppy instead and you got super pissed off."

Gus remembers. She was perpetually angry with Shannon back then. And with Levi. Annalee keeps talking.

"She had the manual for the camera too. Her hands were shaking so much she couldn't read it. I asked if I could help.

She told me the adapter wouldn't fit. She said she needed to copy a video from the camera onto a memory stick. This little orange thing she kept holding up like it would magically do what she wanted it to do. She was almost in tears. We sat in the living room. I read the instructions while she followed them. We got it working and we copied the video."

"What was on the video?"

"I don't know. We didn't look at it. She just copied it to that USB stick, then she erased the memory card in the camera."

"Did she do anything else?"

"She checked on you, said goodbye to the dog, and then she had to get going. Kept checking her watch. She said she didn't know when she'd be back. She just took the camera and left."

An image surfaces in the back of Augusta's mind. She can see her mother talking to Annalee in the living room. They're deep in conversation. Distracted. Gus sees herself tiptoeing across the hall without either of them noticing. Then the memory fades.

"I always felt bad I didn't ask what was wrong."

"And where was I when the police came?"

"In bed."

Gus is confused. "All night?"

"I guess so. Like I said. I sort of passed out. You were in your bed when the cops showed up. We found your great-grandmother in your mom's address book and that's where the police took you. My parents helped me lock up the house and took me home."

Gus feels muddyheaded. The pungent smells of shampoo and hair spray are making her woozy. Annalee gets her a glass of water from the sink. Gus downs it as more questions than answers bubble up in her brain.

What was Shannon up to?

And how did she, Gus, end up in the car with her mother?

Maybe she wasn't there.

"That's everything I remember. I really hope it helped."

GUS IS ON AUTOPILOT AS SHE PULLS OUT OF THE MALL, LEAVING
Annalee waving from the window of Supercuts. Levi's asleep
beside her. Snoring. Gus takes the eastbound ramp to Ottawa.
To the city. As she joins the flow of late-day traffic on the 417,
she gets a call.

It's Haley-Anne. One of her former clients drove by the
house and wants to put in an offer before the listing goes up.
It's a developer friend of hers. And it's a good offer. Enough
to cover the bank loan and real estate fees. Haley-Anne says
she'll come by later with the paperwork so they can discuss.

It all happens way too fast. By nine o'clock that night, Gus
is signing the real estate contract and Rose's rambling house
on Island Park Drive is officially sold. The closing date is in a
month. It's mid-July and even though Gus only showed up on
Rose's front step a month ago, she is gutted. She will miss this
old house. Miss how the sun washes over the kitchen table in
the morning and how the moon lights up the walls of her cozy
upstairs bedroom. At first, she almost doesn't sign because she
can't stand the thought of some family moving into the house
and making it their own, as if Rose and Shannon and Levi
never existed. Never walked its hallways or slept under its
roof. But Haley-Anne assures her that won't ever happen.

And now Gus must ready herself to leave. To move on.
Let go of what was never really hers in the first place. Relief

and sadness rinse through her in equal parts as she locks the front door when Haley-Anne leaves.

The real estate agent didn't care about the broken backdoor screen or the red marker staining the living room wall or the lack of curb appeal. In the end, none of it mattered. The house was sold without the buyer ever stepping foot inside. It was to be torn down. The developer was starting from scratch. Building something new.

And so were Gus and Levi.

31

PEQUEÑO POLICIAL

ᑍ

MID-AUGUST, AFTER TWO MONTHS OF INHABITING HER great-grandmother's house, Augusta moves into a small residential motel off Richmond Road, six blocks from Rose's. She tells herself it's temporary. Takes from Rose's only what she arrived with. The exceptions are the dog's dishes, Rose's garment bag of cash, her gun and her Buick, Augusta's childhood trunk, and the Russian nesting dolls. And, of course, Levi. The rest is off in an estate sale to cover closing costs.

On their morning walks, Gus and Levi pass by the house where Haley-Anne's smiling face still beams from a SOLD sign on the front lawn. It's not being demolished until the fall so Gus occasionally picks weeds from the garden or pulls up the crabgrass that spiders between the paving stones leading to the front steps. She knows her efforts are futile but does it just the same. It feels right. Mostly, though, they just walk past. She lets Levi eat a few of the neighbor's tiger lilies, then they head back to the motel.

She doesn't mind the dimly lit motel room. It's got a single bed, dresser, table and two chairs, a bar fridge, hot plate, and bathroom, shower only. Reminds her of her room at Rose's. It's bedbug- and cockroach-free so it'll do for now. She keeps most of her things in her blue trunk in the corner. She lines up the nesting dolls on the windowsill, stuffs a few hundred dollars in her wallet, and leaves the rest tucked away in the garment bag inside the vinyl-covered spare tire in the Buick's trunk. She stows Rose's gun in the glove compartment.

"Pets are tolerated. Noise is not."

Anita Hubble gives her the lowdown. She's the hotel manager.

"No pooping on the property and no barking after ten."

The turkey flesh under the woman's armpits flaps as she talks. Hubble is seventysomething with a long braid of gray hair that snakes down her back. Gold hoops hang on her sagging lobes and there's a tattoo of Jesus on her bicep. She's an old hippie. Walks around in a floral muumuu that drapes from her low-hanging breasts like a monk's robe. She lives behind the office through a door with a half top that she keeps open when she's inside watching *The Price Is Right*. A bell sits on the ledge of the half door in case someone needs her.

"Ring once if you need me. Twice if the place is on fire."

Hubble likes to impart game show wisdom.

"A tube of toothpaste is cheaper than a tube of Pringle chips but pricier than a pack of chewing gum."

There are other short-stay tenants at the motel. There's a family from Syria who just moved to Canada, a couple whose furnace leaked oil all over their basement, and a construction worker from out east working a short-term contract. It's a temporary stopover where people come to get their bearings. Figure out their next move.

Getting back to their new digs after a walk, Augusta sits on the bed. Levi snuggles next to her leg. She listens to the hum of the leaky air conditioner in the window. Not sure what the future holds.

Then a voice from the past calls.

Miss Santos. Only she says "Yanna" so it takes Gus a second to realize who it is. Yanna says she went by Rose's house looking for Gus. Saw the real estate agent's phone number on the SOLD sign and called it. Haley-Anne was the one who gave her Augusta's cell phone number.

"I saw you in grocery in Kemptville."

Gus remembers. This was back when she was staying with Rory.

"I'm sorry I didn't say hello."

Gus isn't sorry. She had zero interest in talking to Miss Santos then and now.

"I call to make sure you okay. You be careful."

"I'm okay."

"No. Careful of company you keep."

Gus doesn't know what the woman's going on about.

"Why did you call me, Miss Santos?"

"That night your mother die. Rose send me to collect your things."

Gus doesn't say a word.

"Pequeño policial. He was at your house. Looking about. Took boxes. Took things. Your mother's things."

"Policial, you mean police?"

"Sim. Yes."

Gus thinks back to Rory telling her how the police took care of their own.

"They were just doing their job."

She doesn't feel like getting into this with her.

"Not they. He. One man. Pequeño policial. Little police-man. I talk with him that night. He let me get your things from your room. Then he tell me to go. Leave. Take nothing of your mother's. He help me load car. Pushy little policeman. He not nice. He rush me. Want me gone. Didn't like him. Didn't want him in your house but not my place to say."

Gus connects the dots. Kep goes missing and her mother dies in a car accident. Shannon's connected to the crime so a policeman goes back to their house to get rid of anything that might implicate Shannon further. It fits but it doesn't. Yanna cuts in.

"I see him with you. I remember face."

"Where?"

"In grocery. You with that little policeman."

She's talking about Rory. Gus isn't sure what to say, but a question lingers in the far recesses of her mind. A question she's wanted to ask Miss Santos ever since she found her blue trunk.

"You said you got my things that night. But why didn't you ever tell me about my blue trunk? I found it in Rose's basement."

"I sorry. Thought it best you move on. Forget. I stow for future. When you ready to remember and not so much a child missing mother."

Gus is struck by Yanna's unexpected thoughtfulness. Per-haps she isn't a black crow after all. Perhaps Augusta's child's-eye view of Rose's nurse was skewed by the terrible loneliness that continues to warp many of her memories from back then. Yanna was probably right to put aside her things until she was ready to remember. Gus is ready now.

She might have said goodbye to Yanna. She might have just hung up. She's not sure. Her mind had already moved on to Rory Rump. He was at the accident. Then later that night, he was at their house in Hintonburg. And conveniently, he was right there when she was run off the road. Always there. Helping. Protecting. Taking care of things.

She was not in her right mind, you know. Never got the help she needed.

She wasn't herself.

She never hit the brakes.

Drove straight into that lake like she meant to.

Always there. Bringing flowers. Planting seeds.

Good old dependable Uncle Rory.

THE NEXT MORNING, AUGUSTA DRIVES TO KEMPTVILLE BEFORE the sun comes up, Levi in tow. She parks under the heavy bows in a narrow overgrown lane a few hundred yards down the road from Rory's property. Dog's asleep. She waits.

Right on cue. Rory's red Honda passes by. Off to work. She gives it ten minutes just in case he forgot something. Leaves the sleeping dog behind and hikes down the lane, through the scratchy buckthorn toward the back of his property. A broken-down garage sits hidden in the bushes. So deep she'd never seen it before. Not even when she chased Levi through the property when they stayed at Rory's. She peers inside the dirty windows. Can't see through the grit. She pulls on the door. It swings open. Hinges creaking. There's a car under a dusty beige tarp, a greasy lawnmower, compost bins, long-forgotten garden tools, and a collection of plastic planters full of dry soil and rotting roots. She peeks under the tarp at the car. It's black. Gus takes a panoramic shot of the inside of the shed before heading through the bushes to Rory's house.

No time to waste. He usually comes home for lunch.

She tries the back door. Locked. She pushes lightly on the kitchen window. Not locked. She swings it open, pops out the screen, and boosts herself over the ledge and inside, thankful that Rory's house is hidden from prying neighbors' eyes.

Gus scans each room quickly. Takes photos of each as she goes. One after the other, not sure what she's looking for. In Rory's bedroom, there's a desk in the corner. An old computer sits on the floor, unplugged. It's not her mother's. A mess of bills and lottery tickets and baseball cards litter the compartments of the desk. She runs her hands under the drawers. Nothing taped to the bottom like in the movies. Next, the den. She spots the photograph he showed her. The one of him as a kid with his childhood friends. His friend, the one he said went off the rails, is a foot taller than Rory. He's got a ball in one hand, resting against his hip. She hadn't noticed it before. It looks like a football only with flatter ends.

Once in PE class at boarding school, they played a game with a ball like that. Rugby. Todd's words come to her.

Junie said they were teenagers. A couple of players from the annual high school rugby tournament that was in town.

Gus checks her phone. The photo of Gracie's gravestone. She was born in 1995. Rory would have been in high school around that time.

She runs her fingers across the yearbooks on Rory's bookcase. Two dusty trophies prop up the books. Rugby trophies. She pulls out the yearbook for the class of '94. Sits on the sofa and leafs through the pages of fresh-faced high school students. At the back she finds the team photos. Football, soccer, volleyball.

Rugby. The North York Lions. In block letters above the team's name are the words *1994 Champions, McCormick Cup, Elgin, Ontario.* She searches row by row and finds Rory. He's in the back. Scrawny. So young. He's wearing a white jersey with a green-and-gold crest on the chest. Rory Rump's position is listed as a scrum half and assistant captain. He's peering over the shoulder of another boy who sits front and center. This kid is bigger than the rest of them. Wide shouldered, angular face with piercing eyes and black hair.

She grabs the framed photo of Rory and his chums.

Yes. The older one is the same kid in the team photo. Only in the yearbook he's closer to sixteen, maybe seventeen. Rory looks scrawny but his buddy has gotten bigger. He's bulked up. But what stands out most is his ear. How had Manny described him?

Jet-black hair. Big man. Stocky. High cheekbones. He was sporting a cauliflower ear. The left one, I think. Or was it the right one?

She checks. Yep. Left ear. She looks at the row of names printed below the photo. It's Desmond Oaks.

She didn't see this coming. Rory knows Desmond Oaks. They were friends. Went to the same high school. Played on the same team.

She examines the team photo closer. Dezzie Oaks, as he's listed, is the hooker and team captain. Looking at young

Rory, pity catches in her throat. He's got one hand resting on Dezzie's shoulder. Trying to be a part of his world. But Dezzie sits center stage holding the trophy. He's the star. Rory's his backup. Her pity sours as she sees what else the pair of teenagers might also be.

A leader and a follower. A captain and his assistant. A rapist and his accomplice.

It all comes together as she stares at the trophy from the tournament in Elgin.

Smaller one held her while the bigger lad raped her. All she could do was stare at the green-and-gold crest on the front of his shirt.

Green-and-gold crests adorn the uniforms of the team in the photo. She sees Rory for who he really is. A background player but a player nonetheless. Always the sidekick. At Depot when her parents were cadets. Their best man. Their next-door neighbor living down the hall from the newlyweds. Even the RCMP put Rory in a supporting role as a second-rate school crossing guard.

Gus closes the yearbook. The scent of Old Spice is everywhere.

Here and back there.

⁂

She's five. They've just moved to Hintonburg. Shannon is having a party. Their first Christmas in the new house. Rory arrives. Cigarette and Old Spice hugs for Gus. And a present to go under the tree. He stands at one end of the dining room table near the food, shuffling foot to foot, nibbling chips and drinking Budweiser from a can. Still works in the county so he doesn't know any of the officers she's invited from HQ.

He's not one of them. These are Shannon's new colleagues. Her friends, not his.

Some have brought casseroles of layered bean dip or trays of shortbread cookies with bright green icing and sprinkles. Some kiss Shannon on both cheeks. Some squeeze her hands in theirs. The table fills with Christmas cheer. The guests get louder and more red-faced.

Gus is in charge of the buffet. Keeping it stocked with mini paper napkins and toothpicks for the olives and clearing away the dirty plates. She hears Rory tell the same bad joke to anyone who comes near the buffet. He waves from his corner if he's introduced to a new arrival, but he never looks to Gus like he's joined the party.

When it's time for bed, Gus pretends to go up but instead watches from the top of the dark stairs through the railing. Watches as the wobbly guests laugh and dance and spill red wine and talk with food between their teeth and put their arms over each other's shoulders like they're lifelong buddies. Later they stumble as they put on their boots and coats and hats. Until the last of them leaves.

All except Rory. Gus sneaks down the stairs and peeks down the hallway. Shannon and Rory are in the kitchen. It's a mess of dirty platters and plastic wineglasses. Wearing his winter coat, Rory's gathering paper plates and shoving them into a green garbage bag near the sink. Shannon's putting leftover cookies in a Tupperware container. He turns toward her. Puts his hands on her waist. Shannon jumps, spins around, and slaps him across the face with a dishcloth. She has wine eyes.

Shannon grabs the garbage bag and takes it out the side door, leaving Rory alone in the kitchen. Gus watches as he dips his finger into the icing of a half-eaten cake and licks it. His mouth is tight, like a scolded child's. Shannon comes back inside. Mumbles something to him, then turns her back and begins to wash the dishes in the sink. He waits for her to look at him. She doesn't so he slips on his boots and leaves through the back door. Once he's gone, Gus watches as her mother stops washing the dishes, turns, and leans against the sink. Drying her hands with a dishcloth. She sighs, stares up at the ceiling. Then she yells.

Why the fuck did you leave me, Charlie?

Gus runs up to bed and hides under the covers.

❧

Rory has likely loved Shannon since the day they met in cadet training. And even with Charlie gone, she didn't want him. Must have hurt. And if he was connected in some way to the rape of June Halladay and Shannon found out, she would have never forgiven him. Would have hated him. That thought, more than the rape, has probably haunted his nights.

Gus almost feels sorry for Rory.

The sound of gravel crunching under tires startles Gus. Lost track of time. Rory's home for lunch. Gus darts down the hall and slips out his bedroom window as the screen door in the kitchen slams. She tumbles to the grass and races across the lawn.

As she pushes through the buckthorns, she can see the yearbook lying open on the sofa. Right where she left it. Open to the page with the rugby team photo. Lying right next to the framed picture of Rory and Dez. Childhood friends.

32

OLLIE

GUS PULLS INTO THE PARKING LOT BEHIND THE LOW-RISE apartment. She parks in the same spot as before in visitor parking. She grabs the gun from the glove compartment and places it inside her satchel. Then she holds out a dog cookie for Levi. He snaps it from her fingers. She rolls her eyes. Tells him she'll be right back. He knows what that means. He's not invited. Levi sulks and grinds his teeth into the cookie. She locks the car doors.

Skirting the building, Gus peers around the corner and scans the pool deck. No Dez. The pool has been filled since her last visit. A half-deflated inner tube bearing a yellow smiley face floats on the murky water. The smiley face is twisted into a smirk. Dry leaves lift in mini-tornados along the walkway, circling Augusta as she walks toward the building.

She climbs the stairwell. Retracing her steps to apartment 202. Before knocking, she takes a deep breath. A breath that vibrates loudly, causing her to take a step back from the door. Fear is catching in her throat. She almost turns to leave, but stops herself. Steadies her mind by gathering the random pieces swirling around her brain. Gus lays them out in front of her, one after the other.

Dez and Rory knew each other.

That doesn't make Dez dangerous. But he could be.

Her grip tightens on the satchel. She glances down. The gun is in sight. Easy to reach.

Dez also knew Gracie. Said he didn't.

Unless it wasn't him at the bank.

But who else could it have been?

The cauliflower ear. The rugby photos.

Rapist? Grease monkey? Father?

Whoever he is, Dez lied when they first met by the pool.

He was playing a game. Pretending.

Gus needs to know why.

And what else he knows.

She steps toward the door as something far more powerful than fear courses through her body. Deep in her bones, she knows the only thing that matters is the truth. She needs to do this for herself. And for Shannon.

Gus knocks. Waits. As she waits, a weightlessness prickles her body. She knows her actions have disturbed the balance in someone's universe. A balance built on quicksand. And now she's hovering at the murky edges of that universe, and someone doesn't like it. So much so that they drove her off the road, shot at her, gave dear Renata a stroke, and dragged poor Manny behind a car. And that someone is more than just a little off balance. They're in deep.

And they're dangerous.

But Dez? Doesn't add up. He might be angry over being cheated out of money and burned in a fire, but the guy has trouble getting out of a lawn chair. Gus scans for other threats. There's the rookie cop, but Officer Friendly seems more like a glorified babysitter than a hatchet man. Stanton's just a washed-up paper pusher playing the big shot. Lars is a control freak, yes, but he wouldn't drive fifteen minutes out of his way now that he knows they're over for good. Plus he can't track her location anymore. Uncle Rory? Meddling. Definitely overprotective and lying to cover up a past he'd rather forget. A rape he's haunted by. Certainly a violent past, but a sustained taste for violence? She just can't see it.

Gus knocks harder. Still no Dez. The front window is open a crack. She leans toward the open screen. The apartment is dark. She calls inside.

"Mr. Oaks? It's Augusta Monet. We need to talk."

Nothing. A door opens two down. A creepy wisp of a man with fishbowl glasses pops his head out. He squints and wipes his nose with the back of his hand.

"You can stop making that bloody racket."

"Oh, I'm sorry."

"Those two good-for-nothings are out."

She walks toward him. He cowers and is about to shut his door.

"You mean Desmond Oaks?"

He leaves the door open a sliver. Looks her up and down. She's pretty sure he isn't wearing anything but stained boxers.

"What's it to you?"

"I'm his social worker."

"I seen you before. Sitting by the pool with hamburger face."

He stares at her chest.

"You're a young one. Fresh."

Her skin crawls.

"You said those two? Dez lives with someone?"

"That layabout brother of his. Tommy."

In her periphery, Gus sees something move at the end of the balcony. She turns but whoever was there has turned tail.

"Thanks for your help."

She takes off running down the balcony.

"All hurry and no suckie."

Gus shakes off the urge to gag as she races to the top of the metal stairwell. Looks down. Spots a hand letting go of the bottom rail. She takes the stairs two by two. Rounds the side of the building. Surveys the parking lot. Whoever it was is gone. Levi's barking. He saw them. If only the dog could talk.

Sitting in the car, Gus jots a note in her notebook. *Little brother, Tommy.* Another lead. Likely the toddler standing between Rory and Dez in the framed photo. She makes a note to look into Tommy Oaks.

The sun is blinding. It obscures her vision. Intensifying her other senses. From across the parking lot, Augusta feels eyes on her. From the thicket of trees. Levi lifts his head and sniffs the hot breeze.

"You feel it too, don't you, Levi?"

Levi's whiskers quiver. Gus feels her own internal radar switch to high alert. Hands gripping the steering wheel. Heart pulsing against her ribs. She starts the Buick's engine and pulls the car out of the parking lot without glancing toward the trees.

"Let's go see how Manny's doing."

They drive out of the city, and back into the country, this time heading to the town of Perth. And despite crisscrossing the county all day, following trains of thought, Gus feels like they're heading in the right direction now.

She's careful this time. There's only one hospital in the small town that sits about an hour southwest of Ottawa. She calls ahead to make sure Manny hasn't been released. He's still there. Must be a slow recovery.

Once in Perth, Gus checks her map. Finds the location of the hospital. Parks on a residential street about six blocks away. There's no way she's risking any further harm coming to Manny. She leaves the dog behind in the locked car and walks. If she is being followed, they're after her. Not her dog. She enters through a laundry room door at the back of the hospital, dekes down a staff hall, and takes a service elevator to the main floor. There's no way she's being followed now.

Gus buys carnations at Bluebell's Flower Shop in the concourse, then heads to the admissions desk. The woman tells her that Manny's in the ICU. Room 677. No visitors. Family only. Gus smiles. Says she'll go leave the flowers with the ICU nurses' station. The woman tells her it's on the second floor. Coming off the elevator she follows the signs leading to room 677. Heading away from the nurses' station, through the double doors that say no entry. She almost makes it when a cart blocks her path. A nurse asks if she needs help.

"I'm Mr. Clocktower's daughter."

Gus scoots past as if she knows where she's going. The nurse watches her. Gus finds the room.

"Hey, Dad, it's me."

Gus calls into the room, loud enough for the nurse to hear.

Manny looks like shit. Much of his face is scabbed over. One leg's in a cast, knee to foot, and she can see pavement burns on his thigh where his hospital gown has fallen open. A morphine drip seeps from a tube into his arm. Whoever did this meant business. Manny turns as she enters.

"Manny? It's Augusta. Monet."

"You brought carnations."

She places the flowers on the windowsill. Not sure he recognizes her. She gives him a hint.

"We met a while back. Just before your accident."

"We did."

"I came to your trailer. We talked."

"Miss Monet. Yes, I remember."

He points to the foot of the bed. His toes poke out the end of the cast. She reaches down to cover his toes with the blanket, tucking it gently under his feet. She sits on the bed.

"I'm so sorry, Manny. I should have come to see you sooner. This was all my fault."

He takes her hand and squeezes it.

"You were just looking for the truth. The people who did this to me. They were looking for something else."

"You saw who hit you?"

"Saw them? They told me they'd drag me till I talked or died."

"Talked?"

"About the money. The withdrawal from the girl's account. The bank drafts."

"They wanted to know about Gracie's money?"

"I told them I saw her put them in the mailbox across the street. I told those fellows that money was long gone and I didn't know where to."

"Can you describe the men?"

"I didn't tell them about Ollie."

"Ollie?"

"My friend. I didn't tell them a goddamn thing."

Manny lets go of her hand and sighs as he rides a wave of morphine. Gus tries to make sense of what he's telling her about Gracie and the bank drafts. She recalls what he said when they first met.

She had me put each one of those bank drafts in a separate envelope instead of all in one. Maybe she mailed them before she died.

Manny hadn't told her the whole truth.

"But I thought you weren't sure what she did with them."

Manny looks at Gus. He knows exactly what Gracie did with the bank drafts. He tells her she never put them in a mailbox across the street. He lied to his attackers to protect the truth and his friend Ollie. Ollie's the postmaster that Manny sent Gracie to see when she left the bank.

Gus and Manny talk awhile about the weather and the food at the hospital. He likes the vanilla pudding. She promises to come see him when he gets out. Asks if he needs anything. He says he needs her to stay safe.

As she makes her way out of the hospital, the same way she came in, Gus is on high alert. Watches the couple coming

out of the parking garage. The meter maid ticketing a car in a
no-stopping zone. The old man sitting in the wheelchair having a smoke. She ducks into a bus shelter. Stakes out the back
entrance awhile to see if anyone comes out after her. A janitor
comes out. Dumps a bucket of dirty water. Goes back inside.
She waits a half hour. Four buses go past. Coast is clear. No
one's tailing her.

The whole way back to the car Gus berates herself. She
knows she messed up. Number one rule of a private eye, at
least in the movies, is to follow the money.

Gus jumps in the car. Levi's spread-eagle on his back. Snoring. Good old dog. She crisscrosses Perth's grid searching for
the town's post office. The one where Gracie must have gone.
To see the postmaster. Ollie. Gus stops to ask directions from a
local who's watering his lawn. He tells her it's two blocks down
on Foster between Wilson and Gore. Can't miss it. White brick.

A woman in her fifties stands behind a shiny granite
counter next to a cash register. She's arranging a display of
stamps commemorating the upcoming eclipse of the sun.
Mousy blond hair. Peach lipstick matching her peach cash-
mere sweater set. Glasses on a string around her neck. She
looks up. Augusta asks if Ollie still works there. The woman
carefully removes her glasses and rests them against her collarbone. She crinkles her nose.

"You mean Mr. Oliver Trunk?"

"I guess so, yeah."

"And what is this pertaining to, young lady?"

"It's private."

The woman swivels her head. Shouts over her shoulder in
a brassy voice that belies her delicate peach exterior.

"Oliver! There's a girl to see you."

Peaches stares at Augusta's auburn hair.

"That your natural color?"

Gus nods.

"Hmm. What do they call that color?"

"Red. And is yours natural?"

The woman's smile thins.

A little man moseys from the back office. He wears a wrinkled suit. No tie. Midsixties. Boyish face. Humor-tinged eyes. She likes him immediately.

"You the girl who's been looking for me her whole life?"

Peaches rolls her eyes and goes back to arranging the eclipse display.

"Can we speak in private, please?"

Gus doesn't want to stay out front. Near the large windows. In full view of anyone who might drive by. He invites her into his office with a sweep of his arm.

"Oliver Trunk at your service. How can I help, my dear?"

She's glad he's not the touchy-feely type. He keeps his distance, leaves the door open a crack. A gentleman. All business.

"My name's Augusta Monet."

She reaches out to shake his hand. He seems taken aback. Maybe he's not used to young women shaking hands. But it's only for a second. Then he takes her hand and shakes it warmly.

"Well, it is nice to meet you, Miss Monet."

Gus tells him about her mother. Then about Manny. Then Gracie and the bank drafts. He'd heard what happened to his old friend, Manny. Nodding before she even finishes.

"So Gracie did come to see you with the bank drafts?"

"Manny sent her directly over. Knew I'd take care of her."

Gus respects the bond the two men clearly share. Something about Manny and Ollie brings to mind how she imagines her father might have been. A good man. A man of integrity who would never betray a trust when it was given to him to hold on to. Gracie put her faith in these two men and they stayed true, and quiet. And yet, for some reason, they both seem to trust Augusta.

"Can you tell me what happened when she came in?"

"Gracie Halladay. She brought to mind a wee bird. Twitchy. She was uncomfortable in her own body. Like she had an itch needed scratching, only she couldn't get at it. Despite being nervy, she was a strong-minded little waif. She knew what she wanted and wasn't leaving till it was done. She had that stack of envelopes. Manny had called to let me know she was coming. She wouldn't let go of them. She wanted them sent by registered mail, each and every one. Signature required so as to make sure they got in the right hands, you know. She had all thirty-four names and most of the addresses written on a piece of paper and she had notepaper that she wanted to put in the envelopes, along with the bank drafts Manny mentioned. We had to look up a few addresses and postal codes in the registry. Easy enough. I addressed them all for her and she double-checked and affixed the postage to each envelope herself. Then she sat right over there at that corner table, wrote something on those pieces of notepaper, and sealed each one herself. At one point she asked me for scissors. I left her alone to get things how she wanted them and that was that. The letters went out that day."

Gus looks over at the small wooden table in the corner. It's still there. She can picture Gracie hunched over the table, dark hair hiding her face, as she carefully tends to each envelope.

"You didn't see the bank drafts or the notes?"

"None of my business. Miss Halladay paid the postage and fees in cash. Then she sat in the lobby until the depot truck came and took them away. She said she needed to see them go with her own eyes. She even gave a little wave when the truck left. Not sure if she was waving at the driver or the letters. Like I said. Twitchy.

"I promised her I'd keep track of the letters myself to make sure they got where she wanted them to go. I told her I'd let her know every time one of them was signed for and delivered. She didn't want the names of the people kept on record anywhere. I told her I'd keep a list of names locked up in my safe until they were all checked off and then I'd burn it. That seemed to satisfy her. Even though she died the next day, God rest her soul, I still kept track. I still checked off each name on that list as I got confirmation that it'd reached its destination. It was my sworn promise to do so. My postmaster's creed. Neither snow nor rain nor heat nor gloom of night. Swift completion. That kind of thing. And you know what else? Every one of those letters got delivered. All but one."

He leans toward a safe in the corner of his office, turns the combination, and opens it. He pulls out a clipboard holding a list and lays it on his desk. He looks at it. Augusta sees that it's a list of names with checkmarks next to each one. Even upside-down, she catches a glimpse of the names at the top of the list and recognizes them. James and Alison Pratt. Ollie picks up the clipboard and scans the list.

"Thirty-four and only one came back a few weeks later. Marked return to sender. I've kept that one in my safe going on five years now."

He slides an envelope out from under the list and places it on the desk, facedown.

"Just in case I ever tracked down the person she meant it for. Like I said, I promised her. It wouldn't have been right to toss it, or worse, open it. Against the law to open someone else's mail. It says so in the Canada Post Corporation Act. I never did find that last person. Not until today, when she walked right into my post office."

The blood rushes from Augusta's brain. He hands her the letter. Gus doesn't take it at first because she's not sure why he's handing it to her. She looks around for the person who must have walked in before her.

"It's you. You're the last one. See?"

Ollie's smiling and waving the envelope closer to her.

"I found you. Or I suppose, more accurately, you found me."

Augusta takes the envelope. More out of politeness than a desire to touch it. She still doesn't understand what he's telling her or why he's handing it to her. She turns it over and looks at the front of the envelope.

It's postmarked March 31, 2013. There's a stamp across the envelope. *Return to sender. No forwarding address.* Under the stamp is the address where she used to live with her mother. Their last known address. 95 Hilda Street. It was never changed or updated because her mother died and no one thought to forward her mail to Rose's house.

The envelope is addressed to *Miss Augusta Monet.*

Augusta hovers somewhere between the linoleum floor below Ollie's desk and the quivering branches of a birch tree just outside his window. She floats there, unable to be where she is. Ollie clears his throat to bring her back to earth.

"You did reside at 95 Hilda Street at one time, I presume?"

"Yes, with my mother."

"We couldn't find an address for an Augusta Monet at the time, but we did find one for Shannon Monet. Gracie said that was your mother so we sent it there, hoping your father and you still lived there. Turns out it was an old listing."

Augusta stares at the envelope. Oliver Trunk puts on his official voice.

"Miss Monet, it's my sworn duty as a member of Canada Post to follow the letter of the law so before I can let you walk out of here with that envelope, have you got any ID?"

Gus doesn't remember showing Ollie her ID or watching him check her name off the list or walking out of his office or getting into the Buick. Time gets compressed when the past and present collide. Gus sits in the car with the sealed envelope lying on the passenger seat next to her. A girl on a red bike rides past down the sidewalk, the wheels of her bike sounding *click, click, click*, as the plastic tailings attached to the rims whip around in circles. A sound she knows. A blue truck drives by. A color she remembers. A cat skitters under a black car parked next to a bright yellow fire hydrant. The world has become overexposed and mind-numbingly loud. She can't catch her breath. She glances in the rearview mirror, then up and down the street. She doesn't know this town. This block. This curb. She needs to get out of here. Now.

THE WINDOWS ROLLED DOWN, HAIR WHIPPING AT HER FACE, Augusta starts to calm down as she drives faster. Levi sticks his head out the back window. Cruising down the highway, her breathing returns to normal as she absorbs the enormity of what's just happened.

At this very moment, she is sitting next to an envelope.

An envelope addressed to her from the ballerina in the Polaroid.

From Gracie Halladay to Augusta Monet.

A correspondence that inexplicably reached across time and landed next to her on the seat of her great-grandmother's rusty Buick.

A letter from a ghost.

33

STU

༄

THE SKY IS A WHITE SOUP. AUGUSTA STEPS TO THE EDGE OF the black lava crater. Levi is on the far side. She hollers at him to stay back. His tail wags. He steps into the liquid surface, paws sinking. She waves her arms frantically. He jumps back. Suddenly, she's sinking too. In seconds, the muck is at her knees. Levi barks as the black sludge sucks her in deeper. She's up to her waist, then her chest. The more she struggles, the faster she sinks. Then someone grabs her arm at the elbow. Grips tight. She turns. It's a child. Gracie Halladay. Dressed in a ballet tutu. She's trying hard to pull Gus out, only she's not strong enough. She has to let go. Gus is swallowed by the warm slurry. The only sound she can hear as she goes under is Levi barking.

Augusta gasps for air as she's sucked out of the darkness and into the motel room. She's lying on her bed. Fully clothed. She tries to shake off the fog of the nightmare. Her eyes are blinded by the bright morning light streaming in through the

door. Then the barking starts up again. In the distance. It's Levi.
There's a squeal of tires on pavement. Her brain snaps to attention. The door's open. Levi's outside. Gus jumps out of bed
and stumbles out the door and into the courtyard. She scans
the parking lot. Across the street, Levi dashes into oncoming
traffic. Before she can open her mouth to scream for him to
stop, she spots Stu Lashey running into traffic, waving his arms
at oncoming cars. Horns blare. He's wearing a police uniform.
He holds out both hands to the cars. They screech and stop.
Levi makes it across, scuttling over to Gus, wagging his tail and
panting. Stu waves the traffic on then jogs over to them, sweating and wide-eyed. Gus kneels and embraces Levi as he licks
her chin. Tears in her eyes, she looks up at Stu, who blurts out
the obvious.

"Your pup almost got hit."

"How the fuck did he get out?"

"No idea, I just saw him bolt across the street."

"I was asleep."

"You left your door open."

Gus flushes.

"You saved Levi."

"All in a day's work, ma'am."

He salutes. She realizes Stanton hasn't called him off yet.

"And you're here because?"

She's almost glad he's still tailing her since it looks like
someone else is too.

"You left me a message. Said you wanted to talk."

The wheels in her brain slowly rewind. She found his number. Called him late last night. Asked to meet in the morning.

Then everything before that comes rushing back.

Perth. Ollie and the envelope. She remembers driving back to Ottawa. Back to the motel where she sat outside on the metal chair by her door until midnight, under the green glow of the overhead lights. The envelope from Gracie in her lap. Levi lying at her feet on the cool pavement. Finally mustering the courage to open the envelope. Inside she found a bank draft wrapped in a note. A lock of black hair fell into her lap. A token. Like how a mother keeps a lock of her newborn's hair. A strange gesture, but Augusta understood it. Gracie wanted to include something of herself in the envelope.

Gus removed the note from around the certified bank draft. Then she flipped it over. Stunned by what she saw there. The draft was made out to cash in the amount of five million dollars. She looked closer. Squinted to make sure she wasn't miscounting the zeroes or misconstruing the words printed on the front. Nope. She wasn't. Five million bucks. She shoved the bank draft in the back pocket of her jeans and looked around to make sure no one was watching her.

The motel parking lot was empty. Dull buzzings emanated from the air conditioner units in each window. A faltering breeze circled the motel courtyard. It lifted a stray lid from a discarded takeout cup and danced it across the pavement, then flitted it into the air and spirited it away into the night.

Gus opened the note. She could feel Gracie's warm breath on her face as she stared at the childlike handwriting scrawled across the paper. Gracie's fingers touched this paper. Her words were chosen carefully. Written slowly. Smudged by her hand as it grazed the ink. Words written five years ago in the corner table at the post office. A dispatch from the past.

Dear Augusta,

I hope this money helps you to not be sad. It is because of me that your ma is dead. She was nice to me and they killed her. I would have stopped them but I didn't know how.

Yours,
Gracie

There's a P.S. at the bottom of the note.

Don't tell anybody about the money or he will come
for it.

Gus stared at the words. One phrase in particular. She read it over and over. Her heart thudding across it like a record skipping.

They killed her. They killed her. They killed her.

The meaning of those three words sank deep into her soul as the world around her altered. The pavement warped. The green lights glowed hot. The cool metal chair turned her skin to gooseflesh as a terrible truth materialized.

"You okay?"

Gus snaps back to the present. Constable Lashey is crouched down, stroking Levi's belly. Gus rubs her eyes. Her stomach rumbles and she decides they need to have a chat.

"You hungry?"

"Always."

She showers while he calls work to tell them he's running late. They walk a few blocks down to a burger joint called The Works. They tie Levi to a bench outside where they can see him and they grab a table at the window. Order burgers, fries, and coffee for breakfast. Sitting across from him, she's suddenly struck by the fact that he's not wearing his usual undercover getup.

"What's with the uniform?"

"Lieutenant Stanton reassigned me to patrol. I'm officially off the case of Augusta Monet, and company."

He nods toward Levi. Then he blushes ever so slightly.

"So since I'm not tailing you anymore, I think that means you call me Stu."

"Stu it is."

She looks at him. Their eyes meet. She knows he likes her. She goes for it.

"I need you to get me a copy of the accident report. My mother's accident."

He doesn't say anything. She keeps going.

"I know Rory was there when my mom's car went into the lake."

"He told you that?"

"Yeah. And I saw him there. I must have."

"You were there?"

"I think so. Unless I just dreamed it."

She likes that he doesn't smirk or roll his eyes. Let's her find her way. Gives her space to tell him as much or as little as she wants.

"Listen, Stu. Rory was there when my mom died. And I know for a fact that he's done stuff in the past that could get him in deep trouble. Bottom line, he's no innocent bystander."

Stu fiddles with one of his starched cuffs. He seems uncomfortable in the stiff uniform. He looks up at her.

"I'm on thin ice with Stanton as it is. I could lose my job."

Their food arrives. Gus is suddenly ravenous. She takes a huge bite, barely chews, then bites off another hunk of hamburger. Real food. It's been weeks since she's had food that wasn't either microwaved or eaten straight out of a box or can. She glances out the window at Levi. He's staring at her burger and licking his lips. Hopeful and loyal. She wishes she could trust people as much as she does that dog. Maybe she has to try. Lashey did save Levi's life. She leans in.

"I got a note from Gracie Halladay."

"Who?"

"A dead girl. She died in the Elgin fire."

"Weird." Stu rubs his chin.

"You can't tell anyone. Not Stanton, no one."

She takes the note from her satchel and reads it to him. Paraphrasing a little to leave out the part about the money.

"'Dear Augusta, I hope you are not too sad. It is because of me that your ma is dead. She was nice to me and they killed her. I would have stopped them but I didn't know how. Yours, Gracie.'"

"Holy shit."

That's all he says but it's not his words. It's in the way his eyes flicker with recognition. He knows the words tell a terrible truth. Gus decides to tell him everything.

Almost everything.

About how she suspects it was Rory and his friend Dez who raped June when they were teenagers. How Shannon tried to watch out for Gracie when June died. How Desmond Oaks is Gracie's father. How June, Gracie, and a missing kid named Henry were all connected by evidence her mother left for her. And how, even though it's likely Shannon never intended it, that evidence holds the secret to her own death. Last but not least, Gus tells him that the note Gracie sent her five years ago confirms her mother's death was no accident. She was murdered.

Stu listens. No comments about her being in over her head. He just listens. Relief washes over Gus with every word. It feels good to talk this out. Feels good to say out loud that her mother didn't kill herself. Shannon didn't choose to leave her all alone in the world. Someone took her from Gus when she was just eight years old. And Stu is going to help her find out who those someones are.

"If this Gracie person is dead, how'd she leave you a note?"

"It's been in an envelope at a post office in Perth for the past five years. Fluke, really."

"Just a note, that's all?"

She stuffs the note back into her satchel. That's when she remembers the five-million-dollar bank draft, made out to cash, that's tucked in her back pocket. She'll tell him about that later. For now, she'll follow Gracie's instruction to not tell anybody about the money.

"And a lock of hair."

He grimaces. "She says they killed her. So who's they?"

"That's what we're going to find out."

"We?"

She smiles, takes a bite of her burger, then stuffs a handful of fries in her mouth. Ketchup drips down her T-shirt. He dabs the corner of his paper napkin in one of the water glasses on the table and hands it to her. She looks down. Flushes. Takes the napkin. The server tops up their coffees and asks Stu

if everything's okay with his burger. He hasn't touched his.
He nods toward Gus and smiles.

"Just distracted."

Gus looks up. Cheeks bulging with fries. The server winks.

"Can I get you two lovebirds anything else?"

"No thanks. We're good."

"Pay at the counter when you're ready."

She places the bill on the table. Once she's out of earshot,
Stu leans in closer.

"I'll look into the report."

"You're the best. Oh, and while you're at it, see what you
can find on a Tommy Oaks?"

"Who?"

"See if he's in the system. Maybe Thomas or Tom Oaks.
Desmond's brother."

She begins to pick at his fries now that hers are all done.

"You know if I do all this, it makes me your accomplice."

She blushes. He brings on the dimples and she giggles like
a schoolgirl.

"You gonna eat that?"

He pushes his plate over to her side of the table. She chows
down on his burger. Between chews she remembers one more
tidbit.

"I'm pretty sure Kep Halladay had at least one cop on his
payroll back then so be careful. They could still be around.
Might not want the past biting them in the ass."

His phone buzzes. Stu glances at it then grabs the bill off
the table and checks his watch. He holds up his phone.

"Work. I should really get going or I'll end up on traffic
duty."

She nods toward two uniformed cops sitting in a far booth. "We've been seen together so be careful."

She's only half kidding.

"No worries. They're cool."

She continues eating. Stu walks to the cash register and pays the bill. He stops to chat with the other cops for a moment. His back is to her so she can't hear what he's saying. One of the cops says something about it all being good. Then Stu heads out, hip-checking the door and giving Levi a pet on the top of the head before strolling down the sidewalk. The server clears Augusta's plate, leaving Stu's for Gus to finish. They both watch as Stu walks away.

"Nothing like a man in uniform. He your guy?"

"Hope so."

The server smiles and walks away. Gus folds the rest of Stu's burger inside a paper napkin for Levi. The two cops wink at her as she leaves and she's pretty sure Stu made up some story about them being on a date and not to tell anyone since he's supposed to be working. Part of her feels like they were on a date. She likes the feeling.

As Gus and Levi walk back down Richmond toward the motel, she offers Levi tiny morsels of the patty in the palm of her hand. Trying to teach him.

"Gentle."

Levi grabs the last morsel from her hand, nipping her palm. He gobbles it down. She shakes her head, about to scold the dog when she spots the door to her motel room standing open. They cross the parking lot, passing by the office. Hubble, the manager, emerges. Hands on wide hips.

"Your uncles came by."

Hubble isn't making eye contact. Something's up.

"Uncle Rory?"

"Didn't tell me their names. They said they wanted to wait in your room on account of the one's skin condition."

Right away she knows who that was. Dez. Gus stares at the woman.

"So you just let them in."

"Like I had a choice. One was a cop. Wearing short pants, mind you, but a cop."

"Did they have a warrant?"

Gus barks the question like she's starring in a police drama. Hubble shrugs.

"How'd your uncle get so burned up, anyways?"

Gus turns her back on Hubble and heads to her room.

It's trashed. Hubble is right behind her.

"How was I s'pose to know you had crazy kin?"

Gus drags Levi inside and shuts the door in Hubble's face. But she can still hear the woman shouting outside and banging on the door.

"Housekeeping is not dealing with that mess. And your security deposit is toast."

Gus ignores her. The minibar has been toppled and emptied. The bed flipped over. The drawers tossed from the dresser. Her trunk tipped over, half-open. Clothes everywhere. Her so-called uncles were looking for something. It has to be the bank draft. She flashes to the P.S. on Gracie's note.

Don't tell anybody about the money or he will come for it.

Only no one knows about the bank draft. No one but a dead girl and a dog. She stares at Levi. He perks his ears as if to say, *Wasn't me.* Ollie? He'd take it to his grave. Gus thought she was being sneaky, but maybe she was followed to Perth.

She closes her eyes. She can see herself walking to the Buick outside the post office. As she gets into her car a truck passes. A girl rides by on a red bike. A car with tinted windows is parked across the street near a bright yellow fire hydrant.

A black Impala. Shit.

She opens her eyes. She saw everything, but her mind was whirling so much she wasn't thinking clearly. It didn't register. It was right in front of her. The same Impala that ran her car off the road.

Snapshots begin to form a montage of images in her brain. A black car parked at the shady end of the parking lot of Dez's apartment. A black car knocking into her bumper on the high-way. A black car under a tarp in Rory's garage at the back of his property. A stakeout car. A getaway car. A decoy. Maybe she's seen too many old movies, but she's sure it's the one that's been following her this whole time. She caught a glimpse of the license plate from the ditch when she was run off the road. An A and a V. Gus checks her phone for the photo she took of the car in Rory's garage. The license plate is clearly visible. AVMN 618. Same car she saw in Perth.

One in short pants. One with a skin condition.

Rory and Dez.

Her uncles.

Ollie. Fuck.

A quick phone call to the Perth post office and Augusta's worst fears are confirmed. It *was* Ollie who spilled the beans about the bank draft. Peaches doesn't tell her this outright, but

Gus knows it has to be true when she hears the horrific details that unfolded after her visit with Ollie the day before.

Peaches clocked out like usual at five. Oliver was fine when she left. He said he'd lock up. Peaches found him this morning. He had almost bled to death. Someone had cut off some of his fingers with a pair of pruning shears. All except one. Whoever did it got him to open the safe. Peaches blurts out things she's likely been told not to talk about, but she doesn't seem to be in control of herself. Her voice is a high-pitched whine that comes in snotty heaving waves.

"Did they get the list before he destroyed it?"

Before Peaches can answer, someone tells her to hang up. Likely one of the investigators on the scene. She does and the phone goes dead.

Gus trembles uncontrollably. She feels responsible. She led them right to Ollie. He's been horribly mutilated and it's all her fault. Ollie, Renata, Manny. She's played with these people's safety, with their very lives. Thought she was being clever. Elusive. Careful. But she was really just completely out of her league. Every road she's traveled, every person she's visited, they've been watching and following.

And these uncles of hers: an invalid and an overweight truant officer. It seems ridiculous. Responsible for assault and mutilation? Doesn't add up. Then she remembers what that creepy neighbor at Desmond's apartment building said. Dez has a younger brother. Tommy. Maybe he's their grease monkey.

Gus rights her bed and sits down. She calls Stu, hoping he's found something on Tommy. No answer. She doesn't leave a message. Not even sure what she would say. She feels a wave of dread wash over her. Her mind bounces in a million directions. What about Annalee and Todd? She's dragged Stu into this mess too, and now he's in danger. She calls him back and leaves a message.

"Call me when you get this. I just want to be sure you're okay."

She hangs up. Levi jumps up beside her. She looks at him.

"Some other people might be in danger, Levi. And I have to warn them."

Next she calls the Home Hardware where Todd works. Relieved when he comes to the phone. Alive and well. Gus tells him she was just checking on him. Warns him to watch his back. Strange things have been happening to the people she's been speaking to lately. He says he will. Tells her to watch hers too. She does the same with Annalee, who also appears to be safe and sound. Maybe Gus was successful in losing the tail when she went out to Kanata. Maybe they haven't been watching her 24/7 and they didn't see her talking to Todd or Annalee. But poor Ollie wasn't so lucky.

Gus grabs her satchel and car keys. Thankful she hid Rose's gun in the glove compartment of the Buick or they would have found it. She's also still got Rose's cash. Shoved in the wheel well. Good thing Hubble didn't let them rifle through her car too. Gus and Levi walk over to the motel office and she taps Hubble's bell.

"I told you it's up to you to clean up that mess."

Gus ignores her.

"My uncles. Were there two or three of them?"

"You don't know how many uncles you have?"

"Please. How many men did you let inside my room?"

"Two. Now we done with the twenty questions?"

Gus turns, crosses the parking lot, and she and Levi jump in the Buick.

Destination Elgin.

There's someone else she needs to warn.

34

ALISON

✑

Gus circles several blocks, takes a couple of narrow back alleys, waits behind a garage, then takes a detour through a grocery store loading zone. She almost gets lost, but eventually weaves her way through neighborhoods she's never seen before and finds a sign for the 417. She hops on the highway, positive no one's following her this time.

Levi by her side on the front seat, they head south toward Elgin.

Once she hits the 416 south, she feels like she can breathe now that she's out of the city. Reassured by the clear blue sky and open spaces. By a sporadic herd of sheep dotting a hillside. By cows grazing under shady oaks. By winding rows of wood rail fencing and vast hayfields peppered with plastic-wrapped bales that look like giant marshmallows.

Two hours later, Augusta is turning onto the gravel drive-way beside a long white picket fence that surrounds the Pratt homestead. It was easy to find. She drove up and down the roads bordering the land James said was his until she found a mailbox marked J&A Pratt.

There's a large blue-and-white farmhouse at the end of the driveway. A truck is parked beside the house. Two black horses graze in the adjacent field. Chickens mill about the dirt yard. A large barn is set back from the house. A woman comes out onto the front porch. Shields her eyes from the midday sun.

Gus gives her a little wave, stops the car, and gets out.

James Pratt emerges from the barn leading a white horse by the reins. Jocko. He spots her, looks over at his wife who is descending the front steps. The couple meet between the house and barn. Gus approaches them.

"This is the girl I told you about. The one asking about Elgin."

"I was passing by and saw your name on the mailbox."

The woman offers Gus her hand, after drying it on the dishrag tucked in the front of her apron.

"Name's Alison. And you've already met my husband, Jim." Alison has farm girl written all over her sun-spotted face.

"Augusta Monet."

"Pretty name. Czech?"

"Georgian."

"Exotic. Georgia's near Turkey, right? I'm a bit of a geography buff. It helps with the Sunday crosswords."

"No, the state."

Jocko blows air from his nose. Jim does too. Then he mumbles, "Just passing by, eh? There's nothing down that road but a dead town. Like I told you."

Levi barks from the car. Alison peeks around Gus.

"Better let that one out before he does his business all over your front seat."

The second Gus opens the door, Levi takes off like a shot after the chickens. They flutter away, some landing on fence posts, others on a wagon out of Levi's reach. He barks. Circles. Then sits and waits.

"Was there some reason you came by, dear?"

Gus doesn't want to scare them. Alison links her arm inside her husband's. Jim is itching to get on with his chores. Jocko stomps one foot.

"You've lived here a long time?"

Alison looks at Jim and pulls him a little closer.

"Oh, generations. You looking to move to the area?"

"No. I was just curious if this was always your address. Maybe you had a post office box."

Jim pipes in. "You said yourself you saw the mailbox, so I think you've answered your own question."

"I'm sorry. Yes, I did say that."

Jim's getting impatient. "You looking to send us a Christmas card or something, young lady?"

Alison slaps Jim's arm lightly and gives him a scolding pout. "Manners, Jim. Let the girl speak."

Gus gets to the point. "Did you happen to get an envelope from Gracie Halladay a few years back? Maybe five years ago?"

Her question strikes a nerve. Both their faces freeze in half smiles. They give each other sideways glances. Jim fields this one.

"Don't see how that's your business."

"Now, Jim, be nice."

Alison pulls on his arm. Seems to be her way of keeping him in check. Like he does with Jocko's reins. Gus feels she owes them some clarity.

"I only ask because she sent me one too. With a lock of hair."

Gus skirts around the bank draft for now. Still not sure who to trust.

The horse dances. James holds the reins tighter. Still suspicious.

"If she had, you wouldn't be telling us about it."

"And if she hadn't, you wouldn't know I shouldn't be telling you."

Alison tries not to smile. She whispers to her husband, "She's got you there, Jim."

"I got a fox to roust. Go on then and tell her what you like, Allie. I know there's no stopping you."

James hikes himself into the saddle with incredible ease for a big man. He clicks his tongue, then horse and rider gallop down the lane and across the field. Alison winks at Gus. "Tea?"

Ten minutes later, Gus is sitting in the couple's country kitchen sipping Earl Grey tea from a gold-rimmed china teacup. Gus feels completely at home sitting at the large oak table near the hearth. Reminds her of Rose's kitchen. An earthy breeze flows in through the screen door. The sharp smell of yeast floats out from underneath a tea towel covering a bowl of dough set to rise in the window. Alison gives Levi a large bone to gnaw on. At first he's not sure what to make of it, but soon he discovers the sweet marrow bulging from one end and sucks on it like a baby with a bottle.

Alison tells Augusta about the envelope from Gracie Halladay. The note and the lock of black hair. Alison signed for it herself. Almost fell over when she saw the bank draft for five million dollars. The note said it was for royalties owed to them by her grandfather. That they were to tell no one. They never did. Until now.

Gus tells Alison that she got a bank draft too. Same amount. Alison smiles. She figured as much. Then Gus tells Alison about her mother's death, about boarding school and inheriting her great-grandmother's house and about finding the evidence from Shannon's wall.

They drain a pot of tea and eat an entire tin of homemade oatmeal cookies.

"Jim and I both grew up in the county. We've lived on this land our entire marriage. Jim took over the eastern ridge of his father's farm thirty-five years ago. Then when his father died, the whole farm was ours. Hard work, long hours, raised a family. They were prosperous years till the drought came. It lasted five summers and sent us deep into debt along with every other farmer within a hundred miles. Kep Halladay offered us a lifeline. A way to keep the land that had been in Jim's family for generations. He offered a pretty penny too. Enough to pay off all our debts, put in a fancy irrigation system, and get things up and running again. All he wanted were the mineral rights. It seemed like the only way to save the farm. And as far as we knew, there wasn't any value in those rights, so we sold them. Thirty-two other farmers took the same offer we did from Halladay."

As Alison shares her story, an image from Shannon's wall fills Augusta's head. The deed of trust. The one with the thirty-three names on one side and Kep Halladay's on the other. James Pratt's signature likely among them.

Alison recounts how a few months after signing away the rights, Kep Halladay hit pay dirt. Discovered a vein of shale, inked a deal with the gas company, and the fracking started.

Gus can see the headline from the newspaper clipping.

"Prominent Tycoon Inks Landmark Mineral Rights Deal."

Alison gets a little choked up when she talks about how the groundwater became contaminated. How their fields went fallow within a year and the debts started mounting again when the farm yielded not one ear of edible corn that year. How James had to get a job at the Tim Hortons on the 401. They took out a second mortgage. Alison picked up a few grave-yard shifts at the chocolate factory in Smiths Falls. They hung on for close to a decade. The bank was about to foreclose.

Then the envelope arrived from Gracie Halladay.

"Like pennies from heaven. Millions of them."

Jim and Alison told folks her great-uncle had passed away in England and left them a fortune. They put the money in a bank in Whitby. Far enough away from the county so as to not raise any eyebrows. They paid off both mortgages. Put a new roof on the house. Paid for a major sanitization proj-ect to clean up the fields and well water around their house. Couldn't get the farm back up and running, though. That was too big a clean-up job. But what they did manage to decon-taminate meant they could live in their house safely with a few animals. Run a hobby farm. Small operation. They even took their first holiday. To Tuscany.

"We still pinch ourselves for how it all worked out."

Then Alison gives Augusta her take on why Gracie did what she did.

"That girl was righting wrongs. Most of us had our suspicions that Halladay knew the mineral rights were worth more than what he paid for them, but there was no proof. It was just too big a coincidence. Him buying the rights, then he finds the shale right after. None of the thirty-three ever talked about it. Most had to just up and walk away. Leave their dead fields where they lay. Board up their farmhouses. Move in with relatives. We heard some of them retired to greener pastures some years later. Florida. Arizona. I'm guessing Gracie Halladay took the money her granddaddy made off our land and gave it back to each and every one of us. Poor sweet thing."

James Pratt ambles in through the back door as Alison finishes talking. He wipes sweat from his brow and downs a big glass of water before adding his two cents.

"Gracie Halladay was cursed the day she was born into that family. The whole lot of them lived under a dark shadow that goes all the way back to the days of old Jacob. Even that godforsaken house he built way up on that hill. The place is cursed. Now look at it. Left to rot."

Gus doesn't understand.

"Didn't it burn down in the fire?"

"Not so much as seared by a stray ember."

Alison pipes in. "It's too far outside town. Up on Lockheath Hill just beyond the cemetery. Quite the mansion. It overlooks the entire valley. That was the idea old Jacob had when he chose the spot. He wanted to look down on the common folk."

Gus kicks herself. She already knew Halladay House was outside Elgin. Renata told her as much. Kep was sent to live there after his parents died. With his grandfather in a mansion outside town.

Augusta pulls her pen and notebook from her satchel. Poised to write. "Where exactly is it?"

"Oh, you can't get to it anymore, dear. It's inside the zone."

Gus nods at Alison. Knowing she'll figure it out later. First she's got to tell them why she's really come to see them.

"Someone has the list."

They both stare at her. Clearly they don't know about the list.

"There's a list of names. The postmaster kept it. A list of the people Gracie sent letters to. A list of people who got those bank drafts."

They look at each other. Clearly understanding this is serious. James puts his arm around his wife.

"What would someone want with this list?"

"You should leave. These people are dangerous. They cut off a man's fingers for that list. I think they want the money. All of it. I've been investigating and I think one of them is Gracie's real father. My guess is he thinks the money rightfully belongs to him."

Alison looks confused. "That Todd lad?"

"No. Someone far more evil."

Alison gives her husband a knowing nod and then busies herself with clearing away the empty teacups. Jim sits across from Gus.

"We're staying put."

"But you can't."

"It's our land. Our home."

Alison chimes in without looking up from the sink. "We got a rifle or two."

Gus can tell from the look on Jim's face that they've spent

their whole lives fighting to stay on this land. They've poured their blood and sweat and tears into this piece of dirt. They've raised their children here. And they won't be scared off by threats or thugs. As Jim said, this is their home. It's sacred ground.

Gus rises from the kitchen table. She smiles and thanks Alison for the tea and cookies and for sharing. But a question needles at her. One she's not sure anyone but Gracie can answer.

"Do you know why she left me money and not just the farmers on this list? The farmers Kep wronged."

Jim shrugs. Alison shakes her head, then a thought comes to her. "Perhaps you were wronged too."

They wish her well and tell her to be careful. She tells them the same. Jim and Alison watch from the front porch as Levi and Gus head for the Buick. Jim's arm around his wife. Alison calls out, "Don't get stuck in the mud or you'll never get out, honey."

Gus knows Alison means the mud in the driveway. But as she pulls away slowly, Alison's words follow her and take on new meaning. The muddy past has her in its grip. She comes to the end of their driveway and checks her rearview mirror. The couple are still on the porch watching her go. Gus turns left toward Ottawa. Right leads to the barricade. A dead end and the town of Elgin beyond. She knows she can't go that way with them watching.

Gus drives toward the highway and finds an abandoned barn about four miles up the road. She parks behind it and settles in for a nap. She'll wait there until dark. Drive back down the road. Past the Pratt homestead. Headlights off. Park in the lane under the willow and go in by foot.

Shouldn't be that hard to find it.

35

HALLADAY HOUSE

GUS RESTS HER CHIN ON THE BACK OF THE SEAT AND LOOKS at Levi. He's already snoring on his back, hind legs wide, eyes rolled back in his head. As the sun sets, the lavender fields turn a deep purple. Levi twitches as he dreams. Gray eyebrows gently lifting. Whiskers quivering. He's getting old. Sleeping more. Stumbling a little when he jumps in the car. Old bones weary. Joints stiff. Appetite waning. Gus has no idea how long dogs live. Her mother said every year of theirs was like seven of ours. So that would make him about eighty-four. An old man. Levi sighs as if he knows she's pondering his mortality.

Unable to sleep, Gus waits until she can barely make out the looming shadow of the barn against the night sky. She drives back toward the Pratts' farm. Slowly. Turns off the headlights. Passes their mailbox. The porch light glows yellow. The kitchen light is still on. The blue light of a television glimmers from another window.

Gus finds the dirt lane. Same spot under the weeping willow where she first parked when she met James Pratt on his horse. The day she first met Stu. She checks her phone. Six new messages. Stanton and Stu have both been calling. Rory must have given her number to Stanton. She leaves her phone on silent and grabs Rose's gun from the glove compartment. She checks the chamber. One bullet. Forgot to reload it. She puts it in her satchel. Levi wakes up.

The night sky is alive with stars. A full orange moon sits close to the horizon. Perfect. She checks her map. Remembering what Alison told her.

Up on Lockheath Hill just beyond the cemetery. It overlooks the entire valley.

She finds Lockheath Hill. It's a couple of miles due south. The willow is alive in the breeze. Gus emerges from its bows. Heads southwest. Levi ambles ahead, nose down.

Despite the moon lighting the way, the going isn't easy. The fields are thick with purple loosestrife. Gus wades through thigh deep. She reaches a barbed-wire fence strung across cedar posts. Launches herself over, cutting a knee and half falling into the grassy ditch on the other side. Levi squeezes through a gap by a post. Leaves a swath of golden hair hanging off the barbed wire. They follow an overgrown tractor path. The ground begins to rise. She knows she's close.

A stench hits her nostrils. Acidic but sugary. Reminds her of bathroom disinfectant used in cheap motels. She calls out to the dog. He's wandered off.

"Levi, come."

He bounds out of the dark. Rubs against her leg. She pets his head.

"Good boy. Now you stay close."

Gus can make out a small pond and some large metal piping glistening in the moonlight. She quickly grabs Levi's collar. He's a swimmer and that smell is definitely coming from the pond. They make their way up an incline. Once they're clear of the pond, she lets go of his collar. She looks up ahead and begins to walk up a hill. A looming shape rises on the horizon as they crest the ridge of the hill. A wide valley stretches out before them. On the far side atop a high knoll, backlit by a dark blue sky, she can see the mansion. Its peaked gables jutting skyward like fangs.

That has to be it. Halladay House.

Gus stares in awe. Levi looks ahead, then races toward it.

"Levi, wait."

He doesn't. She runs after him, the loosestrife lashing her shins. She loses sight of him in the deep grass, but she can hear him rustling through the weeds up ahead. Then nothing. In no time, she spots his shadow on the front steps of the house.

How did he get there so fast?

She races up the hill. Up the long driveway leading to the house. The place is boarded up. Gus climbs the rickety steps. Looks like no one's lived there for decades. She reaches out to grab Levi's collar, but he wiggles between her legs, heads down the steps, and runs around the side of the house. She gives up trying to catch him. It's become a game in his little brain. If she ignores him, he'll be back.

Gus approaches the front door. Spidery leafless vines drape across it like chains barring anyone from entering. It hasn't been opened in years. She spots a piece of metal at the door's center. Lifts the ivy. It's a door knocker in the shape of a lion's head. She reaches in her back pocket and pulls out her phone. Flips through the photos. Finds it. In the security image of Henry. Same brass knocker. As she suspected, the photo was taken right here.

Gus looks up at the porch ceiling. Trying to figure out the angle of the security camera that the image was taken from. Nothing but cobwebs. She turns, her back to the door. The view from the porch, even by moonlight, is breathtaking. She can see for miles. The valley below and more beyond. She's not positive but that might even be the outskirts of Elgin in the distance. It's hard to tell because there are no lights in the town.

The wind kicks up and dark clouds crowd the orange moon. The moody sky darkens. Shadows disappear and Gus is plunged into total darkness. Maybe hiking out to the middle of nowhere at night was a mistake. She might not be able to find her way back. She looks up at the sky. The clouds look thick and steadfast. The house creaks in the wind. Gus shudders. Bad things happened in this place. June died here. Henry disappeared here. And Kep. His dark energy radiates from the depths of this place.

Levi barks from behind the house. Three sharp barks. Then nothing.

"Levi."

Nothing.

"Levi."

Gus jumps off the steps and races around the porch toward the back of the house, keeping her hand along the siding to find her way in the dark.

"Levi, come!"

Nothing.

She stops. Something's wrong. She tries her angry voice. "Come here right now."

Not a sound.

Gus presses her body flat against the house, then creeps along the siding. Her mind reels with images of Dez's char-broiled face coming out of the darkness. Rory by his side. They kill her, dispose of her body, and no one ever finds her. Levi's probably already dead. And then they'll search her body and find the bank draft because she foolishly still has it tucked in her back pocket like it's nothing more than a pack of chewing gum.

Gus shakes off fear's tight grip. She contemplates turning and running in the direction of her car, but she can't bring herself to do it. To leave him behind. He's her dog. Her Levi. Gus reaches the back of the house. She steps away from the house into the backyard, groping in the dark like a blind person. She feels ridiculous and reckless and small and alone. She wants her dog.

The clouds part. The moon becomes a spotlight on the yard. Gus can make out shapes. Shed. Trellis. Low fence around a tangled garden. Then the smell hits her. Rotten garbage.

Out of nowhere, something knocks her square in the chest and she tumbles onto her back. It's Levi. He licks her face. Licorice breath.

"What have you gotten into, dog?"

She hugs him tight. Relieved to feel his warm furry body, but also aware that the clouds might close in again at any moment. Gus takes hold of his collar and pulls herself to her feet. She attaches his leash and drags him back the way she came. He doesn't want to leave. Likely found some disgusting garbage to eat and wants more.

"Let's get out of here while we still can."

They're down the front yard, away from Halladay House and partway across the valley when the clouds blacken the night again. But she's got her bearings now so they push forward. She wants to put some distance between them and that creepy house. Her mind twitches with thoughts of her mother being out here alone.

Then something completely unexpected happens.

The earth gives way under Augusta's feet and before she can figure out what's happening, the ground opens up and swallows her whole. Levi yelps and scrambles away in fear. Her feet hit bottom. She's standing neck-deep in a hole. Gus panics. She scratches at the earth to free herself. Levi circles and whines. She manages to grab hold of a root, then she kicks her way up and out. She's covered in dirt, more stunned than hurt. Levi licks Augusta's face and presses against her. She catches her breath, then gathers her wits and heads back to the car. She follows the landmarks she memorized. Barely able to make out the cluster of three dead elm trees, the rotten hay bale, the broken fence post third down from the lone pine. And finally, her willow where Rose's Buick sits waiting.

Something about being almost buried alive has shaken Gus to her core. But it's not fear that's been stirred up. It's a fresh sense of resolve that flows through her veins. Maybe it's adrenaline or maybe it's the fumes from the pond. Either way, she knows her work here isn't done just yet. She grabs the flashlight from the glove compartment and leaves the dog behind. Two things she should have done earlier. She cracks the window of the Buick and heads out. Levi settles down to sleep. He's tuckered from their hike to Halladay House and happy to be left in peace.

Gus starts to walk, feeling herself drawn there. Pulled as if by gravity or magnetism or maybe simply by a twenty-year-old's stupid curiosity. Whatever pulls her is a force beyond her control. And yet it's one she fully embraces as she lets herself be led by the hand of that eight-year-old child who just wants to walk beside her mother without fear, knowing all the world is a safe place and a mother can protect you from anything.

36

LOIS GREENAWAY'S DANCE ACADEMY

❧

As she gets closer, Gus can make out the distant out-line of the water tower on the edge of town. She turns the flashlight off each time the moon slips out from behind cloud cover. She can see the layout of the streets in her mind's eye. She enters from the east side, but instead of heading straight down Main toward ground zero, she takes a side street. Passes a hair salon and a small general store. A two-by-four has fallen away from the front door of the general store. It stands slightly ajar. She pries it open. Black soot gets sucked outside on the breeze, escaping its dark prison. Gus covers her mouth until the cloud scatters then shines the flashlight inside. Every nook and cranny is dusted black. Floor. Countertop. Cash register. Shelves. Looks like a scene from a black-and-white movie. Colorless. Abandoned.

Gus explores Elgin as the moon drops closer to the hori-zon. She peers into windows. Pulls open unlocked doors.

Wanders into a church, a pet store, an antique shop, a bowling alley. Even breaks into a few houses. Slowly the ghost town comes alive. She can see the people who lived there. Hear their voices. She can imagine how they moved through these streets. How they worked and lived, laughed and cried.

None of them came to clean up or salvage personal belongings. No one was allowed back. They went to the fair and never got to go home. Left behind their businesses, their homes, their best dresses, their silverware, their family photos. The county boarded up and barricaded the whole town. A red X was spray-painted across the doors of the buildings that remained standing. Those that didn't get burned to the ground. Checked and then left uninhabitable. Dredged inside and out with thick black ash.

But that wasn't why the residents stayed away. It was because of what they couldn't see. The poison. The danger. The toxic air. The air Gus is breathing right now. And when there's a strong southerly wind, the air Alison and James Pratt likely breathe too.

Gus realizes her feet have led her back to the building next to the mortuary. Lois Greenaway's Dance Academy. She tries the door but it's locked. Won't budge. Plan B. She wrenches the plywood from the front window. It's spongy with rot and comes away easily. She breaks the window and runs the flashlight along the ledge to clear the remaining shards. Holding the flashlight in her teeth, Gus hoists herself up, hikes one leg over then slips inside. It's dark. She turns on the flashlight. Surprised. There's barely any soot. Just a light dusting on the floor near the front door. The dance academy looks like it was just closed up for the day.

The beam illuminates a small lobby adjoining an office. Benches line either side. A nameplate is screwed to the office door. Engraved on it are the words *Lois Greenaway, Academy Director*. She peers in the office. Looks like Lois just popped out. Dregs of coffee congeal in the bottom of a mug on the desk. Forms are neatly stacked next to the mug. Multicolored file folders are arranged in dividers on a bookcase topped with trophies. Framed photographs of tiny dancers adorn the walls. Some pose in groups. Others alone. All of them stand next to their instructor, Lois Greenaway. A life displayed in photographs. In some she's in her twenties, then thirties, forties, fifties. Posing with her young protégées. Besides the slight crinkling at the corners of her eyes, Lois barely changes over the decades. Her waist stays trim. Her long brown hair remains styled the same way. Swept up into a chaotic nest on top of her head, fastened with long sticks as if her skull's been impaled. Her wide smile looks practiced and perfected, yet genuine. Thick rims of black mascara highlight her fake eyelashes. Ruby red lipstick rims her full lips. She's beautiful. She exudes enthusiasm. And her compassion and zest for life are evident in the lift of her chin, the flawlessness of her posture, and the simple gesture of a manicured hand resting lightly on the shoulder of a young dancer. Lois must have been a dancer herself. The wall in her office bears witness to a career dedicated to something she loved. Lois would have come back for these pictures if she hadn't died in the fire. Now, they're all that's left of her.

The dance academy's mail lies unopened in the inbox on her desk. Gus sits in Lois's chair. Opens drawers. Pens, elastics, thumbtacks, highlighters, packages of nylons, cough drops, and a flask of whiskey. She leafs through the mail. Mostly bills and invitations to dance recitals. But there is one handwritten letter addressed to Lois Greenaway from Lana Henning. Gus hesitates. Remembering how Ollie said it was illegal to open someone else's mail. Probably doesn't apply to someone who's dead. Besides. Breaking and entering. Trespassing. What's one more crime? She rips it open and reads.

Dear Lois,

I was sorry to hear in your last letter that you are still suffering with those terrible headaches. My dear sister, you really should check with your doctor to make sure the cancer hasn't come back. On that note, good news here on Roger's colonoscopy. All clear. How is Edgar's asthma? I'm sure his new inhaler is a blessing but I do wish you would leave that godforsaken town before it kills the both of you. Roger thinks you could start a dance studio here in Thunder Bay.

Oh and you'll never guess what happened to yours truly Friday. I won the bingo jackpot. Eighty-six dollars. Only that Margie Wilkins made a fuss and said my dauber wasn't regulation. Regulation, my ass. Whoever heard of such a thing. Jealous cow. She needs to mind her own beeswax.

The letter goes on. Detailing the minutiae of Lana's daily existence. A letter from a sister to a sister. The return address is 125 Cottonwood Crescent, Thunder Bay. Gus photographs the envelope then places the letter back in the inbox.

She continues snooping. Opens Lois's filing cabinet. Finds a collection of green, blue, pink, and purple folders. Each marked with a different girl's name. She finds a pink folder marked with the name Gracie Halladay. Inside is a photo.

Gracie's wearing the same pink tutu and butterfly wings as she was in the Polaroid on Shannon's wall. Only this one's taken against a photography studio backdrop.

Gus takes a few pictures on her phone of the file's contents. The photo of Gracie is attached to an application form to attend the dance academy. On the form, beside the question about *any allergies or medical conditions to be aware of,* Gracie's mother wrote *sensitive to much of life.* There's a complaint form in Gracie's file as well. Filled out anonymously.

> *The incident that occurred at Saturday morning's ballet class was inexcusable. Our daughters were traumatized. It is obvious to all of us that Gracie Halladay is a disturbed child who should be barred from attending any further classes. If you know what's good for your business, you will take immediate action. Otherwise, you will suffer the consequences.*

A threat. Dated March 17, 2002. From more than one parent, apparently.

The year of June's death.

Gus hears a noise outside. A wood board snaps as if someone stepped on it. She shuts off her flashlight and silently slips off the chair and under the desk. She hears a light thump on the floor, then glass crunching. Someone's come in through the window. Then silence. She waits. A lock clicks and a hinge whines. Footfalls crunch on the gravel outside. They get farther away until she can't hear them anymore.

Gus waits fifteen minutes before coming out from under the desk. She steps slowly into the lobby, gun in one hand, flashlight in the other. The dance academy door stands open.

The moonlight slants across the lobby floor. There's something lying near the doorway. A furry black lump. She clicks on the flashlight, inches closer, and leans in. It's a dead possum lying peacefully on its side. No blood, just dead. She notices there's a seam down its belly that's been sewn shut. She leaves it where it lies, stepping over the possum and slipping out the door. Coast looks clear. Time to get out of town.

Gus jogs back to the car. She's happy to see Levi's sleepy eyes peering up at her as she jumps into the driver's seat beside him. Gus locks the doors and pulls the Buick out from under the willow. She drives away from Elgin and Halladay House and whoever it was who left that dead animal in Lois Greenaway's Dance Academy lobby. Gus rolls past the Pratt place, headlights off, then a few miles up the road takes Highway 15. Levi nestles next to her as they float through the night toward the city that shimmers pale yellow on the horizon.

An hour and a half later, Gus pulls into the motel parking lot as the dark blue sky hovers on the edge of dawn. She's been up all night. She gathers her things as Levi slowly wakes. She opens the glove compartment to put the flashlight back inside. Something tumbles out. Lands on the floor. Gus picks it up. It's a small book. Wasn't there before. She examines it. A pink diary. Worn cover. Small tarnished silver lock.

She turns to Levi. He yawns.

Gus presses the clasp. The book opens. In the soft glow of daybreak, she reads the words written across the cover page.

She recognizes the childlike handwriting.

Diary of Gracie Anne Halladay.

37

POSSUM

ᘒ

GUS IS FAST ASLEEP AGAINST THE CAR WINDOW WHEN SOME-
one knocks lightly on the glass. She jolts awake. So does
Levi who was sleeping next to her. It's Stu Lashey. Levi jumps
to his feet and leaps at the window. Gus opens the car door.
Levi barrels across her lap and races past Stu to pee. Gus spots
the diary. It was under Levi. With Stu turned toward Levi,
she shoves the diary in the glove compartment. Then she gets
out of the car.

"Thank God you two are okay. The lady at the front desk
told me someone trashed your room. I was looking for you all
night. Thought something happened to you, Red."

"Went driving to clear my head."

"I called a million times."

"Oh, sorry. My phone died."

While Stu leans over to pet Levi, Gus reaches back inside
the car to grab her satchel. She quickly pulls the gun out of
her bag and shoves it under the driver's seat. If Stu sees it, he'll

worry. When she turns back, Levi is growling. Gus taps the top of his head and he stops and heads across the courtyard.

"Guess he's not happy about missing his supper. Sorry, old boy."

They head for her room. Sit out front together once she's fed Levi.

"Did you get the accident report?"

"I'm working on it. But I did get my hands on this."

Stu pulls a photograph from his jacket and hands it to her. It's a press photo. Kep Halladay and a teenage girl. Flanked by two boys. Rory Rump and Desmond Oaks. The girl is holding a trophy and wearing a sash. Harvest Queen. '94. Stu points to the girl.

"That's June Halladay."

Gus looks closer. She's never seen a picture of June. The girl is lovely. Blond like her father. Sweet smile. Blue eyes wide and innocent. Chin tucked as if shy, but eyes sparkling with confidence.

"I've got a friend in records. This was evidence in a sexual assault case in '94."

Sexual assault case? Gus realizes that June had indeed confessed her secret to someone other than Todd. And Todd likely never knew it.

"So it was them?"

"File said the girl withdrew the charges. But Rory was initially named as the accused."

"Not Dez? But the bank manager told me that Gracie said Dez was her father."

Stu shrugs.

"All I know is the file said Senator Kep Halladay was the

one who bailed him out. Not the team. Not his own family. The accuser's father. You said Halladay had a cop on his payroll. Well, the way I see it, it doesn't matter how many years go by, you're always gonna owe a debt like that. Sooner or later you gotta return the favor."

Augusta follows Stu's train of thought.

"You think my mother was the favor."

He doesn't answer.

"And Tommy Oaks. Anything?"

"Not yet."

Gus feels sick. They go inside. Levi is curled up in the corner. He grumbles when they enter. Gus shoots him a look, then softens.

"Sorry about him. He's still getting used to being away from Rose's. Misses her bed, I think."

Her room's a total mess. She can't deal with any of it right now. Gus ponders their conversation. She doesn't want to believe what her gut is telling her. Her head spins, and her stomach lurches.

Stu tries to help her clean up a little, but she's exhausted. Gus nearly throws up. She's been up all night and hasn't eaten since yesterday. Stu makes her a cup of chicken noodle soup and puts her to bed. He eventually stretches out beside her, on top of the covers, while she buries her head under them. He watches TV. The comforting hum of a hockey game blankets the room. The buzzer sounds. The crowd chants. The commentator shouts. The cheering fades as she drifts off to sleep.

MOONLIGHT SLANTS THROUGH A GAP IN THE THICK BLACKOUT curtains of the motel room. Gus wakes, hot and stiff-necked.

Stu's asleep beside her. She slips out of bed. Still wearing yesterday's clothes. Or maybe today's. She's not sure what day it is. Her room is a slightly neater mess. Stu did his best. Sweet of him to stay. She feels bad for what she's about to do. He's been kind and helpful. But she needs him here in Ottawa. Needs that accident report.

She pulls a hoodie over her T-shirt, puts on her jean jacket, then grabs her satchel from the bathroom. Doesn't remember how it got there. Doesn't remember much about the past few hours or how it turned to night so quickly. Gus finds her notebook and pen in the bottom of her bag. Scribbles a note for Stu. Brushes her teeth, then steps over Levi as she heads for the door. The dog stirs, lifts his head, and looks at her. He lets out a small whine. She shushes him, and he huffs through his nostrils, lowers his chin, and pouts. Stu hasn't moved. She leaves the note on the dresser.

Back in a couple of days. Please keep an eye on Levi for me. One cup of kibble, twice a day. Sorry about this, but I'll explain when I get back. Red.

She slips out the door and drives to the bus terminal. Thunder Bay is too far for a road trip, plus she's got some reading to do on the way. After finding a spot in the paid parking lot of the Catherine Street terminal, Gus grabs Gracie's diary from the glove compartment and some cash from the trunk. Leaves the gun under the seat, knowing it's probably not a great idea to travel armed.

Nestled in a seat at the back of the bus by the window, Augusta Monet hurtles out of town, west toward Toronto, then all the way around Georgian Bay and along the shore of Lake Superior to Thunder Bay. Farther than she's ever been in her whole life. Yet closer than she could have imagined to the people who once lived in the small town in Leeds Grenville County called Elgin, Ontario.

For now, the less Stu knows, the less trouble he can get into. Especially if he's caught snooping into old records. She wants to trust him, but she's used to going it alone. Wandering this life on her own. She's still that eight-year-old girl who doesn't fully know how to trust. And the terrible shit that's now coming up about Rory tells her that her instincts might have been way off. So she's treading lightly and holding on to what she's got. An address, a bank draft in her back pocket, a diary, and twenty-four hours to kill.

Augusta doesn't know who planted the diary in the car or why. Perhaps it was the mystery man lurking around Elgin. The one who left her a dead possum. She hopes the answers lie somewhere in the pages of the small pink book.

Gus can't bring herself to open the diary for the first leg of the trip. She stares out at the passing scenery. She eats chips and thumbs through the images on her phone. But as the sun sets, she's ready. She turns to the first entry in Gracie Halladay's diary. It's dated September 16, 2002. Two weeks after June's death. Gracie was just seven. Augusta's hands shake. She rests her knees up against the seat in front of her, scrunches down, and pulls her hoodie over her head and begins to read.

Dear Ma,

Miss Lois says you are up in heaven now and you are looking down at me. I don't like that because I can't see you.

When I look up all I see is clouds and no Ma. Gracie's eyes are pearls. Gracie's hair is licorice. That's what you used to sing to me every night. Gracie's smile is sweet as pie. Gracie's kiss is heaven. You were right and I wish I could take it back. I ask Miss Lois and she says you are in heaven now. I should never ever have kissed you, Ma.

Gracie

The diary has only a few entries. Some about how much Gracie misses her mother. Some about her animal friends. Crude sketches of birds and raccoons and squirrels are scattered along the margins of each page.

Gus connects deeply to the little girl's heartbreak at being motherless. But much of the diary, she can't relate to. Little Gracie's world is a dark one. She speaks of strange men's voices, of shadowy passageways, of wandering mysterious gardens, of hours spent hiding or locked away, talking to the dead. Gracie writes of imaginary friends. All of them wild animals. She writes of the conversations they share, of the secrets she tells only them, and of the comfort they give her when she's scared.

One entry in particular catches Augusta's attention. It's dated July 21, 2003. A few days after Henry was reported missing.

Possum came back to life today, Ma. Once I got his insides out and put in his eyes, he spoke for the first time. He has the funniest laugh. Possum is my favorite. But don't tell Rabbit or she'll be jealous. Possum watched me dance and put on my nightie and brush my teeth and say my prayers.

Possum is a good friend. He told me he can't wait till Henry comes back. Henry is going to like Possum.

Gracie

Gus can barely turn the pages. A lump growing in her throat. But she can't stop. With each sad entry, all written to her dead mother, the years go by. And Henry never comes back. Some entries are months apart. One year turns into two, then three, then four. Gracie grows up little by little, but her handwriting and her sentiments remain childlike. She rarely writes of her grandfather. Mostly she inhabits an invented world where animals come to life and people are absent. Other than the rare mention of a visit to see Miss Lois or to play with her son, Edgar, she appears to spend most of her time alone. At one point she writes about a nice woman taking her for ice cream, but it's a short entry that's mostly scribbled over. Gus recalls what Rory told her about how her mother got transferred for kidnapping Gracie.

Later Shan tells Stanton she was just taking her for ice cream on account of it being the anniversary of her mom's death and all.

The "nice woman" in Gracie's diary was her mother. Gus is sure of it.

Gus turns to find the last entry. It's well before the end of the book. She flips ahead but the rest of the pages are empty. After four years of writing in the small diary, Gracie simply stopped. At the age of eleven. This last entry is dated August 3, 2006. The date catches Augusta off guard. She gasps out loud. The woman sitting next to her on the bus looks over. Gus sinks deeper inside the cave of her hoodie and pulls the diary close so the woman can't see the pages.

She takes a deep breath.

The entry was written the day before Augusta's mother died.

The day before Kep Halladay disappeared, apparently murdered.

It's short and sweet, like the others.

> *Dear Ma,*
>
>   *Today I was sitting in the tall grass out front when I saw the police lady's car coming down the road again. Remember I told you about her. She took me for a chocolate sundae one year after you went to heaven. I had sprinkles on mine. She had hot caramel sauce and peanuts.*
>
>   *But this time, I lay down in the grass so she wouldn't see me. She drove away. I saw her another time. She got out of her car and came right onto the front porch. Grandpa and her were yelling. I heard her say Henry's name. And your name too. Grandpa went and got his shotgun and the police lady left. I don't like her yelling or Grandpa getting so mad. I see her sometimes when I go out at night. I see her watching the house. I wish she would leave us alone.*
>
> Gracie.

38

LANA

Stepping off the bus in Thunder Bay, Augusta shields her eyes from the morning sun. She breathes in the dewy lake air, flips through the photos on her phone. Finds the picture she took of the letter she found in Lois Greenaway's inbox. Checks the address.

125 Cottonwood Crescent.

Gus jumps in a cab. Fifteen minutes later, the cab turns onto a crescent lined with rows of emerald ash. It rolls slowly down the street. Before even seeing the number on the house, she knows which one it is. The front porch is dripping with pink wisteria clusters. Just like the ones draped over the front of Lois Greenaway's Dance Academy back in Elgin. She imagines the sisters shared a love of wisteria, sending seeds in their letters to each other.

Gus pays the cabbie and approaches the front door. Taking a deep breath, she knocks. A shadow crosses the peephole. Augusta puts on her best girl guide smile. The door opens a crack, still chained. A wrinkled eye peers out. A woman. Early seventies. Robe pulled high around her fleshy neck. Same eyes as Lois. Same dark eye makeup rimming her eyes.

"Can I help you?"

Her aging voice claws for uniformity.

"Are you Lana Henning?"

"Who's asking, dear?"

"My name is Augusta Monet. I was hoping to talk to you about your sister."

Lana's eyes flit upward. Accessing a memory. Gus prompts.

"Lois Greenaway. She was your sister?"

Lana nods. Gus waits for her to say something. Anything. The morning breeze wafts down the neck of Augusta's hoodie, sending a chill down her stiff spine. And yet she feels strangely hot. Feverish almost. Sitting for too long on a stuffy bus, thinking too much about everything she's uncovered, not sleeping for the last twenty-four hours. She's getting sick.

"You work for the gas company?"

It's going to take more than a smile to get Lana to open this door. Gus reaches inside her satchel and pulls out Gracie's small pink diary. She holds it up.

"I found this. It belonged to Gracie Halladay."

"Where?"

"Elgin."

Lana looks at the diary. Puts a hand to her mouth. Then she closes the door. Shit. That was a mistake. Gus puts the diary away. She isn't sure what to do. Knock. Go round back. Leave. She's come too far. Then she hears the chain rattle as it's being unlatched. The door swings open. Lana's wearing a white terry cloth bathrobe and fluffy kitten slippers. She motions for Gus to come inside. The smell of coffee brewing almost brings Augusta to her knees.

"Cuppa?"

Gus nods eagerly like a bobblehead. Lana motions for her to take a seat in the front room as she heads to the kitchen. A dark blue linen sofa sits in front of the large bay window. Gus leaves her sneakers at the door and sits. She scans the room. Reminds her of Rose's house. A cabinet displays a collection of porcelain dolls wearing pink and yellow dresses with petticoats. Each holds a porcelain parasol in one delicate hand. In the corner of the room is an antique desk with a roller-top similar to Rose's. A blue-and-orange Persian rug lies across the center of the floor. Orange throw cushions accent each end of the blue sofa.

Gus hears the light jingling of a bell. A black-and-white cat wanders into the room, spots Gus, and freezes. Wrinkles its nose then darts across the carpet and skitters up the stairs. The bell on its collar continues jingling even after it disappears.

Dishes clink in the kitchen. Gus rises and walks over to get a closer look at the framed photographs on the mantel. Wedding photos. Some baby pictures. An old black-and-white shot of a family. Two parents and two young girls. One photo catches her eye. She recognizes Lois immediately. Late fifties, standing between a young man and a girl. The girl is Gracie Halladay. She's about eleven years old. About the time she stopped writing in her diary. When her grandfather went missing and Lois took her in. Gus doesn't recognize the young man in the photo. He's the only one not looking at the camera. Slightly vacant gaze. Gus roots through her satchel for her notebook. Flips pages. Finds a name. Edgar

Greenaway. Could be him. He died in the fire, along with his mother, Lois Greenaway.

Next to this photo is another one of Lois with a woman around her age. The family resemblance is obvious. It's Lois and Lana. The sisters are posing in a large square crowded with people and surrounded by skyscrapers. Colorful billboards tower behind them. Their arms are raised as if they can't believe where they are. They're both glowing. In their early twenties.

"We were so young."

Gus jumps. Lana is right behind her. She giggles and hands Gus a coffee mug. They both sit, one at each end of the blue sofa.

"The pair of us had all these grand ideas about how life was going to turn out. Big Apple dreams. We thought we'd get discovered at a soda counter like Lana Turner and both end up with leads dancing on Broadway. We thought we'd never look back."

"You were both dancers?"

"For a spell."

They sit in an awkward silence. Gus was hoping the diary and some light chitchat would open Lana right up, but nothing's that easy. Lana is far away. Gus tries to get her to come back.

"I understand Lois took Gracie in after her grandfather disappeared."

Lana hesitates then nods.

"I'm sorry if it's painful to talk about your sister."

Gus glances at the pictures on the mantel.

"Is that her son, Edgar?"

Lana nods. Words seem to be stuck in her throat. Gus

realizes how presumptuous it was of her to come here. To just get on a bus and arrive unannounced. She's a stranger who has no right to sit here asking this woman questions about her dead sister and her dead nephew. But she's here. Shannon would tell her to stay the course. Gus squares her shoulders. Figures it's only fair to put her cards on the table.

"My mother was a cop. She was the first officer to arrive after June Halladay's accident. I know she always felt protective of Gracie after that. Like Lois did. I'm just trying to figure out what happened the night Kep Halladay went missing. Maybe Gracie confided something to Lois about that night. And Lois shared it with you? You see, my mother was killed that same night and I think her death had something to do with Kep's disappearance."

Augusta's voice wavers at the mention of her mother's death, but she pushes on.

"I know all this must sound crazy, but anything you can tell me would help. Anything about Gracie or Kep Halladay or Elgin."

Lana looks down. Examines the age spots on the backs of her hands. Considers them carefully as if they were a map to a foreign land where she once lived.

Then the woman lifts her chin.

"Oh, dear child, I can tell you everything there is to know about Elgin. My sister and I were born and raised there."

Lana's eyes brighten as she looks over at the picture of her and her sister.

"She always said it was better to be a big fish in a small pond than a minnow in New York City. That's why she stayed and started her dance academy."

"I've been there. To the dance academy. I broke in actually."

"Well, aren't you a go-getter. How'd the old girl look?"

Lana sits forward in her chair.

"Pretty much the way Lois left it, I think."

"You sure you're not with the gas company?"

"I'm pretty sure."

"Well, even if you are, that settlement money is long gone."

Lana sits back with a sigh, tucks a stray strand of hair back into the messy bun on top of her head, and tells Augusta all about her sister.

"She and I were the best of friends. Both married local boys in our late twenties. One marriage held tight. One came undone. Only two months into it, her Bernie ran off with the dentist's wife. Lois was pregnant with Edgar and left to fend for herself. Only good thing about Bernie was his teeth, she liked to say. Lois wasn't one to be blue for long. She started giving dance lessons out of the local bowling alley and she worked part-time at the mortuary giving makeovers to the dead. She made ends meet any way she could and built up her savings so she could open her own studio. Lois never remarried. She was laser focused on that business of hers and on that son of hers. Edgar was born with an affliction that caused his mind to never fully grow up, but Lois felt blessed to have him in her life. She liked taking care of people. Took care of that boy and took Gracie in when no one else would have dreamed of it.

"Then Roger got an offer to go work in Thunder Bay at the new generating plant and what with Elgin dying a slow death, it was time for us to move. It broke my heart to leave Lois. We wrote every week without fail for years. We told each other everything. The good, the bad, and the oh so ugly. Distance made no difference. We were two peas."

Lana pauses to sip her coffee. And again, that faraway stare appears. Just like Renata, Manny, Todd, and even poor Ollie, Lana has the look of someone burdened by what they know. An aura of déjà vu seems to wash over Lana as she slips into the past, fully immersed in her memories of Lois.

Gus knows in her heart that she's meant to be sitting in this very room, at this exact moment, across from this woman. Her doubts from earlier dissipate. A fog lifts. She can see her mission clearly now.

She is meant to help others make peace with the past. To rid themselves of regret or doubt or fear or whatever has settled deep into their bones. And she knows that if she does this enough times, she'll learn how to do it herself.

Gus sits back.

Lets go of what she thinks she knows.

And gets ready to listen to the stories and the secrets passed between two sisters.

Lana and Lois.

39

LOIS

ONE THING I CAN TELL YOU ABOUT ELGIN IS THE PEOPLE IN that town were as small as it was. Small-minded and fearful. Always whispering about curses and the darkness they believed lived inside that little girl, Gracie. A bad seed, they called her. Hogwash, all of it. Something awful might have brought that baby into this world, but June Halladay loved that child and she was a good mother. No one to help her and a child to raise. Living in that big house with that wretch of a father, Kep Halladay. She did her best. Who could fault her for turning to the bottle? The small minds of Elgin, that's who.

"And little Gracie. Lois wrote about her often. About how none of the girls talked to her or held her hand when they skipped off to the water fountain. None of them giggled in her ear to make her laugh. She had no friends because she was wrong, and no one wanted a wrong friend. Lois shushed the girls if they made fun. She let wee Gracie sit in her office when her mother was late. And when June didn't show up 'cause she was waylaid on some barstool, Lois took Gracie to the mortuary where Lois worked as a cosmetologist. Although on account of Ernie the mortician's bad arthritis, Lois was really so much more than that. A jack-of-all-things charnel so to speak. She did most of the heavy lifting back then. Taught the child all about embalming and sewing skin and covering flesh with makeup. Even let Gracie insert the odd trocar or apply the occasional swipe of blush or eye shadow to a cadaver."

Gus has to ask.

"What's a trocar?"

"Oh, it's a surgical instrument used to draw fluids out of the body cavity."

Gus regrets asking. She tries not to gag as Lana goes on.

"When Gracie was seven, they turned against her for good. All because of the rabbit incident. Gracie eventually told Lois what really happened.

She was sitting in the grassy ditch, waiting for her mother. Waiting and worrying about walking into ballet class late. A rabbit hopped up. Her pink leotard was getting damp with dew. She knew the girls were going to point if her bum was wet. But she didn't move for fear of scaring off the rabbit. The pair of them just sat there waiting and events unfolded as they sometimes do. Suddenly. Sadly. Turning life sideways. Lois couldn't protect the little girl after that."

Lana swallows hard. Gus leans closer. Recalling how her mother shared this same desire. To protect Gracie. Seems Shannon and Lois had that in common. The little ballerina got inside both their hearts. The woman's eyes glisten and her voice trembles as she goes on.

"June had been in town, drinking at the local watering

hole. She'd lost track of time. And when she sped home to pick up Gracie for dance class, she likely didn't see her sitting there in the ditch. She didn't see the rabbit dart out into the lane. A light thump was likely all that registered as she hit the brakes and saw her daughter stand up, distraught. June figured it was because she was late so she honked for her to get in. Gracie climbed in clutching the small bag she kept her ballet shoes in.

"A few minutes later, June dropped Gracie in the parking lot of the academy. June never came inside anymore. It was two hours later when June found out what her daughter had done. Two hours of sitting in her car trying to sleep off the booze.

"A few months earlier, June was drunk and hit a school bus and her father made the charges go away. Luckily none of the kids on the bus was hurt. A week after that she took out a fire hydrant. The senator made some more calls. June got a slap on the wrist for that hit-and-run. The same folks who turned their backs on her when she got pregnant now said June deserved to be thrown in jail.

"People would spot her sitting in her car, passed out or staring into space. Sometimes talking to herself. Sometimes crying like a baby. They whispered that she was unstable. Unfit. Unwelcome. But what could they do? Kep Halladay was her father."

Gus recalls Renata Corrigan's description of young June.

Leggy and pretty with long yellow hair . . . joined the cheerleading squad and had lots of friends.

How far and how fast June had fallen in her young life. Gus feels a crushing sadness for the young mother who tragically became the town joke seemingly overnight. Unwanted and unloved. Maybe a curse she'd carried with her from the day she was born.

Lana clears her throat, bringing Gus back to the room. She's getting to the nitty-gritty of her story and she wants her audience to pay attention. To bear witness, alongside her, to what truly happened.

"So that day, June got back to the academy and everyone was outside waiting. Gracie was standing next to Lois. The other mothers were shielding their children behind their backs. June knew there was trouble. Gracie tried to go to June when she saw her, but Lois gently held her shoulder. She had no choice. June didn't want to get out of the car, but she had to. Some of the mothers couldn't hide their smirks. One particularly nasty piece of work had her hands on her hips and a gleeful look in her eye. June approached, and the moms circled. A wolf pack surrounding their prey. That's when June saw the blood on Gracie's dance shoes. She ran to her daughter and asked if she was hurt. Lois held up the plastic bag. Inside was a blood-soaked rabbit. 'What the fuck?' June said. That set off Penny Dickenson who said, 'What did you just say in front of my child?' And June repeated what she'd said, and the circle tightened. Penny wouldn't let up. She called Gracie a freak. One of the other mothers chimed in and said the girl was just like her mother. Rotten to the core. Lois couldn't find any words for June. They both knew Gracie wasn't welcome anymore. She never really had been. June grabbed the plastic bag with the dead bunny and took Gracie's hand. The circle parted and the two of them walked to their car and drove away.

"The story of the dead rabbit wafted across town like cheap perfume. It eventually seeped into the nostrils of Kep

Halladay. He was livid. He called June a drunken embarrassment. He'd never covered for her out of love. He didn't care about June or Gracie. He did it to protect his reputation. To preserve his status as the head of one of the county's most prominent founding families. But now, even June's child was becoming a stain on his good name. The two of them were bad for business. Bad for his political aspirations.

"Then one terrible Monday in September of 2002, one of Kep's problems was taken care of."

Lana pauses. The memory catching in her throat. Gus knows the date. Knows what's coming. She's on the edge of her seat, eyes focused and intense, hands very still, heart racing. Lana finds her voice again.

"Gracie was playing in the front seat of June's car and someone had left the keys in the ignition. June had gone down to collect the mail from the box at the end of the lane. For seven years, she'd made the morning trek. Likely hoping that a letter might come from Todd.

"When she was finally able to talk about that day, Gracie said she was pretending to be grown-up. Her grandfather had taught her how to turn the key in the ignition and shift the stick into drive. Her gangly legs made it so her feet could just reach the pedals. She liked that he wanted to teach her something. The car rolled down the hill. Gracie said she put the brake pedal flat to the floor like he'd shown her, but the car wouldn't stop. I imagine June saw what was happening and ran to help her daughter. They think she tripped and went under the car. They found the car across the highway in the ditch. Gracie still in the driver's seat. June under the car. She'd been dragged across the road. She was dead. One of Gracie's legs was crushed. The doctors reset the bones, but she always walked with a limp after that.

"Despite the death of Kep's only daughter, nothing really changed. The show went on at Halladay House. The weekend parties with his bigwig friends continued. Then the boy who'd been billeting at the house disappeared. Gracie was eight. She almost seemed more upset by this than her mother's death. He was her friend and he left her without saying goodbye. Before he disappeared, she would go on and on about how Henry was going to take her to Egypt on an archaeological dig. Once he was gone, Gracie was never the same. She barely spoke when she stopped by the mortuary.

"Within a year, big oil made its debut in the county. Took only a few months for the farms to bubble over with toxic waste. Half the town hightailed it to higher ground, but Lois stayed. She couldn't abandon her dance academy. Her life's work. Her hometown. Even after she got those sores on her tongue and Edgar's asthma turned into chronic obstructive pulmonary disease, a part of her felt she couldn't leave because of Gracie. Couldn't leave that girl all alone up there with her grandfather and his cronies.

"Then two years later the old man was gone. Disappeared off the face of the earth. It was the summer of 2006. I heard the news and my heart leapt. Little Gracie was free. What went on in that house didn't matter anymore. It was done, along with Kep Halladay. Children's Aid saw fit to let me foster the girl. Gracie was eleven when she came to live with me and Edgar. Didn't want any more disruptions in her life so we stayed in Elgin. We were a family, the three of us. A family for seven years."

Gus is so caught up in Lana's story that her brain only now

faintly registers the shift that just happened. Lana leans back. Her robe falls open a little, exposing her thigh. Only for a split second before she can pull it closed. But in that second, Gus sees the large mottled scar on her leg.

There's a clank in the kitchen.

A hand appears on the edge of the doorframe.

"I'll be there in a minute, love," the woman calls out to the kitchen with a toss of her brown hair.

Augusta slowly places her coffee mug on the side table next to her, hands shaking slightly. A realization slowly dawning. Then she looks into the eyes of the woman in front of her.

A leg that's been badly burned in a fire.

A loved one hiding out in the kitchen.

The pieces fall into place as Gus replays the subtle and unconscious shift that just took place in the story.

The shift from "her" to "me."

Lana, no longer the storyteller.

Her sister sitting in her place.

She was there all along.

Only it's just now that Gus sees her for who she really is. "Lois?"

The woman tucks a stray lock of brown hair into the loose bun piled on top of her head, looks up, and smiles.

40

EDGAR

ꙮ

Sorry, dear, I'm just so used to being dead it's become a habit. You see, Lana got some money from the gas company on account of me and Edgar being dead so we sort of had to stay dead. 'Course when we moved in with her and Roger, she shared every penny with us. What little there was. Then when Lana and Roger retired to Myrtle Beach last year, they wanted us to come along. What with my cancer meds and prescriptions and doctor appointments, I couldn't afford to live stateside with no health insurance, so we worked it out. Lana and I do look alike. With a couple of pieces of my sister's ID, I became Lana. No one's the wiser. Lana doesn't charge me hardly any rent to live here and winters we keep the heat low so the bills don't get out of hand. A good old hot water bottle goes a long way to taking the chill off. We make do."

Gus smiles at Lois. Miss Greenaway. Alive and well. Sitting right in front of her. Despite having left everything behind that she held dear, despite having no way to go back home to Elgin, she makes the best of her circumstances. Seems it's always been her way. To see the good in things and people. Like little Gracie and June.

A floorboard winces in the kitchen.

Someone else is waiting to reveal themselves. Gus thinks she might know who.

"Edgar?"

Lois smiles and shrugs.

"My boy. My family. I've told my sister, Lana, that if I win the lottery, we'll be down south in a heartbeat. Look out sandy beaches and sunsets, here we come."

Lois laughs and wiggles in her chair like she's dancing the hula. Her robe parts slightly. Gus sees the scars. Tries to fit the pieces together.

"I'm curious. Why did everyone in Elgin think you died in the fire?"

"We disappeared without a trace. What else were they to think? They were all at the fair and our house was blown off the face of the earth by the blast. As luck would have it, we were at the edge of town on our morning walk when things went boom. We got showered with burning debris and a piece of hot plastic stuck to the side of my leg. We peeled it off and ran home to look for Gracie. But the house was flattened. She was gone. My car was parked around the corner, behind the dance academy. It was still in one piece, so we wasted no time. We didn't stop driving until we got here to my sister's place. That town wanted to be left alone. It wanted everyone gone. It just seemed easier to play dead and leave it all behind."

"Gracie was in the house?"

"Poor lass. She'd just turned eighteen the day before. She

didn't want to come for our morning walk. She stayed behind. Something about a sore belly from too much birthday cake, but I knew better. That girl liked to be by herself. Alone with her thoughts. She didn't really know how to be around other people. When we saw the house was gone, we knew she was gone with it. Gracie just wanted to be left alone. I suppose she got her wish in the end."

There's another louder noise from the kitchen.

"You spying on us, Edgar?"

Lois peers toward the kitchen entryway. A cherub-faced man in his twenties is peeking around the kitchen doorframe. Wide-eyed, his round cheeks billowing as he chews. Gus gives him a little wave. He waves back.

"You want to see Elgin before the fire? Edgar can show you."

Gus nods. Lois smiles at her son.

"Can't you, dollface?"

Edgar giggles and disappears back into the kitchen. Lois rises and tightens her robe around her waist. She's still lean. A dancer's frame. Gus follows her through the kitchen. Peanut butter cookies sit cooling on a rack. She leads Gus down a small flight of stairs to a landing, out a back door, and into a small backyard. Edgar is already running across the yard toward a large shed in the back corner.

"Don't be shy, Eddie, my sweet. She's a friend of Gracie's."

Lois crosses the yard. Gus follows. Edgar has ducked inside the shed. Lois steps through the open door and waves a hand for Gus to come inside.

"My Edgar has his gifts."

Gus steps inside. It's dark. She's praying she's not just been lulled into a false sense of security and is about to enter some sort of kill room or improvised prison cell. It takes a moment for her eyes to adjust to the dark interior. There are no windows. There's a large table in the center of the shed. A switch flips and the room is flooded with light. Edgar is standing right next to her. A network of interlacing strings of tiny lights crisscross the ceiling creating what looks like a magical starlit sky. Augusta's mouth drops open. The sight in front of her takes her breath away.

Edgar covers his mouth and stamps his feet. He's happy she likes it.

She can't believe what she's seeing.

Stretched across a large table is an exact miniature replica of a town. Avenues lined with tiny trees, mini park benches, bus stops, street signs, mailboxes, fences, houses, a grocery store, a mortuary, a café. Even the dance academy is there. Miniature cars, bicycles, flowerpots, and fire hydrants dot the neighborhood. It's an entire town, re-created down to the smallest of details. Dozens of tiny bulbs light up the insides of miniature streetlamps and tiny light fixtures attached to front porches. Through front windows, lamps can be seen glowing from the living rooms of houses.

In one corner of the shed, there's a workbench covered with woodworking tools, bits of scrap metal, wood, and colored glass. There's a glue gun and a soldering torch. A set of saws, glass cutters, plyers, hammers, screws, and nails. It's Edgar's workshop. The town is Edgar's creation.

"It's Elgin."

Gus whispers the words, knowing them to be true. She recognized the town the moment the lights came on. Only she's never seen it as it once was. Lois nods from where she stands beside her son. She puts one hand proudly on Edgar's shoulder. He moves away from her touch, crosses the room, and sits himself on a tall stool next to his workbench. He tucks his knees to his chest and bites his lip. He's a big kid. Lois looks at Gus.

"Elgin back in her heyday."

Gus lets her eyes wander down the streets.

"She's beautiful."

Gus imagines Edgar and Lois taking their morning walks past the shady trees. She locates the central square in the middle of town. A tavern, a small department store, a town hall, a community center, a real estate office, an RCMP field office. A hub of activity. All obliterated by the fire.

But in Edgar's model, it's all intact. Nothing is blackened or charred or blown away. There's no crater. He's even built up the base of his model with clay, imitating the topography of the town. Its dips and valleys and the landscape beyond. At the north end of town, the houses thin, giving way to a valley of pastures. The far side of the valley rises to the highest point in Edgar's model. A house sits on the hill.

Halladay House.

"Edgar wanted to include the house where Gracie grew up. To honor her. He knew it well. He played up there with Gracie when they were young. Till I had to put a stop to it. I couldn't risk him being around the goings-on up there."

Gus walks to the far side of the model to take a closer look at Halladay House. It was quite something in its glory days. Velvet curtains in the windows. Bright yellow coat of paint on the siding. A grand driveway of interlocking stones edged with manicured shrubs. A slightly unkempt rose garden around back with winding paths, a stone bench, a trellis, and a pond. Gus peers into the windows of the once majestic, yet slightly creepy mansion.

Edgar comes up beside her and leans in to see what she's looking at. His cheek is almost touching hers.

"He likes you."

Lois smiles from across the shed.

"Hide and see," Edgar whispers.

Gus looks at him. She wasn't sure he could speak.

"Hide and seek?" she corrects. He shakes his head.

"See. See. See."

Edgar points to his eyes. He pokes at them. Lois shrugs. To illustrate his point, Edgar grabs hold of the model of the house and lifts the top floors off the main floor. They come apart easily, revealing the interior of the house. He places the upper section on the floor at his feet.

Gus peers inside the main floor. A top view of the layout of the house. There's a front parlor, formal living and dining areas, and an enormous kitchen. The parlor, likely where Kep entertained his guests, is furnished with a garish array of miniature high-back chairs, plush love seats in rich bronze and plum tones. There's a fireplace with an ornate wood mantel, heavy curtains on the windows, and dark-paneled walls. Despite the attempts to decorate the room in plush grandeur, it's a gaudy room. Smaller than it should be for a house this size. Gus moves closer to the model. Then she sees why it looks so cramped. Edgar has left too much space between the outside walls of the house and the rooms inside. So much that it looks like there's a narrow hallway behind the walls of the entire main floor. But without an exit. Wasted space if it's accurate. Maybe Edgar got the dimensions wrong. Only imagined the walls of Halladay House having this much space behind them. How would he know for sure?

"Hide and see," Edgar says, pointing to a bookcase in the parlor. Gus has no idea what he's talking about, but she nods.

Lois leans in to see what Edgar's pointing at.

"My Edgar has a real eye for detail. Built the entire town from memory. And they called HIM the idiot. Hah. Boy's a genius, if you ask me."

"Why so much space behind the walls?"

Lois shrugs.

"Some sort of attic or crawl space, I imagine. Maybe for insulation."

Gus stands back and admires the model.

"Everything is so perfect."

"Edgar-perfect," Lois says, nodding for Gus to follow her. "Let me show you."

She points to a house on the far side of the table. The other side of the town. They walk over to take a look. It's a pretty blue bungalow with a white front porch. There's a lovely willow in the front yard. So large that it shelters the entire house. The willow is a work of art. Its trunk is made of fine brown twine looped around a frame creating branches that look real. Delicate silk fronds cascade from the branches. Not a trace of glue is visible. It's as if the leafy bows were actually growing from the tree. Lois blows gently and the willow sways like willows do.

"That was our house. Me and Edgar's. And Gracie's for a time. Only we didn't have a weeping willow. Edgar added that. To surround the house. To protect us and our home."

Gus smiles.

"Edgar-perfect?"

Lois's eyes glisten. For a long time, the threesome don't speak. They gaze at the town. Taking in the masterful work of art spread before them. Seeing the perfection and the imperfection in Elgin's narrow avenues. Streets named for nearby towns and cities. Perth. Kingston. Cornwall. Or after things that mattered. Church. Maple. River. Mill. And, of course, there's a Halladay Street that crosses Main. There are two churches and one gas station. There are six starlings sitting in a row on a hydro line. But there's one thing missing. People.

Despite this omission or perhaps because of it, Edgar's world seems incredibly peaceful. Gus wishes she could see the world the way Edgar does. A world where place and home aren't so inextricably interwoven with the people who live in them. Where pain and loss reside elsewhere. Where missing someone doesn't distort the simple beauty of a wide front porch or a weeping willow.

Lois invites Gus to stay for chicken and dumplings. Prepares her a bed on the sofa for the night.

COME MORNING, LOIS AND EDGAR OFFER TO DRIVE GUS TO THE bus terminal in their beat-up orange Volkswagen Beetle. Before getting out of the car, Gus gives Lois Gracie's diary.

"Belongs with her real family."

"I can't imagine how it found its way to you, but I'm grateful it did. Like a gift from the great beyond."

Lois holds it to her chest. She loved Gracie. Did her best to protect the girl. Shannon tried to do the same, in her own way.

"Do you think my mother killed Kep Halladay?"

Lois rests a hand on Augusta's arm.

"No, no, no dear. It wasn't her."

Gus knows she's telling the truth. Shannon's not a murderer. "You know who did?"

Lois shakes her head. If she does, she's not saying.

"Hide and see."

Augusta had forgotten Edgar was in the back seat. He's poking at his eyes again. Lois looks at her wrist even though she's not wearing a watch.

"You'll miss your bus."

Lois gives Augusta a warm hug.

"Take care of you, Miss Augusta Monet."

Edgar leans forward and wraps his big arms around both of them. Group hug.

The two of them watch from the car as she boards the bus. Gus waves from the window. Edgar's in the front seat, waving madly while Lois starts the car and drives away. Gus can picture them stopping for groceries on their way home. Then standing in the kitchen putting them away. Then opening the diary and finding the note she left inside for them. The one wrapped around the bank draft made out to cash for five million dollars.

> *Dear Lois and Edgar,*
>
> *Thank you for being so kind to me. I'm happy Gracie's diary is where it belongs now. This money was also Gracie's. I think she used it to try to right some of the Halladay wrongs. But I think, like her diary, it belongs with the people who truly loved her and took care of her to the end. Her real family. Money doesn't right wrongs. I don't think she knew that. Love is the only thing that can right wrongs.*
>
> *Yours truly,*
> *Augusta Monet*

Gus tries to sleep on the twenty-four-hour bus ride home, but only manages to rest her eyes for a few minutes on the ride to Toronto where she transfers to the eastbound route to Ottawa. No sleep on that bus either. About halfway to Ottawa, Stu sends her a text.

The night before as she lay on Lois's sofa, she almost called Stu. There were a bunch of missed calls from his number. She'd meant to reach out to him so he wouldn't worry. But she'd decided it would be better to explain it all face-to-face.

His text is short.

> Something bad's happened. Where are you?

Her heart skips a beat.

> On a bus back to Ottawa. Is it Levi?
> When do you arrive?
> 8am today.
> I'll meet you at the terminal.
> Tell me what's happened.

He doesn't text back.

> Stu?

No answer. She tries calling. He doesn't pick up.

Gus rests her head against the window and watches as green farmland gives way to vast clusters of suburban townhomes. A few hours later when she jumps off the bus in Ottawa and takes one look at Stu's face, she knows.

Levi's dead.

41

LEVI

❧

STU BLURTS IT OUT LIKE HE'S RIPPING OFF A BAND-AID. "Levi was poisoned."

A crushing pain hits Gus square in the chest. Her legs go numb and she almost collapses. How could she have left her sweet dog to die alone? Without her there when he took his last breath. She wants more than anything to go back in time, forget all about Lois and Edgar and the Halladays. She wants her puppy back in her arms. Stu guides her gently by the elbow. Tells her to leave her car behind in the parking lot. He'll drive. Sitting in the passenger seat of his Grand Am, Gus bites her lip. Finally speaks.

"How?"

"I don't know. I went to feed him yesterday and he wouldn't eat. I thought maybe he was just missing you. But a few hours later, he couldn't walk. All wobbly like he was drunk. I took him to the vet. They said it was antifreeze. They put him on painkillers and said it'd be best to put him down. Only . . ."

Gus stares at him. "Only what?"

"I couldn't. He's not my dog."

"Levi's alive?" Elation floods her heart.

"Barely. I thought you'd want to say goodbye."

"Take me to him."

"Already heading there."

Augusta's mind flip-flops from Rory to Dez, but she can't blame anyone but herself. A terrible guilt racks her bones. This is her dog. Her mother's dog. How could she have been so careless? So stupid. Levi trusted her to take care of him and she failed him miserably. She vows to do everything she can to keep him alive. To make up for not loving him when she was a child. For abandoning him. For everything.

At the vet, Gus asks Stu to wait in the car. She needs to do this alone. The front desk receptionist is tapping away on her computer when Gus bursts into the waiting room. Gus lunges at the desk. The young woman acknowledges her presence by holding up one finger. Augusta's blood boils. She tells the woman her name and Levi's name. The woman stops typing, and without looking at Gus, she picks up the receiver of a phone, presses an intercom button, mumbles something, then hangs up. The woman has yet to make eye contact with Gus, who is ready to leap over the counter and choke her.

"I need to see my dog."

"The surgeon is on his way, miss. If you'd like to take a seat."

Augusta stays put. Bites on the skin around her thumbnail until it bleeds. Finally, a man wearing a blue smock and matching pants comes out from a back hallway. There's a small bloodstain on the bottom corner of his smock. Gus chokes back the urge to push him out of the way and run down the hall to find Levi.

"Ms. Monet? How are you?"

"Not good."

He sees she's in no mood for chitchat.

"If you'll follow me, we can go see Levi now."

He motions down the hall. She follows at his heels.

"Pardon the scrubs. I just came out of surgery. Levi's resting right in here."

He leads Gus into a small exam room that smells like Javex bleach. Levi is lying on his side on a table with wheels. He's covered by a paper blanket the same shade of blue as the vet's scrubs. He's sleeping. She leans in and touches his sweet golden head. He looks so small. Slowly his eyelids flutter open, glassy pupils rolling into place. Recognition floods his eyes. But he barely moves, save for a tiny wag of his tail and sniff of his nose. She strokes his velvet ears.

"Hey, buddy."

"He's not in pain."

"Can you save him?"

"His liver and kidneys are pretty far gone. Only way to save him would be a transplant operation. I have a donor, but Levi's too weak right now and frankly, what with his age, I think it's best to—"

Gus cuts him off. Doesn't want to hear the words.

"So a transplant it is."

"Ms. Monet. We're talking about a very expensive procedure, which he may not survive."

"Where do I sign?"

"I don't think you understand. This will be thousands of dollars."

"I have the money."

She's willing to blow the rest of Rose's cash if it means Levi has a chance. The vet ponders the situation, then turns and searches a cabinet for a form. Asks her to sign in three places and then an assistant wheels Levi from the room. Gus gives her dog one last pet as the gurney rolls out. The vet follows.

"I promise you, we'll do everything we can."

At the front desk, the receptionist asks how Gus would like to pay the deposit. Credit or debit. She finally sees her eyes. Pretty girl. About Augusta's age. The deposit is three hundred dollars. Gus hands over three hundred in twenties from the cash she has on her. The cash she grabbed from the trunk before heading to Thunder Bay. She'll cover the balance with what's left in the Buick. Should be close to seven grand.

The clerk hands Augusta a receipt and Levi's collar. Gus takes the receipt but not the collar.

"You can keep that. He'll need it for when he's better."

The girl stares at her. A second too long. Gus can tell the receptionist is pretty sure this dog's not getting better.

"Okay, so bring it back then."

She places the collar on the counter.

"No. You keep it here."

Gus shoves it away, knowing that if she walks out with Levi's collar, he's a goner for sure. The girl narrows her eyes. Tells Gus she can't hold on to personal items.

"I don't want it."

"Shall I dispose of it for you then?"

Gus grabs at the collar angrily, accidentally shoving her

fingernail inside a fold in the collar and jamming it on a hard object. The dog tags clink. She winces in pain and shakes off her hand. She picks up the collar and stares at it like she just got bit. She lifts the fold. It's actually a Velcro flap. Underneath it, a small pocket runs along the inside edge of the collar. Tucked inside the pocket, she finds a slender orange tube about the size of a stick of gum, only thicker and made of plastic. Must be the hard object she jammed her fingernail against. She pulls the tube out of the collar. Examines it. Tugs on it. The outer plastic shell slides back to reveal a metal square. A connector of some kind.

A memory stick.

The past comes rushing toward her like a freight train. She'd forgotten all about Shannon's camera. And the video Annalee helped her transfer to the memory stick.

"What's that?"

Gus looks up at the receptionist. She forgot she was there. Gus ignores her. Shoves the stick back inside the pocket of the collar and heads for the door with it.

"You're welcome."

Gus doesn't look back. Her mind is racing. She jumps into the passenger seat of Stu's car. He's staring at the steering wheel. Doesn't want to look at her. Assumes the worst. Gus is breathing heavily.

"I'm sorry. I should have kept Levi with me the whole time. I got called in to the station. I thought he'd just sleep."

"He's gonna be okay."

"Really? That's awesome."

Gus puts the collar in her satchel. Stu rubs her shoulder.

"You think maybe it was an accident? He got into a leak under a car or something?"

"He was poisoned on purpose and I can guess by who."

"Rory? Why hurt your dog? What's his end game?"

She needs to throw Stu a bone so he doesn't feel shut out. So he keeps digging.

"Money."

"What money?"

"Gracie Halladay's. There's a list of people she gave her fortune to and I think he has it. I'm on the list so maybe he was trying to get my attention."

"You got money from Gracie Halladay?"

Stu shakes his head in disbelief. Then it dawns on him.

"It came in that letter she sent you. Why didn't you tell me, Red?"

Gus ignores the question.

"I need you to see what you can find out from the detectives working the case at the post office in Perth."

"You mean the guy who lost his fingers?"

"See if they've got any leads. Any security footage."

He raises his eyebrows.

"We gotta turn that money in. It's evidence."

"If I did get money, it's well hidden."

"You're bat-shit crazy, Red."

Gus feels bat-shit crazy. She's desperate to see what's on that memory stick. Alone.

"Oh crap, I forgot to grab the paperwork on Levi."

She sighs. Milking the moment.

"Would you mind? I can't go back in there."

Stu nods. Puts on his cop voice.

"We're not done talking about this."

Gus smiles and nods like she agrees.

Stu hops out of the car and heads for the veterinarian hospital entrance. As soon as he's through the doors, she jumps out of the car and hikes herself over the fence at the edge of the parking lot. She runs down an alley, then crosses three blocks before flagging a cab. She directs the driver to the bus terminal where she left Rose's Buick. In the parking lot, the first thing Gus does is grab the gun from under the driver's seat and shove it in the zippered pocket inside her satchel. Hidden but close. She's not taking any more chances. Then she drives to Carlingwood Mall. Her phone buzzes the whole way. Stu is not impressed with being ditched again.

Gus parks in a dark corner of the mall's covered parking garage. No one's around. She opens the trunk and tops up her wallet from Rose's stash. Last time she was here, she remembers seeing a Radio Shack. When she was buying her phone. She finds it. The sales guy is a slim dark-haired young man. He reminds her of Henry Neil. Clean-cut. Wholesome. He's helpful. Tells her she needs an adapter for the stick, helps her transfer the file from the memory stick onto her phone where he saves it for her. The sales clerk is patient. Doesn't make her feel like an idiot.

"It's a .mov file. Basically a video. You can watch it right on your phone. I saved it to your photo library under videos so just click and play. I can show you how if you like."

"It's okay. I'll watch it later. Thanks for the help."

He gives her back the memory stick, she pays for the adapter, then heads into the busy mall. Gus hasn't eaten for hours and she's totally dehydrated. A major head rush forces her to take a seat in the only spot between a man and woman on a hard sofa bench in the middle of the mall concourse.

Afternoon shoppers float past in all directions. A preschooler tugs on her mother's arm. Sweat-panted seniors march in a pack. Two teenage girls giggle as they dig into a greasy box of french fries from the food court. Smells heavenly. A saleswoman sprays perfume in Augusta's direction. She gags. Nearly passes out. Leans forward. Stares at her phone.

Gus can't wait any longer. She clicks on the video. Hunches forward and wraps her palms around either side of her phone so no one can see the screen. It loads then begins to play. Just static at first. The audio buzzes loudly. The man on her right flinches and gets up to leave. Gus smiles at the woman on her left and mutes her phone. The woman's handbag rests lightly against Augusta's leg. Like her mother's used to when they sat together on the bus on their way to a movie.

The video is stamped, 21:30 August 4, 2006. The date makes her gasp even though she knows her mother recorded the video the night she died. But seeing the date transports her back to that terrible day. Shannon filmed this video twelve years ago. Then she came home, copied it to a memory stick, and inserted that stick inside Levi's collar. She hid it well. She didn't want it found by the wrong people.

Augusta's body shudders involuntarily.

At first the images are so dark it's hard for her to make out what's happening.

But as the video continues, the images become more clear.

It's 9:30 P.M. The hours leading to her mother's death begin to unfold.

And they prove more frightening than she could have ever imagined.

42

SHANNON

❧

THE FOOTAGE IS DARK, BUT GUS CAN SEE SPORADIC MOVE-ments. Then the image jostles. Night-vision mode clicks on. As it does, Shannon's face momentarily appears in the frame as she turns the camera and pushes the button. But it doesn't look like her. Light is dark and dark is light. She looks otherworldly. White eyes and mouth. Green glowing hair. The view swings back to her point of view, across the hood of a car toward a house. She's some distance from the house, but Gus recognizes the sloping dormers and peaked gables and broad front porch.

It's Halladay House.

Dark clouds dance across a light green sky. Lightning flashes on the horizon. A black moon emerges from behind a roaming cloud. Details sharpen. A small figure darts across the driveway and around the side of the house.

Augusta pauses the video. Desperate to hear the audio. She needs to hear if her mother's saying anything. But she doesn't want anyone in the crowded mall to listen in. Gus returns to

Radio Shack. She buys a set of headphones from the same young man. Again, he helps her find the right ones for her phone. Then she heads back to the sofa. Her spot's been taken. She can't wait a second longer. She eyes a space on the carpet behind the sofas between some planters overflowing with plastic ferns. Gus nestles in between the planters where no one can step on her and sits down cross-legged. She plugs her new headphones into the audio jack of her phone, puts in the earbuds, and presses play.

The first sound she hears is her mother breathing. Hard. Augusta's eyes fill with tears. She feels like she's right there with her mother, running across the lawn, camera bobbling. Shannon is holding it waist high. The view is rocky as she rounds the house and spots the figure running into the back garden. A young girl. Limping through the rosebushes. Doesn't look back. Shannon is closing in, then the girl disappears. One minute she's stepping through a trellis and the next, gone. Shannon's lens scans the garden. Left. Then right. She crosses under the trellis. Then she whispers.

Gracie. Where are you?

Gus gasps at the sound of her mother's voice. So alive. So close it's as if she's come back from the dead, whispering in Augusta's ear. The sound is bittersweet. Familiar, yet almost forgotten. Gus curses herself for letting that voice get lost deep in the damaged parts of her soul. But in this moment, it's not her soul, it's her body that yearns for more of that sound. Her gut. Her heart. Her ears. All longing for more of those whispers from her mother's lips. And yet more would almost be too much to bear. Torturous.

A noise comes from the house behind Shannon. Laughter. Men's voices talking loudly. The camera pans toward the house. Shannon's filming through the spidery vines hanging from the trellis. A man is standing outside on the back porch. He lights a cigarette but he's too far away to see his face clearly. Doesn't look big enough to be Kep Halladay. He hasn't seen her so she must be hidden. A voice calls from inside the house.

Benchwarmer? Get back in here.

The man tosses his cigarette on the lawn and goes back inside.

The camera turns back to where Gracie disappeared and scans the garden. It moves forward as Shannon searches for the girl. Gus can hear dry branches snapping under her feet.

Gracie. It's me, Shannon. Detective Monet.

Suddenly the camera jerks, hits the ground, and rolls on its side. Gus holds her breath. Eyes wide. There's scrambling, then the camera's picked up.

Fucking hell.

Her mother curses in a whisper. She must have tripped. The lens is dirty. Shannon rotates the camera so the lens is facing her. She spits on the glass then wipes it with the edge of her sleeve. She's wearing a jean shirt. She's sweating. Her eyes are wide. Hair tousled.

She's alive and breathing.

Gus pauses, rewinds, then plays the image over again. And again. Each time freezing the frame on her mother's face. Gus stares, spellbound. There's a fearlessness and a fire burning inside her mother's eyes.

"What are you doing out there, Mama?"

Gus says this out loud. Oblivious to the shoppers side-glancing at the young woman huddled on the carpet talking to herself. Gus lets the video play on. Shannon turns the camera back toward a gravel path that winds through a derelict rose garden surrounded by a low stone wall. The camera scans the dark corners as it moves along the path. She almost misses it. But something catches her mother's attention. The lens tracks back, then moves forward. Hidden by thorny branches is a small hatch in the ground. It stands open.

Gracie?

The trapdoor was covering a hole in the ground that goes straight down. A well. There's a small ladder on the well's wall. Shannon continues to film as she lowers herself down the ladder. Below ground.

Gus flashes to herself sinking into the earth on her visit to Halladay House. Then she remembers Renata's story about Kep's grandfather building the house in the 1920s.

He named it Halladay House. It was a huge property. Underground he dug a network of tunnels leading from the house to the barn where he operated his distillery. Spidering under his property and beyond.

Gus realizes that wasn't some random bog she fell into that night. And this is no well Shannon's climbing down into. It's the tunnels. The camera settles as Shannon reaches the bottom. The view reveals a narrow passageway. Five or six feet high with a rocky base. The tunnel is reinforced with wood beams. Gus can hear her mother's footsteps crunching over the stones. She's being too loud.

Augusta's entire body bristles as she desperately tries to cross through the invisible membrane between their two realities. Tries to will herself into her mother's world. She needs to be there to watch her back. Protect her. Warn her of the danger to come, even though she has no idea what that danger looks like or when it happens.

Shannon follows the tunnel to a wooden door. She tries the handle. The door creaks open. Beyond it is a corridor lit by tea lights set along beams stretching the length of the house. The foundation is concrete. Shannon turns off the night vision. It's light enough without it. She enters what looks to be the basement of Halladay House. The space is cramped as if she's in the back of a long closet. A noise causes the camera to jump. Shannon pans left, catching a glimpse of a small foot disappearing up a narrow wood staircase. Shannon follows, creeping slowly up the rickety stairs.

Edgar was right. There are spaces behind the walls of Halladay House. Hidden passageways. He'd seen them. Played in them with Gracie.

At the top of the stairs, the camera swings left then right. She's out of the basement. On the main floor of the house. Still behind the walls. No sign of Gracie. Men's voices can be heard talking. Muffled but close. Shannon inches down the passageway. A voice is suddenly right next to her on the other side of the wall. She freezes. Gus tightens her grip on the phone. Staring at the video as the camera slowly turns toward the voice. A small piece of pink cloth hangs from two nails. Shannon's hand lifts the cloth to reveal a hole in the wall. Light pokes through the hole. She moves the lens closer. It's a peephole looking into the front parlor. But only a portion of the room is visible. A fire crackles and light dances on the dark wood paneling.

Hide and see.

That's what Edgar said when he pointed at the bookcase in the parlor of his Halladay House model. This parlor looks exactly the same. The view is from the back of a bookcase right next to the fireplace facing the high-back chairs. A rolling cart laden with bottles of booze sits in front of the bookcase. Edgar and Gracie must have spied on the grown-ups from this very spot. Child's play. But this is nothing close to that. A chill runs through Gus as she sees who is sitting right in front of her. Right in front of Shannon.

Kep Halladay. He sits in one of the big armchairs, legs splayed, leaning forward so his barrel chest is resting on his thighs, red face looking like it might implode.

Gus can't breathe. Her body shudders. It's him. In the flesh. He's terrifying. Larger than life. His eyes sparkle a reddish orange reflecting the fire in the hearth. His bushy eyebrows furrow. His gravel voice rumbles like thunder.

You fuckin' lowlifes. This isn't a debate. It's a fuckin' order. That bitch needs her balls chopped off. Cop or no cop.

He sucks on a big cigar, then leans back in his chair.

Another man comes into view. This one sips whiskey from a rock glass. Turns away from Kep, facing the bookcase and Shannon's lens. His face flickers in the firelight. Gus knows him from the deep-set eyes, dark black hair, broad shoulders, crumpled ear. Desmond Oaks. Only he isn't a mass of burnt flesh. He's young. Maybe thirty. Someone else speaks, but he's across the room and beyond Shannon's field of vision. His voice is hesitant, hard to make out, yet something in his tone resonates with her. Gus hopes it's not who she thinks it is.

I can talk to her. Get her to back off.

Kep tosses his cigar in the direction of the unseen man.

You back talkin' me, you little prick? You don't get a say. Not since the day I kept you both outta juvie do either of you get a say in fuck all.

Dez flinches and downs the rest of his whiskey. Kep smiles. Knows he's getting under his skin.

You got a problem, Grease Monkey?

Dez turns to face Kep. His back to the camera.

My debt's been paid, old man. And then some.

Kep rises. He's even bigger than Dez. They stand nose to nose.

You think I like taking care of that half-wit freak you spawned?

Kep grabs Dez by the collar. It looks like he's lifting him off the ground. The other man across the room chimes in.

Easy, boys. Stop clangin' balls.

Dez pulls free from Kep's grip. *This is between me and him.*

Kep laughs and with a dismissive flip of his hand, he sits back down in his big armchair and lights a new cigar. Dez turns away from Kep, facing the camera, resting his drink on the mantel. Trying to control his temper, he speaks in a near whisper.

I've spent half my life doing your bidding, old man. I messed with them brakes. Got rid of that Henry kid when you had no more use for him. And all the while you're getting rich on what that kid found in them rocks.

Dez turns to face Kep.

The way I see it, you owe me, Halladay. And I aim to collect.

The camera is suddenly bumped. The lens turns and there stands Gracie Halladay. Gus gasps. The little girl is right there. Mere inches from Shannon in the narrow passage. Eyes glassy and wide. Pale yellow dress clinging to her bony eleven-year-old shoulders. She heard everything.

Gus covers her mouth at the sight of the ballerina. She's not a Polaroid. She's real. Her little chest is rising and falling. Her cheeks are trimmed with teardrops. The girl hovers a moment, opens her mouth as if she's about to speak, but Shannon reaches out and quickly puts her hand to the girl's face. Gracie pulls away and slips down the passageway, disappearing into the darkness. Shannon follows, dropping the camera to her side.

It's still rolling. Her feet move along the dusty floorboards. The passageway dead-ends at a half wall. Shannon crawls under the wall into a cramped space. She raises the camera. A spiral staircase leads up the side of the house. She films as she winds round and round until she reaches the top, emerging into a small attic room with sloped walls under steep dormers.

Gracie? Don't be scared.

The paint on the walls is peeling. It's light pink. The only window is a small circular one above a bed. On the bed is a tattered rose-colored quilt and a small heart-shaped pillow. A side table stands next to the bed. On the table sit a melted candle on a saucer, a mason jar filled with daffodil deadheads, and a small diary. A circular wool rug lies in the center of the room.

It's a little girl's room. Gracie's room. Large, but claustrophobic and stark. There's no visible door into the main house. The only access seems to be the spiral staircase leading to the passageways behind the walls of the house. It's a hiding place that no one can enter but Gracie. A place she can be alone.

As Gus gazes in wonder at Gracie's hidden attic room, a gaping hole in her investigator's brain opens wide. She crawls through and sees her mistake.

Gracie is still alive.

Goose bumps pop up all over her arms. Her mouth is dry.

Clear as day, Gus now sees her.

The figure limping across the horizon near the Elgin cemetery.

One of Gracie's legs was crushed. The doctors reset the bones, but she always walked with a limp after that.

The knife thrower trying to keep strangers from Elgin.

Gracie just wanted to be left alone and I suppose she got her wish in the end.

The dead possum and the diary left as gifts. Olive branches. *Possum came back to life today, Ma.*

Gracie isn't a ghost living in a ghost town. She's a grown woman living way up in the rafters of a boarded-up mansion, where the dust in the foyer is so thick it's as if no one's disturbed it in years. It is a hiding place. An attic room where no one would ever think to look. Where no one would guess someone still lives. With a secret way in through the tunnels.

"I know where Gracie is, Mama!" Gus shouts. Trying to communicate with her mother through the phone. But she can't. She's in a mall twelve years later. Gus looks up from the video. A woman pulls her child away and hurries down the concourse. Gus is disoriented as she looks around at the bright lights. She stops breathing. Squints.

A floorboard creaks over her headphones, pulling Augusta back into Shannon's world. Her mother is in the attic. Gus is there with her. Shannon moves slowly across the room. Gus holds her breath. The ceiling is lit by a ragged string of bulbs strung across nails. Most are burned out. On the far side of the attic, there's a large table. Shannon moves toward it. Laid out on the tabletop is an array of knives, twine, bags of cotton batten, sewing instruments, a small makeup kit, a toolbox, and a row of jars filled with colored liquids. Blue, bright green, orange-yellow solutions. The lid is off one of the jars of fluorescent-green liquid. There's a bookcase in the corner. It's dark. Hard to see what's on it. She can only make out some large gray shapes.

"What are those?"

Shannon and Gus say the words at the same time.

Shannon steps closer to the bookcase. Suddenly, the camera jerks back as she gasps at what she sees. On each shelf is a dead animal. A rabbit, a possum, a squirrel, a raccoon, and a black bird. Some are missing limbs. Others have partially crushed torsos or mangled ears. They've been cleaned and sewn back together. Then crudely stuffed with cotton. It's all a little too Frankensteinian.

What the fuck?

Just as the words come out of Shannon's mouth, a floorboard winces behind her. Gus lets out a tiny cry. The camera spins around as a flash of Gracie's yellow dress disappears down a trapdoor where the circular rug had hidden it. As Shannon lurches for the handle, a bolt clicks. She pulls but the trapdoor won't budge. Shannon moves fast. Across the room toward the spiral staircase. Down the way she came in. The camera swings at her side. Gus shivers. Blood throbs at her temples. The image is dizzying to watch, but Gus can make out the planks of the spiral stairs and then the floorboards of the narrow passageway behind the parlor.

Shannon's trying to get out of there before Gracie can tell on her.

Gus holds the phone closer, her grip tightening. She's terrified for her mother. Wants her to be safe. Even though Gus knows she's not going to be okay, she holds out hope that this video somehow proves her mother escaped or was saved or ran away or is being held hostage. Anything but dying in a car wreck.

The camera lifts to eye level. Shannon pauses at the entrance to the stairs that lead to the basement and the ladder out to the garden. Kep's voice echoes from the parlor. She hesitates, then moves down the passage. She's not leaving. Gus shakes her head.

There's the apple of my eye. Come over here, Gracie. Let's get a look at you.

Shannon inches toward the voices. Pulls aside the pink cloth covering the peephole and presses the lens close. Kep is still sitting in his armchair. Dez sits in the chair next to him. The third man still isn't visible, if he's there at all. Gracie stands next to Kep. Head hung. Eyes down. Tiny shoulders slouching.

Buck up, girl. Make yourself useful. Fix me a drink.

Gracie shuffles toward the rolling cart that serves as the parlor's bar. It's directly below the bookcase. Her back is to the two men. She's facing Shannon's lens. Her lips are pursed tight as she grabs ice from a bucket, slips two cubes into a rock glass, then pours soda over the ice.

Dez looks relaxed. Less combative than before. The men have reached some sort of agreement.

Get it done before the weekend and I'll throw you two a party to celebrate your release from the shackles of my employ.

Kep chuckles and sucks on his cigar. Dez grins.

You know I'm always up for a party, Mr. Halladay.

Gracie pours whiskey into the glass then adds a splash of fluorescent-green liquid from a tiny bottle. She stirs the drink with a plastic stick, then quickly puts the bottle back in the pocket of her dress.

The third man pipes up from across the room.

I'll do it.

Dez and Kep both laugh. Dez shoots a look across the room.

You ain't got the stones, Benchwarmer.

Gracie plunks a cherry into the drink, then turns and takes it over to her grandfather.

'Bout time.

He grabs the glass and waves her away. She doesn't move. Instead, Gracie leans in and gives him a kiss on the cheek. Kep cringes. Wipes off his cheek. Gracie stands her ground. Nods to his glass.

Okay, okay.

He sips. She smiles and waits. He sips again.

It's good. Now stop embarrassing yourself. Go make my friend here a drink.

Gracie shuffles back to the drink cart. Her expression blank. She slowly places two cubes of ice into another rock glass. She's listening. Waiting. Not really paying attention to what she's doing. Then she hears it and her hands freeze.

Her grandfather coughs lightly.

He downs his drink in one gulp. Trying to clear his throat as he puts his cigar in the ashtray next to him. Coughs again. Then he slowly turns a reddish-purple color. He opens his mouth. Nothing comes out. He drops his empty rock glass and grips the arms of his chair. Tries to cough. He can't. Can't speak or catch his breath or make a sound. He thumps one fist into his chest.

Dez slowly rises from his chair, clearly surprised by what's happening. He backs away from the senator. Kep sputters foam from his mouth. His veiny eyes bulge as he rises from his chair.

Gracie carefully steps away from the bar cart and moves left. Out of frame. A few seconds later, she can be seen skirting the edge of the room, behind the chairs. Behind her grandfather and Dez. She moves as if floating. Light, quick steps. Like a dancer. Only with a limp. No one notices her leave the room.

Gus leans in closer, her nose almost touching her phone. Mesmerized by what's happening.

Kep suddenly manages to catch his breath. He sucks in a

huge gulp of air, then nothing. He can't exhale. He's frozen. Then he spits blood. Staggers to the bar cart, grabbing for water. The ice bucket crashes to the carpet. Bottles teeter off the cart. Blood streams from his nostrils and fills his mouth. He's right in front of Shannon's lens. He abruptly throws up, bending forward out of frame. Then he rises, lifting his bloodstained chin. He takes a breath. Then another. Throwing up seems to have helped. Cleared his airways. Gotten rid of whatever was poisoning his bloodstream.

Dez hasn't moved. He's behind Kep, watching his recovery progress. A look of resolve washes over Desmond Oaks as a decision bubbles up from deep inside his dark pupils. He glances at the other man in the room, then suddenly and swiftly, Dez removes his belt and wraps it around Kep's throat. Squeezing hard. Kep claws at the belt, but Dez holds tight. Kep flails and scratches, but his strength has been compromised by toxins that continue to rack his body with spasms. Seconds then minutes go by as the life slowly seeps from Kep's body. Then he goes quiet as his eyes roll back in his head and his limp body slips to the carpet. Dez is panting from the effort. The third man is silent. Dez straightens and loops his belt back into his trousers, then he smooths his hair.

Then it happens. *Beep. Beep. Beep.* Shannon gasps and whispers, *Shit.*

Gus gasps too. Shannon's watch is beeping. Dez freezes. He heard it too. He looks toward the bookcase, leans in, and sticks his finger in the peephole. Gus is right there with her mother. They both hold their breath. Paralyzed. Terrified. Caught.

"Run!"

Gus shouts at the video playing on her phone.

Shannon runs. The camera swings at her side as she races down the passage to the basement stairs. Gus feels like she's running by her mother's side. Heart pounding. Sweat forming on her brow. She can smell her mother's fear. Sense the adrenaline pumping through her body. Shannon flies down the stairs, through the tunnel, up the ladder, and out into the garden. The lens is pointing behind her as she sprints across the wide lawn beside the house. The men are shouting. They're outside. On the front porch of the house. One of them is coming across the lawn. Shannon is at the ditch, then across the road. A car door swings open, the camera bounces then comes to rest on the seat facing Shannon. She's fumbling to get her keys in the ignition. The engine roars, she shifts into first. Dirt and rocks can be heard blasting the underside of the car as she speeds away. Her hand reaches for the camera. The video cuts to static and Gus is wrenched from her mother. Sucked out of the tiny screen on her phone and yanked across space and time. Hurled twelve years into the faraway future. Left behind, like a dropped glove on the floor of a shopping mall. Lost, helpless, and alone.

Gus is on her knees. Ears buzzing with the sound of static. Someone touches her shoulder. She jumps and pulls away sharply. It's a security guard asking if she's okay. A couple of shoppers are gathered behind him. Gus trembles violently. Her heart's pounding. She needs to get away from their staring eyes. Gus shoves the phone in her satchel and struggles to stand. Her legs are asleep. She gets up too fast.

Head rush. Stars.

Everything goes black.

43

MAMA

SPIDERS CRAWL ACROSS HER SKIN. SCRAMBLE INSIDE HER nostrils. Her body rocks gently. She can't move. One spider bites her wrist. Her stomach churns as a siren wails.

Augusta opens her eyes. She's curled under a blanket on the floor. Behind the front seat of a car. The blanket's coated in dog hair. The car door slams. The engine turns over. She feels the car back up, then drive forward. Fast.

There's a voice. It's her mother. She must be talking on her cell phone.

Thank God you picked up. Something awful's happened.

She sounds scared.

I'm in my car.

Pause.

No, not on the phone. I need your help.

Pause.

You're the only one I can trust. Please, you have to meet me.

Pause.

Bruce Pit. The parking lot by the lake. Ten minutes.

Pause.

Thank you, Rory. You're a lifesaver.

She hangs up. Keeps driving.

Augusta tries to call out to her mother. Tries to suck air into her lungs, but she can't. Her body is jostled as they hit a bump in the road and the past falls away.

She opens her eyes and she's no longer under the blanket. No longer in the back seat of her mother's Corolla. No longer eight years old.

She is twenty-year-old Augusta and she's lying on a stretcher in the back of a moving ambulance. A paramedic sits next to her. A tube runs out of her arm tickling her skin like a spider. Cool oxygen flows from a mask to her mouth.

"Take a deep breath. That's it. Don't worry. You passed out in the mall, but you're gonna be just fine."

In the ER, a nurse checks her blood pressure and heart rate and gives her a juice box with a straw. A doctor shines a pencil flashlight into her eyes and holds her wrist to check her pulse. Tells her she's likely dehydrated, but just to be sure they're running some blood tests so she's told to sit tight.

Finally, they leave her alone behind the curtain and Gus has a chance to check her satchel. The gun is still there. Hidden in the inside pocket. Phone, check. Memory stick, check. Right where she left them in the bottom of the bag. The nurse pulls back the curtain.

"Do you have someone we can call?"

The nurse is wearing scrubs covered in tiny rabbits. The rabbits remind Gus of Gracie. She knows she should tell the nurse to call Stu.

But she doesn't.

"My uncle. He's with the RCMP in Kemptville. Constable Rory Rump."

HALF AN HOUR LATER, RORY POPS BEHIND THE CURTAIN THAT hangs around Gus's ER station. She's sitting on the edge of the bed eating a soda cracker.

"What in the heck? I've been trying to get hold of you for days. You hurt? You sick?"

He feels her forehead.

"Dehydrated, that's all. I'm okay."

"They told me you passed out. Break any bones, hit your head?"

"I'm good, Uncle Rory."

It's the first time she's called him Uncle Rory in years. They're both pretending. He's playing the doting uncle. She's playing the helpless little girl.

"You're coming to stay at my place. No argument, young lady."

Gus smiles sweetly. Just what she wanted. To be alone with Rory. She picks up her satchel. Rose's gun is safely tucked out of sight in the zippered pocket inside.

ON THE DRIVE OUT TO RORY'S, GUS FEELS HER EYELIDS GETTING heavy and her plans getting more muddled with each passing mile. She hasn't slept since the night she spent on Lois Greenaway's sofa in Thunder Bay. It's been more than thirty hours. She rolls down the window to wake herself. Sleep can wait.

At Rory's, Gus curls her feet up underneath her and

snuggles under a blanket on the sofa in his den. Rory props a pillow behind her. The teapot whistles in the kitchen. As soon as he leaves the room, she reaches for her satchel, unzips the inside pocket, and pulls out the gun. Places it by her hip under the blanket. Then she grabs her phone. There are a few missed calls from Stu. And Stanton. And a voice message from the animal hospital. She listens holding her breath. The message is short, but sweet. Levi made it through surgery. He's resting. Not out of the woods yet. They're keeping him sedated.

Gus ends the call, then opens the voice memo app on her phone and presses record. She places the phone facedown on the coffee table.

A few minutes later they're sitting next to each other, sipping peppermint tea. Rory tells her the nurse in the ER said peppermint tea helps with dehydration and digestion. Gus sits with her teacup in her lap. Enough chitchat. She dives in.

"Can I ask you something?"

"Shoot."

"Did my mom call you the night she died?"

"Say what?"

"If Shannon was in trouble, I think maybe she'd call you. She always said we could count on Uncle Rory."

Gus sips her tea, hoping that buttering him up will open the floodgates.

"Now you mention it, she did call me."

Rory said they hadn't talked in months.

"Why'd she call?"

"Something was bothering her. Wanted to meet. 'Course I went, only she didn't show and well, you know the rest."

He casts his eyes down to his tea. He hasn't touched his.

"I found a video she took that night."

He looks up too fast.

"Video?"

A wave of fatigue hits Gus. All she can hear is Kep Halladay's threatening growl.

That bitch needs her balls chopped off. Cop or no cop.

Her mouth is dry. Gus takes a big sip of tea, but it's more chalky than hydrating.

"People know you raped June Halladay and they think you're Gracie's father."

His jaw drops. She keeps going.

"But I don't believe it. I think you were set up to take the fall. Desmond Oaks bullied you your whole life and I think he still is."

Rory hangs his head. She continues. "I can't imagine how hard it's been for you all these years. Knowing what he did. And you a police officer."

His eyes well up.

"Uncle Rory, please just tell me what happened to my mother."

The room lurches. Augusta grips the arm of the sofa. Her vision darkens at the edges, then returns to normal. She reaches out to put her teacup on the coffee table but somehow it drops to the floor. Rory's face warps. He doesn't move to help her or to pick up the teacup. Just stares at her. Very still. Too still.

That's when she knows she's fucked this whole thing up. Completely underestimated him. Gus searches under the blanket for the gun. Her hands are jelly.

"I'm sorry, Little Monet."

She finds the gun, pulls it out from under the blanket, and

points it in his direction. He easily takes it from her hand and tucks it into the back of his belt. Straightens his uniform as he stands. Her father, Charlie, suddenly flashes across her mind. Wearing the same uniform but with a hole blown through the chest. Only twenty-one. Just a year older than she is right now. Both of them so young. Too young to die. She wonders if she'll see twenty-one.

Rory grabs her phone off the coffee table, turns it over, and sees the record button flashing. He shakes his head, presses stop, and tosses the phone across the room. It lands under the dining room table. Then he rifles through her satchel and finds the memory stick. Pockets it and then leans over her. She tries to squirm away. He takes her by the shoulders and tips her gently onto her side. She can't get up.

"You rest awhile. I'm gonna take care of everything. You'll see. I failed you big-time, kid. And I failed Shan too. But I'll make things right if it's the last thing I do."

Rory heads to the kitchen. She can hear him talking to someone. He's on the phone. Keys jingle. A screen door slams shut. Gus rolls herself off the sofa and onto the floor. A car engine starts up. Gravel churns under the wheels.

Then nothing. He's gone.

Augusta doesn't have much time. She needs to get the drugs out. She grips the edge of the coffee table and pulls herself to a sitting position. She puts her finger down her throat and vomits down the front of her T-shirt. She doesn't care. Some of it's out. Augusta drops off the sofa to her knees and crawls to the kitchen. She hauls herself to a standing position in front of the sink. Splashes cold water on her face. Cups the faucet and drinks.

There's a bottle of pills open on the counter next to the teapot. She tries hard to focus on the label. Zol-something. It rings a bell. Her mother took something beginning with a Z once in a while to help her sleep.

Throwing up into the sink, Gus realizes what Rory's done. This whole time he's been making her think her mother was crazy and off balance and suicidal so Gus would stop believing she was onto something. She lifts her head. Woozy. She needs to stay awake. Gus staggers to the fridge. Opens the freezer. Sticks her head into the icy air. The cold starts working. The fog begins to lift. Inside the freezer are two frost-covered pizzas and a bag of french fries. She grabs the fries and brings the cool bag to her forehead, but as she does she gets clocked by something hard inside the bag. Lars used to hide things in the freezer inside the frozen peas. Drugs. Guns. Stolen Rolex watches. She opens the bag, sticks her hand inside, and pulls out a VHS tape bound in cling wrap. She unwraps the plastic. Written on the label of the tape is one word:

Shan.

Gus stares at the four letters. It takes her brain a few seconds to put them in the right order. To register their meaning. But when it does, her sluggish heart skips a beat. She hugs the tape to her chest and staggers to the den. She leans down and puts the tape into Rory's old VCR. Grabs the remote. Turns on the TV and presses play. At first there's just static. Then an image comes into focus. It's stamped, 23:25 August 4, 2006. A little over an hour after Kep's murder.

The view points toward the roof inside a car. Then it tilts down to the door handle, then swings around to Shannon. She's sitting in the driver's seat of her Corolla, holding the camera with both hands. She's placing it on the passenger side of the dashboard. From the seat next to her, she grabs a sweater and drapes it over the camera, leaving the lens uncovered. The angle is wide. Shows the entire driver's side.

Headlights cross the back of Shannon's head. She checks the rearview mirror. She's got a look in her eyes that says nothing can stop her. Shannon gets out of the car and stands with her back against the open car door, looking toward the car that's pulling up behind hers. The headlights blast her eyes so she has to shield them.

The car pulls up and stops. A door shuts. Footsteps. Rory comes into frame, his face in shadow.

Augusta's body begins to shake. She doesn't want to see this. She sinks to her knees in the middle of Rory's den. The weight of what's about to happen is too much.

Rory is going to kill her mother.

There they are. At Bruce Pit. Right where her mother's car went into the lake. Where Shannon asked him to come meet her. Gus is right there next to them. She knows it for sure. She can smell the lake.

What the heck's going on, Shan? Meeting way out here in the middle of the night like criminals.

Shannon takes his hand.

Kep Halladay's been murdered.

Holy shit. You sure?

I saw it with my own eyes.

You were at his house?

Shannon stares at him. Makes him wait.

I didn't say it was at his house.

Rory doesn't speak. Shannon's face changes.

She lets his hand drop. It flops back to his side. Limp.

I videotaped the whole thing.

Rory steps back and a space opens between them. She holds his gaze. He shakes his head in disbelief. Stammers.

This is, this is good. You got evidence.

It was this guy I've seen around Elgin before. I think he does all Halladay's dirty work. His grease monkey. Dez somebody. It's all on the video. Kep's murder. And more. The guy talks about how he took out Henry Neil and June Halladay. All of it.

Rory's jaw clenches.

What are we doing out here? You gotta turn it in.

She shakes her head.

I was trespassing. It'll be inadmissible. It'll get thrown out by any judge. With my history, I'd probably get pegged for the murder. There's physical evidence. My tire tracks. My footprints in the garden. I was inside the house.

What do you need me to do, Shan?

Shannon moves very close to Rory. Intimately close. Then she whispers, almost mouth to mouth with Rory.

Testify, for fuck's sake. After all, Rory, you were there.

Rory staggers backward and nearly chokes on his own spit. Shannon doesn't take her eyes off him.

And even though she's foggy-headed, that's the moment Gus is dead certain that Rory was the third man in Kep's parlor. Up until then, she'd clung by her fingernails to the fragile belief that she might have been wrong. That is wasn't him. But Shannon knew it all along and now Gus lets go and knows it too. She is overcome by a deep sense of foreboding.

You can do it, Rory. Tell them who he is. What he did to June and Henry and Kep.

I can't. I'll go to jail. I didn't try to stop him. I couldn't save any
of them.

Like you couldn't save Charlie?

Rory looks like he's been gut punched.

Shan.

Shannon looks into the darkness surrounding them.

It should have been you, not him.

Rory stares at her. Sees the hate in her eyes when she looks
back at him. The disgust. He covers his face with his hands.
A broken man. A man whose fantasies have been shattered.
He can't look at her any longer. It's too agonizing. Can't face
who he's become in her eyes. He sobs. Then Shannon makes
a strange sound. He opens his eyes.

Shannon is inexplicably lifted off her feet. Her body arches
back over the open car door. She's choking. There's a leather
belt around her neck pulling her back hard. Shannon's arms
thrash behind her. She punches and gasps. Fights so hard her
elbow smashes the car window.

Rory stumbles a few steps back. Eyes wide. He moves
away from her. Hand over his mouth as he watches. And does
nothing. Then there's a hideous snapping sound like a branch
breaking. It's her neck. Shannon's lifeless body wilts to the
ground where she lands in a crumpled heap on her knees,
head tilted to one side. Her face is vacant. Her eyes wide. Rory
drops to his knees. Cradles her wobbly neck in his hands. Sobs
and moans. Behind him a figure appears. Dez. He's looping
his belt back into his pants.

Find that fuckin' video. I gotta go bury the old man's body.

Rory stops crying and looks up at Dez with the slobbery
face of an abandoned child.

What? No, you can't go.

Dez ignores him and grabs the car keys from Rory's hand and walks away. Rory blubbers.

You, you can't leave me out here, Dezzie.

Figure it out, Benchwarmer.

A car engine starts. Headlights streak across Rory's back. He sits there awhile, holding Shannon's lifeless head in his hands. Then he leans toward her and kisses her mouth. Picks her up in both arms, piles her body into the front seat of her car. Fastens her seat belt around her. He searches her pockets. Finds her cell phone. He stands up and dials. Puts on a phony voice.

There's been an accident. A car went into the lake out at Bruce Pit. Send help.

He hangs up and pockets the phone. He wipes the tears from his cheeks and takes a deep breath. He reaches across Shannon and turns on the ignition. That's when he spots the camera on the dashboard. He looks straight into the lens. Lifts the sweater covering the camera.

Fuck, fuck, fuck.

Rory picks up the camera. The view swings toward the back seat, then he turns it off. Everything goes black. But just before the video cut off, Gus is sure she glimpsed something else. She rewinds the tape and presses play. Rory picks up the camera and swings it toward himself. As he does, Gus presses pause. The image freezes. She did see something. A small hand clinging to the seat behind Shannon. Her own eight-year-old hand.

She can smell his aftershave. Old Spice.

The past crashes like a tidal wave into her tranquilized brain.

Her mother is driving. Only her head's bent sideways like she's sleeping. Gus looks out the back window. Uncle Rory is standing at the top of a hill. They're going too fast. Water slams the front windshield. The car floats. Then begins to sink. Gus pounds on the back window. Rory spots her and starts to run down the hill. She scrambles over the seat, shaking her mother's shoulders.

Mama. Mama. Wake up.

44

TOMMY

GUS IS DRAGGED BACK TO THE HERE AND NOW BY THE sound of crunching gravel in Rory's driveway. A car door slams, then another. Still dazed, she scans the room. Spots her phone under the dining room table. Wills herself to her feet. She can hear voices outside. Her legs are wobbly. She glances through to the kitchen and sees two men coming up the back steps of the porch. Before they catch sight of her, she ducks. Gus crawls under the dining room table just as Desmond and Rory enter the house.

"She's in there."

Dez comes into the den first. Nothing like the feeble creature she met by the pool. He moves with a swift lurching stride that belies his mutilated form. More monster than man. He snarls, "The fuck she is."

Rory dekes around Dez and stares at the empty sofa. The static on the TV. He races into the back bedroom. Checks closets, the bathroom. Dez leans against the dining room table.

Rory emerges from the hall utterly baffled. Eyes flitting to Gus behind Desmond's legs.

"I swear on my life, Dezzie, I gave her a boatload of pills."

Dez moves on Rory fast. He grabs his collar and slaps his face hard three times. Rory's lip splits. Blood trickles down his quivering chin.

"Dezzie, forget about the girl. We don't need her anymore. I didn't tell ya before 'cause I wanted it to be a surprise, but I found it. It was in her purse. I got your money for ya, Dezzie."

Her brain screaming for her to stay put, Gus tries not to move a muscle. Wills herself to sink into the floorboards, disappear. Turn to stone. Anything but remain crouched under a table in full view of Dez if he turns around. Dez lets go of Rory's collar. Doesn't turn. Rory holds his attention.

"I hid it for safekeeping."

Rory darts over to the bookcase of trophies and yearbooks. He searches in between the yearbooks, tumbling several to the floor. Dez sighs impatiently.

"You never could do nothing right. Couldn't even pop a woody when I was done with June. Never been nothing but a benchwarmer."

A split second after he utters those words, blood sprays the hardwood floor at Dez's feet. His knees buckle then he corkscrews to the floor. Body twisting. Head smacking against the hardwood. Facing Gus. Seeing her for the first time. Eyes perplexed. Sputtering dark liquid from his deformed mouth. Like an upended turtle, Dez flaps about, trying to get up.

Rory softly places the gun on the coffee table. Rose's gun. The gun he'd taken from Gus and tucked in his belt. He picks up the championship trophy and walks over to Dez. Then he smashes it down on his childhood friend's skull. Over and over. Until Dez's mutilated head is nothing but a mound of brains. Blood stipples Rory's face and the front of his police uniform. He licks his split lip. Then matter-of-factly, he flicks off bits of brain matter dripping from the trophy as if this is something he does every day. His eyes are blank. He speaks to Gus without looking at her.

"You can come out now."

Gus lets out the breath she's been holding for what feels like forever. Her head is clear. Shocked back to sobriety. Completely untranquilized. She crawls out from under the table, keeping it between her and Rory. Eyes Rose's gun behind him on the coffee table. Rory places the trophy back on the bookcase, then he turns to face her.

She nods toward the static buzzing on the TV.

"I found the tape. The one you marked Shan."

He looks over at the TV. Into the static. Narrows his bloodshot eyes as if he's trying to see beyond the waves of black and white rippling across the screen. The color drains from his cheeks. His mouth drops open and he slumps down onto the sofa. His eyes dart back and forth, and then Rory starts pounding his fists into his forehead. Gus doesn't move for fear she'll trigger his madness to spill across the room toward her. He pounds and rocks and stammers.

"I pulled you out of that lake, got you home, put you in your bed, safe and sound. That's what Uncle Rory did. All I've been trying to do is protect you, Little Monet. But you started nosing around and Dezzie wouldn't let up about the video. He wanted to know if you had it, what you knew, and who you talked to."

Gus inches along the table toward the kitchen. Rory's manic.

"But it was that bloody money that drove him off the deep end. He'd kept his eye on that Halladay girl for seven long years, then he started playing daddy just to get his cut. He played the long game and lost. Lost his dignity. Lost his face. He wasn't gonna stop till he got every last cent. And you led him right to that list. A list with your name on it."

Rory stares at the static on the TV. Then he looks up at Gus for the first time since sinking onto the sofa.

"Shan set me up. She was trying to get me to confess. I burned that camera of hers out back in the fire pit. After I made that copy. I thought I might need it one day. In case them two tried to pin it all on me. But you saw. Dezzie's the one who killed her. Not me. It was all Dezzie."

Gus is at the far end of the table. Ready to run. His eyes are pleading for forgiveness. His soft belly quivers as he breathes hard. She meets his gaze and in a split second, all of what Uncle Rory was falls away and Gus sees the real Rory. A pathetic, spineless nothing of a man. He's desperate to see a glimmer of sympathy in her eyes, but all she can give him is utter disgust. The same look her mother gave him just before she was killed.

"Fuck you, Uncle Rory."

He picks up Rose's gun. A chill runs down her spine. He cradles the gun for a moment, then waves it at the TV.

"That was our first kiss. Me and Shan. I watch it sometimes when I'm missing her."

Augusta's body shudders violently. Fear and loathing rip at her stomach as she tries to will him to shoot himself. Instead, Rory tosses her his car keys. She catches them.

"Go. Get far away from here while you can. Once Tommy finds out what's happened, he'll come for the both of us."

There's a sudden pop like a firecracker.

A fierce jerk of Rory's head sends a chunk of his hair floating to the sofa. Gus stares as a stream of blood flows from under his hairline and travels down the side of his face. He tries to stand, but a second pop rips a hole right through his neck. His tongue sticks out, eyes spasm as he pitches over the coffee table. Dead before he hits the floor.

The shots came from the kitchen. Gus flattens herself against the dining room wall. The kitchen floor groans. He's in the house. She searches for a way out. The window in the den. Visible from the kitchen. She'll never make it. She needs a weapon. Spots Rose's gun on the sofa where Rory dropped it. Too far. She's cornered. She looks down at the car keys in her hand. Better than nothing. She grasps the key ring, sticking the keys out between her fingers. Holds her fists up in front of her.

Then Stu appears in the kitchen doorway. Gun raised. He lowers it when he sees her. Relief floods her body. She tosses the keys on the table and runs to him. Wraps her arms around his neck. Pressing her cheek against his solid chest, breathing him in.

He pulls her arms gently away and surveys the room. He steps toward Rory and that's when he spots Dez, lying on the far side of the dining table. He inhales sharply, then moves closer and takes a knee beside the bludgeoned lifeless body. Shaking his head as he checks for a pulse in one of Desmond's wrists. Gus comes up beside him.

"You don't know how glad I am to see you, Stu."

Then he rests his chin on his knee. He's breathing heavily. Eyes shut. Gus doesn't know what's happening. Why isn't he calling for backup? Maybe they're on the way. But he's not moving. He's sniffling. Crying. Gus gets a sick feeling in the pit of her stomach.

"Stu?"

He stands. Turns to face her. Tears running down his cheeks. She stumbles away from him, pressing herself against a corner cabinet.

"Who did this to my brother?"

He chokes on the word *brother*.

Suddenly, Augusta sees what was right in front of her eyes this whole time. It all comes flooding back in a terrible onslaught of sights and sounds and smells that barrage her senses like shards of glass slicing through her insides.

A young rookie holding up a badge that she never got to see up close.

Wearing a uniform those cops at the diner knew was fake. She'd read their interaction all wrong. They weren't saying *it's all good* that he was on a date. They didn't know him. She can see now why he was looking down at his uniform. They were telling him the costume looked real. The shirt, the badge, the belt. *It's all good.*

She hears him making the mistake that she didn't catch.

Lieutenant Stanton reassigned me to patrol.

Gus sees the office door at RCMP headquarters bearing the sign that says SERGEANT MARTY STANTON, HEAD OF YOUTH SERVICES.

He'd slipped up because he didn't know Stanton. Didn't

know she was a sergeant not a lieutenant. He's been pretending to be a cop.

That layabout brother of his.

Gus flashes to the man who ran off when she was talking to Desmond's neighbor. Likely the same man whose rock-hard chest she ran into behind Dez's apartment. The one whose face she never saw, but now remembers smelled of sandalwood soap. Just like the rookie had when she'd gotten close to him out near Elgin the first time they met.

Gus smells that earthy aroma now on the man who's just killed Rory. Who's been following her and faking like he's a nice guy just to get close to her. Levi sensed it before she did. Sensed his facade crumbling as he got more desperate. That's why the dog growled at him at the motel. He knew.

And of course, Rory knew him. She saw the recognition on his face outside the library in Kemptville. But not, as she thought at the time, because he was a fellow cop. He knew him from way back. Augusta sees the little boy in the picture on Rory's bookcase. Perched between the two older boys on the milk crate, making a peace sign and smiling at the camera. Childhood friends. Brothers.

Her bones rattle violently as these sights and sounds and scents begin to mix with the faces of Renata, Manny, Ollie, and Levi to form one horrific and vicious deception carefully designed to infiltrate her life, gain her confidence. Her trust. And it worked. She let her guard down. She confided in this man. Trusted him. Left her dog with him.

Stu isn't here to save her.

Stu doesn't exist.

"Tommy?"

"Red."

"You cut off a man's fingers. You poisoned Levi."

He wipes his runny nose on the back of his hand.

"Oh my God, he's just a stupid dog. What about my brother? Look at him."

Gus looks down at what's left of Dez.

"That monster killed my mother."

"Rory strangled her. Dez told me. He saw him do it."

"He lied."

Tommy flinches at her words.

"It's your fault I poisoned your dog. You took off. Dez said it was the only way to get you running back to me. He said it was on me that you got away and it was on me to get you back. I fuckin' let him down."

Tears streak his face. He twitches. Like he's struggling to hold his shit together.

"Where is it, Red? Where's the money?"

"I burned it."

"You're lying. That post office dude said it was all in bank drafts. Multimillion-dollar bank drafts. You still got it. You told me as much."

He raises the gun and points it at her. His hands are shaking so much he has to grasp the gun with both hands.

"Where'd you hide it?"

She stares him down, unwavering.

"You're the liar."

He fires. Just misses her ear. She pees. Her ears ring.

"That money is my brother's. He earned it. It's mine now."

Tommy's jaw clenches. Behind her back, Gus feels for

something sharp in the corner cabinet. Fingers touching a heavy gravy boat.

"I don't want to hurt you, Red."

Gus launches the gravy boat at Tommy's head as hard as she can. He tries to block it. It knocks the gun from his hand and bounces off his jaw before crashing to the floor. A gash explodes from his chin as he stumbles to one knee. He's dazed. It's her only chance. Gus grabs the keys off the table and makes a break for the kitchen. Tommy dives for her ankles. Grabs hold. The momentum sends her belly flopping onto the floor. He drags her into the dining room. Flips her over. Gets his hands around her throat. Her tongue feels like it's popping out of her mouth. She swings her arm at his head with all her strength. He screams and lets go of her neck. Eyes wide, he reaches for the car key embedded in his cheek. It's gone right through to the inside of his mouth. He tries to dislodge it. It's stuck between two teeth.

Gus squirms out from under him. He yanks out the key. Spits blood and turns to grab her. But stops. Gus has Rose's gun aimed right at Tommy's head. He winces as she pulls the trigger and it clicks. Empty.

Damn it.

Rory used the last bullet.

Tommy spots his gun under the dining room table. He goes for it. Gus makes a run for the back door. She gets across the den, through the kitchen entryway, past the fridge, the table, the trash bin. Each stride knowing Tommy's bullet is about to rip through her back. Gus gets halfway across the kitchen when she sees Stanton in the window of the back door waving for her to get down.

Gus drops like a stone.

A gun fires.

Everything goes deadly quiet. All she can feel is the sting of shattered glass cascading around her head and shoulders. She lies still amid the shards as they prick her skin and bounce off the kitchen floor like freezing rain.

In the silence, a slow and steady sound grows louder and louder.

Stronger and stronger.

Thump-thump, thump-thump.

It is the steady beat of her heart. Strong and full and alive.

And it's not just her blood that courses through her veins as she lies on the cool linoleum.

It's Shannon's.

Her beautiful, brave mother.

Augusta breathes deeply.

Mama. I see now. I see it all.

45

MARTY

TOMMY SURVIVED STANTON'S BULLET. THE MEMORY STICK found in Rory's pocket and the VHS tape from his freezer were both key pieces of evidence at the trial of Tommy William Oaks for the murder of Rory Rump, assault and battery of Oliver Trunk, and the attempted murder of Augusta Monet. The videos clearly detailed the factors that motivated his brother, Desmond, to murder Kep Halladay and Shannon Monet and go after her daughter, Augusta. The videos also implicate Gracie Halladay in her grandfather's death, but as far as everyone's concerned, she's long dead. And the Halladay fortune has disappeared. Augusta showed the police the location of the black Impala in Rory's garage in the woods. The one Peaches saw across the street the day Ollie was attacked. She ID'd the car and picked out the faces of two of the three men she saw sitting in it earlier that day. Rory and Tommy. She said that she couldn't identify the third man on account of his face being a total mess. Dez.

Gus was called as a witness at Tommy's trial. She recounted what happened at Rory's house right up to the moment when Tommy was handcuffed to a gurney and taken away by ambulance.

The rest is between her and Sergeant Martina Stanton. Marty, as Augusta calls her now.

GUS WAS SITTING IN THE PASSENGER SEAT OF STANTON'S CAR. Two RCMP officers were stretching yellow crime scene tape across Rory's back porch. Stanton got in the car. They both stared out the front window as the team cordoned off the property. Gus was grateful, but curious.

Why were you out here anyway?

Stanton looked at Gus.

It was something you said. It stuck with me. I decided to look into the 911 call from the night of your mum's accident. It turns out it came from her number. Only there was no cell phone found at the scene. I checked the evidence box. Nothing. I tried to track down the 911 recording and the file had been deleted.

Gus turned to look at the policewoman who saved her life.

What did I say that stuck with you?

That Rory told you he was there that night. He pulled her out of the vehicle. At first, I brushed it off. I thought he was trying to impress you. Only it didn't sit right. None of the officers on the scene mentioned him being there. It felt more like a slipup than a white lie. And then you said I had a tail on you. That got my ears perked too.

Gus nodded. Stanton continued.

So I tracked down the department Hansel just so he could have a look-see. That's what we call the tech guy who's good at finding little crumbs of data. A hacker type. Long story short, he found that deleted

911 call. It came from your mom's phone all right, but it wasn't her voice. It was our good buddy, Constable Rump. I'd recognize that weak-ass chirp anywhere.

No phone at the scene. Deleted call. I knew he was up to something. But I didn't know what or how deep. I came by here to confront the SOB, then I see him lying in a pool of blood in his den and some fella's pointing a gun at your back. First time I ever discharged my weapon. After thirty-five years on the force.

During the trial in Ottawa, Augusta took to meeting Marty for breakfast at the Capital Diner before walking over to the courthouse together. The older woman's graying sideburns and rumpled sweaters reminded Gus of a slightly disheveled schoolmarm. Marty helped ease Augusta's nerves about testifying. And Gus helped Marty see the big picture. Stanton's hard edges had definitely softened since making her decision to take early retirement after being awarded a Special Service Medal from the RCMP for her actions that day at Rory's.

When the trial was over and Tommy got a life sentence, both of them knew it was time they parted ways. They didn't need each other anymore. Besides, Marty was moving to Winnipeg to be closer to her son and her grandchildren. The two women said their goodbyes and walked away from each other. Then Marty turned and chased after Gus. She gave her a big bear hug.

I'm proud of you. And they would be too.

46

AUGUSTA

꿍

EVEN AFTER A YEAR, THE HAIR ON LEVI'S BELLY HAS NEVER quite grown back after being shaved for his surgery. He's put on some weight. Drools a little and favors his left hip when he walks, but he's doing pretty good for a thirteen-year-old mutt. Ninety-one in human years.

It's autumn and Gus has found a cozy apartment in Wellington West just a few blocks from Island Park Drive. The developer who bought Rose's house tore it down and built a modern duplex in its place. All glass and sharp angles. Just like the one that replaced the house in Hintonburg where Gus lived with her mother. Seems that's what happens to the old houses in her family. It's as if they never existed. But Gus is okay with them being gone. With no one living there in her place. She can hold them in her memories and visit them anytime. There they can belong to her and her alone.

Gus gets a job at a local pet shop selling chew toys and dog food to the neighborhood canine lovers. She knows most of the regulars by name and their dogs' names too. Best part of the job is that she can bring Levi to work. He sits in the window watching the world go by and occasionally someone asks if he's for sale. He's not. When he feels up to it, he lumbers over to greet a customer. Most days he just people-watches and naps.

Monday is her day off. If it's sunny, Gus and Levi usually walk the neighborhood. Buy a raspberry cassis donut at Suzy Qs and a takeout coffee from Bridgehead. The baristas know how she likes her coffee and Terry at Suzy Qs always has a treat in his pocket for Levi. They head over to the Byron path to sit on their favorite bench and soak up the sun.

On this one particularly cool Monday, Missy saunters toward them. She's a lanky goldendoodle with a serious crush on Levi. Gus chats with Raj, her owner, while the dogs nose each other's private parts. Raj and Gus discuss how the leaves are already turning and the nights are getting cooler. Then Raj and Missy move on down the path.

Levi sniffs the air. Then he taps her leg with one paw. Gus knows what he wants. She pulls the raspberry donut from its bag, breaks off a morsel, and holds it out to him.

He nips at it and she pulls her hand away before he can snap up the morsel.

"Gentle," she scolds. Then, ever so softly and slowly, Levi lifts his chin and brings his mouth close to the piece of donut and gently takes it from her fingers. She smiles as he gulps it down in one piece.

"Who says you can't teach an old dog?"

Augusta pets the top of his furry golden head. Again, he lifts his nose and flares his graying nostrils.

Gus smells it too. Smoke on the air. Coming from some-one's backyard. Burning leaves or maybe warming themselves on this cool fall day by their fireplace.

The smell transports her back in time. Just over a year ago. The day after Rory and Dez were killed. When she couldn't stop herself from jumping into her great-grandmother's old Buick and heading out on the highway one more time. Levi couldn't make that road trip. He was still in the hospital. So she was to go it alone. But she didn't feel alone. Even the car seemed to know where she wanted to go.

Back to Halladay House.

47

GRACIE

❧

AUGUSTA PICKS UP THE GAS CAN AND STRIDES DOWN THE hill through the purple loosestrife, across the dusty road and up the steep incline toward the house. She takes the long gravel lane until it reaches the flagstone path. She's deep in the shadow of the house now. She climbs the front steps. The rotting cedar planks creak. She crosses the veranda, bracing for a cave-in that doesn't come. The front windows are boarded up. The front door is draped with ivy. Gus pushes aside the ivy and it falls away in one great swath of dead vines. She wipes dirt from a small window in the massive door and peers inside.

Dust churns a ghostly dance in the foyer. To the left is the front parlor. Its furniture is shrouded in flammable sheets. Bird wings flutter somewhere deep inside the house. An enormous dusty staircase ascends from the foyer to a second-floor landing. It looks like no one has stepped foot on those stairs in years.

Names swirl around Augusta's mind. Pirouetting like the dust. The names of the places and the faces that brought her to this moment. But standing at the front door of Halladay House, one name dances above them all. Gus knocks and calls out.

Gracie?

She waits. She knows, even if she's right and Gracie is here, that this isn't the way in. She's trying to be polite by knocking on the front door, but now she just feels ridiculous. She leaves the gas can sitting on the porch and walks around the side of the house. She knows the real way in.

Gus heads to the back garden. She spots the trellis. Walks through it. She finds the corner by the low stone wall. Sees the hatch in the ground. She pulls it open and climbs down the ladder, then makes her way through the dark tunnel into the basement. She reaches the narrow hallway below the house. Climbs a small staircase then works her way along the passage to a door.

Then Gus pauses.

She knows that behind the door is the spiral staircase leading up. But the other way, down the walled passage, is where her mother peered into the parlor that fateful night. Gus works her way down the passage toward the peephole. She examines the dusty floor at her feet, smells the musty air, and leans toward the hole, her heart beating steadily. Her mother was right here, peering in. Gus can't see much. It's too dim. She can only make out a few shadowy shapes in the parlor. Then Gus turns away from where her mother stood that night. She runs her fingers along the passage wall as she makes her way to the door at the far end. She opens it and climbs to the top of the staircase. Once there, she slowly opens the door to the attic and steps inside.

Hello?

A chill runs through her as she looks around Gracie's room.

The room her mother videotaped more than a decade earlier. Not much has changed. The small bed is neatly made. Under it is a row of plastic grocery baskets. Some are empty. Some are filled with canned beans and tuna and packages of black licorice. The licorice Levi had on his breath. On the side table by the bed are a can opener and a mason jar of fresh wildflowers. Purple loosestrife. The ceiling is still strung with small bulbs and in the corner, still there, is the large table with Gracie's knives and jars of colored liquid. The tools of the mortuary trade.

Taught the child all about embalming and sewing skin and covering flesh with makeup.

Gus approaches the table. There are bits of animal hide and spools of coarse thread strewn about next to the tinted batch of liquids. She picks up one of the jars. A greenish-yellow liquid. Embalming fluid. Poison. She looks at the shelves where the collection of dead animals is displayed. Fox, squirrel, raccoon, black bird. Possum is back.

They're all there, except the rabbit.

A creak startles Gus and she spins around. There's no one there. Then she hears another soft creak. It's coming from the corner wardrobe. She places the embalming fluid slowly back on the table and steps toward the wardrobe. The door moves ever so slightly. It's her.

Augusta is suddenly overwhelmed by a deep sense of shame. She feels like a child caught spying on her best friend. Without invitation, she's thrust herself into Gracie's very private world. Into her personal space. Without her permission.

Shame quickly gives way to fear. There is no seven-year-old ballerina hiding in that wardrobe. There is a woman who's been living in an attic for over five years.

Reality dawns.

Gus is alone with Gracie Halladay. A woman she doesn't know. Up high in the rafters of a boarded-up mansion that no one ever visits. She could disappear without a trace. Her mind races. She wishes Levi was by her side right now. Augusta eyes the knives on the table. The wardrobe door inches open a crack. Gus almost screams, but instead she runs.

There's no way in hell she's waiting around to see what's coming out of that closet.

Gus dives for the circular rug at the center of the room, rips it away, pulls the trapdoor open, and jumps through the opening. She lands in a heap on the floor below. She's up fast and running down the hall. She finds the staircase leading down to the main level. She takes the stairs two by two, misjudging the last step and sprawling face-first across the dusty central foyer. She rolls onto her side. In the murky light of the parlor, she glimpses a pair of shoes sticking out from under a sheet draped over one of the large armchairs.

She looks up the stairs. Hears no footsteps.

Curiosity gets the better of her.

Gus pulls herself to her feet and steps into the parlor. Slowly, she crosses the carpet toward the armchair. It sits across from the fireplace. Exactly where it was in Edgar's model and in Shannon's video. Kep Halladay's chair. Gus reaches out, takes hold of one corner of the sheet covering the chair, holds her breath, and yanks. As the sheet cascades to the floor, a dust cloud wafts up. She closes her eyes, waving away the dust particles. As they dissipate, she squints, not fully processing what her eyes are seeing.

Propped against the cushions of the armchair, wearing a

suit and tie and dress shoes, sits a bizarre, desiccated, life-size mannequin. Stray hairs jut from its bald head and a ghoulish lipstick smile is painted across its ashen face. Gus can't take her eyes off the grisly figure, the face a patchwork of stitches, the eyes black.

Her mind flashes to Gracie's embalming fluids, sharp knives, spools of thread, and dead animal hides. Could it be?

She leans closer and suddenly grasps the horror of what actually sits in front of her. This is no mannequin. It's a human cadaver. Drained, stuffed, strung together with coarse thread, and preserved by fluids. She gags. It's him.

It's Kep Halladay.

The stairs groan behind her. Gus jumps. She tears her eyes away from Gracie's handiwork and races from the room. Without so much as a glance up the stairs, she does a sliding run across the foyer and lunges for the front door. She struggles with the dead bolt. Finally gets it to budge and wrenches open the dusty door. The oppressive August heat assaults her lungs. She lurches out the door and trips over the gas can. Both Gus and the gas can tumble down the front steps. Landing on the flagstone path, Gus rolls over, flat on her back, staring up at Halladay House. She freezes.

A figure moves toward the front door.

Adrenaline has Gus pinned. She wants to get up and run, but she can't.

The woman's face is hidden in the shadows, but Gus can make out her arms. She's cradling a dead rabbit. Stroking the rabbit's head.

The two women are just a few feet away from each other, but Gus can feel the vast expanse between them. She pictured them being kindred spirits. Orphaned sisters. Bonded by a mutual hatred for this house. She imagined they would burn it to the ground together. But this house is not what she thought it was. It's more than a house of horrors. It's a reliquary. A macabre shrine where the past has been carefully, almost lovingly, preserved. It is a sad and lonely prison where a little girl continues to punish herself by living among the dead.

Gus realizes that this house is not hers to burn. And the past is no longer her burden. Gracie is not hers to save. Nor was she her mother's. Gracie never belonged to either of them.

Gus carefully gets to her feet. She slowly moves to turn and leave, but then she remembers the envelope in her back pocket. The letter for Gracie. The letter Lois slipped into her pocket when she hugged Gus at the bus terminal. Lois knew it could only have been Gracie who left the diary in the Buick. She knew she'd survived the fire. Maybe she always knew. For she was the one who likely chose the words on Gracie's headstone.

She will remain forever alive in our hearts.

Gus is pretty sure the envelope contains some cash and a plea to come home to her family, but she hasn't opened it. It's addressed to Gracie Halladay. The return address on Cottonwood Crescent is clearly marked on the front.

Gus steps cautiously toward the porch. Gracie cowers back into the shadows as Gus gently leans toward her, placing the letter on the porch steps. She rights the gas can, leaving both for Gracie.

As Augusta crests the hill beyond the house, she looks skyward toward the puffy white clouds trimmed by golden sunlight. Gus pushes through the purple loosestrife, letting it scratch her legs. The farther she gets from Halladay House, the more the past seems to loosen its grip on her heart and a sense of peace begins to wash over her entire being. With each stride she feels herself walking toward the present, breathing in the pungent aroma of the weeds, letting her fingertips graze the purple buds, sending tiny seeds floating up behind her.

The faint smell of smoke wafts on the August breeze.

Real or imagined, she's not sure.

ACKNOWLEDGMENTS

WHEN I TOLD MY FAMILY I WAS WRITING A NOVEL, THEY said, *Of course you are.* Their belief in me, their constant support, love, and enthusiasm are my fuel. I'm lucky.

Lucky to have Andy Sinclair by my side. He puts up with my half-listening and waving him off when I'm writing. The man never complains. In fact, he does the opposite. He's my personal booster. He's okay with being Mr. Tallo and he always lets me take the driver's seat. Without him along for the ride, this novel would never have been written and the journey wouldn't have been half as much fun. Here's to three more decades, my love.

I'm lucky to have a life overflowing with strong women who inspire me to tell women's stories and who each in her own way informed this novel. Kathleen, who was the mother I needed even if she didn't always think she was. My multi-talented sister, Louise, who continues to love me despite the fact that I used to pull her red hair. Maggie, for her beautiful, open heart. Sue and Lori, who knew me at eight and will always be a part of my stories. Chantal, for her love and wisdom and for always being there to read pages before they're ready.

Vivi, whose unwavering faith in me means more than she'll ever know. Jen, who devours books and was there to support me when this one was just a dream. Jamie, for lifting me up with lots of kudos when I most needed them. And LA, my writer-in-arms, for letting me have the river view, for the camaraderie, advice, writing talk, and healthy snacks. I'm immeasurably grateful to all of you.

And I'm luckier still to have had an early champion and mentor in Tom Shoebridge. He believed in my writing before I did. His early encouragement has helped light the way, even years later.

I want to thank Stephen Parolini, *The Novel Doctor*, who read my early draft, gave me great notes, and offered a discerning, reassuring glimpse at what this novel could become.

I also want to thank my editors, Emily Taylor and Sarah Stein, for guiding this first-timer through the editing process with grace and patience, for encouraging me to retain and strengthen the heart in the story, while still embracing the creepy stuff. Thanks for loving Gus and Levi as much as I do. And to the team at HarperCollins, from design to copyediting, the creativity and talent and attention you have poured into the making of this book has been overwhelming.

My awesome agent, David Halpern, is the best. He's been my sounding board, editor, advocate, and champion for the past six years. His easy manner, his kindness, his humor, his intellect, and his brilliant advice have made this foray into novel-writing an unexpected delight. His team has always been generous with their time and their ideas. I still can't believe he agreed to represent me. Lucky for me, he did.

And last but most definitely not least, I'd like to thank another amazing woman in my life. My sweet daughter. My Alex. She is my reason. My reason for writing, for getting out of bed in the morning, for telling stories. She is my best friend, my daughter, my heart. It is through her eyes that I can see the mother, the woman, the writer that I might still become.

This book is hers.

All except for a tiny corner reserved for my sweet pup to chew on. My Levi. Gone, but never forgotten.

ABOUT THE AUTHOR

KATIE TALLO GREW UP IN OTTAWA, ONTARIO. AFTER STUDYing Film and English at Carleton University and Television Broadcasting at Algonquin College, she was invited to attend the prestigious Women in the Director's Chair in Banff. For the next two decades, she wrote, produced, and directed short films, documentaries, feature films, and television series. Her films toured festivals across North America. In 2013, she won the Mslexia Novel Competition in the United Kingdom for unpublished fiction. Katie lives with her husband, Andy, in the Wellington West neighborhood of Ottawa.